Master
OF THE
HALL

The Eden Hall Series by Veronica Heley

THE *Eden* HALL SERIES

Master
OF THE
HALL

VERONICA HELEY

ZONDERVAN®

ZONDERVAN.com/
AUTHORTRACKER
follow your favorite authors

Sign up for our *Fiction E-Newsletter*. Every month you'll receive sample excerpts from our books, sneak peeks at upcoming books, and chances to win free books autographed by the author.

You can also sign up for our *Breakfast Club*. Every morning in your email, you'll receive a five-minute snippet from a fiction or nonfiction book. A new book will be featured each week, and by the end of the week you will have sampled two to three chapters of the book.

Zondervan *Author Tracker* is the best way to be notified whenever your favorite Zondervan authors write new books, go on tour, or want to tell you about what's happening in their lives.

Visit *www.zondervan.com* and sign up today!

To find out more about Veronica Heley and her books,
visit www.veronicaheley.com.

ZONDERVAN®

Master of the Hall
Copyright © 2006 by Veronica Heley

Requests for information should be addressed to:

Zondervan, *Grand Rapids, Michigan* 49530

Library of Congress Cataloging-in-Publication Data

Heley, Veronica.
    Master of the Hall / Veronica Heley.
        p. cm. – (The Eden Hall series ; bk. 4)
    ISBN-10: 0-310-26560-6
    ISBN-13: 978-0-310-26560-3
    1. Sands, Minty (Fictitious character) – Fiction. 2. Administration of estates – Fiction. 3. England – Fiction. 4. Domestic Fiction. I. Title. II. Series: Heley, Veronica. Eden Hall series ; bk. 4.
PR6070.H6915M37 2006
823'.92 – dc22

2006007268

Veronica Heley asserts the moral right to be identified as the author of this work.

Interior design by Michelle Espinoza

Printed in the United States of America

06 07 08 09 10 11 12 • 18 17 16 15 14 13 12 11 10 9 8 7 6 5 4 3 2

Master
OF THE
HALL

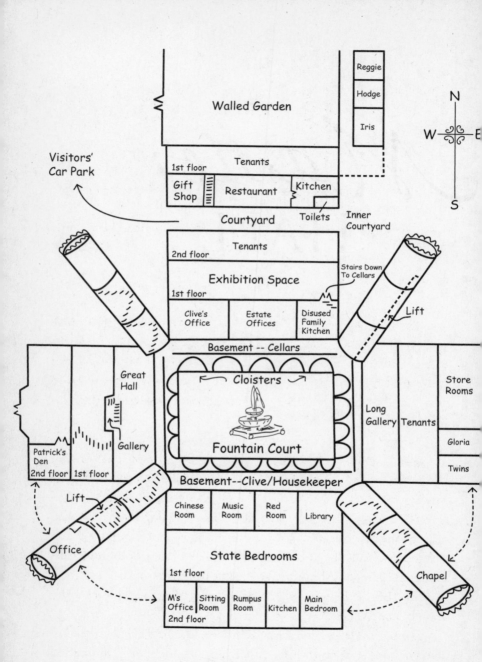

Eden Hall

Chapter One

It was a bad decision. Minty knew it straight away. And what would it lead to? A victory for God, or ... a descent into hell.

Something flickered at the back of the other woman's eyes. Was it triumph?

These two women had a history. A couple of years ago Minty —heartsick after a miscarriage— had returned home to find a music festival being staged at Eden Hall. The notorious star Maxine had not only taken over Eden Hall itself, but had corrupted the hearts and minds of everyone around her. She'd even dared to desecrate the family chapel.

Now she was back, and asking for a job!

Minty walked over to the library window, giving herself time to think. She was worn out. How many times had the twins got her up last night? And how was she to deal with Patrick's desire for more children? She really couldn't face being pregnant again, but she dreaded telling him that. She loved him so much; he was everything she'd ever wanted in a man. She realised that her present behaviour must be frustrating for him, but she didn't know how to explain ...

She shut off that line of thought. It was no use going round and round in circles. There was work to be done.

She pushed back the heavy velvet curtains on either side of the tall windows, to let as much light as possible into the library. A stand of heavy-headed chrysanthemums had been arranged behind one of the leather settees, scenting the air. Something about the flowers stirred a query at the back of her mind. She must investigate, later.

The late afternoon sun warmed the magnificent sweep of lawn below the great house. Down, down to the lake, and beyond. There had been a storm a couple of nights ago which had stripped the last leaves from the trees in the Park and brought down a great oak on the other side of the house. Patrick was in mourning for the oak, because he often took an early morning walk in that direction. She hadn't yet had time to visit the site.

The splendour of the library lay in shadow behind her, with only a few gleams of gold lightening the darkness of the ranks of leather-bound books. Above the marble fireplace was the portrait of Minty's mother, that pale flower who had died young. Minty's likeness to her mother was very marked in that both were fair-haired with piercing blue eyes, but Minty's chin announced a stronger, more resilient character, and the cross she wore on a chain round her neck was no mere ornament.

By contrast, the former pop star Maxine was a creature of the shadows, with a capacity for evil. She was adept at playing games. Despite the damage to her face, she was still a beautiful woman. She'd once boasted she could take Minty's husband away from her. So what was she really after now?

Minty—Mrs Araminta Cardale Sands—had inherited the beautiful but run-down Eden Hall some years ago, and after a struggle had begun to make the stately home pay its way. She'd married her childhood sweetheart in the teeth of opposition from her family, who had thought she could do better than a country solicitor, and it had proved to be the best thing she ever did. After a traumatic miscarriage, they'd produced twins who were now two hurtling bundles of energy.

Looking after the twins took up all her time. If she'd had no other responsibilities this might have been all right, but lately Patrick had begun to hint that she was neglecting the Hall and, perhaps, him as well.

She'd given him short shrift. "I'm short of sleep, that's all. I don't understand why you keep on about it. Haven't you always said that running the Hall is my concern, not yours?"

Patrick was not only a solicitor with a thriving practice in a nearby town, but also a businessman with many outside interests, and it was unusual for him to interfere. Yet he had persisted, the upright line between his eyes deepening. "I can't watch you running yourself into the ground and not say anything."

She'd ended that discussion by walking away, muttering that it was ridiculous to say that she was spoiling the twins. If she hadn't been so tired, she'd have lost her temper with him. She'd been to all the boring weekly business meetings at the Hall. Well, perhaps not the last two, because one of the twins hadn't been well and the other had been playing up. But apart from that ...

Oh, and they'd had a stomach upset after she'd taken them to the toddlers' group in the village. And perhaps ...

She grimaced. Perhaps she hadn't been for quite a while. But Patrick should mind his own business.

When Chef's daughter had offered to take the twins out into the Park for an hour, it had been on the tip of Minty's tongue to refuse, because she'd been looking forward to doing that herself. Then she thought what a pleasure it would be to have an hour to herself to snatch some sleep, and agreed to let them go.

But Patrick's nagging — yes, he had been nagging! — made her drag herself along to the tower office, instead of diving under the duvet.

She wasn't going to the office to check up on things. No, of course not. Just to pass the time of day with Iris, her wonderful personal assistant. Only, Iris hadn't been there, and Toby Wootton, he of the triangular face and misleading appearance of fragility, had paperwork spread over every surface, including the floor. Toby was in charge of the publicity and promotional material for the Hall, and very good at his job he was, too.

"Hello, stranger," he said, which made her wince. "No twins today?"

"They're out in the Park with Gloria—Chef's daughter—you know? It gives me an hour's peace and quiet."

She drifted to the window which gave onto the Park. A flight of ducks took off from the lake. Was that a tiny scarlet-clad figure running round the far verge, followed by one in blue? Being chased by a laughing Gloria? Minty wished she was down there with them.

Toby was amused. "Those two have enough energy to run a nuclear power station. Did you realise they've learned to operate the lift? You remember you asked if they could sit quietly in here with me and do some drawing while you helped Serafina with the housework? I didn't realise they were plotting something until I heard the lift doors opening and saw them disappear inside."

This was frightening news. If they could operate the lift, the twins could roam wherever they wanted through the great house and even . . . horrors! . . . stray onto the driveway in front of passing traffic!

The four wings of the centuries-old Hall had been built in a square round the Fountain Court. To solve the problem of access at different levels, there was a staircase in the tower at each of the four corners. Minty and Patrick occupied the top floor overlooking the lake, but were gradually spreading into rooms on either side. As soon as the twins became mobile, Patrick had had the staircases partitioned off, with handles on each door at adult shoulder height. The tower which housed the office on its top floor also contained a lift, but everyone had thought the operating panel too high for the twins to reach.

Minty checked the height of the buttons on the lift.

"They dragged that chair across and stood on it." Toby was amused. Toby wasn't married and didn't have to worry about what children could get up to.

Minty looked across to the door leading to Patrick's sanctum in the adjacent wing, which he allowed nobody else but Minty to enter. A month ago Patrick had had a combination lock put high up on that door.

Minty couldn't think straight. "We can't move the buttons on the lift. What can we do to stop them getting out?"

Toby humoured her. "There's a lock on the door into your rooms, isn't there? Any idea where the keys are?"

"Of course. I'll see if I can find them. Sorry. Short of sleep."

There was a slightly uncomfortable silence, then Toby—who'd stopped work on his papers—said, "If you're looking for Iris, she's gone off somewhere with Clive. I'm a bit bothered, actually, because there's a couple of women coming for interviews this afternoon. Also, Chef's been phoning through, wanting to talk to her. Iris didn't say where she'd be, did she?"

Minty shook her head. This was something else to worry about. Clive Hatton, their Administrator, had made it clear he'd no intention of marrying Iris. Unfortunately, that otherwise sensible woman believed one day he'd change his mind. She'd had other men interested in her—in particular their delightful if rotund accountant—but she'd never wavered in her devotion to Clive. Maybe they'd gone off somewhere to ...

Minty stopped that thought. Once before Iris had put Clive before her loyalty to Minty and the Hall. Surely, she wouldn't do that again?

"What's that about Chef?" Chef—Florence Thornby—had been one of the mainstays of the Hall for ages. Minty rather thought Patrick had said something about Chef recently, but she hadn't taken any notice because it was no business of his what Chef did.

Toby shrugged. "I don't suppose it's anything. I'm a bit bothered about these two women, though."

"What jobs have they come for?" Minty realised she ought to have known, but she didn't mind showing her ignorance to Toby, who was an old friend. Well, not so old, really. He'd been at school with Patrick. He was also looking at her in a slightly hangdog way, almost furtive. Was he, too, up to something?

When she didn't feel so tired, she must find out what was worrying him.

He scrabbled to find some papers on Iris' desk. "One of them wants a job in the gift shop. School leaver. Doris in the gift shop says she knows the girl and thinks she'd be all right. Actually, Doris is pretty desperate for help in the run-up to Christmas, so if the girl's not got two heads, we should take her." He showed Minty an application form filled out in a round hand.

"The other wants ..." He frowned, checking through the application form. "I'm not sure. Office skills? Computer literate. I don't think we've got any vacancies in the Estate Office at the moment, have we? Iris hasn't said anything about their needing help. She must have forgotten they were coming."

Minty smoothed back her unruly fair hair, and looked down at her white shirt and blue jeans. She wasn't exactly dressed to interview people, but did that matter? "I was supposed to be having a rest, but I suppose I could see them."

The phone rang on Iris' desk, and Minty picked it up. Someone from the Estate Office reported that two people had arrived to see Iris. The voice thought that Iris had gone off in her car with Clive and hadn't come back yet. What were they to do?

Minty made a decision. "I'll see them up here."

Toby raised his hands in horror. "Can't you take them somewhere else? It's taken me all afternoon to get this lot sorted."

VERONICA HELEY

Minty regarded the sea of papers with bemusement. "What is it, anyway?"

"New brochure. You know."

She didn't know but hadn't time to investigate. She turned back to the phone. "The house isn't open to visitors today, is it? Take them along to the library. I'll be there in five minutes."

She scooped up the two application forms and picked her way through the papers to the lift, leaving Toby to his sorting.

Reaching the courtyard down below, she wondered whether she ought to have gone and changed her clothes, brushed her hair, and put on some make-up. She didn't exactly look the part of Lady of the Hall at the moment, did she? Patrick had complained recently that she ought to spend more time on herself, but really she was too exhausted to care.

One of the girls from the Estate Office was hovering in the doorway of the library, anxious to get back to her work. Or to leave early, perhaps? Minty thanked her and said she'd show the applicants out herself. A movement on the opposite side of the courtyard caught her eye. Who was there? The house was closed to visitors today, so … but the movement was not repeated, and she dismissed it from her mind.

The library was dim, with the shutters only half open. Minty put the paperwork down on the vast desk in the centre of the room and went to pull the shutters open and let up the blinds. The sun was bright outside, but inside the room shadows masked the glory of the stuccoed ceiling and the gilt tooling on the leather-bound books.

A dark-haired teenager was standing nervously by the desk, while the other woman had faded into the background. The younger applicant was eighteen and trying to look older, wearing a black trouser suit which had probably been bought for the interview. Her hair was brushed and her nails well shaped and not bitten. Minty got her to sit down and went through her application. The girl was nervous. She'd left school in the summer. She'd considered going to college

13

but couldn't bear the thought of more lessons, and anyway she'd got a boyfriend who was working in one of the pubs in the village, so she didn't want to go far from home. She'd helped Doris out in the shop a couple of times on Saturdays, and she'd really liked it, with all the pretty things they had to sell. And yes, she'd been taught how to manage the till and she could start straight away.

Minty thought the girl might stick with the job for a year, with luck. But, as Doris was desperate for help, Minty said she'd get a contract sorted out ready for the girl to start immediately. The girl was pleased, red-cheeked, smiling. She bounced out of the room, saying she knew her way out.

Minty waited for the other woman to approach the desk.

And drew in a long breath.

"I know you."

The ex-pop star Maxine cast down her eyes. "No one else did."

Maxine's own hair had been a light auburn in colour, cut short because it was a trifle on the thin side. Most of the time she'd worn wigs. Her clothing had been flamboyant. She'd been a sex symbol who despised and dominated her back-up group and dancers. For her most famous act she'd dressed like a Goth in black and purple, with a metal brace on her teeth.

Minty glanced down at the application form and read off the name. "Judith Kent."

"My real name."

Judith Kent was dressed in a plain grey sweater over a calf-length brown skirt. She wore sensible shoes and carried a dull brown handbag, rather the worse for wear. She wore glasses which were no fashion statement, and her hair—or it might be a wig?—was mouse colour, not particularly thick, and cut to frame her face without being in any way come-hitherish.

On her very last day at the Hall, and entirely through her own wilfulness, her face and arms had been extensively burned by contact with a toxic plant. Now her skin looked smooth, but maybe that was the result of skilfully applied make-up. There had been some damage. Missing eyebrows had been flicked on with a skilful hand. The eyelashes were sparse. In the past she had worn a musky scent, but now she didn't seem to be wearing any at all.

The low, seductive voice was the same, as was the slender figure and classically perfect profile. She had camouflaged herself, but she was still a beautiful woman.

She sat opposite Minty, completely at ease.

Minty fidgeted. It might seem to an onlooker that it was Minty being interviewed, not the other way round.

Minty suppressed a shiver. The woman could do her no more harm, could she? Granted, Maxine had nearly destroyed everything that was good in the Hall. She'd even threatened Minty's marriage at one point.

Minty looked down at her hands. She'd crumpled the application form between her fingers. She put the form down on the desk and straightened it out.

"Why ...?" She tried again. "Why are you here?"

"Where else would I go? It's taken a series of skin grafts to look even as good as this. My voice isn't what it was, and I don't have the stamina for the club circuit. My agent, the accountants, the recording companies ... they don't want to know me any more." She shrugged. "I had everything once, didn't I? Now all I've got is a second-hand caravan and a couple of hundred pounds. The caravan's in your car park, by the way."

Minty wanted to say that the wages of sin were death, but couldn't bring herself to crow over someone who'd lost so much. Pity fought with outrage. She bit back some hasty words and shook her head. "How could you think I'd help you, after what you tried to do here?"

"I didn't succeed, though, did I? You stopped me, and yes, I'm glad that you did. In my old life, I could have had anything I wanted, and none of it satisfied. I tried drink, drugs, sex, chasing new sensations ..." She shrugged.

Minty couldn't restrain herself. "You performed a Black Mass here in our chapel. Don't deny it!"

"All that's behind me."

Minty stood to end the interview. "I don't believe you."

Judith flicked a slender gold chain out from the neck of her sweater. On it hung a tiny gold cross. "You wear a cross. So do I."

Slowly, Minty sat down again. Was it just another ornament?

Judith nodded. "I saw the light, as they say."

Was she sending herself up, or did she mean it? Minty said, "You can't expect me to believe that."

"It's true." She looked away. "It's not easy to talk about it, even now."

Minty was silent, waiting.

Judith's tone became mock-serious. "Well, there I was in hospital, being persecuted by this woman in the next bed. She'd been blinded in an accident, but she wasn't going quietly. She demanded that the chaplain visit her every day. She was a right pest, you know? As if I wasn't in enough trouble, she wanted me to read to her from her Bible. The nurses were always too busy, but I wasn't, was I?"

Judith's tone slid out of self-mockery into sincerity. "You can imagine how I felt after the things I'd done ... the thing I'd become. I treated her to a right mouthful, but she went on and on at me and one of the nurses told me she was dying, so in the end, I read her a bit. Just to keep her quiet, you know?"

Her voice became reflective. "She wanted me to read to her about a man being forgiven, even though he'd committed terrible crimes. I read on and on, and when she fell asleep, I took her Bible back to my own bed with me and I read some more. That night she died and I still had her Bible."

Judith seemed to be telling the truth, but she wouldn't meet Minty's eyes. "When the chaplain came, I tried to give it to him, said I'd no right to it. He said she'd no family, that I should keep it. I don't know how, but he got me to talk, to confess. Gradually, the load was taken from me and I began to live again. He baptised me in the chapel at the hospital. Then it was time for me to move on. Only I didn't know where.

"He said that being sorry for my sins wasn't enough. That I should try to make up for the evil I'd done. I kept thinking of this place. I told him about it, about you and what I'd tried to do here. He said I should pray about it, that maybe God wanted me to face up to my sins by returning here and offering to work for you.

"So I drove here by easy stages. I arrived in the village a week ago and then lost my nerve, couldn't get any further. I parked the caravan down by the river and mooched around, asking for a job. Any job. I'm not up to heavy work, as you can probably see, and there wasn't anything else. But there were all sorts of rumours flying around about the Hall ..."

"What rumours?" Judith was adding to Minty's unease.

Judith waved her hand. "That the Hall was heading for disaster. Then someone in the village said you were short-handed, and it seemed an opening was being made for me. If you turn me away, I don't know where I'll go, or what I'll do."

Again came that flicker at the back of her eyes. Or maybe it was just the flash of her spectacles? As the sun faded from the sky, the room had become darker. Minty leaned forward to switch on a table lamp.

Judith flinched as the light struck her face. Then she made herself turn towards Minty, exposing her face to the light. Now Minty could see that her skin was far from flawless. She was filled with pity for the girl.

"My new face. Do you like it?" Judith's tone was hard.

"But Maxine—Judith—we have no need of a singer here."

"Those days are gone. I'm computer literate, took all sorts of courses between hospital visits, till the money ran out. I could help to look after your children."

Minty recoiled. "I'm not letting you near my children."

Tears came into Judith's eyes. Minty remembered that Maxine had been an accomplished actress. Perhaps she could cry at will?

"You don't trust me." Judith got to her feet. "I suppose I can hardly blame you, though I thought, if you really were a Christian, that you'd give me a chance to show that I've changed." Her voice broke.

No, Minty didn't trust her. And yet—it would be against her better judgement—wouldn't it be right to offer a helping hand? What would Jesus have done? Forgiven her? He'd forgiven those who'd truly repented, but there was a big question mark in Minty's mind. She'd experienced Maxine hell-bent on destruction. Several times she'd been almost seduced by Maxine's softly spoken words.

Also, Minty wasn't Jesus, and she had to think of the broader picture.

Suppose she found Judith a place under someone who could be trusted to look after her? Florence, their chef, was a strong woman and a practising Christian. She was always in need of help; but Judith had said she wasn't up to a physically demanding job, and she certainly didn't look it. What was it that Chef wanted to talk to Iris about? Something Patrick had tried to tell her ... no, it eluded her.

Minty turned over the application form while Judith stood on the far side of the desk. "Office work?" said Minty. "References?"

Judith smiled derisively. "I completed the courses but I've had no work experience. I got hold of a copy of your brochure on the Hall. Suppose I learn it by heart and take parties round?"

She had a point. They had volunteer stewards in every room, but no one to take parties around. It would undoubtedly be an asset to the Hall if they did. But Toby's mother, Venetia Wootton, was in charge of the stewards at the Hall and had observed the desecration Maxine had wrought in the chapel. Venetia would never agree to employing Judith. Venetia was a Christian and committed churchgoer, true. But she was not that flexible. Also, her only son Toby had once been smitten by Maxine, and even though he'd recoiled from her when he'd seen the signs of satanic practices in the chapel, Venetia wouldn't want him coming into contact with the girl again. And neither would Minty's old friend Carol, who'd had her eye on Toby for a long time.

Minty pushed the application to one side. "I think I'd better ask my husband about this. See if he can suggest something."

Judith looked down. "I thought your husband was a country solicitor who never interfered with the running of the Hall."

"That's true, but ..."

"You have everything, and I have nothing. You have this beautiful house and adoring servants. You have a faithful husband and twins, an heir and a spare, as they say. I could make a start here, in the library. There's dust on all the bookshelves, and the books aren't in any sort of order. I could do something about that for you."

Minty looked around her. What Judith said was true. "We can't start spring-cleaning the house until after Christmas when we close to visitors for three months. Every few years we have a specialist come in, take down the books, and examine them page by page for damage. It's true you could do that, but not till you've been trained."

"I could catalogue them. I could find out how on the Internet. I have a laptop. If you'd trust me, I could even make a preliminary assessment if there's any damage that needs looking at."

Minty bit her lip. The books did need cataloguing. Patrick was the only person who ever took a book out from the library, and goodness knows what was lurking in bottom drawers and at the back of the shelves.

"Just give me a small wage to start with. Enough to buy food. Let me keep the caravan in the car park. That's all I ask. For the Lord's sake, if not for mine."

Minty covered her eyes, putting her elbows on the desk. When in doubt, pray. It was difficult, but not impossible. She had to try. *Please, Lord. Tell me what to do. I can't judge ... I'm bewildered ... I'm so tired, I can't think straight. Would You forgive her?*

She took her hands away from her face. "Would you be prepared to come up to the chapel with me now? To swear on the Bible that you mean to follow Christ in future?"

A faint smile. "Of course. I thought you'd want something like that." Her voice roughened, deepened. "I have changed, you know."

"You say you've been here a week. Did you go to church last Sunday?"

A slight hesitation. "Yes, but only when no one else was there. I was afraid someone might recognise me and ask me to explain myself. I wasn't sure I could."

"You'd find the vicar sympathetic. He's old for his years and he's seen all sorts. Besides, there's my uncle ... he's retired now, but he still helps with the services ... you might find he's got more time to help you."

Judith reddened. She said, low down, "I was ashamed."

Minty believed her. She glanced over the application form. "Give me the name and address of the college where you learned IT skills, and of the consultant and the chaplain at the hospital."

Judith filled in the details. Minty still wasn't sure that she was doing the right thing, but she said, "Subject to my taking up your references, I'll put you on probation for a week. Minimum wage. You can keep your caravan in the car park. But you leave if there's the slightest hint of trouble. Right?"

"One more thing," said Judith. "You won't tell anyone who I am, will you? I need a clean break with the past."

"I can't promise. One or two people may have to know."

"I'm relying on you."

Minty felt wretched. She was almost sure she'd made a mistake, and what Patrick would say, she didn't like to think. Something flickered at the back of Judith's eyes. Triumph? And then it was gone.

Chapter Two

After Judith left, Minty sat on alone in the library. She was almost sure she'd regret what she'd done, but she had prayed about it, hadn't she?

She switched off all the lights and made her way back up to the tower office. Toby had vanished, his papers had been cleared from the floor, and the place was deserted. She went through into her own office. The place seemed very quiet, which meant that the twins hadn't returned from their afternoon walk yet. Minty started to worry about them and then told herself not to be so stupid. They wouldn't come to any harm in Gloria's company.

She pulled the phone towards her and rang the college where Judith said she'd been studying. The principal was still at her desk, luckily, and happy to give Judith a glowing reference.

"We get a lot of mature students, usually women returning to work after they've had their family. Judith Kent was an excellent student and passed all her exams with flying colours."

Minty imagined the principal was a white-haired, competent woman in a business suit, with a brain that went *click, click, click!* to produce facts and figures as required. A human computer. What Minty really needed was a gossip to tell her what Judith was like as a person, not as a showpiece passer of exams. It didn't seem she was going to get it.

"She did the college credit, and I'm pleased she's landed herself a job straight away."

"On the social side," said Minty, "how did she interact with other students?"

"Kept herself to herself, just as she should."

"No personal relationships after hours?"

"What the students do after hours is no business of mine."

"No, of course not. But I need to know ..."

"I am sure she will be extremely capable at whatever she undertakes. Now, if that is all ...?"

"Thank you. You've been most helpful."

In a way, the principal had been helpful, more because of what she'd not said, than because of the actual words spoken. She hadn't said any of the usual things, such as that Judith had been a popular student, well liked by all. Minty guessed that Judith probably hadn't been popular with the other students. She would have considered herself a cut above them, and in fact she probably was, in some ways. She'd been standoffish, probably. Not a social bunny. Possibly chilly. Even slightly sinister? Or was Minty reading too much into what the principal had not said? A second opinion wouldn't come amiss.

Minty dialled the hospital which had given Judith a new face, and there she came up against a brick wall of a different character.

"I'm afraid we can't give out any information about our patients unless you are a relative. You aren't, are you?"

"No. I'm thinking of giving her a job, but ..."

"I'm sorry. No one but relatives ..."

"What about her consultant? Would it be possible to ..."

"Not unless you're a relative."

"I understand all that, but ..."

"In any case, he's on leave at the moment."

"Oh. When does he get back?"

"After Christmas sometime. In any case, he wouldn't be able to discuss one of his patients with you, unless ..."

"... I was a relative. Thank you."

"You're welcome."

Minty put the phone down with a bang. Yuk. Scream!

Judith Kent had appeared to be giving a lot of information on her application form, but in fact, the leads she had given led nowhere.

Minty decided to have one last go, without much hope.

She dialled the number of the vicarage where the hospital chaplain lived. The phone rang and rang. And rang. A voicemail service clicked in.

Minty gave her name and telephone number. "Judith Kent has given your name as a reference for a job here at Eden Hall. I'd be grateful if you would ring me back this evening about it."

At that point the twins erupted into the room, with shiny eyes and cheeks pink from exertion, followed by a laughing Gloria. All thought of doing any more business was at an end. Play-time. High tea time.

Six o'clock. Was Patrick going to be late?

The phone rang while Minty was feeding the twins. Normally she let it ring, but today she had Judith on her mind, so she asked Serafina, her wonderful housekeeper, to take over from her, and took the call. It was lucky that she did.

"Mrs Cardale Sands? This is the Reverend Tom Briggs speaking. You rang earlier, asking about Judith Kent?" A young-sounding voice, perhaps not too sure of itself.

"Yes, I ..."

"I'm afraid I haven't long, have to be out again in fifteen minutes." Overemphatic now? Perhaps he wasn't too keen on talking about Judith? Or was Minty reading too much into his brusque manner?

"Yes, I appreciate ..."

"I cover two hospitals, you see. The Royal, of course, and ..."

Minty cut in quickly. The twins were making a racket because she'd left them at table, and Serafina was trying to quieten them. If only Patrick had been on time, he could have helped, but it was already well after six and he was late. "She came to me for a job today, saying you'd advised her to ..."

VERONICA HELEY

"Yes, she told me all about you. An interesting situation. How do you feel about it? Are you sure you can cope?"

Minty blinked. This wasn't quite what she'd expected. "I'm not sure that I ..."

"I advised her to get herself a spiritual director and gave her a couple of names for her to follow up."

"Weren't you her counsellor? Didn't you sort her out?"

For the first time, there was a pause in the rat-a-tat of his words. Then, in a guarded tone, much slower, he said, "I did what I could, but in such cases it is advisable to have an ongoing relationship with someone who has had dealings with such matters as part of their ministry."

"And you don't?"

Another hesitation. "This is the first such case that has come my way. I was about to ask the bishop to suggest someone who could take over from me, when Judith was discharged from hospital and left the area."

"But you did baptize her?"

"The bishop wasn't terribly happy about that, either. But we all felt—it's a team ministry, you know, and we all discussed the matter—that it was the right thing to do. She was repentant, she did ask for baptism, and she did seem to understand what that meant. Only, she needs to be carefully guided, steered, ... what's the right word? In touch with someone who can look after her through the next stage of her life, and possibly for as long as she lives. And now, I really must go."

"Pray for me," said Minty. But the chaplain had already hung up.

Minty returned to the supper table with much on her mind.

The twins were being extra rowdy, and it would probably be a struggle to get them to bed at their usual time.

Seven o'clock. Patrick was more than usually late.

Most people knew him only as a conscientious and successful country solicitor who'd been fortunate enough to marry the heiress of

Eden Hall. Few knew that he was a wealthy man in his own right, buying and developing property for affordable housing.

Minty's father — Sir Micah Cardale — had founded an educational trust to which he'd devoted the last years of his life. Minty had been expected to take his place on the Board, but running the Hall and producing twins had forced her to relinquish the position. Entirely on his own merits, Patrick had been asked to take her place as a trustee. In addition, he sat on the Parish and County Councils. All of which took up much of his so-called leisure time.

He was also a devoted father who never missed the twins' bath time if he could help it. Tonight the twins had had their baths and were in the middle of their bedtime story when they vanished from Minty's side. They had ears like foxes and could hear their father's car as soon as he turned off the main road into the drive.

Minty abandoned their book, checked that she was reasonably tidy, and followed. She could hear the doors banging along the suite as the twins shot through the rooms to greet him at the far end. Then the doors closed in reverse order, accompanied by stifled giggles. Patrick enjoyed their new game as much as they did.

He opened the door into the big family kitchen and came in with the stiff-legged gait of a man whose long overcoat hid a child clinging to either leg.

"Where, oh where, are those little rascals hiding tonight?" he demanded in a loud, carrying voice. He was a tall, spare, dark-haired man. He had no opinion of his looks — which had never been much to write home about — and he had a superficially easy-going personality which hid a steel core. He also had an elegance which made him stand out in any company.

He bent to kiss Minty's cheek, but she turned her head to kiss his lips instead. That checked him, for they were not usually demonstrative in front of others. He had rather hard grey eyes which saw more than most people, and in that moment he registered that something had alarmed her.

Serafina sang out that supper would be on the table in a minute. Serafina had had a chequered career. She'd been born in the Middle East, but after a loveless marriage and the loss of her children, she'd had a short but torrid love affair with Minty's father. Disowned by her family, who'd beaten her almost to death, she'd been taken into Sir Micah's household, where she'd settled down to look after him. After he died, she'd chosen to stay on to take care of Minty and Patrick, even though she'd been left a fortune by Sir Micah and could well have afforded to buy and live in a place of her own.

Serafina was almost as broad as she was high, always dressed in black, and doted on the twins. Just lately she'd been talking about going to visit her family, but Minty didn't think it would ever happen. After all, what could they have to say to one another after so long? And she was needed at the Hall.

Serafina raised her voice. "Has anyone seen the twins? How strange they are not here to greet their father on his return home."

More giggles from under Patrick's long coat. He dropped his laptop and mobile on the space at the end of the kitchen table that was kept clear for him, and said, "Phew! Isn't it hot in here? I must take off my coat! One button ... two buttons ... three!" He threw off his coat and looked down with mock surprise.

"What's this? Two children hiding beneath my coat? I wonder where they've come from. Do I know them, I wonder?"

He sank into his chair at the end of the table, and the children clambered onto his knees. The chair had once been a rocker—until the twins had rocked it so hard it had tipped over. Now a strong bar kept it steady.

The boy wriggled under Patrick's jacket until his ear was pressed close to his father's heart. "Boom, boom!" he shouted. "Boom, boom!"

He was the elder of the two, a well-built, flaxen-haired adventurous child who took after Minty in looks and character.

The girl had her fingers in Patrick's waistcoat pocket, extracting his pocket watch. She was smaller and slighter, with Patrick's dark hair and grey eyes—and his more cautious approach to life. With precise movements she set the watch chiming. "Ting, ting, ting!"

The children had been christened with appropriate family names, but since this enchanting game began, they had refused to answer to any names except Boom and Ting.

"Well past your bedtime," said Serafina, amused but worried about keeping supper hot.

"Two minutes," Patrick begged. And to the twins, "So what mischief have you been up to today?"

"Went to the Park ..."

"With Gory and ..."

"... chased ducks."

"Gory fell and ..."

"Bluggied her knee and ..."

"... said a funny word."

"We saw Reggie ..." Reggie was the Hall's Houseman and Jack of all Trades.

"... and had a biscuit from a tin with a lady on it ..."

"... Gory washed her knee, all bluggy ..."

"... we came home and Mummy wasn't here."

Patrick looked up at Minty, not worried, but curious. She'd switched on the iron and was tackling the never-ending pile of children's clothes. "Gloria took the twins into the Park for an hour, and then some people came for an interview. I'll tell you later."

He nodded and stood up, one child on either arm. "What an exciting day. And Gloria was all bluggy, was she? I hope she wasn't permanently damaged." He glanced at the big old clock hanging on the wall. "I've a committee meeting in an hour, so off we go to bed."

The twins started to wail, of which he took no notice. Minty switched off the iron. "You eat. I'll put them to bed."

"My treat." He carried the twins through the main bedroom, across the tower which housed the family chapel, and round the corner into the twins' bedroom. Two sturdy wooden cots stood in the middle of the floor with mobiles hanging overhead. The cots had been roped together, with the "gates" between permanently lowered. By the door was the narrow bed on which Minty spent the nights when the twins wouldn't settle.

By this time the twins had stopped wailing. He laid them one in each cot, while Minty covered them over with their duvets. They might stay in their own cots, or they might change over. So long as they were within touching distance, they didn't mind who slept in which one.

Patrick murmured a prayer over each sleepy head. Minty kissed both of them and followed him back to the kitchen.

"What's up, Minty?" He pulled out a chair from the table, while Serafina deposited a plateful of sizzling hot lasagne before him.

Minty looked at her watch. She'd have to be quick. He was rarely at home in the evenings nowadays. If it wasn't a District Council meeting, it was a parish meeting, or ... whatever. She was a bit fed up with being left alone in the evenings, if the truth were known. She never could get to sleep till he was back, and the twins started acting up any time after midnight. She kept going on coffee and the hope that one day soon she'd get a good night's sleep.

"Nothing much. You remember that pop star, Maxine, who caused us so much trouble? Well, she's a changed woman, has become a Christian, came to me for a job. I think she's sincere, so I said yes. Will you be late tonight?"

"What?" He put down his fork and checked Serafina's face, which was registering as much surprise and alarm as his. "Minty, was that wise?"

"Eden Hall needs a small army of people to keep the Hall open to the public, and as you've often pointed out, it's my affair who I employ, not yours. Serafina, do sit down! I hate it when you hover, and your food's getting cold."

Minty had to make herself relax, because if the truth were known, she wasn't sure it had been wise to take Maxine on, either. Also, there was that disturbing hint Maxine had made about the Hall heading for disaster.

Patrick took a long, deep breath. Then let it out. "I accept that it's your right who you employ here, but my instinct tells me it means trouble."

"Mine, too," said Serafina, but started to eat.

Minty's instinct was telling her the same thing, but she wasn't going to admit it. She shrugged. "I'm sure it'll be all right."

Patrick said, "You look tired. Has Gloria agreed to move in and help Serafina look after the twins while we're away?" He yawned. "I'm tired, too. I'm really looking forward to a few days away. No phones, no emails, no meetings, no crises. Brussels first — and I promise it will only be half a day of meetings while you catch up on your sleep or go shopping — then we can wander wherever we wish. Perhaps visit Bruges? Gentle walks, pretty views, trips on the canal and in the horse buggies, good food. Have you packed yet?"

She'd forgotten he'd planned that they should go away for a few days. "I know I promised to come, but I really can't leave the twins at the moment. Once they get back to sleeping the night through, it'll be different."

He wasn't going to lose his temper. He very rarely did. But his eyes probed hers. "If you didn't pick them up as soon as they stirred at night, they'd soon learn to turn over and go back to sleep again." His tone was even, hiding disappointment. "I don't want to take a holiday without you. Won't you reconsider? We haven't had a proper break since the twins were born."

"Gloria can cope with them for an occasional afternoon, but not all night and day."

"Have you asked her?"

"I haven't, because it's out of the question."

"All right. One more try. I don't and won't interfere with the way you run the Hall, but people have been trying to tell me that all is not well here. Even your old friend Carol stopped my car in the High Street and asked if I could get you to ring her. She said it was important, that she'd been trying to get hold of you for ages. Why haven't you returned her calls?"

Minty had made friends with ginger-haired Carol at college. When Minty inherited the Hall and half the village, Carol's antique dealer father had opened a branch in the High Street, installing her as manager. While Carol described herself as a "ditzy blonde," she'd proved to be a good businesswoman and, somewhat surprisingly, had been accepted by the locals. She also had her eye on Toby Wootton.

Minty moved the food round her plate. "The twins keep me too busy to answer the phone here, and I can't have them playing with my mobile, so I've put it away for the time being. I've left messages for Carol on her answerphone. If it's a problem to do with the Hall or the village, she must take it to Clive."

He shrugged, picked up his fork, and started to eat. He probably hadn't eaten since breakfast. Serafina had a hearty appetite, but Minty was too tired to eat. She was out of sorts, irritated — no, angry — with everyone and everything. Judith had summed up Minty's situation well. She had a beautiful house, which ran like clockwork thanks to Clive and Iris in the office and Serafina upstairs. She had a loving husband who'd given her an heir and a spare, which meant she didn't have to struggle through another pregnancy just yet ... so why did Patrick keep criticising her? It wasn't fair.

Minty pushed her plate aside. She'd just have another cup of good coffee and that would keep her going. Patrick was already rushing through the last few mouthfuls, glancing up at the clock, wondering if he'd make his meeting in time. Serafina asked if anyone wanted second helpings.

Minty shook her head. She'd hardly touched her plate. "Another month and the twins will be two mornings a week at playgroup instead of one. Maybe they'll be sleeping better then, and I'll feel better about leaving them."

Serafina said, "Tsk! Patrick's right. You spoil them. Let some-one else look after them for a couple of nights, and they'll soon sleep through."

Minty's colour rose. "It's me they want when they wake up."

Patrick shook his head but said no more. He cleared the last crumb from his plate and reached for his mobile. He hugged Serafina and thanked her for supper. He blew a kiss to Minty and made for the door, saying he'd be late and not to wait up for him. Then returned for his overcoat and laptop — he really was one of the most absent-minded of men — and finally left for good.

Serafina clattered plates together. "You want to talk about it, Minty? It's not just the twins playing you up, is it? You've been edgy for days. I don't want to leave you like this when I go to visit my family."

Minty ignored that hint. Surely Serafina wouldn't leave her while Patrick was gone.

"Nothing's wrong." She helped herself to a cup of strong coffee. "I could do with a few days by myself." Now Judith had come, there was even more reason not to leave the Hall. She would lie down on the bed in the twins' room for a couple of hours, though it was unlikely she'd be able to sleep.

She dozed and woke and dozed again. She dreamed she was fac-ing Judith, who was laughing at her ... and then she was on the top of the tower and as it crumbled beneath her, she was tumbling down with it ... falling headlong, twisting and turning ... knowing she'd forgotten her parachute ... had forgotten ...

Voices shouting at her that it was all her fault and ... she was hiding behind a door and listening to voices shouting, arguing because she hadn't done what she ought to have done ... and now the people who'd been shouting were rushing at her and she was fleeing through the library and the other State Rooms till finally she reached the Chinese Room ... where the tiny figures on the painted wallpaper joined in the hunt and she was the size of a doll and running, running, panting, without enough breath even to call for help and suddenly she was falling through the floor, down, down ...

Light flooded the room.

She sat up, banishing her nightmare, breathing hard. Patrick had opened the door from the tower, throwing a band of light across the room. She'd had a bad dream, that was all.

The twins! She started up, fully dressed apart from her shoes. Two mounds appeared to be sleeping in one cot, but as usual Boom had shed his duvet. When had he moved over? She hadn't heard him waken. What a bad mother she was, sleeping when he might have needed her!

Patrick hovered over the cots, easing Boom's duvet over him. He whispered, "They're fine. I've just switched the baby alarm on."

She'd forgotten to do that, too. She was furious with herself ... with him ... with everyone. Shards of the nightmare clung to her brain. She'd been in the tower and it had fallen, fallen ...

She pushed the nightmare away and it faded from her mind. Something still lurked in the corner of the room. A shadow, of course. She was imagining things, just as she'd imagined a figure watching her from the shadows in the courtyard earlier on.

Chapter Three

Patrick was leaving the room, holding the door open for her. She was thirsty. She picked up her shoes, and followed him. "What's the time? Eleven? You're late."

He led the way through the tower to their bedroom. "Ructions at the church council. The chairman couldn't make it, so without benefit of a referee, the two ladies who run everything in the village slugged it out over eleven rounds. I got my head bitten off when I tried to intervene."

He could still laugh, but it wasn't much of an effort. "I nearly forgot myself and called them Mrs Fattypuff and Mrs Thinifer to their faces. Most of it seems to have been about a cancellation of something here at the Hall, but they soon got on to the subject of one another's weaknesses. It would have been entertaining if I hadn't been so tired."

He would have put his arm around her, but she slid away from him. She said, "I'm thirsty. I'll just get myself a drink."

"I'll get it for you. What do you want?"

"I can get it for myself." She went through their bedroom to get a drink of water from the bathroom. Her ears were stretched to hear movement from the twins. She shut the door, shucked off her clothes, and stepped into the shower. It didn't seem to help much. Clean nightie from the cupboard. Towelling robe from behind the door. Where were her slippers?

When she returned to the bedroom, Patrick was sitting on the side of their big four-poster bed. He'd made no effort to undress and had his hands in his pockets, his eyes half closed. The bed was inviting, the willow-patterned curtains held back by silken ropes, the duvet and pillows freshly laundered.

It struck her all over again what an attractive man he was. What fun they'd had in that bed in the old days, playfully teasing, gently loving, breathlessly passionate. She was tempted even now to nestle up to him, to tell him what ailed her and trust him to put it right, just as she had done as a little girl when they'd first met, she aged four, and he six years older. He'd taught her to read and write and promised to marry her when they both grew up ... and they had eventually married and it had been good, so good.

But — she sighed — she daren't think about that now. She was too tired.

"Minty." There was a world of patience in his voice. "How long is it since we slept in the same bed?"

He'd chosen the wrong moment to reproach her. She loved him, yes; but she had no reserves of energy left to show that she did. Feeling guilty, she lashed out. "Are you feeling neglected just because I'm needed by the twins? Isn't that a bit childish?"

His mouth tightened, but he maintained the same even, reasonable tone. "Aren't you encouraging them to call out for you unnecessarily? You don't even start the night here with me any more, though we have a perfectly good baby alarm. I'm more than willing to spell you at nights."

"It's me they want when they wake up."

He passed his hand across his eyes. "This is all wrong. I miss you horribly. Lately I feel there's a barrier growing up between us, and I can't seem to break through. I know you're tired and not sleeping properly. I've tried to be patient, but when I try to talk to you about anything important, I see you decide not to listen."

"If it was important, of course I'd listen."

"But you don't. I've prayed about this, hoping you'd join me in the chapel early in the morning and last thing at night, as you always used to do. But you don't. You're always too tired. Chef had a word with me this morning. She's really unhappy about things, too. Why don't you go down and sort it out? Then Gloria's been hoping that you'd offer her a full-time job looking after the twins. She could start tomorrow. I'll gladly pay her wages."

"You should have consulted me before ..."

"I have. You don't listen. Serafina is worried about you, and so am I. She doesn't want to leave you like this, but ..."

"You've been discussing me behind my back? How could you!"

He patted the bed beside him. "Sit down for a minute."

"I'm looking for my slippers." She pounced on them. "I'm tired. I expect you are, too. We'll talk in the morning."

She walked out and returned to the twins' room. Ting had moved over to the cot in which Boom usually slept. She'd dragged her duvet with her. Clever Ting.

Minty sank onto the bed and let herself lie back with a groan.

Pictures whirled through her tired brain ... Patrick feeling neglected ... that upset her, but ... why couldn't he be more understanding? The Hall ... surely nothing could really be wrong ... Judith Kent ... the shadow in the courtyard ...

Minty shot upright, gasping, forcing the nightmare from her mind. The same one? Somebody watching her from the shadows? Or the one where the tower crumbled beneath her and she fell ... being chased by tiny figures? Sometimes it was one and sometimes the other. She knew she was overtired. She supposed she ought to see the doctor about it.

She drank some water, checked on the twins, who were back in one cot again, and lay back, trying to slow her heartbeat down. If only she could get a good night's sleep.

The twins woke her at seven. It was a wonder they hadn't woken earlier. They were full of beans, but Minty felt as if she'd hardly slept at all.

Minty dragged herself out of bed, got them washed and dressed, and pulled any old clothes on for herself, longing for the first cup of good coffee to perk her up.

Patrick was due to leave for the airport at eleven that morning. He didn't appear at breakfast; Serafina said he'd breakfasted early and was out and about somewhere. Minty was out of sorts, for the cafetière of coffee was empty and Serafina said they'd run out of ground coffee and Minty must have some decaffeinated instant instead.

Minty didn't go looking for Patrick but assumed that as usual he'd gone for a walk in the grounds after a stint in the chapel. He'd probably visit the fallen oak. He'd loved that oak. A pity it was no more.

The twins were full of energy, as usual. Minty could hardly keep up with them. After breakfast, she played bears with them under the rugs in the rumpus room. Once this had been the family's sedate dining room, but it had long since been turned into a nursery. Situated next to the family kitchen, it was convenient for all purposes. On the rare occasions nowadays that Patrick invited people for a meal, they'd eat informally in the kitchen, or more formally, in the Great Hall down below.

When they were all tired of being bears, Minty felt a headache coming on, so she settled the twins down in the kitchen for their midmorning milk and biscuit under Serafina's eye.

She wasn't avoiding Patrick, of course. This was her usual morning routine. Some more coffee would help. Good coffee, this time. If they'd run out of ground coffee, she'd have to find time somehow to go into the village and get some more. Meanwhile, she'd make her peace with Patrick by offering to help him pack.

He was in their bedroom, with his airline case open on the chaise lounge near the windows, sliding a couple of books under his clothes; he never went anywhere without books.

It was a cold, grisly sort of day, the trees in the Park below indistinct in the mist. Inside, Patrick had put on the bedside lights to see what he was doing.

Minty subsided onto the ottoman at the end of the bed, rubbing her forehead in an effort to banish her incipient headache. "I was going to pack for you."

Patrick was wearing one of his good grey suits and a white shirt with gold cufflinks. He looked elegant and remote.

She was, as usual nowadays, wearing the sort of old clothes you could tumble around on the floor in, clothes that didn't matter if they got torn. Any minute now the twins would come rushing through the door, demanding attention. Her ears were stretched to hear them.

Patrick would have chosen a good suit to wear because he had a business meeting in Brussels this afternoon — something to do with the educational charity her father had founded, on which Patrick served as a trustee — so he had to appear well dressed. She was glad she'd given up the charity work. She had more than enough on her plate as it was.

He inserted his laptop into the side compartment of his case. "I gather you're not prepared to come away with me. I thought you'd enjoy a few days away, especially since it was your father's charity that got me involved in the first place."

She thought she heard the twins pounding along the floor and filtered out Patrick's words. She'd heard it all before, anyway. He'd only taken up with her father's charity because she hadn't wanted to be involved, and he seemed to have made a success of doing ... something or other with it ... and now another charity wanted him to look at ... something or other ... and there were a lot of difficulties that she didn't understand and didn't want to have explained to her. She wasn't interested. Nowadays all that was his job, not hers.

She tuned back in to hear him say, "... I can see you're not listening. Well, after Brussels, I've decided to take my holiday as planned. I've told your uncle Reuben I'll be away for a few days and not able to give him his usual game of chess. If you've time, you might drop in on him, see if he's taking his medication. Which he probably isn't. And before you ask, yes, I did raise the subject of his getting a pacemaker fitted, and he told me to get lost." He was smiling to himself.

She ignored all that about her uncle; Patrick was overreacting, as usual. She usually dropped in on the Reverend Reuben Cardale after taking the twins to the toddlers' group. He was good for another ten years, despite developing a heart murmur.

What she couldn't understand was why Patrick was being so cheerful. She'd half-expected him to be angry because she'd put her children first. For some reason it had never entered her head that he'd take time off without her.

In her mind she explored the possibilities of his going away for a few days. Was this really what she'd wanted all along? Without him always at her elbow, wouldn't she feel more free to concentrate on the twins? Was it relief she was feeling? Or dismay?

She removed herself from him and went to make the bed. "Fine by me." She pummelled the pillows into shape.

He collected his passport, tickets, and mobile, and tucked them into his pocket. "One last word. I agree it's your job to look after your family and the Hall, but it's my job to look after you and the twins. I wouldn't be doing my job if I went away leaving you like this, especially with Serafina going away for a while. So I've taken it on myself to ask Gloria to move into the guest room to help you with the twins, full-time."

"What!"

"It will give you the rest you need so badly, and a chance to sort out what's wrong at the Hall."

"How dare you interfere with—"

"No one else will stand up to you, and you're heading for a nervous breakdown if you go on like this. You might consider cutting down on coffee for a while. I've heard it can prevent a good night's sleep. I've left my schedule on my desk, in case you decide to join me in a couple of days' time . . . that is, if you can work out how to get into the room."

He collected his coat and airline bag and waited to see if she'd turn round, but she was trying to discover whether she felt more surprised than outraged, and didn't move. When she failed to respond, he left the room without another word. Without even kissing her goodbye.

"Good riddance!" she said, through her teeth. "How dare he!" She scanned the room, checking for what he might have forgotten, but there was nothing. "Does he really think I'm going to desert my post and run after him? No way!"

The room looked unusually tidy. The pile of books he usually kept by the side of the bed was considerably reduced. He'd have taken his reading notes and Bible with him, together with the poems he'd been studying. All that was left was his book on antique furniture and the latest novel that he hadn't liked much but was persevering with. Oh yes, and his notes on the history of the Hall, which he seemed to think might have been built on an earlier foundation—possibly even that of an abbey. He was always saying that when he got time, he'd like to do some research on it. She shrugged. He never would have time.

She braced herself. Do without good coffee? Nonsense. It was the only thing that kept her going. She needed coffee to get through the day. Instant just didn't do it for her.

It was, of course, quite out of the question for her to hand the twins over to Gloria for more than an hour at a time. Any minute now they'd come rushing towards her, screaming, "Mummy!"

She looked at her watch. The twins hadn't broken in on her conversation with Patrick, which was alarming. What had they got up to while her back was turned?

She found them in the kitchen, which smelled of the little cakes Serafina had just been baking. Gloria was sitting at the table with the twins, who had a large tub of crayons before them, and were busy "drawing," or rather scribbling on large sheets of paper. Serafina was poking around in the huge walk-in fridge.

Serafina gave her a warning look. "Minty, good news! Gloria's going to help us look after the children full-time. Her fiancé's brought over her things and she's going to have the bedroom next to the twins."

Gloria was a buxom wench, daughter of their marvellous chef. She was a nice girl, engaged to a driving instructor who lived in the next town, and had recently trained to be a nursery nurse, hoping that a job would materialise locally. Minty liked her and felt that she could, on the whole, trust the children with her, but she didn't like Gloria being foisted onto her, willy-nilly.

Gloria smiled up at Minty, confident that she was welcome. "I can't tell you how pleased I am to get this job. Mum's thrilled, too. She said you're looking tired."

Which didn't help. How was Minty to get rid of the girl now?

It was a dagger to her heart that the twins didn't seem to have missed her.

Boom pointed to the scrawl on his piece of paper. "Look, Mummy. Gory's knee all bluggy!"

"Look, Mummy. 'Fina, making a cake!"

Gloria was enjoying herself. "Boom, suppose you use this red crayon for the blood. Ting, try the black for Serafina's dress."

Minty did her best to smile. "Lovely, Gloria. I hope your knee's all right now."

Serafina was making a list. "Some more cheese, fresh vegetables, fruit, especially bananas. What else do we need from the village?"

"Ground coffee," said Minty.

"I'll do the shopping in a minute, if you like," said Gloria. "I could take the twins and we can have a go on the swings on the Green afterwards."

"Swings! Now!" The twins screamed their approval, causing Minty and Serafina to cover their ears. Minty made herself another cup of instant coffee and downed a couple of aspirins to keep her going.

Gloria firmly told the twins she'd take them when they'd finished their drawings and to stop their nonsense. For a wonder, they did.

Minty wondered blankly what she should do with herself for the rest of the day, since Gloria had usurped her responsibilities. She could do the ironing, of course. But that would be boring. She could go to see Carol. Or Chef. Not because Patrick had asked her to. No, of course not.

The Hall was open to visitors today from noon. Patrick would by now have made his way through the courtyard, with a smile and an appreciative word for the stewards who would be marshalling people around the great house. He'd probably have shared a joke with Chef in the restaurant and paid Doris in the gift shop a compliment on the way she'd arranged her stock on his way out. Then he'd have got into his second-hand Volvo, an old but trusty car, and by now be driving himself, competently, swiftly, to the airport. He could have afforded to buy himself a top of the range four-by-four, fitted out with every expensive gadget known to exist, but he'd never been the sort to flaunt his wealth.

The twins would miss him. Minty told herself that she wouldn't. It would be heavenly not to have to worry about what he was thinking, on top of everything else.

She was used to his being out in the evenings. If it wasn't something to do with his busy solicitor's practice, it would be a meeting of some sort. Even when he was home, he'd have papers to look at in the evenings. Occasionally, when he was working late, he'd even stay overnight at his tiny cottage on the outskirts of the nearest town "for a bit of peace and quiet."

He could talk about responsibilities! Wasn't he neglecting his wife and children, too?

Something was nagging at the back of her mind. What had she forgotten to do?

Ah, she hadn't told anyone what she'd done about the interviews the day before. The Administrator, Clive Hatton, would be annoyed if he learned about them from someone else. Also, she needed keys to lock the door from their rooms into the tower office so that the twins couldn't get at the lift.

She took her mug of instant coffee and went through the rumpus room and the formal sitting room into what had once been her own office, but which now held the old dining room furniture as well as her desk and computer. The room had a slightly dusty smell, as it was hardly ever used nowadays.

Where would the keys be? In her old desk, surely. She tried various drawers without finding them. She would ask Serafina if she knew where they were, but for now she must see Iris or Clive about the interviews yesterday.

Normally it was just Iris and Toby who worked in the tower office; Toby was at his desk, yes. Also Iris, her unflappable PA, who was looking unusually flushed. Iris was sitting next to Clive Hatton at the coffee table by the windows. He was ignoring Iris, as he always did in public. Minty held back a sigh. When would Iris realise that Clive never intended to marry her?

Their astute accountant—Neville Chickward—was not there, but perhaps that wasn't so surprising, for Clive and he had never got on particularly well, and it can't have helped that Neville still hankered after Iris.

But what was this? Judith Kent was being ushered out of the lift by a burly, no-nonsense figure of a man. Reggie had once been Minty's father's driver and good friend, and was now their trusty Houseman, responsible for everything that Clive didn't do around the Hall.

Reggie's grasp on Judith's arm was that of a policeman bringing in a suspect. Judith was looking pale but was not resisting him in any way.

Reggie saw Minty first and sketched a wave. "Mrs Sands." In private he called her "Minty," but not in front of Clive Hatton, who liked to play the part of employer to Reggie's servant. "Sorry to bother you," said Reggie, "but this needs sorting out. I told this woman yesterday to move her caravan from the car park, but now she says you've given her a job and told her she can stay there."

Judith fixed her eyes on Minty. She wasn't pleading for Minty to take her side. She didn't even look as if she was expecting it. Rather, she seemed to be enduring the scene.

Minty flushed. "That's right, Reggie. I'm sorry I didn't have time to tell you yesterday. And, Clive—" she turned to him with an apologetic smile—"I know I ought to have got in touch with you about it last night. My fault. I interviewed two people yesterday and took them both on. There's a young girl to help Doris in the gift shop, and Miss Kent is going to be working in the library for a while, cataloguing the books. She has nowhere else to stay, so I've said she can leave the caravan in the car park. If it causes you problems, Reggie, perhaps you can find somewhere else for her to leave it?"

Reggie might have come out of a London slum originally, but in many ways he was a better judge of human nature than the highly educated and well-connected Clive Hatton. Reggie wasn't going to query Judith's appointment in front of the others, but he signalled his uneasiness to Minty with a long, frowning look and a snap of his eyebrows.

Now he released Judith's elbow and stepped back. "Can do. If you'll come this way, miss?"

Judith met Minty's eyes for a moment, her expression bland. Something that was not quite a smile moved the corners of her lips. She hadn't spoken during the confrontation though she seemed aware—very much aware—of everything that was going on. She knew that Toby was looking hard at her. How, Minty wondered, did the woman do it? Everyone in the room had been concentrating on the newcomer, and yet she hadn't spoken a word. Now she bowed her head and returned to the lift with Reggie.

Clive said, "You shouldn't have had to bother interviewing people, Mrs Sands." He half rose from his seat and gestured to an empty chair beside him. "If you'd only told me you wanted someone to catalogue the books, I could have found a qualified person to do so. I don't suppose that poor creature will last the course. Failed teacher, is she?"

It was clear to Minty that Clive didn't particularly want her to sit down with them, but she did, and caught a sharp glance pass between Iris and Clive as she did so. Neither of them was happy about her joining them. So what were they up to? Again, Judith's words about the Hall riding for a disaster echoed through her mind.

Toby had his head down, immersing himself in his work. And what was worrying him, anyway?

Minty took the chair Clive had drawn out for her, wishing she'd thought to change into something less casual. Iris was looking immaculate as always, from expensive smooth haircut, through designer black suit, to well-cut shoes. Iris' Chinese ancestry helped her hide her feelings, but Minty knew her pretty well. It was clear to her that Iris and Clive had been having some kind of an argument when she'd walked in on them. Would Iris tell her what it had been about?

"Well," said Iris, getting to her feet, "busy, busy. Did you want anything in particular, Minty?" She picked up the papers on the table in front of her and went over to her desk, but not before Minty's sharp eyes had seen that the top one bore the curlicued font used for letterheads by one of the local Powers That Be.

Mrs Chickward was county stock, knew everyone, and worked tirelessly for charity, promoting events which were usually held at the Hall. Her nephew, Neville, was also the Hall's excellent accountant. Now what had Patrick said about the meeting last night? That Mrs Chickward had been having a row with someone about ... what? Something that had been cancelled at the Hall?

"Is that from Mrs Chickward?" said Minty, wondering what important event that good lady had been writing to the Hall about.

Iris whisked the letter out of sight. "Nothing for you to bother about."

Clive smiled at her, revealing good, slightly too large teeth. Someone had once said he was a Hooray Henry with brains. He was the younger son of a county family, but his elder brother would eventually inherit the estate, so Clive had had to make a living for himself elsewhere.

Minty had never liked him particularly, nor he her. But he ran the Hall efficiently, and they got on well enough. Now he smoothed back his already smooth fawn-coloured hair, and enquired after the twins. "Quite a handful, aren't they?"

Minty nodded, but her mind went back to the library yesterday. There had been a big stand of chrysanthemums between the long windows, and something had knocked at the back of her mind then about flowers in November.

"Wait a minute," she said. "What about the Christmas decorations? Aren't they usually up and running by now? There were none in the library yesterday. Has something gone wrong with the arrangements?"

"You don't want to worry your head about that," said Clive, rising to his feet. "It was a hassle dealing with amateurs, so we decided to bring in the professionals this year. I'm sure it will improve visitor numbers."

Minty bit back a sharp reply. She hadn't been consulted about this. All right, the Christmas decorations festival had been a lot of work, but the displays had been created by volunteers from different flower clubs, each taking on a different room. Sponsors had paid for the cost. True, a programme had had to be drawn up and printed, and special arrangements made for parties, but ...

"I wish you'd told me," she said. "I don't think I'd have wanted to cancel it." She had a nasty thought. Hadn't Patrick said something about a cancellation upsetting the people in the village? Now, if that was true, it was serious. Everything locally was managed either by Mrs Chickward or by her bête noire, Mrs Collins, who was built like a sergeant major and possessed the same bullying tendencies.

Perhaps Minty ought to call on them to find out what had gone wrong? But not with the twins in tow, because they couldn't be trusted to respect Mrs Chickward's knick-knacks.

"Ah, well," said Clive, pushing his chair back against the window. "Got to get on. Contracts for the two new people to be drawn up. Usual terms, I suppose? I'd better alert our housekeeper that someone is being allowed to work on the books in the library, or there'll be ructions, eh? Nice to see you, Mrs Sands." He disappeared into the lift.

Chapter Four

Minty rubbed her forehead. The aspirin was beginning to take effect. Another cup of coffee—even if it was instant—and she might feel well enough to tackle whatever was next on the agenda. Or perhaps go back to bed and catch up on sleep?

Now there was an attractive proposition.

Meanwhile, Iris was busying herself at her computer. As was Toby. What was that he'd said about a new brochure? She hadn't seen the proofs. Clive must have taken it on himself to get the brochure updated. The job of running the Hall had fallen to him by default since the twins were born ... not that this was a scenario which Minty particularly liked. She'd always thought Clive efficient but a bit of a lightweight, whose morals were not quite what they should be.

Come to think of it, his morals with regard to Iris were definitely not what they should be. How long had their affair been going on? Two years? Longer? And Clive seemed happy to continue that way, whereas Iris ...? Minty no longer knew what Iris felt about it.

Iris picked up some papers and made for the lift. "You all right, Minty? I've got to ..." She waved at the lift, without explaining what it was that she had to do.

Minty started. "Yes, of course. Thanks, Iris. Short of sleep, you know. Gloria's got the children today, thank goodness."

Iris nodded, smiled, and disappeared into the lift.

Toby stopped work but didn't raise his eyes from his computer screen. Minty looked longingly at the door to her rooms—oh, to stretch out on the four-poster, with the curtains drawn for a couple of hours—but instead went round to perch on the end of Toby's desk. "So what's wrong, Toby?"

He shook his head, still not raising his eyes from the screen. "Nothing."

Minty realised that she really hadn't a clue about what was happening day to day in the house. It was slightly alarming, in view of what Patrick and Judith had said. But if anything had gone seriously wrong, she'd have been told about it ... wouldn't she?

They hadn't told her about cancelling the Christmas decorations. What else hadn't they told her? From somewhere she found the will to continue. "Toby, who pays your wages?"

He raised eyes full of distress but didn't reply.

"I'm going to find out, you know," she said, hoping she meant it, wondering if she'd the stamina for it nowadays.

He gulped. Opened his top drawer, pulled out a folder, and thrust it at her. "The new brochure. It's going to press on Monday, after Iris proofreads it. I've just finished sorting out the photos — which ones, where they go, that sort of thing."

She was alarmed. "What's wrong with it?"

He turned his eyes back to the screen. "I really can't say. I showed a copy to Carol in the village and there was a terrible row. The thing is, it really isn't my problem. I don't know enough about it."

"About what?" Minty riffled through the pages, but couldn't see anything to cause her concern. Introduction to the Hall, its history ... the Eden family history ... maps ... detailed descriptions of the rooms. It looked very much like the old brochure to her, though perhaps it had been expanded here and there.

Toby said, "Can you bring it back tomorrow? Perhaps you could show it to Patrick? Oh, he's off somewhere, isn't he? I've got to get on. Clive's overbooked the restaurant for some corporate functions, and it's going to take me ages to get it sorted."

Minty realised she was being told to go away and play. She hesitated. What was all this about Carol? She was really sorry about the Christmas decorations being cancelled. Mrs Chickward must be furious, since she'd been one of the chief movers in that event. What rumours, exactly, had Patrick and Judith heard?

Toby reached for his phone and punched in numbers.

She'd been dismissed. At that moment the phone rang on Iris' desk. Since Toby was already on the phone, Minty picked it up.

An alto voice, authoritative. "Is that you, Iris? Venetia Wootton here. Is Clive around? We've a small problem in the library." Venetia was not only Toby's mother, but also ran the team of volunteer stewards who looked after the Hall on open days.

Minty grimaced. "Venetia, it's Minty. I think I know what you're going to say. It's all my fault for not keeping you in the loop. I'll be down in a minute to explain."

Returning to her own office, she put the file into the top drawer of her desk. She listened out for screams from the twins — there were none, and Minty didn't know whether to be pleased about that or sorry that they weren't missing her — before returning to the tower and taking the lift down to the ground floor.

Visitors were already moving around the rooms with brochures in their hands, keeping behind the red ropes which separated them from the beautiful furniture which had been collected over generations by the Eden family and added to by Minty's stepmother when she opened the house to the public.

As Minty passed through the State Rooms against the flow of the sightseers, she nodded and smiled at each of the stewards with their official badges. They all knew her, of course.

A frail little woman with white hair was the official steward for the library that day, but Venetia, blonded hair carefully banishing grey, was also there, standing by the fireplace, tapping her foot. Judith Kent had taken a pile of documents out from one of the long narrow drawers at the bottom of one of the bookshelves and was standing nearby with hands folded and eyes downcast. On the giant desk was a laptop, already opened up and running.

The little group was attracting a considerable amount of attention from the visitors.

"I'm so sorry, Venetia," said Minty. "I know I should have rung you last night, but the twins ... shall we go into the cloisters for a moment?"

Venetia nodded and they passed out of the library into the base of the tower and from there into the stone-built arcades of the cloisters around the Fountain Court. It was chilly and the sky was spitting rain now and then, so all three hugged themselves to keep warm.

Minty said, "I've asked Judith to catalogue the books in the library. They haven't been touched for years and we really have no idea what we've got."

"Yes, Minty," said Venetia, trying to be patient. "I follow your reasoning, but I can't have people wandering in and out as they please. Security! Common sense! She hasn't even got an identification badge!" Venetia hadn't recognised Judith as Maxine, then.

"You're quite right," said Minty. "I should have thought. Sorry, Venetia. Sorry, Judith."

Venetia was calming down. "Well, I can see she gets a badge all right. But it would be best if she does her work when there's no visitors around. From noon on Wednesday till five on Sunday the library must be on show."

Minty nodded, her brain working overtime. "Judith, there's a big table in my office on the top floor. Could you take a pile of books up there while the Hall's open to visitors? Then you can work on them in peace and quiet."

Judith nodded.

Venetia smiled. "Problem solved. You're so good at solving problems, Minty. We've missed seeing you around. Will you and Patrick come to supper one night next week? Not Wednesday. District Council. I'll check the diary and ring you to make a date."

"Lovely," said Minty. "Now we'd better rescue Judith's laptop and get her a badge."

"I'll give her the code we use to access the building, and a set of keys so that she can get into the library after Reggie's locked up in the evenings," said Venetia.

Judith nodded, and her lips contracted momentarily in what might have been a smile in anyone else.

Minty felt a moment of wild dismay. Had she really arranged for this strange woman to be given the code and keys which would allow her access to all parts of the Hall? Again, she noticed that Judith had been at the centre of the argument without saying a word herself. Her ability to influence others was still operating at full strength, it seemed.

One problem solved. How many to go? Perhaps she'd pay a visit to Chef, because Toby had suggested that Chef had a grievance. Emerging into the courtyard, Minty was accosted by a familiar figure: Neville Chickward, their accountant, wearing a padded jacket which increased his already considerable girth.

"Minty!" His face lit up. "Someone said you were out and about, so if we could have a word?"

Neville was a free-lance chartered accountant with an office in the village. He was responsible for keeping the Hall's finances in order and had an office in the north wing. Minty knew he'd been working on a proposal to form a limited company to run the place. There'd be all sorts of benefits, he'd said, for tax purposes, etcetera. He was proposing that she be chair, with Patrick and himself acting as secretary and treasurer. Minty realised that this would make sense, but so far Patrick had resisted being drawn into the affairs of the Hall, and she really didn't want him to be drawn in, either. An added complication was that Clive Hatton had already intimated that if they were going to form a company, he ought to be managing director.

Then there was the ongoing problem that Neville was still yearning after Iris, who was still yearning after Clive, who yearned after …

who knew what? A girl from a county family with a bit of money on the side? Clearly he was not yearning after the daughter of a man who ran a Chinese restaurant in the village.

She didn't know what she ought to do about any of this, so Neville's asking for a word triggered alarm bells. "I'm so sorry, Neville. I've been so busy with the twins, you know, and now I'm just on my way to —" she wondered where she could be heading out of his reach, and had an idea " — to inspect the great oak that was struck by lightning in the storm the other night."

"You'll freeze," said Neville, taking off his padded jacket and handing it to her. He had a good three-piece suit on underneath. "I'd like to see it myself. Patrick says it was probably older than Eden Hall."

Hodge, the head gardener, appeared at her elbow, reminding her of the dwarf Rumpelstiltskin, who had the habit of appearing at appropriate moments. "I'll come along of you, then. I've been meaning to talk to you about that there old oak. The master's been right sorry about it."

Hodge always looked as if he'd grown out of the ground rather than been born into it. Patrick said he thought there'd probably been a Hodge tilling the soil hereabouts since Roman times or even before. As for telling Hodge what he could or could not do ... even Minty handled him with care.

She did a double take. Hodge had called Patrick "the master"? What on earth? She'd never heard him called that before. By Hodge, of all people. Hodge admired the Queen, and if he were ever by some chance to be called into Her Majesty's presence, Minty had no doubt that he'd bob his head to her ... but to no one else. He would have been a republican if he hadn't thought so much of the Queen.

Minty didn't approve of his calling Patrick "the master." Patrick didn't own the Hall and had no authority to give orders. She owned the Hall and she'd earned the title of the Lady of the Hall.

When they'd first married, everyone had called Patrick by his Christian name. He'd not gone around giving orders, though he was the sort of man whom people did go to for advice in times of trouble, and of course he always mucked in when there was a job to be done, like clearing a blocked drain or moving furniture. Once or twice she'd heard him referred to as "Mr Patrick." But ... *the master*? That was a title which had to be earned. And it had come from Hodge, of all people!

Hodge was leading the way, chuntering on about what the Park Ranger wanted to do with that there old oak, and how it wasn't what the land needed. Hodge had a running feud with the very capable Ranger, whose territory extended over the many acres of parkland, right up to the lake below the house. The Ranger thought he should be responsible for the greensward which sloped up from the lake to the house, but Hodge maintained that he'd always had the job of mowing that there bit, and he wasn't going to give it up, not nohow.

Another source of friction was the flock of sheep which the Ranger had introduced to keep the grass nibbled short in the Park, but which Hodge swore were always breaking into "his" territory. Once upon a time Minty had wanted to throw the Park open to visitors free of charge, but the Ranger had vetoed this as being too expensive, citing the amount of litter they'd have to clear up, and the cost of having to employ personnel to clear visitors out of the Park at sundown. Naturally, Hodge had taken the opposite point of view. For the moment, the Ranger had his way, so maybe Hodge was looking for a way to even things up.

Minty and Neville followed Hodge through the inner court where the family and staff cars were kept, and past the sheltered knot garden, climbing the hillock to the marble folly which looked down over the slope to the lake below. On the far side of this incline lay the remains of what had once been a giant of a tree but was now a sad ruin, the split stump riven and twisted. The trunk had been almost as thick as Minty was tall, and the ruins of a wooden seat lay crushed beneath it. This was where Patrick had been accustomed to sit and think.

Minty shook her head. "What a shame. Is the tree completely dead?"

Hodge nodded. He took off his cap in homage to the departed.

Minty could see why Patrick had liked this place. The ground sloped away on the south side to the lake, and to the boundary of the Home Farm on the east. A massive sky seemed to bear down upon them, with a threat of sleet or snow in the wind. There wasn't a house in sight. Some people might find it bleak, but it was a quiet place in which to worship God. She sorrowed for Patrick, that he'd lost a place which had been so precious to him.

Neville was shifting his feet in his good shoes. "I'm glad to have seen it, but it's a bit boggy around here, isn't it? Mind yourself, Minty."

"What? Oh. Yes, there's a spring rises hereabouts, I think. It makes the ground very wet. Hodge, I suppose the tree had better be cut up?"

Hodge looked doubtful. "That's what that fool of a Ranger says, but the master's fond of this place. Says he can think better here."

"Well, what would you do with it, Hodge?"

"You tell that Ranger to keep his hands off it. The master and I, we'll put our heads together, and mebbe we'll come up with something."

Minty set her teeth. If Hodge referred to Patrick as "the master" again, she'd hit him. She noticed that Neville was shivering. She was warm enough in his coat, and Hodge never seemed to feel the cold. "We'd best get back. The twins will be wanting me."

She hoped Neville wouldn't raise the subject of Iris on the way back and, in fact, he didn't. She sorrowed, gently, for him. If only Iris ... ah well. You couldn't force people to love one another, however much they might seem to be suited.

When they got to the courtyard, Neville said, "Minty, I know you've been busy, but have you had time to look at my memo about the future of the Hall?"

"Neville, I don't know what to think about it. I realise what you've suggested makes sense, but I need to talk to Patrick about it. He's not keen to get involved in the running of the Hall." She ought to have added, but didn't, that she wasn't keen that he should, either.

"He's got the clearest brain I know."

She nodded. It was true. "Sooner him than Clive Hatton."

"You might want to give Clive something, some kind of title, or shares? Some stake in the future of the Hall."

That made sense, but Minty still didn't want Clive to have too much power.

She handed Neville back his coat. "Thanks, Neville. You are such a kind man."

Neville wasn't paying her any more attention. Iris was crossing the courtyard ahead of them. She caught sight of them and waved to Neville, who waved back. Both were smiling, not the forced smile of acquaintances, but the warm smile of two friends pleased to have caught sight of one another. Iris vanished into the house.

"Thanks, Minty." Neville didn't comment on seeing Iris, but got into his car and drove off.

Minty wondered what that little encounter was all about? Had she missed something? Iris and Neville had always been so awkward with one another in the past, he wanting more than she could give, and Iris uncomfortably aware that she couldn't give it.

Minty stopped thinking about it. The twins would be looking out for her, and she was dying to see them again.

❧

The twins were glad to see Minty, but had had a good time in the village with Gloria and didn't seem to have missed their mother at all. Minty couldn't make up her mind whether she was sad or glad about that.

Lunchtime. Minty ate a sandwich while the twins spooned up mince and carrots — sometimes they refused to eat carrots, but today Gloria had them pretending to be rabbits, and carrots were back on the menu. While she ate, Minty had a quick look at the file which Toby had given her ... she couldn't see anything wrong with it. A couple of typos. If it had been left to her, she'd have reversed the order of a couple of things, but no, nothing screamed at her for attention.

Frustrated, she pushed it aside as Reggie arrived with two awkwardly shaped packages, wrapped in layers of paper. "Special delivery for the twins and ..." Reggie gave Minty a sidelong but penetrating look, "... a word in your shell-like, Minty?"

"Of course, but not now. I haven't ordered anything, have I?" The packages looked suspiciously like children's tricycles.

"Not in here!" Serafina was clearing the table. "Take them in the rumpus room."

Once next door, Reggie produced an enormous folding penknife and carefully started to cut the packaging away, watched by whooping, screaming twins and a laughing Gloria. Serafina couldn't bear to be left out of the fun, so she also came to watch.

Minty was grinning. This was what life was really all about. All morning she'd been dealing with horrid grown-up problems instead of doing what came naturally, which was having fun with the twins. She began to tear open the second package, helped by Gloria wielding a knife she'd fetched from the kitchen.

"Who sent them?" she asked, trying to read labels.

Reggie half saluted. "Mr Patrick, to keep the young 'uns amused while he's away."

Boom was jigging up and down, his eyes on the knife. "Let me!"

"Not till you're older." Reggie folded up his knife and stowed it deep in a pocket. Boom transferred his attention to Reggie's pocket.

"I *am* older," insisted Boom.

"So am I," said Ting, dancing around, soft dark hair curling around her ears. She looked adorable. Minty wanted to catch them both up and smother them with kisses.

The twins weren't taking any notice of her. Two shrieks practically lifted the roof as Reggie pulled away the last of the packaging on his bundle to reveal ... yes, a small-size tricycle. The twins had ridden tricycles at the toddlers' group in the village but hadn't got any themselves. By this time the room was knee deep in corrugated paper.

"Trike! Me first," yelled Boom, reaching for it.

"Patience! There's one for each of you." Laughing, Reggie fended him off, while Minty and Gloria disinterred the second machine.

"I'm bigger!" yelled Boom, who was nothing if not obstinate.

The tricycles were the smallest size on which a small child could push themselves around. There were pedals on the front, but the twins' feet wouldn't be able to reach them for a while.

One was red and the other was blue. Boom always wanted blue, and Ting always wanted red. Each had a hooter instead of a bell, and a basket on the handlebars, into which Ting immediately put her favourite teddy bear. Boom wasn't waiting for anything but got straight on the saddle and would have pushed himself up and down the room if it hadn't been for all the wrappings strewn around.

"Wait till I get my camera!" cried Serafina.

"I'll take them down to the Long Gallery, shall I?" said Gloria. "They can ride around there to their hearts' content and do no damage."

"Not till five o'clock," said Minty, with regret. "The house is open to visitors today."

Boom had found the hooter. *Perp!*

Minty put her hands over her ears. Reggie was signalling that he wanted a word. She said, "I'll come down and find you later, all right?"

He obviously didn't think it was all right, but nodded, gathered up an armful of discarded packaging, and took himself off.

Minty helped to clear a track round the room for the children to ride their bikes. What fun this was! She wanted to laugh, and she wanted to cry. Patrick should have been there to see. Why hadn't he waited to get them delivered till he was back?

A little voice said at the back of her head, *That's Patrick all over.*

He knew Minty was hardly capable of standing on her own feet at the moment. His solution was to give the twins a present which would keep them occupied and happy. He was selfless.

The phone rang, and Minty was nearest, so she picked it up. It was probably some sales call. She didn't know why she'd bothered to pick it up. Perhaps because she hoped it might be someone who might give her some advice about Judith.

Snap! It was the Reverend Briggs again. "Is that Mrs Sands? I'm so sorry, I may have been a little short with you yesterday, but we'd had a bad day at the hospital, not that you need to know about that. I was talking to the others in the team this morning, telling them that Judith had actually contacted ... are you still there?"

"Yes, yes." Minty made shushing noises to the twins, but they were too excited to listen. "Hold on a moment. I'll take this call on another phone."

She sped through into her office and switched the call through. "I'm here. Sorry about that. The twins were rampaging and I couldn't hear myself think. You've got some more information for me about Judith Kent?"

"N–no. Not exactly. It's just ... I don't know how to put it, but ... well, I'm the most junior member of the team and actually, we didn't all agree that I should tell you but ... Judith is a very strong personality, and perhaps it's only right to warn you ... though really it's nothing to do with how well she can do a job of work for you ... but ..." He obviously took a deep breath to spit it out. "She can be most attractive to the opposite sex."

"You're trying to tell me that she might attempt to seduce someone here?"

"I suppose so. Yes."

"Was it you she tried to seduce at the hospital?"

"No! How could you think such a thing?"

"Easily," said Minty, grim-voiced. "I know her of old, remember. If it wasn't you, it was one of your team, right?"

"Certainly not! That would have been most unethical." But he didn't sound too sure of himself. "If you must know, there was talk about her and a junior doctor. I'm sure it went no further than flirting, and anyway, she's left now and he's going out with one of the nurses."

Minty was inclined to say, "Oh, yeah?" But didn't. She thought the Reverend Briggs wasn't quite as innocent as he'd tried to make her believe, either. It sounded to Minty as if he had a slightly grubby conscience about Judith. Why else would he be making this follow-up phone call? In Minty's opinion, Judith had all the sex appeal of Mata Hari, and the lack of morals to go with it.

The Reverend Briggs was right in one way; Judith's sex appeal was not a good enough reason to refuse her a job. Minty couldn't imagine herself going to an Industrial Tribunal and saying, "I couldn't give this woman a job because she might have seduced my husband." Minty might feel like using that excuse, but it wouldn't stand up in law.

There were only two good reasons why Minty could refuse Judith a job. First, was she competent? The principal of the college had said she was. The second reason was not so easy to put into words.

"Tell me one thing," said Minty. "Do you think she has put satanic practices behind her?"

An indrawn breath. Then, "Yes, we really do think so."

"All of you think that? The whole team?"

"Yes."

"Then I'll have to take my chances on the rest. Thank you for warning me."

Minty put the phone down, in no mood now to play games with the children. A greater game was afoot, a game of life and death.

She looked in on the twins. Gloria was happily supervising them. In the kitchen, Serafina was busy preparing supper.

Minty went through the kitchen into her bedroom. The willow-patterned curtains hung straight at the sides of the great bed, but Patrick wouldn't be there this evening to share it with her. She could lie down on it now and rest ... or ... she could spend some time in prayer. Somehow she felt that prayer was more important at that moment than snatching half an hour's sleep.

Prayer for Judith, and for herself. Prayer for everyone and anyone that Judith might come into contact with.

Chapter Five

Minty slipped into the family chapel. Patrick had reminded her that she'd been missing out on her daily prayers, and he'd been right, as usual, bother him!

After the rededication following Maxine's desecration of the chapel, Patrick had installed indirect lighting to focus on the altar and the plain cross that hung on the wall above.

There were three chairs set before the altar. Like the chairs of the Three Bears, Minty thought, bemused with fatigue. Big chair for Daddy, middling chair for Mummy, and little chair for Serafina, who liked a low seat. Beside the altar was a low table bearing a Bible and a vase of glossy, red-berried holly. A flower-embroidered kneeler lay before the altar, but Minty sank into the nearest chair, the one with a high, carved back and strong arms. Patrick's chair, normally.

He'd have his laptop out during the flight. Saving time, saving work. He'd arrive early, with all the appropriate paperwork, for his afternoon meeting in Brussels. He'd listen to other people, speaking little himself, though what he said would always be very much to the point. He'd probably make everyone smile, or even laugh. He could be witty. But pithy.

Meetings, meetings. He spoke French well enough, and German even better. Since she wasn't with him, perhaps he'd dine with colleagues that evening, drinking little, not eating very much. He was far too thin.

She began to weep. She didn't know why. Tears of tiredness, perhaps.

Or of sorrow, because she'd let Patrick go without a kiss or even a kind word? Or perhaps of despair, because she knew she'd neglected to keep in touch with her dearest Lord and God? Or a mixture of all three?

There was a big gap between the way she wanted to be—constantly praying, always in touch with Him, learning from Him, praising Him—and the poor, half-crazed creature she'd become. She didn't know how it had happened.

The twins were forward for their age. They tumbled about, experimented, fell down and hurt themselves, yelled for help and consolation when they needed it. They were healthy, happy children. Was Patrick right, and had she encouraged them to rely on her for everything, when they ought to have been learning to cope with life by themselves?

She caught herself up. She'd been about to fall asleep, instead of praying, which was what she'd come here for. Wasn't it?

She seemed to have forgotten how to pray.

This was ridiculous. You don't forget how to pray. It was easy, as easy as falling off a log ... log ... log ...

She woke to find two warm, sweetly bath-scented pyjama-clad little bodies pressing up against her.

"Kiss Mummy goodnight now," said Gloria, lifting one twin up to be kissed by Minty, while Serafina fielded the other.

"Mummy-Mummy-Mummy," murmured Ting, giving Minty a soft, wet kiss.

"Perp-perp!" said Boom, valiantly trying to keep his eyes open. He hugged Minty, went limp, and subsided into Gloria's arms.

Minty tried to rouse herself. "Your good night story?"

"All done," said Gloria, who was still, incredibly, smiling at the end of what must have been a tiring day. "And our prayers said."

Serafina carried a sleepy Ting away, saying, "Minty, come and get something hot inside you. Gloria and I had our supper with the twins."

Silence as the door closed behind them. Minty sighed deeply, wondering at the feeling of comfort that surrounded her. The light was still on over the altar, and it was completely dark outside. She had a strange fancy that she'd been watched over during the hours she'd been asleep.

What time was it? Seven o'clock. Had she really been asleep all afternoon?

Lord, help me to remember You are always here, waiting for me to turn back to You. Don't let me get so busy, so wrapped up with the children, that I forget You again.

Not much of a prayer, though it was something like one of Patrick's that she couldn't quite remember at the moment. Something about having a busy day ahead but *please, Lord, don't forget me, because I don't mean to forget You, even in my busyness, though I know, being only human, that I may well do so.*

She turned off the light and went through to the kitchen with coffee in mind. But there was still no ground coffee for the cafetière.

"Didn't Gloria get me any ground coffee when she went into the village? I need something to wake me up."

"Decaffeinated, if you must," said Serafina, putting a plateful of chicken curry and rice in front of her, and adding a salad on the side. "Patrick thinks you're drinking too much strong coffee and not eating enough. Coffee never stops me sleeping, but I said we'd try it, so you'd better go on decaf for a bit."

Minty shook her head in disbelief. "You think I'm incapable of managing my own life?"

"Hmph!" said Serafina. "You've not been capable of anything except running around after the twins for months. You've even stopped sleeping with that good man of yours! Don't think he complained because he hasn't got a complaining bone in his body. Or rather," said Serafina, trying to be fair, "of course he complains all the time, about the weather, or a meeting that goes on too long, or there being none of his favourite cereal for breakfast. But he never complains about anything important. Eat!"

Minty picked up a fork and started to eat. It was best to let Serafina finish her rant; she didn't often let fly, but when she did ... oh, boy!

"That's another thing," said Serafina. "It's only natural that the children should try to take over your life. I've had four and lost them all, and I should know. Selfish little animals, always seeing how far they can go before they're stopped. It's only natural behaviour, but if they're to grow up to fit into society, they have to be taught that rules apply to them as well as to other people. Those are two good children that you've got there. Loving and kind to one another, which children aren't usually. But you've let them make a rod for your back and nearly killed yourself in the process, not to mention failing to be a proper wife to Patrick, and letting the Hall go to rack and ruin."

Minty suspended operations on her food. "It's not going to rack and ruin, is it?"

Serafina sat down, letting out a long sigh. "I don't know, and that's the truth. It's just a feeling I get, the odd silence when certain things are mentioned, the way Chef and Reggie don't smile so much. And that Iris ...! She's a disgrace, the way she runs around after young Hatton."

Minty pushed her empty plate away. "Being a mother is a full-time job."

"From today it's part-time. Gloria stays. She's moved into the spare room next to the twins, though I told her she's not to go in to them during the night unless they start screaming. She's to work nine to five, five days a week, weekends off unless we arrange otherwise. And she's to have the baby alarm switched over to her room."

Serafina pushed a bowl of fresh fruit and some cheese towards Minty. "Are you going to join Patrick at the weekend? He rang through to me an hour ago to say he'd arrived safely and to remind you to water his plants."

"You think something's wrong at the Hall, but you still want me to take a holiday?"

Serafina nodded, clattering plates into the dishwasher. "You need to step back, to get the full picture. As I do. A few days off will do us both good."

Minty was half amused and half perturbed. She really couldn't believe that anything much could be wrong at the Hall, but she supposed she ought to check. She shivered. The central heating was on; one of the first things Patrick had done when he married her was to insist on their rooms being properly heated, even though the rest of the Hall had to be kept on the cool side to avoid damaging the antique furniture.

Suppose she did take a wander around the Hall to check up on things? Gloria was cosily making herself at home in the room next door to the twins, so she could go out with a clear conscience. First she must find some warm clothes to wear. November nights could be bitterly cold.

But before that she must check on the twins. She opened the door to their room and heard their soft breathing. Good. They were fast asleep. Leaving the door half open, she tiptoed in. As her eyes grew accustomed to the dim light, she saw they'd pulled the tricycles close to their cots. She covered Boom over with his duvet again. Like Patrick, Ting slept neatly without disturbing the bedclothes. She kissed them both and murmured a prayer over each. Patrick usually said a prayer over them when they were asleep at nights. Now it was her turn to do it.

Gloria popped her head round the door to say, in a soft voice so as not to wake the twins, "Everything okay, Minty? I'm just next door and will listen out for the twins, if you want to get a good night's sleep."

"Thank you, Gloria. I appreciate it." Minty changed into a warm jumper and clean jeans. A soft thick jacket went over all. Serafina had retired to her own room. Minty could hear her television turned up high as she passed through the suite.

She checked. There was a light on in her office. Why? It was nearly eight in the evening. No one should be there at this time of night.

Judith was there, sitting at the dining table, with her laptop in front of her. She gave Minty one of her calm, considering looks, and switched off her laptop.

Minty asked, "You shouldn't still be working, should you?"

Judith shook her head. "I was downloading a programme for the catalogue. It's taken some time."

"You've had a rough first day. I'm sorry about that." Minty reflected that she seemed to be apologising to everyone that day.

Judith leaned back in her chair. "Reggie's found me a place to put the caravan at the back of what used to be the stables. I don't think he recognised me."

Minty suspected that he had, but she said nothing.

"Venetia didn't recognise me, either, but she still doesn't like me."

"That's my fault. I'd forgotten to tell her about you."

"It was instinct. Her beloved Toby hankered after me in the past. He will again, given half a chance."

Minty had noticed that, too. She rubbed her forehead. Was her headache coming back? "I had an illuminating phone call from the Reverend Briggs earlier. He wanted to warn me about you—and men."

Judith half smiled. "He rather fancied me but didn't dare do anything about it."

"Oh, Judith. Which of the team was it you seduced?"

Judith laughed. "You don't really want to know, do you?" She put on a mock-serious face. "'Dear Judith, run away and play. It would be most unethical for me to have an affair with you.' Word for word, that's what he said. Pathetic, isn't it?"

Minty knew she should condemn Judith's morals, but the girl had such charm that she found herself laughing, even as she shook her head. "What about the young doctor you fancied?"

"Got himself a dolly bird nurse."

"Before or after you got your claws into him?"

"Does it matter?"

No, it didn't. But ... "Who have you got your sights on here? Toby really isn't up to your weight, is he? Too easy a mark. So who else do you fancy?"

"Not Clive," said Judith, entering into the spirit of this extraordinary conversation. "He doesn't really like women, does he? Correction: He likes a certain type of woman who'll understand him completely without letting him know it. He'll go for good hips and old money. He'll provide his wife with a couple of children, give the children some ponies to play with, and probably get into debt trying to keep up appearances. He won't marry Iris, that's for sure. I could have a fling with him, but I probably won't. There'd be no fun in it."

She'd summed Clive up well. "Failing him? Toby's out. Who else? Tim, the Estate Manager?"

"Got a little wifey at home that he's devoted to, and a baby on the way."

"Reggie?"

They both laughed at that.

"Reggie'll marry an older woman some day and probably settle down to run a pub in the village here. He doesn't like me, anyway."

"That wouldn't stop you," said Minty, enjoying this game.

"No, it wouldn't." Judith acknowledged the hit. "But not Reggie. Perhaps I'll make a play for Hodge, the gardener?"

Minty was amused. "He's a widower, but cracking on a bit for you, isn't he?"

They both knew who Judith was aiming for: Patrick. But neither was going to mention his name first.

"What do I want?" Judith seemed to be communing with herself. "I want what you have. You lead such a privileged life; you don't know what it's like to have to fight your way out of the pit. My father drank and abused me. Mother drank and took drugs. They'd have sold me to a pimp if I hadn't proved I could earn money by singing."

Minty grimaced. "You're pressing the wrong button. I was rejected by my father after my mother died, and brought up in a city slum by relatives who did their best to break my spirit."

The spark was back in Judith's eye. "Then that's how you knew how to fight! We have more in common than I thought. You know, you're the first person to deny me what I wanted. I admire you for that."

What an odd conversation. They were talking as equals. "Judith, what is it you've heard about the Hall?"

Judith's eyes went left and right, and a faint frown appeared, echoing the upright line that sometimes was seen between Patrick's brows. "The people in the village don't trust me, and they certainly didn't want to talk to me about the Hall, so it's really just what I've overheard other people say when they didn't realise I was listening. It's something to do with the antique shop that Carol, that friend of yours, runs in the village. Also people are saying that you don't care about them any more, that you never stop to talk to anyone if you do have to go into one of the shops."

Minty winced. Was that really how she appeared to the villagers nowadays? Of course she was always in a hurry, always having to think first about the twins. Didn't they understand that? It appeared not. "Thank you for telling me."

"A pleasure," said Judith, in the same flat voice. Then her lips twitched, and so did Minty's.

Judith laughed without sound, then unplugged her laptop and stood up. "Reggie's connected me up with electricity and water, so I can cook something tonight instead of eating out. He's a good man, I think."

She spoke as if it was a rare thing to find a good man.

"There's plenty about," said Minty, thinking of Patrick.

"Not that I've come across. Good night, Mrs Sands. I won't call you by your first name. We aren't friends."

"Not yet," said Minty, realising that she had begun to like Judith.

The girl hesitated. "Which is the quickest way out? I assume the front door's locked at this time of night?"

"At night we use the door from the north wing that leads into the outer courtyard, opposite the restaurant. Gloria's listening out for the twins tonight, so I'll come down with you, show you where the light switches are. Do you have a torch? No? It's good to have one in case you miss your way. I'll find one for you."

Judith nodded. "May I use a rest room first?"

"There's one off the tower office. I'll show you."

Waiting for Judith, Minty found a couple of torches and then approached the door to Patrick's den. She knew the combination for the lock, of course. But something he'd said ... she tried the usual numbers and they didn't work. Ah, so he'd changed the combination, had he? How annoying of him.

He'd left a message for her not to forget to water his plants. He had green fingers and a passion for plants. She'd always meant to let him have a part of the Park for a garden just to himself, but it had never happened. He always had big troughs of indoor plants in his den. Azaleas at the moment.

She stared at the door, wanting to kick it open, knowing the ancient door was too stout for any onslaught she might make on it.

Judith had returned and was watching her. "Is that the door to your husband's study? I hear he's fled the nest. Is he so scared of me?"

Minty told herself to calm down. "I was supposed to go with him, but I can't get away at the moment. Let me show you how to summon the lift and open the doors before switching off the lights in here."

They went down to the ground floor in the lift and out into the Fountain Court around which the Hall was built. Dim security lights reacting to sensors switched on as they passed through the shadows of the cloisters. There didn't seem to be any moon as yet. Nor anyone lurking. Minty brushed her hand across her forehead. That nightmare . . .

"Spooky," said Judith. "Glad I'm not doing this alone."

"Mm?" Minty was thinking about several other things at once: would Gloria hear the baby alarm if the twins woke up and cried, why had Patrick changed the combination lock on his door, and why was she traipsing around in the dark with Judith when she could be safely tucked up in bed?

There was another combination lock on the door into the north wing, but this time the usual numbers worked.

Judith nodded. "Venetia gave me those numbers."

Minty showed her where the light switches were as they threaded their way through the oldest parts of the Hall, built in far-off Elizabethan days. The dark panelled walls made the darkness even more intense, but the lights here were on a timer.

Then out into the dimly lit outer courtyard. The restaurant was dark, as was the gift shop. "The security lights here go off at eleven," said Minty. "Where's your caravan? Round the back of the restaurant?"

Judith was having difficulty closing the door behind her, and before she could reply, someone or something, moving fast but barely seen, bore down on Minty . . . Was that an arm raised, a weapon, something as black as the night?

Minty had half turned to help Judith with the door and, sensing a threat, threw herself at the wall so that the weapon, whatever it was, missed her head and shoulder, instead catching her a glancing blow on her hip. She stumbled to the ground, the breath knocked out of her body as she fell. The dark shadow—whatever or whoever it was—ran on and on, out of sight.

"Why, whatever's the matter with you?" said Judith, having finally pulled the door shut.

Minty tried to say, "Someone tried to kill me!" But found she couldn't speak.

Chapter Six

Judith helped Minty up. "Do you make a habit of falling over your feet?" She sounded amused.

Minty pushed her hair back from her face. Her hands were shaking. "Didn't you see?"

"What?" Judith didn't wait for an answer but started off across the courtyard. "I know my way from here, I think."

The courtyard itself was fairly well lit with security lights. To the left lay the inner courtyard, where family and staff cars were kept and deliveries made. The inner courtyard was in darkness; presumably the security lighting there had failed. It was from there that the dark figure had come, rushing out at her, arm upraised.

Had he been holding a weapon? A stout stick? Something dark?

It might have been a she ... no, the figure had been taller than her ... though ... she wasn't thinking straight. Whether it had been a he or a she, they'd meant business.

The figure had shot out of the inner courtyard, struck at her, and disappeared in the direction of the visitor parking lot, and the drive ... which led to the road.

There was no function being held at the Hall that night, so there was only minimum security lighting in the courtyard and beyond. As far as Minty could see, the car park—which was also lit at night—looked deserted.

She tried to put weight on the leg he'd hit. She could do it, just. With an effort. She leaned against the wall, trying to breathe deeply, telling herself that the pain would soon ease off.

There should have been at least one light operating in the inner courtyard. She couldn't think straight, but her fevered brain was sending her a message. She must tell Reggie about the defective light. Reggie would know what to do about it.

It was a dark night. Minty shivered, thinking that eyes might be watching her from the shadows. She couldn't detect any movement. He — it must have been a he — had moved so quickly, had been dressed in black or something else dark. She'd had only the most fleeting of glimpses of the figure, couldn't really describe him.

She recalled her nightmare ... someone had been lurking, waiting to ambush her ... but that had been in the Fountain Court, not out here in the open.

This had all the quality of a nightmare, but she hadn't imagined it. Her hip was fiery with the blow he'd dealt her. Someone had lain in wait for her, to mug her ... or perhaps to mug anyone who might come along. The restaurant was busy most nights of the week, but not tonight, as it happened.

Normally there would be people coming and going in the courtyard until about eleven at night, or even later. A drug addict in desperation for another fix might well decide to lurk in the courtyard to mug a late-night visitor to the restaurant. He could probably rely on getting a mobile phone and some credit cards. Even a wad of cash.

But they'd chosen the wrong night, for there'd been no one around because — for a wonder — the restaurant was closed tonight. If they'd picked on Judith, they'd have got her laptop. Instead, they'd struck too soon and got away with nothing.

She must ring the police ... except that she hadn't got her mobile on her. She'd stopped carrying it a couple of weeks back, when Ting had learned to press the buttons and accidentally got through to the emergency services. She'd put it somewhere safe ... she wasn't sure where.

Minty pushed herself off the wall. Judith was by now out of sight round the corner of the kitchen. The mugger had disappeared in the direction of the drive and the main road. So he wasn't following Judith at the moment. But perhaps he'd not been alone? Perhaps Judith was even now being mugged round the corner?

Minty cried out, "Judith, wait for me!" There was no reply. Minty set out to follow her, limping, setting her teeth. She must warn Judith to be careful and then tell Reggie about the light.

She turned the corner into the alleyway, which was deserted. On one side was the blank wall of the kitchen, and beyond that lay the walled garden. On the other side—thank heavens—were lights and noise; at least there were some signs of life here. What had once been extensive stabling had been converted into three estate cottages, all occupied by people who could help her. The security lighting was brighter here, thank goodness.

Minty looked back over her shoulder. Nothing moved behind her. She didn't fancy returning to the house by herself, but would see Judith safely to her caravan and then find someone to escort her back.

The first cottage belonged to Iris, but the windows were dark, so she must be out. A television blared from the second; that was Hodge's domain. He wouldn't thank her for disturbing him at this time of night. Although his heart was mostly in the right place, he could use a good selection of Anglo-Saxon words when upset, and he liked his television, did Hodge.

Reggie, the Houseman, lived in the third cottage; she couldn't hear any television, but there were lights on inside.

Judith was disappearing round the end of the walled garden. She hadn't even bothered to switch her torch on yet ... ah, now she'd reached a large caravan which was parked in the lee of the walled garden. She'd left a light on inside and the curtains drawn—sensible girl.

Minty called out to her to "Wait!" but Judith didn't hear. She was using her torch to help her see where to unlock the door. In an instant she had vanished inside.

Thank goodness, she was safe.

Minty sagged against Reggie's door and felt for the knocker. It took all her remaining strength to lift it and let it fall.

Reggie opened the door. "Why, Minty! Whatever ...? Come on, let's get you inside."

His door opened straight into a small living room, which he kept scrupulously tidy. His hobby was mending clocks, and one was in pieces on his dining room table, while he listened to some jazz on the radio.

Reggie took her arm and helped her inside. Minty collapsed into his armchair. "Thank heavens you were in, Reggie. I've been mugged!" She started to laugh, recognised a note of hysteria, and made herself stop. She took in a long breath. "There's a light not working in the inner courtyard. Someone shot out from among the cars there, aimed a blow at me, and ran off in the direction of the drive. He was so quick, I hardly saw him, and Judith didn't see him at all."

Reggie snapped off his radio. "Judith?"

"We were just leaving the north wing. She was behind me. But she's all right. I saw her go into her caravan."

"You're hurt? Where? How bad is it?"

She tried to laugh, but the pain in her leg was fierce. "I'm hurt, yes. But not enough to send me to hospital. He hit me here on my hip. I'll have a nasty bruise there in the morning. Mainly, I'm in shock."

"Will you be all right here if I go and have a look-see?"

She nodded. She didn't want him to leave her, but of course he must. Common sense ruled out fainting or screaming or any other of the things she'd like to do.

Reggie armed himself with a stout walking stick, which was large enough to be called a cudgel, and a powerful torch. "I'll get Hodge from next door and we'll have a look around. Minty, you bolt the door behind me and stay here till I get back."

"But . . ." He'd gone. Minty staggered to the door to bolt it behind him, and with an effort retreated to the armchair. Now she worried that Reggie and Hodge might fall victim to a whole gang of thieves and be beaten to a pulp, and then what?

To her enormous relief Reggie was back, alone, within ten minutes. "It's me, Minty. Let me in."

Once inside, he reported, "There's no one out there. There's a smashed light bulb in the inner courtyard, but that could have happened at any time. Kids mucking around, probably. Whoever hit you must have been a loner, chancing his luck. I thought he might be hiding out in the car park, but there's no one there. Hodge is furious because I've made him miss five minutes of his programme. I'll get onto the police."

He pressed buttons on his phone.

Minty explored the tenderness on her hip. "I've been thinking. I know we have to report it, but I expect he or they had a car waiting and didn't wait around to see if they could catch anyone else once they'd failed with me. The thing is, Judith Kent was right behind me and didn't see anything. I can't give much of a description. Someone taller than me, wearing dark clothes? That's about it. They picked the wrong target, didn't they, because I wasn't carrying any money or a mobile or anything."

He got through to the police, reported the incident, and put the phone down, frowning. "They've logged it, but there's no one who can come out to investigate for a while." He stood over her, checking for damage. "You didn't bang your head or anything? Shall I take you to Casualty?"

She shook her head. "I'm fine. Look, I can move all my bits and pieces, including my toes. I'll take some aspirin and get an early night."

"I'll make you a cuppa. I've got some aspirin somewhere." He busied himself in the kitchen at the back, calling back to her, "Just our luck. It's about the only night for weeks that we haven't something on in the Hall."

Reggie was a big, capable man who'd been brought up in a back street in London and left the City only to become the trusted driver and friend of Minty's father. After Sir Micah's death, he'd stayed on to become the mainstay of the Hall, and Minty's very good friend. He pushed a mug of sweetened tea into her hands, together with a couple of aspirins.

"Drink up. It couldn't have been Maxine—her that calls herself Judith—that mugged you?"

"You recognised her, didn't you? No, she couldn't have been behind me and in front of me at the same time."

"Whatever possessed you to offer her a job, Minty?"

"I was sorry for her. She's got nothing left but that caravan, and she swears she's turned over a new leaf and become a Christian."

"You believe her?" It seemed Reggie didn't. He was pulling at his lower lip, frowning, glancing at the door and back to her.

Minty sighed, forced herself to sit more upright and sip the hot tea. "I'm not sure. Sometimes I think I do, and then ... I don't know. I agree that she still has a capacity to do a lot of mischief, but she has an honesty that I admire."

"You always look for the best in people, but sometimes they're not worth it."

"I know, I know."

"Best take care, especially with Mr Patrick away. What does he think about your having Judith here?"

At least Reggie wasn't calling him "the master."

"He's doubtful about it. So is Serafina. I may have made a bad mistake in offering her a job, Reggie, but on balance I think she deserves a second chance." She forced the aspirins down and drank the hot tea. Almost, she stopped shaking.

"That's another thing. Patrick thinks I've been neglecting things at the Hall. I can trust you to tell me the truth, Reggie. Have I?"

"Mm, I was meaning to have a word about that. Of course you haven't so much time for the Hall now. Those twins!" He chuckled. "Young limbs! But Gloria can handle them, I reckon."

"So what have I been missing? Do you think Clive is on top of things?"

He ran his hand over the back of his neck. "He's making the Hall pay its way, if that's what you mean. He's good at that. He's not so good with people." He looked at her as if expecting her to make some kind of connection, but she had no idea what he meant.

She would never have expected Clive and Reggie to be soul-mates, but did that matter? Minty persevered. "I gather the Christmas decorations event has been cancelled."

Reggie shrugged. "Clive's got a stack of private functions booked up. He wants to make a big impression, so he's got an interior designer to theme the decorations, so it all looks alike. Coordinating it, as they say."

Minty could see the sense in that, but wouldn't it have upset all the dozens of people who'd been involved in decorating the State Rooms for the past few years? She must speak to Mrs Chickward in the village about it as soon as possible, soothe any feathers that had been ruffled. "Do you know why Chef's upset?"

He screwed up his face. He knew, all right. "You'd better talk to her about it."

"Do you know why Carol's been trying to get in contact with me?"

He took a big breath of air. "I don't *know*, but I can guess. Coupla times she's given me letters addressed to you, marked Private and Confidential. I handed them to Iris to give to you."

Minty hadn't received them, but then, she'd handed responsibility for her correspondence over to Iris ages ago. She could trust Iris. Couldn't she? She didn't want to criticize Iris to Reggie. "I've been so busy; perhaps Iris has been overzealous."

Reggie nodded, frowning. "Carol wondered if you'd got them, but she said to me the other day that she's washing her hands of the whole business."

"What does she mean by that?"

He moved his big shoulders uneasily. "Ask her, not me. But if I was you, I'd take a good look at the new brochure."

This didn't make sense. Minty tried to think in what way the new brochure could have been worrying Carol.

She thought back, testing various ideas in her mind. Some antiques had been damaged during the short time Maxine had been in possession of the Hall, and as Carol employed a couple of excellent furniture restorers, the remedial work had been put her way. But all that work had been completed ages ago.

Minty rubbed her forehead. Wait a minute. Carol had also been making an inventory of furniture at the Hall. Perhaps Clive had been querying payment for this? How absurd. Carol wouldn't rip them off.

She felt worn out. "I'll try to speak to her tomorrow. Now, Reggie, if you'd see me safely across the courtyard?"

"I'll see you up to your rooms, Minty. I'm not taking any chances. Mr Patrick would have my guts for garters if any harm came to you while he's away."

He took her arm, and for once she was grateful for his support. She'd been badly shaken by her experience. That, on top of sleep deprivation ... she must look in on the twins on her return ... and then, there were Patrick's plants to attend to, if she could get into his den. Why had he changed the combination on his door?

Reggie saw her to the lift and safely through into the suite. He insisted on searching all the rooms—except Serafina's, from which the television set was blaring—and she was grateful that he did. The twins were fast asleep. Soft music was coming from Gloria's room next door to the twins.

Minty popped her head round Gloria's door. "Everything all right, Gloria?"

Gloria was lying on the bed, watching television and talking into her mobile—to her fiancé?—but spared a moment to say, "Everything's lovely. The twins haven't stirred."

"Thanks, Gloria."

She turned back to Reggie. "I'll be all right now. Thanks for looking after me."

Reggie disappeared, and she made sure the door from the tower to the stairs was locked behind him. Also that at the other end of the suite. Memo: must find the keys from these rooms into the office to stop the twins getting at the lift ...

She was physically tired, but her brain was still active. She went through her quiet rooms, limping a bit, turning off lights, checking that everything was in order. Which it was, except that ... except that Patrick wouldn't be coming home that night. It was ridiculous to miss him so much, because he was so often out at nights, anyway.

This time it was different. She looked across the kitchen towards his big chair at the end of the table and imagined she saw him sitting there, cuddling the twins ... or laughing up at Serafina. Then she seemed to see him standing by the door, watching her with that private, slightly crooked half smile of his. When had he stopped smiling at her that way?

She didn't want to think about that.

She went through into their bedroom, and now she seemed to see him sitting on the side of the bed, waiting for her, being patient. Not smiling this time, but watching her, assessing her mood perhaps?

He shouldn't have been so patient! He ought to have shaken the truth out of her and then ... but no. That wasn't his way, was it?

She had to admit that the place wasn't the same without him. Even if he was often out at nights, he was always there in the background, supporting her ... defusing tense situations ... teasing Serafina ... ready with the commonsensical reply, or a joke. He could cut through a tangle of contradictory statements in a trice. He was — he had been — always there. And now, he wasn't.

Her hip was hurting like blazes. She put some arnica cream on it and went back to the kitchen to make herself a second cup of tea. Not coffee. She couldn't go to bed. Not yet. She wandered into her office, leaning against the window, trying to see if there was a moon.

The answerphone light was blinking on her desk. Almost, she let it be, because she'd got into the habit of having all communication with the outside world channelled through Iris. But she picked it up, thinking it might have been Carol trying to contact her.

It was Patrick, who'd left a message for her earlier in the evening. "All's well here, Minty. I hope I'm not speaking German. I seem to have been switching languages all evening, and now I'm not sure which is which. The preliminary discussions went well, but I may have to come back again a few times before everything's finalized. Don't forget to water my plants, will you?"

That was all. She slammed the phone down. It was all too much. Everything was too much. Patrick was too much.

What was more, she rather thought she'd left her favourite sweater in Patrick's den, together with a box of chocolates, half eaten, and her needlework box. The twins were always shedding buttons, and she was accustomed to doing running repairs at all hours of the day and night.

Why had he shut her out of his room?

She went to stare at the door. The combination had always been the same: four figures. Her birth date, followed by his. She tried it again, and it still didn't work.

She tried his year of birth. No.

Hers. No.

The twins'? No.

Part of the main switchboard number for the Hall. First part. Last part. No.

Her mobile phone number. Ridiculous. Too many figures. She tried it anyway. First part, second part. Third part. No.

His mobile number. First part, second part, third part. No.

She kicked the door, said a bad word, and limped away. Giving up for the night.

Her bed yawned invitingly. She made herself shower first, and crawled in. She knew she ought to have looked back in on the twins. She ought to have spent time in prayer in the chapel. *Dear Lord, forgive me. Sorry. I ache all over. I'm so tired, so upset, so sorry for myself!*

She began to laugh, because of course this was nothing but self-pity. *Please forgive me, Lord. Help me to do better tomorrow ...*

She woke when she heard somebody banging at the door of her bedroom. Two shrill voices were yelling, "Mummy, Mummy!" Two horns were going *Perp! Perp!* Was there any way to dismantle those horns? How could Patrick have inflicted them upon her? Her hip hurt. The bruise was coming out nicely.

The twins were still in their pyjamas. They rode into her room on their brand new tricycles, determined not to be parted from them. They had to be prised off their saddles, kicking and screaming, to be washed and dressed.

They rode the trikes into the kitchen and insisted on eating break-fast while riding round and round. Serafina couldn't even coax them to sit at the table with an offer for one of them to depress the plunger on the toaster—which they normally fought to do. The noise was horrendous. *Perp! Perp!*

"Mummy, you're not looking!"

Crash!

Wail. "Mum-my!"

"You bumped me!"

"Didn't!"

"Did!"

By the time Gloria arrived to take charge, Minty was reaching for the aspirins. It was raining, so Gloria couldn't take the twins outside to play, especially since they refused to be parted from their trikes.

Normally Minty would have suggested that they go down to play in the Long Gallery, which had been designed not only as a some-where to hang the pictures collected by generations of Minty's family, but also to act as a place for indoor exercise in bad weather. But they couldn't use it till the cleaners had finished with it and they couldn't use it after noon when the doors of the house would be opened to the public.

Minty had a brainwave. "Why don't we take the trikes down to the cloisters, where they can ride around while being sheltered from the rain?"

She helped Gloria insert the twins into outdoor clothes—much against their will—and found something warm for herself to wear. Together they descended via the lift to the ground floor. Yes! The cloisters were ideal. *Perp, perp!* sounded even louder down there.

There was a stir at one of the doors leading into the north wing, and Reggie emerged with a policeman in tow. "To see you, Mrs Sands, about last night." He never used her first name before strangers.

"Mrs Sands?" The policeman seemed undecided as to whether Minty or Gloria might be "Mrs Sands."

"I'm Mrs Cardale Sands, yes." Minty asked if they could stay where they were as she told him what had happened, because she needed to keep an eye on the twins, whose steering was somewhat erratic. The policeman said he didn't mind.

Reggie didn't disappear as she'd expected him to, but folded his arms and leaned against a pillar, as the policeman said, "I understand you reported an intruder last night. Would you like to tell me what you thought happened?"

What she *thought* had happened? She didn't understand him. She went through it again, and he made some perfunctory marks in his notebook.

"I understand no one else saw this mystery intruder. There was a search made immediately after, and nobody was found."

Her eyes widened. Did he think she'd made it up? Why? Ah. Judith hadn't seen anything. "I assure you, the assault was very real."

The policeman was stolid. "Ms Kent was right beside you, she says. She didn't hear anything, or see anything. She turned round and found you'd stumbled and fallen against the wall. Right?"

Minty stared at the policeman. "She was struggling to close the door at the time."

"I've tried that door. It seems to me to close quite easily."

Minty reddened. "Would you like me to show you the bruise on my hip? He aimed for my head, you see, but I was turning back to help Ms Kent at the time, and he caught me on my hip. Not on the side nearest the wall. The other side. I couldn't have got that bruise if I'd just fallen against the wall."

The policeman smiled patronisingly. "I understand you've been overdoing it, not been sleeping properly. I know what it's like to have youngsters run you into the ground. You hardly know whether you're coming or going." He snapped shut his notebook. "Well, let's hope it doesn't happen again, eh?"

Meaning he thought she'd been wasting police time. Minty felt humiliated.

Reggie narrowed his eyes at the policeman and seemed to be on the verge of saying something, but didn't. He took the man away, leaving Minty to fume. She told herself it would be no good kicking anything to vent her frustration, but that is what she wanted to do. Judith had neatly, oh so neatly, made Minty out to be a hysterical woman who didn't know which end of the week it was.

What could she do about it? Nothing.

Well, it was over and done with, and if the policeman thought she'd been wasting their time, well ... it wasn't the end of the world, was it? There was no point in dwelling on it.

She must do something, anything, to take her mind off what had happened.

The twins wanted to stay where they were, and Gloria was happy to look after them, so, controlling herself with an effort, Minty decided to take the lift back up to the office. There were always decisions to be made about events at the Hall and maybe—just maybe—she ought to check up on what had been happening recently.

Chapter Seven

Iris wasn't in the office. Query: Was Iris now on better terms with Neville? It had looked like it down in the courtyard, but Minty, fresh from that disastrous interview with the police, was inclined to doubt the evidence of her eyes. Perhaps she'd have a word with Iris later about Neville. And perhaps she'd leave well alone.

Toby was alone in the office.

"Hi, Minty. Finished with the stuff for the new brochure? We're running short, so the sooner we can get it to the printers, the better."

"It looks all right, but I need a little more time to study it properly. Have you seen my mobile anywhere? I really must contact Carol."

For some reason, this seemed to alarm Toby. "You really don't want to get involved, do you? At least, speak to Iris or Clive first."

"Why? What's going on, Toby?"

He avoided her eyes. "Nothing." He concentrated on his screen, picked up the phone, and dialled a number. "Busy, you know? Look, Carol's been having a hard time lately, but I don't think you can do anything about it. I'm sure Clive's right. In theory, anyway." He didn't sound convinced.

"They've had words? About what?"

Toby was already speaking to someone about a party booking for December.

Minty looked at the door to Patrick's den. She remembered now that that was where she'd left her mobile. Bother.

She swung through into her own office. Judith Kent was there, busily studying a large tome. She looked up but didn't smile.

It occurred to Minty that it would be more appropriate if Judith were to work in one of the rooms in the north wing, on the other side of the courtyard. Judith wouldn't then have to traipse the books all the way up to the top floor every day, or be a constant reminder to Minty that she might have been foolish to take her on.

The two women held one another's stare for a moment. Minty broke eye contact first, moving to her desk. "Judith, did you really not see anything last night?"

Judith flushed, her skin showing the damage that had been done to it. "No, I didn't. I didn't realise you'd been hurt. I'm sorry."

Minty believed her. She tried on a smile. "Judith, will you give me a minute? I need to use the phone on a private matter."

Smoothly, without comment, Judith rose and went to join Toby in the tower.

Minty wondered, *Now why did I send her out? I don't need to hide the fact that I'm phoning Carol. Do I?*

"Eden Antiques, may I help you?" It wasn't Carol's voice.

"May I speak to Carol, please."

"She's not here this morning, I'm afraid. May I help you?"

"I'll try again later."

Carol was often out on buying expeditions in the surrounding countryside. She could be anywhere within a radius of thirty miles. Minty tried Carol's mobile.

Carol answered.

"Carol, it's Minty here. Where are you? Can we meet?"

There was a babble of voices in the background, and a pause in which Minty began to wonder if Carol would decide to speak to her. But eventually she did. "Hello, stranger. What's brought this on?"

"Patrick said you wanted to talk to me. Letters appear to have gone astray. I know it's my fault we've not been seeing one another so much lately . . ."

"My letters have gone astray? Right." Carol sounded as if she hardly believed Minty's excuse. "So you're on to the problem, then?"

"No, I'm not. Tell me."

More babble in the distance, and a voice yelling for Carol, who half covered over the phone to say to someone else, "I'll be with you in a minute." Then, hurriedly into the phone, "I'm just finishing up here. Meet me at the Five Ways pub, in half an hour?"

"Will do," said Minty, looking at her watch. The line went dead.

Judith Kent walked back into the room and resumed her work without comment. Had she been listening at the door? Probably. Did it matter? No.

The folder containing the proofs for the new brochure was sitting in plain view on Minty's desk. She weighed it in her hand. She didn't know what was wrong with it, but she was beginning to think that something was. Who to ask? Toby knew. She went back into the tower office, but Toby was still busy on the phone and didn't look up when she entered.

She transferred her gaze to the door leading into Patrick's room. Had he known something was wrong with the brochure, or was he simply trying to help Carol sort out whatever the problem was between two old friends?

Minty caught her bad hip on the edge of the desk and said, "Ouch!" Then walked over to the door and tried a combination that had occurred to her in the night.

She might be wrong. She'd been wrong every time she'd guessed the combination yesterday.

Slowly she keyed in the day and month of her marriage to Patrick.

Had she guessed right?

Eureka! The door clicked open, and she went in.

Patrick had a very private side to him. Every now and then he needed to go off somewhere by himself and be quiet. His early morning walks in the Park had been one way of doing this, and he'd spent some time in the chapel every day, while this room was his private sanctum. Even Serafina didn't come in here without an invitation.

His books were all around. There were piles of paperwork on his desk.

Ah-ha. In the centre of his desk lay a photocopy of Judith Kent's application form. Now when had he done that? She'd given the original to Clive to process, hadn't she? Patrick must have photocopied it before he handed it over, perhaps when he came back from his late night meeting? Or early the next morning before he went off to Brussels? Why? There was nothing odd about it, was there?

She told herself that Patrick never did anything without a reason. He had a cool, logical mind with an occasional twist to it that made him an excellent advocate.

She riffled through the papers and files on his desk. He'd said he'd left his schedule there, but she couldn't see it. Had he forgotten to write it out for her? No, if he'd said his schedule was here, here it must be. She wasn't looking in the right place for it, or failing to see what he intended her to see. The answer probably lay in one of the folders on his desk, but she hadn't time to look through them now.

She muttered to herself, "The facts, man! What are the facts?"

Carol might supply some.

Minty collected her sweater, popped a chocolate cream into her mouth, and rescued her mobile phone. With her hand on the door to the tower office, she hesitated. Iris and Clive seemed to have been having some kind of row with Carol, and Toby wasn't telling her anything. Suppose Iris—or Clive—or both of them, had now returned to the tower office. If she went back that way, she might run into them, and they might put pressure on her to let the new brochure go through straight away, and somehow Minty had a feeling that that wouldn't be a good idea.

If she told them she was going to meet Carol that morning, they might try to persuade her not to. Toby had been trying to tell her

VERONICA HELEY

something about this, without going into detail. Another infuriating man! Why couldn't these men come straight out with it and tell her whatever it was she needed to know?

Minty was determined to see her old friend, but she couldn't face the hassle that might arise if she had Iris and Clive going on at her.

So she'd leave Patrick's den by another route.

She made sure that the door to the tower office was properly shut and locked and left the room by the far door into the rest of the early-Elizabethan wing. These had been the rooms her stepmother had made her own when she lived at the Hall. Now they were used only for the occasional guest.

Minty made her way down the imposing oak staircase to the Great Hall, attacked by bad memories which a visit to this part of the house always brought to mind; it had been a tumble down these stairs which had caused her tragic miscarriage. She paused on the half landing, shook her head at herself, and thrust away another bad memory. As a small child she'd stood there, overhearing the news of her mother's death, and, watching from above, had seen her father turn to stone while his secretary poured poison in his ear.

Minty tried to be positive. She had good memories of this part of the Hall, too, hadn't she? Patrick had walked down those stairs, one step behind her, the first time she'd appeared in public as the Lady of the Hall. What a night that had been! Then on the eve of their wedding, she'd hosted a dinner party here in the Great Hall with all her friends about her. Including Carol and Carol's antique dealer father.

Minty exchanged a smiling word with the steward on duty at the front door.

He asked, "How are the twins? I hear they've learned to operate the lift."

"I'm going to put it out of commission till I can work out how to stop them escaping."

He laughed, indulgent. "It keeps us all young, having them around. Before you go, can you say when we're getting the new brochures? We're nearly out."

Minty had already noted that the pile of brochures on the table in front of the steward had shrunk to almost nothing. "I'm on my way to see someone about it now."

That made the steward feel better, but only put more pressure on Minty.

She got through the courtyard without being stopped by anyone, and started up her car. Just as she was turning out into the drive, Reggie came rushing along behind her.

"Minty, a quick word ..."

She thrust her head out of the window. "Sorry, Reggie. Can't stop. Catch up with you later."

She put her foot on the accelerator. She thought he was calling after her that it was important he speak to her, but it was even more important that she see Carol, so she left his worried face behind. He'd probably only wanted to tell her he'd changed the smashed light bulb in the inner courtyard, or something.

She wasn't used to seeing Reggie so doleful. He always used to have a happy face and whistle as he went about his work. Patrick, too, had been accustomed to whistle when he was working in his garden before they married. But not recently. Perhaps she hadn't given him anything much to whistle about?

The Five Ways pub was to be found five miles away on the out-skirts of a village—almost as big as a town—which boasted a real, live smith who produced weather-vanes and other ironwork to order, a thriving bakery, and a tiny museum open two afternoons a week. It also had the remains of a castle on the hill above. As the song goes, this was "one of the ruins that Cromwell knocked about a bit."

The pub had turned itself over to flashing games machines, but there was a quiet snuggery in which Carol was to be found, her strawberry blonde hair in an aureole against the light from the window behind her.

Carol was wearing a Barbour jacket over a roll-neck sweater and trousers. Minty blinked. Carol was transforming herself from sparky city girl to seasoned country woman. Minty was heartened to see some signs of the old Carol in the huge Victorian opal ring on her right hand, and a number of gold chains around her neck. Carol was mixing the old and the new. There were dark shadows under her eyes.

Minty ordered herself a round of sandwiches and a half of shandy at the bar, paid for them, and went through to the dining room.

Carol didn't rise to greet Minty but instead leaned back in her seat. "So how's Mummy bearing up today?"

Minty relaxed, grinning, for Carol's warm tone showed they were still friends. "Show some sympathy for the terminally tired. Mummy's all worn out, but Daddy's got her some daytime help, so Mummy's playing truant from the Hall, and trying to keep awake long enough to work out why her best friend's in a tizzy."

Carol swished ice cubes around in her fruit juice. "You really don't know anything about it, do you?"

Minty shook her head. "Explain it to me. Preferably in words of one syllable."

"Well, first of all, I know you were quite innocent of any skulduggery—at the start, anyway."

"Skulduggery?" Minty would have laughed, if Carol hadn't looked so serious.

"Don't interrupt. History lesson coming up. You were four years old when you were shot out of the Hall by your daddy who thought he'd been short-changed by your mummy. Mummy dies, Daddy weds loathsome secretary, and you end up living with ghastly uncle and auntie in their city vicarage, right?"

Minty nodded, frowning.

"Your new home is furnished with cheap pieces picked up in junk shops. Auntie and uncle thought more of cleansing their souls for eternity than cleaning the house. I don't want to be mean. I never knew your aunt well, and now she's dead ... well."

Carol shrugged. "As for your uncle Reuben, he's become one of my favourite people now he's calmed down a bit, but he's never appreciated beauty or even a comfortable chair, has he? So — and this is the ·point — you were whipped away from the Hall before you'd a chance to learn much about it, and you weren't exposed to any quality furniture or furnishings while you were growing up. Right so far?"

Minty couldn't see where this was leading.

"Daddy died and lo and behold, Cinderella Araminta became Princess Minty. You inherited the Hall. About which," said Carol, poking her finger at Minty, "you knew practically nothing. You had vague memories, but no actual knowledge. Not of the furniture."

"I remember some things, some of the pictures, our big bed. I remember quite a bit, really, but a lot of it I didn't recognise when I inherited. Well, I wouldn't, would I?"

"My dear Cinderella, you knew so little, you'd have mistaken Hepplewhite for Chippendale. You can't even now, hand on heart, tell me which pieces of furniture had been brought into the Hall during the years you'd been away, and what had been there before. Can you?"

Minty stared. "Well, there are some things but ... no, on the whole I don't suppose I could."

"While you were gone, it amused your wicked stepmama — known to all and sundry as 'Lady C' — to turn the Hall from a family house into a stately home and open it to the public. She'd been a humble secretary before she induced your dear daddy to put a ring on her finger, and she hadn't a clue about antiques, so she employed a so-called expert to buy goods for her and to devise a brochure."

Minty shuddered. "A slimy type." She sought for his name in her memory. "Hertz, that was his name. Guy Hertz. He wanted to go on buying stuff for me, but I didn't like him. He tried to pass off a miniature of an unknown man as one of my ancestors, but the colour of the eyes was wrong, and the hair-style, too. I thought he was trying to pull a fast one, so I told him No Deal. I could never have trusted him after that."

Carol said, "Bully for you. Cut to where my father and I start up the shop in the village. My beloved parent is fond of you. I'm rather fond of you myself, you know. I've been brought up with antiques, and since my father put me in charge of the new shop, I've been soaking myself in them. I found I'd quite a flair for spotting fakes ..."

"Fakes?" Minty drew in a deep breath. "You think there are fakes at Eden Hall?"

"Not your fault, lovey. Not then, anyway. Beloved parent and I had a quiet laugh together after his first visit to the Hall. 'That oak chest in the Great Hall is a bit dicey, don't you think?' You do get the odd bit of diceyness in all old houses. We see it all the time. A young Regency wife throws out her mother-in-law's cherished walnut suite and orders something new-fangled in mahogany. An Edwardian carpenter cuts up the barley-twist posts from a redundant four-poster bed to make lamp stands. Great-aunt leaves her nephew a cherished tallboy in her will, little knowing it had started life in two different centuries.

"The oak chest in your Great Hall started out in life absolutely plain, but in Victorian times someone carved a design into it to make it look more fashionable. We were amused to see that it is featured in your brochure as Jacobean, but we decided these things happen in the best regulated families. Provided you weren't trying to sell it, well ... it was none of our business, was it?"

Minty's sandwich came, and she set about it, while concentrating on what Carol was saying.

Carol said, "Let's pass on to the short but turbulent reign of the evil pop-queen Maxine. She and her entourage did an incredible amount of damage to the Hall in a short space of time. Candle wax, wine stains, cigarette burns, a couple of chairs broken. It was an insurance job, and you asked me to quote you for restoration. I made a preliminary assessment. Most of the stuff you asked me to look at was genuine, but one piece — a pseudo-Regency side table from the Chinese Room — wasn't. The top didn't match the base, and what's more, the wood was wrong, the method of construction was wrong ... oh, it was all wrong."

"That brightly coloured table?" said Minty, her mouth full of sandwich. "I've never liked it, but I thought the fault lay with me, not the table."

"Perhaps you do have an instinct, after all. Yes, it's a fake. Your humble servant consulted her beloved parent, whose brow became as wrinkled as hers. You see, this table wasn't a Victorian replica; that does happen and such things have a value, though not as much as if it were an original. This was a modern imitation, but it is featured in the brochure as a genuine Regency table. Beloved parent agreed that I had to Tell All. I didn't bother you with the bad news, because this was when you'd just become pregnant with the twins after that awful miscarriage and everyone was walking around you on eggshells. I told Iris instead."

Minty flushed. "I see what you mean. If there are any fakes at the Hall, then up to the point that I inherited, I wasn't responsible. But now I am. You're making me feel guilty. I don't think I've ever looked at the furniture critically, as you do. I suppose I ought to take a course in antiques. Oh dear."

"Iris hadn't spotted it and she has a Fine Arts degree; admittedly, her speciality is pictures, not furniture. I'm happy to say that all the pictures bar one appear to be exactly what they're supposed to be.

Anyway, Iris and I talked it over; she would arrange for the fake to disappear into one of the storerooms, while I got on with restoring the rest—which I did.

"Cut to this last winter. The twins were thriving, they hadn't yet started walking, and you had things more or less under control. You asked me, in all innocence, to make an inventory of the furniture at the Hall during the winter months when the place was closed to the public. That was sensible of you, and I give you full marks for that. There hadn't been an inventory for years, and Neville Chickward—I do like that man—very properly wanted to bump up the insurance to cover today's inflated prices for antiques. You thought you were doing me a favour, putting work my way.

"So in January, when the Hall was closed, I started to go through every room, sometimes with my father, sometimes with my restorer, checking every single piece. I found forty-seven pieces of repro and junk masquerading as pricey antiques, most of which are on show in the State Rooms and featured in the brochure."

Minty lost all her colour. "Forty-seven fakes? I'm responsible for passing off forty-seven fakes as the genuine article?"

Carol nodded. "Some are passable reproductions, but yes, about half are fakes. Some of the fakes are falsely stamped with the names of the great and good—which is criminal, by the way."

Minty clutched her head with both hands. She could feel her heart thumping. "Fakes? Criminal fakes? Really?"

Carol said, "Yes. Criminal fakes. I realised you hadn't a clue, probably thought everything was kosher. To do nothing was to invite disaster, because if I could see that things were not right, then other people could, too. It was a wonder someone hadn't shouted 'Fake!' already.

"Something had to be done, but what? I delayed putting in my report, so that I could talk to you about it first. You never returned my calls, even though I left messages saying how urgent it was. I wrote twice. No reply, except for a terse message from Clive to say that he was dealing with affairs of the Hall for you. Beloved parent became restive, pointing out that the longer the deception went on, the likelier someone would yell, 'Stop, thief!' So eventually I made an appointment and went up to see Clive and hand over my report.

"Clive took ten seconds to read the covering page and perhaps thirty to decide what to do about it. He said I didn't know what I was talking about. He said that if I dared make my report public, he'd sue me for defamation. He asked why I was trying to ruin you, when I was supposed to be your friend. He was intimidating, and I was duly intimidated, fool that I am. But I fought back.

"I said that if he didn't accept the report and take the appropriate steps to remove the offending articles, some time or other the truth would get out, and then the Hall would be on the skids, because people would lose confidence in what was on show. If they lose confidence, they'll stop coming to the Hall, and if the paying public stop coming, it's curtains for the Hall and for his job."

Minty washed her face with her hands. "Dear heavens!"

Carol continued, "I asked him to imagine the headlines. 'Heiress dupes the punters, fleeces the friends, violates the visitors.' Write your own tabloid shocker. When Clive had calmed down, he said he was going to get a second opinion. Would I hold my tongue until he'd got an independent expert to do an inventory? I said I would, provided he withdrew the fakes from public view and made sure they didn't appear in any future brochures. He wouldn't promise, and in fact he left them where they were.

"I was very sure of myself," said Carol with a bitter twist to her mouth. "Three weeks ago he sent me a copy of an inventory done by a well-known and reputable firm from London. I mean, they're the tops at this lark. They'd condemned just three of the fakes as repro and everything else had been passed as tickety-boo."

Minty gaped. "But, Carol, you do know your stuff, and your father is the tops. I'd trust you both to the end of the world."

Carol's hand shook as she drained her glass. "It's a nightmare. The following day, Clive sent me an ultimatum; I was to withdraw my report and apologise unconditionally, in writing. If not, he'd make sure the word gets around that I'm an unreliable judge of furniture. If he does that, I'm finished. I might as well close the shop and go back to the City. I don't want to go. I like it here. But if I do recant — which I've thought of doing, believe me — then he'll have me by the short and curlies for ever more."

She found a handkerchief and blew her nose. "To rub salt into the wounds, Toby tells me that the new brochure still includes the worst of the fakes."

So that was why Toby was so agitated about the new brochure! If only he'd come out with it and said ... but would she have believed him, as she believed Carol? Wouldn't she have consulted Iris and Clive about it? Iris would have sided with Clive ... or would she?

What a mess!

Had Reggie realised exactly what was going on? It was possible, yes. And Toby? He spent a lot of his free time with Carol, so ... he must have felt that he was between the devil and the deep blue sea.

Minty tried to read Carol's face. "What's with you and Toby?"

Carol shrugged. "Nice lad. We see quite a bit of one another, being two singles in a village which is a trifle short of young and eligible men and women. He treats me like an elder sister. He gets a crush on a girl about once a quarter and tells me all about it. He knows about my report because he and Iris came in on the end of my row with Clive. Toby thinks I'm right about the fakes, but ... divided loyalties ... what can he do? Clive told him to zip his lip, threatened him with the loss of his job if he so much as set a whisper going that all was not well."

Minty blinked. She thought Toby had managed pretty well, under those circumstances. He'd managed to get Minty interested in the problem without saying a word that Clive could object to.

Minty opened the folder and laid out the proofs of the new brochure. "Show me which ones are wrong."

Carol scrabbled through the sheets. "Here's the oak chest—still down as Jacobean. Well, it is Jacobean, but the carving was done later, so it's not an out-and-out fake. Here's the matching mirrors from the Red Room, with replacement modern glass, if you please. That's not a crime, but it is usual in such circumstances to point out that the glass is a modern replacement if you feature them in a brochure.

"Also in the Red Room, we have the brochure extolling 'a priceless collection of Moorcroft pottery signed by the master William Moorcroft himself.' One or two pieces are just that, but others aren't. How can I tell? Well, William Moorcroft died in 1945, and though the firm staggered on for a while, it finally died the death, was bought out, and only started making quality pots again a few years ago. New designers were brought in, but no pot made after William's death should bear his signature, right?

"Some of yours are unsigned, which is okay; they're genuine Moorcroft, though not from William's hand. They have a value, but it's nothing compared to the pots he made and signed himself. Some of yours are signed, but the signature's wrong. So those are criminal fakes, right?

"Don't pass out on me yet, because there's worse to come. The Chinese Room is where we have the biggest problem. Those spindly chairs and tables are definitely fakes; twentieth century, not eighteenth; you've only got to look at the construction of the frames to realise that. And also ... the nerve! They've kept that fake Regency table in the brochure. Are they mad or am I?"

Minty gasped. "You mean, everything in that room is fake?"

"Everything except the wallpaper and the curtains. So what are you going to do about it?"

Chapter Eight

Minty rubbed her eyes. "I can't think straight. Of course you're right. But how did it happen that the London firm did a whitewash job? Do you think my unbeloved stepmother's 'expert' had something to do with it?"

"Don't see how he could," said Carol. "I can't explain it."

"Guy Hertz was out of the picture long before Clive arrived on the scene. If only Patrick were here … but goodness knows when he'll be back. Perhaps he could make some enquiries about the London firm?"

"Patrick guessed something was wrong. He came into the library to return a book while I was examining the curio cabinet by the fireplace. We joked about how many secret or concealed compartments it might contain. I'd found four, and he found another. The cabinet's genuine, by the way. Everything in the library is all right, except, possibly, the library steps, which are a bit of this and a bit of that — made up from two other pieces of furniture, in my opinion. But still quite valuable."

Seeing Minty's look of incomprehension, Carol added, "Someone mixed and matched oak and mahogany, which is not usual practice, believe me. The steps probably got broken some time in the past, and an estate carpenter made use of wood from another piece of furniture to mend it with. Anyway, getting back to Patrick, before he left, he asked if I'd like a list of the things bought by the infamous Lady C for the Hall. I said yes, but not till I'd finished …"

"So your judgement wouldn't be influenced while you were conducting your examination."

"The list arrived a few days after Clive threw my report out. Yes, your stepmama had bought all the items I'd marked down as questionable. To be fair, there's other things which her expert has bought which seem all right, but he must have cleared a fortune if he got her to pay antique prices for the dicey bits."

Minty pressed her hands to her temples. Patrick had known. Or guessed. One of the books he'd left at his bedside had been on antique furniture. Had he left it out for her to consult? Why hadn't he warned her? Ah, but he'd tried to, hadn't he? And she'd not listened. So he'd attacked the problem from a different angle. He'd freed her from looking after the twins so that she had time to check up on things. She pushed her hair back from her face; she was exhausted. "Reggie has been hinting this and that, but I thought you might have quarrelled with Clive because you hadn't been paid for the work you'd done."

"I haven't been, but that's the least of my worries. To be fair, Reggie has tried to help me. He knows his clocks, doesn't he?"

It was one of the joys of Reggie's life to keep the many clocks at the Hall in working order.

Carol said, "Reggie made sure I had a good look at the one in the Red Room, and the one on the chest in the Hall. Neither of them are in original condition, though still fairly valuable. He'd spotted it, of course. But ..."

"Did the London firm spot it?"

"Apparently not. But then, they might not have sent down an expert on clocks. I bet their bill was something else! I'm glad you know now, Minty, though I can't for the life of me see what you can do about it. Toby says they're running short of the old brochures and really need some new ones."

Minty got up. "I need some strong black coffee. How about you?" Carol nodded.

Minty couldn't think what to do. If Carol was right, then it was folly to leave the fakes and reproduction pieces on show. Sooner or later, someone would be bound to denounce them.

But if they needed new brochures ...? And if the London firm had passed more or less everything as genuine ...?

No, she couldn't allow fakes—or even pieces which were doubtful—to appear in the new brochure. Suppose she removed them from display, then ...? There were nearly fifty! It would leave great gaps in the rooms. The Chinese Room would be stripped of all its furniture. Suppose Carol was wrong!

There was one solution. She could close the Hall early this year, which would give her time to check on the second inventory from the London firm ... yet, who in their right mind would dare query such an august institution? Closing the Hall early might solve some problems, but not all, because Toby had said there were a number of private functions scheduled at the Hall throughout December. And suppose Carol was wrong?

If only Patrick hadn't gone off by himself, she could have asked his advice. She felt her colour rise as she considered her recent conduct to him. She'd stamped on all his offers of assistance, and now he'd disappeared somewhere in Europe, without leaving her a forwarding address. Except, if he said he'd left her a schedule, then that was what he'd done. She just hadn't found it yet.

She paid for the two coffees and took them back to the table. Carol was looking at her watch. "I really haven't time for coffee. I've an appointment the other side of the county at three."

Minty looked at her watch. "Nor me. I've missed the twins' lunchtime. You should see them! Patrick's given them a couple of tricycles, and they insisted on eating their breakfast on them. And the noise they make with the horns. They haven't got bells, but horns. Ting is so sweet ..."

"How is my beloved godchild? I wish you'd call her by her proper name."

Minty bit her lip. When would she learn that women who'd never had a child had a limited patience with stories about other people's children? "Will you let me have a copy of your inventory, and the list of stuff bought by Lady C?"

"I'll give them to Toby when I see him tonight. Oh, and by the way, I popped into the vicarage to see your uncle Reuben yesterday, but he was asleep. Cecil says he's sleeping a lot of the time now. Cecil's worried because your uncle refuses to take his medication, and if he has another heart attack . . ."

Minty nodded. "I know. Patrick warned me. I'll try to drop in on him later today."

They each took one sip of coffee, Minty gave Carol a reassuring hug, and they ran for their cars through the rain.

Minty's journey home was tiresome. It wasn't far as miles go, but the heavy rain made driving difficult, and then—just to add to her misery—a lorry had jack-knifed into a bridge and blocked the road completely. She would have backed and tried another route, if she hadn't been travelling in a slow queue of cars. She pulled out her mobile and rang the phone in her rooms back at the Hall.

Serafina answered, sounding sharp. Minty could hear Boom bellowing in the distance.

"What's happened?" Minty's heartbeat went into overtime.

Serafina was reassuring. "Ting hurt herself, switching on the toaster. She's all right, just a little shocked. We're coping. Where are you?"

"Are you sure? Did she burn herself? What happened?" How could she have left her children in someone else's care! Boom was still bellowing. Whichever twin was hurt, it was always the other who yelled.

"She'll tell you herself. Here you are, Ting. You wanted your mummy and here she is, on the phone."

Ting came on the line, sniffing a bit. "Mummy, Mummy, I want you. The toaster bit me!"

"I'll be back as soon as I can, darling. Is Boom all right?"

Serafina took the phone back. "They're both all right, really. But there is something wrong with the toaster. It gave her a nasty shock, poor little thing."

Minty tried to think. "I used it this morning, didn't I? It was all right then."

"I'll get Reggie to have a look at it. What time will you be back?"

"As soon as I can. I'm stuck in traffic a couple of miles away."

There was no sign of the lorry moving. Some of the cars behind Minty were beginning to try to turn, to retrace their journey. Minty was in her big old estate car, which wasn't easy to turn. If she got mired on a road verge softened by all this rain, it would take a tractor to pull her out. It would be better if she could back her way out, but not with so many cars in line behind her. *Pray*, she told herself. *Just pray.*

It took her ten minutes to manoeuvre her car out of trouble and facing back the way she'd come. She looked at her watch. She was going to be late ... Poor Ting ... She hoped Gloria wasn't put off by all this.

What am I going to do about the Hall? Dear Lord, what a mess! Patrick gone, who knows where, and ... I wish he hadn't gone. I wish I hadn't been so hard on him. I feel so split ... the twins ... the Hall ... what am I supposed to do? Which comes first? I can't cope. I've got to cope. So many people depend on me, not just Carol. It would be awful if Carol were driven out, but ... I don't understand what's going on! Dear Lord, don't let Ting suffer, needing me, and me far away on a wild goose chase ... I wish I'd never asked Carol to meet me ... but no. That was the right thing to do.

Dear Lord, I do realise I'm battering away at You while You're doing all the listening, and are just waiting to get a word in edgeways, but it's so hard to listen when things are worrying me.

There, I'll be quiet for a bit. Concentrate on the driving. This rain! Is that another hold-up ahead? Which other road could I take? There isn't another road. Thank You, Lord. The road's clearing. Just tell me what to do next, will You?

She switched on the heater and concentrated on driving.

By the time she reached the top of the village, the rain had more or less ceased and the clouds were breaking up. A coach full of tourists was causing an obstruction on the one-way road around the Green, blocking the street down to the Hall. Minty pulled into the side of the road and rang the Hall again.

Serafina answered. "Where are you, Minty? Everything's all right here. The twins are watching a video that Gloria's brought in for them."

Minty felt herself relax. "It's been a terrible journey, and now I'm stuck behind traffic on the Green." She found herself looking at one of the superb Georgian houses opposite. A miniature stately home, it was the domain of Mrs Chickward, who, together with the nouveau riche Mrs Collins, ran everything in the local community.

She remembered, with a smile, Patrick's description of them as Mrs Thinifer and Mrs Fattypuff. Very apt. Mrs Chickward was as spare as Mrs Collins was broad in the beam.

Mrs Chickward knew everyone of importance. What's more, the Hall's excellent accountant, Neville, was her nephew and presumably would inherit her wealth in due course. (And what was going on with Neville and Iris? Minty thought she really must find out, or she'd put her foot in it when she next spoke to them.)

Patrick had mentioned that Mrs Chickward had been battling with Mrs Collins about something or other ... about the cancellation of the Christmas decorations? Minty had told herself earlier that she ought to find out what was going on. Only, now she was sitting opposite Mrs Chickward's house with an opportunity to do just that, she discovered she'd really prefer to get back to the Hall and comfort poor Ting ... except that Ting had probably forgotten about her mishap by now.

Minty pulled a face; hadn't she just been asking God what she should do next, and then her car had been stopped outside Mrs Chickward's? God had an uncanny way of pushing you into doing things you didn't want to do, sometimes.

She looked down at her casual garb. Mrs Chickward would be immaculately dressed even if she was not expecting visitors. Minty pulled down the driving mirror to tidy her hair as best she could and thought she presented a very poor image as the Lady of the Hall. She looked dishevelled and heavy-eyed from lack of sleep.

Ah well. No more excuses. The next job on the list appeared to be tackling Mrs Chickward, so she'd better get on with it.

As she rang the bell, she looked back over the Green. When she'd inherited the Hall, she'd had grand ideas for improvements at the house and in the village. Some of these ideas had come to nothing; others had worked out. One of the things that had worked out was the children's playground which she had paid to install at the top of the Green, though it was maintained—at Patrick's insistence—by the Parish Council. The swings, climbing equipment, and slides were well used. Even though it had only just stopped raining, some children were out there playing.

At least she'd got one thing right.

Mrs Chickward opened the door, tall and bony. And disapproving. "Well, well. What brings you here?"

"A guilty conscience, Mrs Chickward." Minty hadn't meant to say that, but Mrs Chickward's rigid expression softened, and she ushered Minty inside.

"We're in the drawing room at the back. Go through and I'll fetch another cup." Minty obeyed, stepping into a room which might have been lifted from a Jane Austen novel, except for the ultra-modern settees and the contemporary art work on the walls. Mrs Chickward's principles might have been formed at her mother's knee, but she was bang up to date with her furnishings.

"You know everyone, I think," said Mrs Chickward. "Tea?"

"Thank you." Minty wished fiercely that she'd taken the trouble to go home and change before she ventured into this circle of smartly dressed women. Jeans and an ancient sweater couldn't compete.

Mrs Chickward was wearing her favourite navy—probably by Chanel or Jean Muir. Venetia Wootton was in one of the understated but classical ecru ensembles that matched her hair, and Mrs Collins—a surprise to see her here in view of the well-known animosity between the two older ladies—was wearing something floaty in black and pink that failed to minimise her bulk.

Another surprise: opposite her was the landlady of the Pheasant Inn, Moira of the gimlet eyes, wearing something a trifle too glittery but nevertheless expensive. Moira and her husband were comparative newcomers to the village but had identified themselves with it and were proving an asset.

Now what could have brought these four together? Something that affected the whole village, obviously. Something like the cancellation of the Christmas decorations season?

Minty steeled herself to face four women's carefully bland expressions. "Have you been talking about the Hall?"

"Would that be so surprising?" said Mrs Chickward, seating herself behind a tea tray and pouring Minty a cup. The other ladies seemed to have been there for some time, judging by their empty cups and a half-empty plate of biscuits.

Venetia seemed embarrassed. "Minty's been so taken up with the twins, she really hasn't been able to cope with ..."

Mrs Chickward lifted one bony hand, and Venetia subsided.

Mrs Collins stirred her half-empty cup. She, too, seemed embarrassed. "Those of us who have had the pleasure of a large family—not that I have ever been blessed with children—but we should perhaps, sympathise with ..."

Mrs Chickward gave Mrs Collins a look. Mrs Collins, her colour rising, also fell silent.

Moira clicked her empty cup down on her saucer. "Well, Minty. Tell us how you see things."

The cup of tea Mrs Chickward had poured for Minty was tepid. She put it down on a nearby pie-crust table which was most certainly a genuine antique. There was no point trying to defend herself. She had neglected her responsibilities, just as Patrick had said. "I put the children first. I got overtired ..."

Four identical nods.

"... and didn't realise that things were going wrong ..."

Four more nods.

"... until Patrick ..."

Four nods, to one another this time. "I told you Patrick would make her see sense."

Mrs Collins excused Minty. "He said it was entirely a matter for her, but ..."

Moira of the sharp eyes cut across them. "So what are you going to do about it?"

Minty was wary. "About what?"

Mrs Chickward stiffened her already straight back. "The cancellation of the Christmas decorations season, for a start."

"It has caused such a flutter, my dear, you must have realised." That was Mrs Collins.

"The gossip ..." Moira overrode Mrs Collins with ease. "... about your friend Carol."

There was a silence filled with unspoken words. All four of them were frowning. So Carol's name was already mud, was it?

Then something unexpected happened. Venetia lifted her chin. "I like Carol." She sounded defiant.

Now there was no way that Carol's friendship with Toby could have gone unremarked in the village. Naturally Venetia would know about it. As Toby's mother, perhaps she'd hoped that one day he'd marry someone from a local family, who'd settle down to produce him a couple of children and immerse herself in good works. Although that was perhaps an old-fashioned point of view, Minty was pretty sure that that was what Venetia would have liked. Venetia's first choice would definitely not be an "incomer" like Carol, who was a city girl and a businesswoman with a mind of her own. So, if Venetia was defending Carol to her peer group, then Venetia was saying not only that she liked Carol, but that she approved of her as a possible mate for her son.

Bland expressions appeared on the faces of Mrs Chickward, Mrs Collins, and Moira, which told Minty that a vital piece of information was being processed, and that these three powerful women were adjusting their viewpoints accordingly.

Earlier, Minty had allowed herself to entertain the suspicion that Carol's judgement might not be trustworthy, but gut reaction now told her that she'd already decided whose side she was on. "I don't know what gossip you've heard, but Carol is my oldest friend, honest and true."

The silence was like a thud in the room. Then Mrs Chickward stirred. "May I refresh your cup, Minty? No?"

Minty could see the others working it out. If Minty and Venetia were both backing Carol's judgement, then the rumours could be discounted. Working back from that premise, as the rumours had originated at the Hall, if Carol was on the side of the angels, then Clive wasn't. Next point; if there had been a disagreement between Carol and Clive, then it must be about the inventory, because everyone knew that Carol had spent a great deal of her time up at the Hall doing it. Which meant, didn't it, that there must be something wrong with the furniture up at the Hall?

Venetia bit her lip. "Clive got me to sack one of our oldest and most faithful stewards because he queried something in the brochure. I wonder..."

"I'm looking into it," said Minty.

"Are you, dear?" said Mrs Chickward. "Then I think we can leave the matter in your capable hands."

Mrs Collins took the last biscuit. She always took the last biscuit. Probably no one else had had any. "To get back to the decorations. They were so much fun to organise. Can't we reinstate them for December?"

"What's done is done," said Moira, her eyes on Minty. "We've got to forget about all that, and look to the future. If the Hall goes down, the village suffers, and so does the pub." Moira had grasped the significance of what was happening. Moira was telling Minty that she was going to be held to her promise to look into things. Moira ought to stand for Parliament.

Mrs Chickward was not one to let the meeting drift out of her control. "No need to look on the black side, Moira. I trust Minty to put things right."

Mrs Collins heaved herself to her feet with an effort. "Must go. Women's Institute meeting this evening. A pity you resigned from the committee, dear Mrs Chickward. Such an interesting programme we have this winter."

Moira armed herself with a handbag the size of a briefcase. "Must go, too."

Venetia was still frowning as she accompanied Minty to the front door. "Has it stopped raining? Minty, if the children can let you off the leash for long enough, I wouldn't mind a word sometime." She disappeared in the direction of her car.

Moira grasped Minty's elbow. "I'm not absolutely sure what's going on ..."

"Neither am I," Minty admitted. "But I intend to find out."

"Good girl. A word to the wise: Young Toby was in the pub at lunchtime with that odd girl that's been wandering around the village.

Lives in a caravan. I didn't take to her, and I doubt if either Carol or Venetia will, either." Moira trudged off down the road.

Minty drew in her breath. Toby had taken Judith to the pub at lunchtime? Had he recognised her? Was he going to fall victim to her wiles all over again? Another tangle.

Mrs Collins wafted herself to the door, winding herself into a gauzy scarf which didn't look warm enough for a chilly November. "About the Christmas decorations ..."

"Moira's right," said Minty. "I can't put the clock back, but I'm going to have a word with Clive tomorrow about this and that. Perhaps I can ring you afterwards?"

"I trust you to put things right, dear." Mrs Collins must weigh fourteen stone, if an ounce, but she always wore high heels and contrived to give the impression of floating rather than walking to her car.

"Humph!" said Mrs Chickward, watching her guests depart. "Minty, no one asked how the children are. You must bring them over one day soon. They can run wild in the back garden while you and I have a chat."

This was an order and not an invitation. Minty said she'd love to, but turning to bid Mrs Chickward goodbye, she was struck by how much the older woman had aged recently. Her dismay must have shown in her face, for Mrs Chickward laughed and patted Minty on her shoulder.

"Anno Domini, my dear. I do seem to get tired easily these days. Perhaps it's time for me to retire. I know I've not been on top of things as much as I should lately. I'm resigning from various committees; late-night wrangles don't agree with me any more. I've asked Moira to consider standing instead. So you'd better sort out the Hall, or she'll move away to a more lucrative pub, and we'll lose her."

Minty considered saying that this was rubbish and Mrs Chickward was good for another ten years, but stopped herself. Mrs Chickward was no fool; and if she was facing the inevitable end with dignity and a strong Christian faith, then she needed approval and prayers, not mindless assurance that she'd live to be a hundred.

Minty said, "I'll bring the children up to see you sometime soon. They'll love your woodland garden."

Mrs Chickward nodded. "One more thing. My nephew Neville is a good boy. He'll inherit everything when I go. I've watched him and all the other children around here grow up. Your Patrick was always going places; that was clear from the start. And little Iris ... who is not so little nowadays. Rather like Venetia with her son Toby, I always hoped that Neville would marry someone from his own background who would give me great-nephews and nieces to spoil, but he's still ... all these years later ... do you think ... not at all what I had wanted for him once, but if that's what he really wants, then ...?"

"We'll have to pray about it," said Minty, alarmed at all these undercurrents. What on earth did Mrs Chickward or Venetia Wootton think she could do to sort out the love affairs of their nearest and dearest?

Mrs Chickward nodded and closed the door on Minty's heels.

The tourist coach had now departed, but her car had been boxed in by two vans. Large vans. There was no way she was going to be able to get her car out.

Now what, Lord?

Try listening, for a change.

Was it going to rain again? She looked round for the owners of the vans which were preventing her from leaving, but the place seemed deserted in the dusk. Lights were being turned on in all the houses that fronted the Green. Across the Green shone the lights of the old church. It was too early for evensong, but it seemed that someone was there.

God is there. He's here, as well, of course. But I might be able to listen to Him better in there.

Chapter Nine

Minty rounded the Green and crossed the road to the church. An electric invalid buggy was parked in the porch. She knew that buggy; Patrick had bought it for her uncle Reuben. On his good days he could walk well enough and even manage stairs, but on his bad days he relied on his buggy, pottering about between the church, the bookshop, and the coffee shop, putting pedestrians at risk with his haphazard driving.

It was cool inside the church, and Minty shivered. Golden stone, old glass tinged with green in the tall windows, pale tablets of marble on the walls. Heavy-set pews. Just one light on in the chancel, and a bowed black scarecrow of a man huddled against a pillar at the back, with a stout stick leaning against the pew in front of him. Minty's uncle at his prayers, or possibly, asleep?

The Reverend Reuben Cardale had been a hellfire-and-damnation clergyman in the City, and as a child Minty had feared rather than loved him. Though his utterances were still more Old Testament than New, he'd become pathetically dependent on her and Patrick, and had settled down well enough to a pernickety retirement.

Minty had wanted him to move into the Hall, but he preferred to occupy a bed-sitting room in the vicarage behind the church. Years ago, the Reverend Cecil Scott had been a curate of Reuben's in his city parish, and Cecil held him in great affection. Cecil encouraged his old mentor to assist with the services, while Minty and Patrick provided the two men with a competent housekeeper and saw to it that the vicarage was kept in good repair.

Carol said he reminded her of her own late grandfather, and had more or less adopted him as such. She bullied him into keeping his hospital appointments; perhaps her care of him explained why the village had accepted her so easily.

He was valued by the village as their local eccentric, and by Minty for his own sake. He was a stern, almost frightening touchstone for right and wrong.

At the moment he seemed to be dozing. Minty slipped into the pew beside him. He was wearing an enormous old coat, which might perhaps have come out of a charity shop, with a huge scarf wrapped round his scrawny neck, and mittens on his gnarled hands. The scarf had come adrift, and he coughed in his sleep.

Minty gently drew the scarf across his chest, and he woke with a start, staring round at the church, and then at her. He attempted a smile. "So I'm still here? I always hope, when I sit down here for a while, that I'll wake up in a better place." He stirred, grumping as he eased legs and back.

"What's the time?" He'd stopped wearing a watch some time ago. He'd probably dropped it, or left it somewhere. "I wanted to see you about something. Ah, I remember. Satan's handiwork, lies are afoot, and the good and innocent are threatened with destruction. 'Save her, Lord, from lying lips and deceitful tongues. The people have not returned to him who struck them, nor have they sought the Lord Almighty. So the Lord will cut them off both head and tail, both palm branch and reed in a single day.'"

Minty tried to disentangle this. "You've heard something about Carol?"

"The price of her is above rubies." He glared at her. "Yet she is bowed down and brought low by their lies."

"I know. I'm trying to do something about it. Let's go up to the vicarage, Uncle. It's too cold for you in here."

He ignored that, switching from prosecuting counsel to pathetic old man. "Patrick said he's not coming back this side of the weekend, so who's going to give me a game of chess tonight, eh? Cecil's starting a new fellowship group, and his housekeeper's always on at me to change my socks and 'Eat up!' I keep telling her that you should always leave the table feeling you could eat a little more, but she doesn't listen, and Cecil takes her part."

Minty stroked his fingers, smiling. He was better looked after now than at any time in his life, but he'd chosen austerity in his youth and found it hard to relax now. In a previous age he'd have been a gaunt monk, praising God in an unheated monastery, hardly noticing what he ate or drank.

With another switch of thought, he smiled and punched her knee. "You should have seen Patrick a couple of weeks back when he brought the twins to church. You couldn't make it for some reason ..."

"Was that the time they had me up all night, being sick one after the other?"

"Was that it? He put them in the crèche, but they got out when he was taking the collection plate around, and ran to him. He picked one up and tried to give her to Venetia Wootton, but she wouldn't let go. So, solemn as an owl, Patrick went up and down the pews with one child on his arm and the other clinging to his leg. Some of the old folks were scandalised, but Cecil ... I like that lad ... he threw away his prepared sermon and talked to us about Jesus asking for the children to be brought to Him for a blessing. Hah! To give them credit, the twins sat down beside Patrick as quiet as mice for the rest of the service, and then fell asleep."

She smiled, appreciating the story. Patrick hadn't told her about that. She'd caught the bug from the twins herself and been up most of the following night, being sick, too, while Patrick attended to the twins. She'd not really been fair to him; he had looked after them often.

He raised both his hands in the air. "Ah, yes. I know what I needed to say to you. My eyesight's not what it was. Perhaps I dreamed it. A woman walked up the street this lunchtime with young Toby from the Manor, and it seemed to me that I knew her."

"It was Judith Kent, who used to be Maxine, the pop star. I wanted to ask your advice about her." Minty told him the story as she knew it, not forgetting that Patrick had asked her if what she'd done was wise. "I don't know whether it was wise or not. Probably not. I think she still has a capacity for making mischief, she's attractive enough to endanger any man she cares to tangle with, and I can't be absolutely sure that she has put the wiles of the devil behind her. Now she's bewitching Toby all over again, and ... I don't know what to think."

He was stern. "Did you consult God before you offered her a job?"

"Yes, I tried to pray, but I'd got out of the way of praying so much recently, and I'm not sure I was really listening to what He said."

He clucked with his tongue. "Child!" He sighed. "Well, you had a generous impulse, I suppose, and we can only pray that it doesn't turn out badly. We must judge her by her actions. 'By their works ye shall know them.' Has she done or said anything which has caused you concern?"

Minty shook her head. "Not really. Except—though I don't see why she should have lied—someone tried to mug me in the courtyard last night. She was right behind me and said she didn't see anything, and maybe she didn't. But the police now have me down as a hysterical female."

"I don't like the sound of that. You wouldn't lie. What did Patrick say?"

"He doesn't know. He'd already gone."

"You must tell him." He became fretful. "These old limbs of mine move so slowly. What use am I to man or beast now? Why does God keep me here still?"

She was struck afresh by his frailty. How much longer would they be able to keep him with them? "You are my wise counsellor, especially now Patrick's away."

"Pray constantly, child. Remember: Seven days without prayer makes one weak."

He said he wanted to go on praying, so—after a glance at her watch—she had to leave him there. She hadn't really got time to do so, but she rushed round the corner to the vicarage to see if Cecil was in, and met him on his way out.

"Minty, have you seen—"

"My uncle? Yes, he's in the church. I tried to get him to leave, but ..."

Cecil half smiled, shaking his head. "We have to have a meal early tonight, as I've got a meeting to go to. He knows very well that our housekeeper gets into a state when he's late for meals, but there you are, he says praying is more important than being on time for meals, and perhaps he's right, though it's me who has to calm her ladyship down." Cecil was not tall, nor did he give the impression of being a heavyweight in any way, but Minty knew he was a man of God.

"Thank you, dear Cecil. Can you cope? I was struck just now by how much my uncle has aged of late."

"I've given up trying to make him take more care of himself. He says he's well past his three score and ten, and he's looking forward to going home."

Cecil didn't mean an earthly home. Minty nodded, brushed her hand across her eyes, and left him to retrieve his charge.

It had started to rain again, but the vans which had boxed her in on the Green had now departed, so she collected her car and made her way back to the Hall, feeling somewhat comforted.

There was no comfort for her at the Hall.

Reggie met her in the courtyard as she was leaving her car. He must have been waiting for her to return, which meant what he'd had to say to her earlier had been no trivial matter.

"A word, Minty?" He drew her under cover from the rain.

There was no one else about, but she dropped her voice nevertheless. "Reggie, I'm sorry that I had to dash off like that, but I had an appointment to meet Carol. You wanted to tell me something?"

He rubbed his chin. "It's about that attack on you last night. I got to thinking about it today. Did you know that Hodge has taken on a part-timer to help out? He'd mentioned it to me in passing like, saying he needed an extra hand in the greenhouses, Christmas rush, garlands to make, all that sort of thing. He usually knows what he's doing, does Hodge, so I didn't think much about it at first. Only, after last night, I began to wonder."

Minty tried to follow his reasoning. "You think that Hodge's part-timer might have attacked me? Why?"

"I don't know. I made it my business to give him the once-over this afternoon, and he's not from the village, I can tell you that. A Londoner, by his talk. A weaselly looking fellow, but Hodge says he's got the makings, knows how to handle plants, not like some who'd knock a pot over soon as look at it. So what's an off-comer like him doing here, I ask myself."

"Why would a complete stranger want to attack me? Unless — wait a minute — you don't think he's got some connection with Judith, do you?"

"Dunno. I'll have a word with Hodge later, see if I can find out where he's staying in the village. Meantime, you'd better keep a weather eye out, right?"

Minty suppressed a shiver. Did this mean she was going to be attacked again?

"Feeling the cold?" said Reggie. "Have you time for a cuppa at my place?"

Minty glanced at her watch. She had time, just, before Gloria left for the afternoon, and she owed Reggie one. "Of course."

They darted through the rain round the corner into Reggie's neatly kept cottage. He provided two large mugs of tea and pushed a biscuit tin towards her. Minty was amused to see the tin had a picture of the Queen on the lid. Presumably he'd fed the twins biscuits from this very tin the other day.

She said, "About Carol. You've guessed what's upset her, haven't you?"

He nodded. "When she started the inventory, I mentioned to her, quiet-like, that I wasn't happy about the clock in the Great Hall or the one in the Red Room, and she knew what I meant. I thought then that the news wouldn't be welcome in certain quarters, but that they'd have to take notice of what she said."

Minty said, "You know Clive's rubbished her report? What did you make of the experts from London? I wasn't even aware there were any around. They must have come and gone in an instant."

He shrugged. "Carol worked a coupla days a week, and it took her the best part of two months to do the lot. She went through the storerooms at the top of the house as well, though she never got far into the basement, since Clive told her not to bother, and anyway, it's locked up right and tight. She had her father or her chief restorer with her all the time, and they really know their business. When they were in doubt, they consulted books and the Internet and brought in specialists. Once she had a chap down to look at the pictures, and another chap came with her to look at the clocks. She did a thorough job, I'm thinking.

"As for the London firm, they sent two youngsters down, armed with little tape recorders and cameras. They went through the place like a dose of salts—all over within four days. They worked from lists. I managed to catch a glimpse of one. It looked like Carol's inventory, only it had been amended with handwriting all over it."

"You think they'd been primed to take special note of the things she was unhappy about? Surely that's not the usual way to appraise furniture?"

"I wouldn't have thought so, no."

"Did you mention the clock in the Great Hall to them?"

"I did. They laughed, saying 'what did I know' about such things."

Minty leaned back in her chair. "What did you think of Guy Hertz, the expert my stepmother used to buy things from?"

"Not much. Some of the things he bought are all right."

Minty eased the muscles in her neck. "I need a quick course on antique furniture. Will you help me? Don't say you know nothing about it, because you do. You know wood for a start. I can hardly tell walnut from mahogany."

"Mr Patrick knows furniture. His stuff is all right, that he brought from his old home." Patrick wasn't there. She only wished he were. Reggie fidgeted. "What would you want me to do?"

"Perhaps when the visitors have gone, you'd go round the Great Hall with me, point out why the clock is wrong, that sort of thing?"

Reggie nodded, and she said she'd meet him there at half past five. She went slowly through the house, up in the lift to the top floor, and along to the kitchen. She opened the door to find a tea party in progress. Or rather, Gloria and the twins were sitting at one end of the kitchen table, with Serafina ministering to them, while at the other end sat Toby ... and Judith.

"Mummy, Mummy, Mummy!" Ting ran to Minty and clasped her leg. "Bad Mummy! Ting wanted you!"

Minty collapsed into a convenient chair — Patrick's chair — and Ting climbed onto her lap, while Boom came to press himself against her.

Minty clasped Ting to her with one arm, while cuddling Boom with the other. What bliss to have their warm little bodies wriggling against hers. "I missed you so much today, little ones. What have you been doing?"

Boom said, "Ting didn't cry!"

Ting showed Minty her tiny forefinger. "It bit me! All the way to here!" She indicated the top of her arm.

"Electric shock," said Gloria, tersely. "I had a look at the toaster. Someone had stuck something down it."

"It was all right this morning," said Minty, worried. "I'm pretty sure I used it at breakfast."

Toby said, "I don't expect you noticed. You've been in such a state recently."

Minty opened her eyes wide. Had she been in such a state that she hadn't noticed the toaster was dangerous? Ridiculous!

Toby and Judith were sitting close together at the far end of the table, almost as if they'd been isolated by the others. Judith was not saying anything, but there was a shadow of a smile on her face. Perhaps Judith had fed Toby with that line about Minty's distracted state of mind?

Gloria said, "They've been fine, really, Minty. Ting got over the shock very quickly. We went to toddlers' group in the village this morning. After lunch we had a little nap, then we played hide and seek and watched a video. And, if you don't mind, Minty, I'll be off in a minute. Seeing my man tonight."

"Of course. Many thanks, Gloria," said Minty, managing to get Boom on her lap as well. Gloria left. Minty looked hard at Toby, who had never before ventured uninvited into the family quarters.

Toby fidgeted. "I was just showing Judith around. She was dying to meet the twins, but they're acting shy. I'm taking Judith out for supper tonight."

"Really?" said Minty. "Carol didn't mention it. By the way, she'll be giving you some papers for me. I'll need them before the weekly meeting tomorrow."

Toby looked disconcerted for a moment. "I'd forgotten I was supposed to see her tonight. Well, I'm sure she won't mind if Judith comes, too."

Minty was pretty sure that Carol would mind, but didn't say so. Still Judith said nothing, but sat and watched and took everything in. It was uncanny, how she could dominate a conversation without speaking.

Boom ignored the visitors. "What we playing now?"

Ting said, "See me ride my trike!"

Serafina dumped a cup of tea and some homemade biscuits in front of Minty. "Let your mummy have her tea, and then she can take you out of here while I make supper."

Where would she take them? They hated being cooped up all day, and it was still raining out, wasn't it? If they got into the lift again ... it didn't bear thinking about.

"Serafina, that reminds me; do you know where the keys are to the door into the tower office? I need to keep that door locked, so the twins can't get at the lift."

Serafina started to stack the dishwasher. "I haven't seen them. I'll have another look, see if I can find them before I go."

Minty decided not to hear that bit about Serafina going. "I'll take the twins down to the Great Hall and they can ride around there." The tea was hot and just as she liked it, but after drinking a mug with Reggie, she wasn't thirsty.

Toby was preparing to go. "Oh, Minty, those proofs? Iris has been asking for them."

Judith spoke for the first time, seeming amused. "Iris came storming in, really angry with Toby because he couldn't produce the proofs. He didn't give you away. He said he must have mislaid them."

Biscuit in hand, Minty stared at Judith, and Judith stared back. There was a subtext here, but Minty wasn't sure she understood it. Was Judith praising Toby? Or warning Minty, or building a bridge of secrets to be kept? Minty said, "Thanks, Toby. I'll speak to Iris about them in a minute. Judith, it doesn't seem a good idea for you to traipse heavy books all the way up here. I'll see if I can find you a desk in the north wing instead."

Judith lowered her eyes, but not before Minty had read a flash of anger in them. Judith understood she was being punished for daring to enter Minty's rooms. Toby probably hadn't realised what was happening, but Judith had. As Toby and Judith passed them on their way out, the twins both pressed their faces into Minty. The message was clear. They didn't like, perhaps were even afraid of Judith.

Minty spoke over their heads to Serafina. "How did those two get invited to nursery tea?"

"Invited themselves. Or rather, she put Toby up to it, I think. Was it wise to give her a job, Minty?"

"I thought it the right thing to do at the time, but ... it's a big worry."

"I almost wish I wasn't going away."

Minty refused to hear that hint, too. "Have there been any phone calls for me?" She meant calls from Patrick but didn't like to mention his name in front of the twins, or they'd start yelling for him.

Serafina was clearing the table. "Not for you, no. He rang to speak to me, though. He's arranged for a car to take me to the station and bought my ticket for me. As soon as you're off, I'm away. A whole week away with no cooking or running around after children!"

"What?" Minty couldn't ignore that. She almost spilled her tea, feeling as if she'd missed a step in the dark. "You really are going? Why didn't you say something?"

"I have, several times, but you didn't want to hear. Two of my brothers and several of my nephews are visiting London and have invited me to meet them. It'll be the first I'll have seen of any of my family for years, but the older I get, the more I wonder about what it's like now, back home. It'll be warmer than here, for a start."

Ting, who was always more responsive to other people's moods than Boom, slipped down from her mother's lap and went to hang onto Serafina's dress.

Minty struggled with herself. She did not, repeat not, want Serafina to go. "I didn't think you'd ever want to see them again, after the way they treated you."

She didn't want to spell it out in front of the twins, but Serafina would know what Minty was referring to. If Minty's father hadn't paid for hospital treatment for Serafina after she'd been beaten up by her family, she'd have been left a cripple to beg on the streets.

The children turned their heads from one adult to the other, trying to make sense of what was obviously an important conversation, but which excluded them.

Serafina said, "I brought my punishment upon myself. In their eyes, I deserved it, and perhaps in my eyes, too. You're right, though. I was surprised when they wrote asking me to visit them in London. They are proud, my family, and I never thought they would forgive me for disgracing them. I showed the letter to Patrick—it was when the twins were being sick all the time and I didn't want to bother you—and he said that I might make even better pastry if I could find it in myself to forgive them, and they to forgive me. It was just like him, to make a joke of it. So I wrote back and said I'd come."

Minty said, "But Serafina ... no, I'm glad for you. Yes, I am, really I am. But ... oh, I'm being horribly selfish. I can't imagine how we'll get on without you, even for a few days. You won't let them whisk you away to visit the rest of your family, will you?" She caught herself up. "No, I didn't mean that. Of course you must go. It's only natural. I can't think straight! Tell me. Where is it I'm supposed to be taking the twins?"

Serafina swept away Minty's cup and plate. "He said you'd work it out, if you wanted to. I must say, it sounds good."

"Where we going?" asked Boom, wide-eyed.

"See Daddy, a course." Ting was ahead of the game.

Boom got off Minty and returned to his bike. "Watch me, Mummy!"

Minty was bewildered. Serafina leaving the Hall for a holiday? It was unheard of. However was Minty going to manage without her? And Patrick thought Minty was going to join him? Travelling abroad with the twins? He must be out of his mind. She supposed he'd left tickets and a schedule somewhere in his desk, but she hadn't seen them. She'd have to have a good look later.

She got to her feet, favouring her bruised hip. Ouch! That hurt. "It's nearly half past five and tourists should have left the house by now. Twins, let's leave Serafina in peace. We'll go downstairs and you can show me how fast you can ride the trikes."

Minty glanced at the clock. It was getting on for the time Reggie had appointed to meet her in the Great Hall. It would be good to have his guidance while she inspected the furniture. Even though she hadn't been trained to appreciate antiques, perhaps, now that she'd been warned, she'd be able to spot something not quite right.

Chapter Ten

Judith was at work in Minty's office and hardly looked up as they passed through. When they reached the door into the tower, the twins drove their trikes at it again and again, *bang, bang!* till someone opened it for them. Iris, looking distinctly put out.

Perp, perp! Boom drove his trike across the office to the lift door, and then continued playing his horn, followed, of course, by Ting, who could easily make as much noise as he did when she tried. She had an air-raid shriek which paralysed hearing at ten paces.

Toby, laughing, summoned the lift for them, while Minty tried to tell Iris that they were on their way down to play in the Great Hall.

"But Minty, those proofs! Toby said . . ."

"Come down with us. We'll talk on the way," said Minty, drawing Iris into the lift after them. Iris came, frowning, fidgeting, but she came.

Conversation was impossible in the lift, for the twins kept up such a racket it was impossible to hear anyone speak. As the doors opened on the ground floor, they went pounding through to the Great Hall. "Hold on a minute!" cried Minty, sprinting ahead to turn on the lights. Tourists and stewards had all left by now, and the room was in darkness.

The wide oaken floorboards shone like silk in the light of the standard lamps.

Minty automatically checked the room for any obstacle that might harm the children as they played. The long narrow table down the centre of the room was flanked by upright dining chairs with tooled Spanish leather seats; they could scoot around those.

Two huge carved chairs stood like sentinels either side of the carved oak chest. They were safely off to one side.

The raised stone lip of the wide hearth would prevent the children riding their trikes into the fireplace, where ancient fire irons might prove dangerous to the young. If they ran into the armoire, it would probably do it no harm, nor would the huge old grandfather clock topple on them if they ran into that.

Perp! Perp! "Race you!" Boom scooted to the right of the table.

Perp! Perrrrrrp! Ting decided to go left.

Iris said, "Minty, about those proofs. I really need them now!"

Minty screamed, seeing the danger ...

The sheen on the old oak floorboards to the right of the table reflected too much. It was like a mirror. Glossy ...

Iris said, "What ...?"

Minty foresaw what was going to happen, her son hurtling along on his trike, getting up speed, hitting the treacherous surface ... what was it? Oil? It would speed him up, throwing him onto the fire irons in the fireplace ... killing him!

He was already caught, sliding helplessly ... yelling for help!

Minty didn't stop to think, but threw herself forward with giant strides ... one ... two ... and on the third step her foot skated along the floor, skidding along behind Boom, who was caught ... sliding helplessly along towards the yawning, gaping fireplace with its lethal fire irons ...

Minty's feet went from under her, she fell, slipping and sliding ... reaching out ... but the little boy was always just ahead of her ...

"Mummy!"

The front wheel of his trike collided with the fireplace just as Minty managed to catch up with him and scoop him off the seat. She fell into the fireplace with him in her arms, clattering, scattering the heavy fire irons. Heart pounding. Legs a tangle. All the breath knocked out of her.

Ting screeched, trying to get off her trike, trying to stand, tumbling over onto the floor.

Time seemed to stop.

Iris dashed forward to snatch the little girl up into her arms, hugging her, eyes wide, face as white as Minty's.

Minty couldn't breathe. Held tight in her arms, Boom was quiet, small chest heaving.

He whimpered. Glorious sound. He wasn't dead.

Minty told herself to try to breathe. Her chest responded, slowly, reluctantly, with care. Her lungs half filled. She tried to sit upright. Failed. Her back hurt. She felt her son's arms and legs.

Boom whimpered again. He was a brave child, who usually only cried when his sister was hurt. He put one hand to his temple. "Hurts!"

Iris stepped carefully across the floor, avoiding the shiny area of boards. Still holding Ting close, she extended a hand to help Minty up.

"Give ... minute," gasped Minty. She couldn't move. What had she broken?

Iris lifted the trike off Minty's legs and set it aside. Ting was weeping, reaching out, calling out for her mother.

"Hurts, Mummy!" cried Boom, still holding his forehead. For all her care, his head must have struck something.

Iris' voice was not steady. "Ting, dear. I must put you down for a moment, to help your mother. Be a good girl, will you?" She deposited the little girl on the window seat. Ting sat like a rag doll with legs dangling, weeping in gulps. Her thumb found her mouth, circled it, and popped in. She hadn't sucked her thumb for quite a while, but it was a comfort in times of trouble.

Minty went on trying to breathe lightly. She felt as if she'd been knocked into the middle of next week, but she hadn't actually hit her head. Had she?

"Mummy, I hurts!" Boom kicked her leg. He hadn't meant to, but he'd jarred her.

Iris said, "Don't try to move, Minty. I'll phone for an ambulance." She bent down and lifted Boom off Minty, saying, "There, there! Brave boy!" She carried him over and set him beside Ting on the window seat. Both children were crying, but quietly now. Boom inched closer to Ting, and she moved closer to him.

With Boom's weight taken off her, Minty tried to move muscles in arms and legs ... they seemed to respond. Neck muscles. Ouch. Her shoulder and back ... had she broken a rib?

Iris was visibly shaking, too. "Where's my mobile? I never move without it ... but ... don't try to get up, Minty!"

Minty shook her head, breathing lightly. She whispered, "Give me a minute. Can't breathe." She'd twisted as she fell, trying to keep Boom safe, and he'd knocked all the wind out of her. She tried to shift her bottom out of the fireplace.

"Don't try to move!" Iris located her mobile on her belt, tried to dial. Failed. "God help me! The battery's down! Just when I need it."

Minty caught her breath. "I'm all right. I think." She could see the children both looking towards her, reaching out their arms, crying, "Mummy-Mummy-Mummy." Imploring her to get up, be normal, be their mummy again.

"Mummy, come!" said Boom, wriggling, trying to get off the seat and run towards her.

Minty couldn't do anything to help him. Now she was crying, too.

"Stay where you are, Boom. Please don't try to move, Minty." Iris ran to the internal phone by the door and punched numbers. "Chef, can you come to the Great Hall? Bring that woman who's done a First Aid course, and if there's a doctor in the restaurant ...? There's been an accident."

Minty felt the edges of her sight were darkening. Was she going to faint? No, she was not going to faint. Not with the twins needing her so badly.

She inched herself forward, straightening her legs. Ouch. That hurt. But she could feel her toes ... and her fingertips where they clung to the stone edge of the fireplace. She hadn't broken anything. Breathe in. Breathe out. It was getting easier to breathe now.

Iris was pushing Boom back onto the seat. Both children were in shock. Iris, too. They were all in shock. What do you do for shock? Hot tea with sugar in it?

But not if you were still sitting in the fireplace like Cinderella. She had to get herself moving again, somehow ...

Florence, their chef, burst through the end doors, closely followed by a hatchet-faced woman. What was her name? She worked in the kitchens. Minty couldn't remember her name for the life of her.

Iris was holding herself together, just, though her voice shook. She spoke directly to Chef. "She tumbled into the fireplace, trying to save Boom from a fall ... mind that patch of floor, it's like ice! I told her not to move."

"I'm all right, I think," said Minty, her tongue fumbling in her mouth. "Just winded. Bruised. Maybe a cracked rib."

Chef, neatly peroxided and accustomed to giving orders, said, "Molly, you look after Minty. Twins, you stop that noise, do you hear? Iris, sit down and put your head between your knees."

The twins recognised the voice of authority in Chef's voice and quietened down, though Ting still hiccupped sobs, and Boom continued to inch his way to the edge of the seat. Iris obeyed, too, sitting beside them and putting her head down.

Chef—Florence—was one of the first friends Minty had made when she came back to the village after her years away in the City. Chef was one of those stalwart Christians whom you could rely on till death. She had a solid body which seemed unbendable. "Where's Gloria? Gone home early? Tck! Never here when she's wanted."

Molly seemed to know what she was doing. Minty surrendered herself to Molly's hands. Chef sat beside the twins, put Boom on her lap, and cuddled Ting while eyeing the treacherous floorboards. "There, there, twins. There, there."

Chef got out her own mobile. "Gloria? Get back here immediately! Minty's had an accident and you're needed." She didn't wait for a reply but shut off the phone, confident that Gloria would obey her.

"No bones broken, no great harm done, but a possible cracked rib," said Molly. "We must take her to hospital for an X-ray."

Minty's body was slow to obey orders, but it seemed she'd live. "No hospital. Check Boom. Hurt his head."

Molly did so.

Iris was into deep breathing, but her colour was returning. Minty shuffled towards the nearest chair on her bottom. Molly helped to ease her up onto the seat. Yes, movement was getting easier. Ting slipped down from the window seat and cast herself into Minty's arms. Minty found she could hold her. Just about.

Boom brushed aside Molly's hands and came to cling to his mother's leg. A nasty bump was rising on his forehead. Minty couldn't make out who was shaking most, herself or the twins.

"Are you really all right? You don't look it," said Iris, who didn't look any too good herself.

Minty said to the twins, "I'm all right, darlings. Really I am. See, Mummy's smiling. Silly Mummy, falling down like that."

"Ah," said Chef. "You don't want the twins to be alarmed. I can understand that, but ..." She bent over to touch the glistening floorboards, then held up her hand.

Minty fought for control, fought to stop the shakes. Fought not to scare the children.

Chef said, "Oil?" She tasted it. "Vegetable oil. Someone's spilt a whole bottle of vegetable oil on the floor. See, there's the empty bottle in the fireplace. A poor quality brand. I certainly don't stock it. Criminally careless! They could have killed you."

So they could, thought Minty. Or they could have killed one of the children. Or just damaged them. Or me.

Maybe that was the point. How well she remembered Judith saying that she wanted what Minty had.

Could Judith have done this? Had she had time? Well, no. She hadn't, had she? Minty had passed her in the office upstairs on her way down.

But Judith had still been in the kitchen when she heard Minty plan to bring the children down here and she could have got the oil—where from? Could she have got downstairs, got the oil—perhaps she had some in her caravan?—spread it on the Hall floor, and then returned upstairs so quickly? Perhaps she could ask Toby if Judith had used the lift just now?

Or perhaps this hadn't anything to do with Judith at all, but had been the brainchild of the weaselly London lad that Hodge had taken on in the gardens? A complete stranger. But why would a complete stranger want to kill her?

Ting was still shaking, sobbing without sound. Boom was dry eyed, but his clutch on Minty's leg was like an iron band.

I could have died! Oh, Patrick, where are you?

The important thing was to comfort the twins and remove them from the scene. Minty said, "Chef, can you get Serafina down here to look after the twins?"

Chef nodded. "Gloria will be back in a minute, but till then …" She used the internal phone by the door and punched in numbers.

Iris was still a bad colour but was now getting angry. "Whichever of the stewards did this, they ought to have seen it was cleaned up before they left. It was criminal negligence to leave it."

Not stewards, thought Minty. *It had all the hallmarks of Judith, though I don't have a clue how she arranged it. But, if it was she, she'll be arriving any second to point out that I'm psychotic, setting up accidents to get attention and harm my own children . . .*

. . . and here she comes.

The door opened with a jerk, and not one but two people entered. Judith and Reggie. Thank God for Reggie.

Chef commanded his attention. "Reggie, just in time. One of the stewards dropped a bottle of vegetable oil on the floor and caused a nasty accident. Minty nearly got killed, saving Boom from running into the fireplace, and it's really shaken her up. Iris, you'd better get on to Venetia in the morning to find out which of the stewards was so careless, but in the meantime, can you get the housekeeper to see that oil slick is cleared up?"

Now, thought Minty, *let's hear what Judith has to say.*

Judith had lost all her colour. She seemed to be in shock but trying to hide it. Her eyes were wide with distress, while her lips said, "What a shame. Things can so easily get out of hand, can't they?"

"What do you mean by that?" Reggie asked.

"Oh, nothing. It's dreadful to think how nearly there could have been a tragedy." She turned away, fumbled for a seat, and put her hand over her eyes.

So, thought Minty, *Judith didn't arrange this. It wasn't her.*

Chef treated Judith to a glare and Reggie gave her a narrow-eyed look, but the insinuation passed over Iris' head, busy as she was getting the housekeeper on the internal phone to clear up the mess.

Minty tried to take control of the situation. "What do you think, Reggie? Will it be safe to allow visitors in here tomorrow?"

"Should be." Reggie was hovering over Minty and the twins. "You look pretty shaken. Shall I whip you off to hospital?"

Ting gave a little wail and buried herself further in Minty's arms. Tears were sliding down Boom's face. "Trike ran away!" The trike seemed to have come off better than anyone else.

Minty made an effort. "No thanks, Reggie. Just shaken up." Then to Judith, "What brought you here?"

Judith cleared her throat. "I needed to collect some more books for tomorrow and heard the little girl scream." But the library was in another wing of the house.

Serafina arrived. She exchanged looks with Chef, who explained what had happened and then vanished, saying she "must get back to work; come along Molly, we're not needed here any longer."

Serafina told Reggie to take the trikes back upstairs, while Iris helped Minty up with the twins and Judith ... but Judith was backing away, taking herself off. Were those real tears she was shedding?

Minty tried to stand up, and slipped. Her shoe, saturated with oil, was skidding even on the untreated boards. Ting gave a piercing shriek and clung fast. Minty steadied herself. With Serafina on her other side, Minty eased off her shoes and set off for the door in her socks.

Iris stopped her. There were tears in Iris' eyes. For once, she was hesitant. "Minty, I know this isn't the right moment, but can I come up and get those proofs?"

Minty made a big effort to turn her mind away from the parts of her body which were hurting. "No, Iris. Not now. We'll talk about the proofs in the Heads of Department meeting tomorrow morning."

Iris' face was a picture. The accident had shaken her. Probably she'd looked into a possible future and not liked what she'd seen. Iris knew—as Judith probably did not—that if Minty died before Boom was old enough to assume charge, then Patrick would be the children's guardian and in charge of the Hall. And Patrick, for all his easy-going manner, wouldn't be as tolerant of people's frailties and mistakes as Minty.

Minty tried to think clearly. So what about those proofs? How much did Iris want the new brochure to go through unchallenged? Could Iris have spread oil on the floor to distract Minty from pursuing the matter of the fakes? Oh, no. Not Iris!

Would Iris go to Clive and complain that Minty was holding up the proofs just to be awkward? Would Judith feed her poison to Iris and Clive tonight? Perhaps by tomorrow they'd be armed with all sorts of reasons why Minty wasn't in a fit state to make decisions about the Hall.

Too bad. Mummy had been bashed about, but Mummy was also the Lady of the Hall and quite capable of running both the Hall and her family, thanks to Gloria. But at this very moment, Minty had to look after the children first.

And then, perhaps, take a precaution or two? Once Gloria was back and the twins soothed, she could perhaps do something to clear this matter up. She said, in a low voice, "Reggie, are you around later this evening? Can I phone you?"

Reggie nodded. She could trust him. And Chef, and Serafina. But maybe not Iris and certainly not Judith. If Minty had died, Judith would be preparing to step into her shoes, to take over Patrick and the children and the Hall, just as Minty's loathsome stepmother had taken over her father and the Hall when her own mother had died.

Minty wanted Patrick so badly it hurt. She despised herself for it. Was she really just a weak, silly woman that she must cry for a strong man when she'd been hurt? Well, rather a lot of her was hurting at the moment, so maybe it was allowable.

She made it to the lift, murmuring soothing words to the twins … a nice hot bath … a warm milky drink … bed. For them, if not for her. She'd need some painkillers to get her through the next couple of hours.

The twins were weepy, hard to settle. Serafina helped Minty strip the children and get them into the bath, which usually calmed them down beautifully. But not tonight. When Minty tried to get into the shower by herself, they cried.

Gloria arrived back, very distressed to hear what had been happening, but the twins would not be comforted by anyone but their mother. They accepted hot drinks but wouldn't eat their supper.

Minty brought out all the soft toys they had been rejecting for some weeks, and eventually they curled up in their cots in a nest of furry animals. Ting's head was actually upon a soft rag doll, and Boom had a large grey rabbit in his arms. Minty smiled, thinking back to her own childhood when she'd appropriated Patrick's own toy rabbit ... and then she lost her smile. She remembered how, when she'd been sent away to live with her uncle and aunt, they'd deprived her of even the comfort of the rabbit. Minty vowed her own children would never suffer as she had.

She stroked their heads and murmured prayers as their eyelids fell, rose again, and fell to half mast ... and finally dropped.

> Now I lay me down to sleep,
> Guardian angels round me keep
> Watch about me through the night
> Wake me safe with morning bright.

Both she and Gloria held their breaths as the twins' breathing slowed. Serafina hovered in the doorway. As Minty cautiously detached herself and made for the door, Gloria said in a soft voice, "I'll keep the door to my room open for a bit, shall I? You must switch the alarm through to my room, and I'll listen out for them so you can get a good night's sleep."

"Thank you, dear Gloria. I know they're safe with you, but if they wake and cry for me, you must let me know immediately. I won't leave the Hall."

Serafina said, "Come along, Minty. It's your turn to get cleaned up now. I want to hear exactly what happened. I'll get you and Gloria something to eat while you have a shower, and then I'm going to give you a nice massage."

Minty took a long shower and ate as much as she could of the chicken and rice dish which Serafina produced for her. Then she lay on the great four-poster bed while Serafina kneaded away, her fingers finding all the sore spots, careful of Minty's ribs on one side, easing tension and making her sleepy.

Minty checked off her worries in her mind. She must remember to switch the baby alarm to Gloria in the guest room. Gloria was settling in nicely, with her own television and video. Her room was already fitted up with coffee and tea-making equipment and snacks in a refrigerator. Thank God for Gloria ... and thank Patrick for arranging her arrival in the household.

Minty's ears were stretched to hear the first cry from the twins, but it seemed they were sound asleep — for the moment — though she couldn't believe they'd last the night through. They rarely did.

Serafina was checking off her own list of worries. "Early bed for you, Minty. I must go and pack, I suppose. I really don't want to leave you while all this is going on, but ... I've promised."

Minty made an effort to think about something other than her own problems. "Of course you must go, Serafina. I'll be perfectly all right now."

Far from getting into bed, as soon as the older woman had gone, Minty took some painkillers and pulled on some warm clothing. She had work to do. She slipped into the quiet of the chapel for a few minutes to pray.

Dear Lord above, thank You that we're all still alive, that You had Your hand over us. Please watch over the children. Help them to recover quickly from their fright. Be with me as I try to sort things out. I know I don't deserve Your love, that I've neglected to talk to You lately. No excuses. I just let everything take me over. Stupid, stupid!

The chapel was always so quiet and peaceful. Serafina had put some dull gold chrysanthemums in the vase on the table by the altar. They glowed. The windows in the old glass shone black against the night sky. It was a dark night outside.

There was comfort here.

Forgive me for neglecting You. Forgive me for my neglect of Patrick. I wish he were here with me now. Forgive me for forgetting that if I neglect the Hall, it affects so many people. Show me how to make better use of my time. Take care of the children ... and of Patrick, wherever he may be. And if You can sort out Iris ... why can't she see that Neville is worth a dozen of Clive? And Carol ...! Don't let Toby make a fool of himself over Judith again, will You?

She thought of Patrick waiting for her in some European city. He might be eating supper in a good restaurant at this moment, tasting some new dish, relaxed, perhaps reading a book? She winced at the thought of travelling with the two young children, but ... *sigh* ... if that was what it took to make them a family again ... But was it right to leave the Hall at this moment?

She bent her head and rested her hands on her thighs, palms uppermost. *Your will be done. Show me the way.*

She stayed there a while, trying not to think of anything at all.

The peace of the chapel entered into her and she closed her eyes, resting upon it.

Allowing the love that God gave her, to heal her.

Finally she stirred. Time to be moving. Time to see if Reggie was able to help her solve a mystery or two.

Chapter Eleven

Minty's rooms were quiet and dark, save for the muted roar of television from Serafina's quarters.

On the kitchen table was a note from Serafina. "Can't find the keys to the end room. Sorry."

The twins slept. They were restless and both had thrown off their covers, but they did sleep. Minty pulled the covers over them again and made her way through the suite to her old office, where Judith had been working. There was a small pile of books on Judith's desk, but the laptop was absent.

What was she going to do about Judith? Had Judith known there was going to be an attempt to harm the children? Well, yes, because she arrived so promptly on the scene afterwards. But how did that tally with her genuine shock and distress when she saw what had happened?

Minty's question and answer time in the chapel didn't seem to have thrown up any solution to that particular problem, except—now that was an extraordinary thing—she suddenly received an image of a shepherd looking for a lost sheep. It wasn't the usual New Testament shepherd. It was the boy David, before his encounter with Goliath, saying that when a lion or bear came and carried off a sheep, he went after it, slew the wild beast, and rescued the sheep.

Did that mean that Judith was a lost sheep, and that Minty was supposed to fight for her?

Frowning, Minty passed through to the tower and keyed in the numbers to access Patrick's room. She switched on the lights, drew the curtains against the darkness outside, and seated herself—not without a wince—at his desk.

He'd asked her to water the azaleas in the plant trough. She touched the earth beneath the plants, and it seemed damp enough. No need to water tonight. Had he asked her to look after the plants as a ruse to get her into his rooms, hoping she'd then look at the things he'd left out for her on his desk? She wouldn't put it past him.

She didn't bother trying to access his well-hidden safe, because it would only open to his palm-print. He kept all his confidential papers and his up-to-date computer discs in his safe, so whatever was on his desk had been left out for her to read.

There were several files on his desk, yes. Plus the photocopy of Judith's application form. Now Minty had time to look at it more closely, she could see he'd pencilled in some queries. He'd queried "Marital status." Minty shook her head. What was he thinking of? Judith attracted men but never tied herself to them.

Patrick had a devious mind. Perhaps he knew something she didn't? Did he think Judith had a husband somewhere? The suggestion was laughable.

Minty shrugged and tackled the small pile of files to the right of the desk. Ordinary manila files. One for the Parish Council—he'd been there on his last night. He'd scribbled a note over his agenda about the cancellation of the flower decorating. Well, Minty was going to have to deal with that tomorrow, wasn't she? He really hadn't needed to nag her about it.

Well, not nag precisely, but ... remind her.

Or perhaps—*sigh*—he'd been right to do so.

Next was a file which looked at first sight to be about the charity which her father had founded to further the education of disadvantaged children. She'd been elected to the Board after her father died but had never been that much interested, especially when she'd realised that the "old boy" network operated, even there. She'd been pleased when Patrick had been elected as well. She hadn't been to any of their meetings for ages, though Patrick had. She seemed to remember that he'd tried to tell her something about the charity needing to be reorganised, and that they'd asked him to be responsible for seeing it through .... Something like that, anyway.

There was nothing new about people asking Patrick to do something difficult for nothing. He was the right man for the job, obviously.

Wait a minute. Hadn't he tried to tell her about some other problem to do with the charity? Or, come to think of it, hadn't he been talking about a second charity that wanted him to do ... something ... she couldn't remember what, except that Patrick hadn't been any too keen to do it. She had a feeling there was something dicey about the second charity, though what that was all about, she couldn't for the life of her remember.

He'd gone to Brussels on behalf of her father's charity, hadn't he?

Either way, this file might give the name of the hotel where he was staying. She opened it, and her mouth formed a soundless "Oh!" There was just one piece of paper in it, not on the letterhead of her father's Foundation, but on that of a much larger, internationally renowned concern. The writer — she looked at the signature — was a well-known personage with royal connections.

She glanced through the letter and frowned. What was it, precisely, that the writer wanted? He was asking for an urgent meeting with Patrick, but to discuss what? There were lots of flattering phrases, such as "a wily negotiator such as you" and "I know you have the patience of Job."

Minty didn't understand why such an important man felt he had to almost beg Patrick to meet him, and yet the tone of the letter did seem to be doing just that.

Minty sat back in the chair. Could she add two and two and make five? If she added into the equation what Patrick had tried to tell her about the work that was taking him to Brussels ...? Had he hinted that this second charity was in financial difficulty and they wanted him to sort it out, because he'd made a good job of reorganising her father's Foundation?

She'd hardly listened. She ought to have done, of course. She was sorry now that she hadn't. If there had been some financial problems in this second, mightily respected organisation, they'd certainly not want to publish the matter, and they would indeed need someone like Patrick to ride to the rescue. Only, it would cost him dear in time and patience.

Equally surprising was the prayer which the writer had appended at the end of the letter. So the important person was an active Christian, too?

She took a deep breath. Patrick had tried to tell her why he was having to go to Brussels, but she'd not listened. Sitting at his desk, she felt a tide of shame rise into her face. How petty her conduct now seemed! When he returned, she would ask him to tell her all about it.

There was nothing to show which hotel he was staying at, so she opened the next file, which was bulkier and dealt with recent work on some of his properties.

She'd known for years that he made money buying old and derelict properties to renovate and put back onto the affordable housing list. He'd started with a family legacy, but what had been a sideline for him in his student days seemed to have grown into a small empire.

Some time ago, Patrick had asked if she'd like to meet a man he thought of appointing to manage this side of his business, but ... what excuse had she made? One of the twins had been running a temperature, had been teething ... ? She hadn't wanted to hear of other people's problems and had said she couldn't make it. She was sorry about that now, because the appointment had obviously been weighing on Patrick's mind. She could have helped by meeting the man and giving Patrick her impression of him afterwards. Patrick had scrawled, "Pray about this!" over some man's CV. Had he been appointed? Minty had no idea. Again she felt shame.

She riffled through the rest of the file. He had several properties in the course of conversion: an old farmhouse and its outbuildings above the village, the last phase nearly completed ... she knew about that because it was local. A derelict hotel in a nearby town had been bought and was being converted into flats, three cottages were being thrown into two, and so on.

No schedule.

There was no file on the work he was doing as a solicitor. He had two partners and apparently both were now pulling their weight and not giving him any trouble. Or at least, she assumed that if there had been a problem there, he'd have left something out for her to read. Probably.

So where were the hotel details?

The top drawer of his desk was locked. Annoying, but not unexpected.

She knew where he kept the key. Correction, she had known where he kept the key. She felt along the top of a nearby bookcase, took down a couple of Moorcroft vases and ...

Moorcroft vases. What had Carol said about some of the Moorcroft vases on the ground floor? That the signatures were wrong?

Well, these vases of Patrick's had come from ... where? She couldn't remember. Yes, she could. He'd brought them back after a visit to his elderly father, who was now living in retirement on the South Coast. They were family pieces, which had belonged to an aunt, but his father had never liked them. They would be genuine. Patrick wouldn't have kept anything that wasn't.

The larger one was full-bellied, rounded, in glorious purple and soft red on the darkest of blue backgrounds. She'd often seen Patrick caress it with his long fingers. She upended it. It was signed, all right.

So was the second, smaller one. She memorised the look of the signature as the key of the top drawer fell out into her hand.

She unlocked the drawer and found only unused stationery.

No diary, no phone book.

Patrick was playing games with her. She depressed the Play button on the answerphone. No messages. Where the dickens was he?

She hit the top of the desk and then nursed her hand. She'd collected bruises all over, and she was beginning to wonder when she should take some more painkillers. She mustn't take anything too strong, or she wouldn't hear the twins if they woke.

God, be with them. Put Your hand over them ... and over Patrick ... the infuriating man!

There was a knock on the door. Reggie.

Patrick wouldn't like Reggie being taken into his den, so she called out that she was coming, turned off the lights, and went to join him in the tower office.

"Thanks for coming, Reggie. My turn to give you a cuppa?"

"Thanks, but I've just eaten. Are you all right? You look a bit pale."

"Best not to dwell on it while there's so much I ought to be getting on with. Reggie, I need your advice about all sorts of things. The most pressing is that the keys have gone missing to the door from this office into my rooms, and the twins have learned how to operate the lift. Can you suggest a solution?"

"Let me think about that ..."

Half an hour later, they took the lift and descended to the Great Hall. Most of the oil had been mopped up, but some had seeped into the old oak of the floorboards.

"That oil won't do no more harm," said Reggie. "But you look like you're due for bed, Minty. Won't you leave your learning till you're better?"

"I daren't," said Minty. "If I've got to stop the new brochure going to press, I need to know what I'm talking about. Show me the clock that you don't like, first."

It was a French boulle clock, with an elaborately carved goddess on top, drapery floating. Reggie gave her a little lecture on it; most of it passed over her head. Some of the words she could capture and keep in her head; some she couldn't. *Escapement* was a good one. Or was it *escarpment*? No, that was something else.

Reggie shook his head at her. "You aren't taking it in, are you?"

"You say it's not eighteenth century but a Victorian copy, and I believe you."

He rewarded her with a grin. "You've got the root of it in you. The brochure says eighteenth, but it should be mid-nineteenth century with a twentieth-century movement. It's still worth a bit, mind."

She sank to her knees in front of the oak chest, and then wished she hadn't. Ouch! How long would she take to heal? "Carol was twittering on about this chest. It's supposed to be Jacobean, isn't it?" She ran her hands over the carving on the front. "How can she tell that that's wrong?"

"You need to know how the Jacobeans used to carve wood. Look at those high-backed chairs round the table. They're walnut, not oak, but the principle's the same. No, it's not the leather seats and backs you need to look at, but the depth of carving on the legs and at the top here ... and here. Run your hands over them. Feel how deep, how *solid* this carved mask is at the top. That's the real thing. Now go back and run your hands over the carving on the chest."

She did so and cried out, "The carving here's shallow. It's hardly cut into the wood at all!"

"You've got it. This oak chest was probably made in Jacobean times, but it started off plain, without any decoration on it. When some Victorian chippy was asked to prettify the chest, there wasn't enough depth of wood there for him to do anything but pick out an itty-bitty pattern on the surface. So it's an early chest that got mucked around with at a later date. Got it?"

"Yes." She forced herself to her feet. "I'm sorry, Reggie. You're right, and I'm too tired to go on. We'll have to continue another day."

"You'll feel a lot better after a couple of days away."

"I'm not going anywhere at this rate."

Reggie nodded, turned away, hesitated, and came back to her. His face was flushed, and he almost stuttered with embarrassment. "N—now, you look here, Minty. Patrick's a fine man. I dunno as any other man could have married you and moved into this great place and given you kids and not let it go to his head. He's respected by all of us, and looked up to, and ... well, if you're thinking of giving him the push ..."

She could feel her face had gone scarlet. "I'm not. Really, Reggie, I'm not."

He chewed on that but was still ruffled, still red-faced. "Sorry. Shouldn't have said. But I couldn't stand by and see what was happening, and me thinking what your father, God rest him, would have said ..."

"My father," said Minty, also embarrassed, but trying for humour, "didn't want me to marry a small town country solicitor, remember?"

Reggie began to get angry again. "Minty, if that's all you think of Patrick ...!"

"No, it's not." She laid her hand on his arm. "Sorry, Reggie. I was just trying to lighten up. I agree with you that Patrick is something else. I wish he were here now."

"So do I," said Reggie, sighing. "Sorry I shot my mouth off. Forget I spoke?"

She wouldn't forget. Since Patrick had gone, everything seemed conspiring to remind her what a wonderful man he was. She was ashamed that she'd pushed him out, because yes, that was exactly what she had done. Now there was a constraint between her and Reggie, and she didn't know how to remove it.

She said, "You know where he is, don't you? You and Serafina—and maybe Chef—all know where he is."

He was unhappy. "He said he'd left you a schedule and you'd join him when you could."

Infuriating man!

Reggie turned out the lights. "I'll come up with you, shall I? Make sure everything's all right and tight." He checked every room. All seemed quiet. Serafina's television had been turned off, so she was probably asleep.

"Good night, Reggie. Thanks for everything. And I do mean everything—including the scolding."

Now he was embarrassed again. "I didn't mean ..."

"Yes, you did, and I deserved it. Thank you."

He ducked his head. "Well ... good night, Minty. Sleep tight."

"And you."

There! It was all right between them once again.

He waited on the far side of the door in the tower till she'd locked up, and then he took the lift back down to the ground floor for the night.

But where, oh where, was this schedule?

She sat on the side of the great four-poster, wishing that Patrick were indeed there, that she could tuck herself in beside him and whisper that she was sorry that she'd been so crotchety of late ...

... and fell asleep...

Ting's screams woke her. She started to her elbow, wincing as her bruised body protested. She was still fully dressed and she'd left the bedside light on. Half past two in the morning. Gloria had said she'd listen out for the baby alarm, but Minty had forgotten to switch it through to her.

Ting's scream was eerily coming through the baby alarm. It was Ting who was screaming, so it was Boom who was in trouble.

Groggily she limped through the tower and into the twins' room. Ting was standing up in her cot, more or less awake and still screaming. Boom was twitching and whimpering, held fast in a nightmare. Minty stroked his face and called his name, holding her free hand out to Ting. Boom had wet the bed. He hadn't done that for a while.

Boom struggled to come out of his nightmare, and when she was sure that it was releasing him, Minty picked him up and gave him a cuddle. Ting was still hiccupping, but no longer screaming. One-handed, Minty made Ting blow her nose and gently washed her face. Only then could she attend to Boom. She changed Boom's pyjamas and washed him, while he stared around, owl-like, hardly aware what was going on. Ting clung to Minty's leg, sucking her thumb. Boom's cot was saturated. Minty pulled off the bedclothes, but both twins started crying the moment she lost physical contact with them, and, heavy with sleep, she couldn't face finding clean linen for his bed.

There was nothing for it. She popped the grey rabbit into Boom's arms, and with an effort, carried both children through into her own bedroom. She lifted them up onto the bed and lay down between them, one arm around each. Ting sucked her thumb rhythmically. Boom burrowed into the pillow with Rabbit.

If they fell out of this bed, they could hurt themselves badly.

Please, Lord. Please, Lord. Please.

She sighed deeply and joined the twins in sleep.

She woke to find one twin bouncing on her legs. "Cockie cock horse! Wake up, Mummy. Wake up!"

Where was the other one? Still fast asleep, arms and legs spread-eagled, his head resting on the grey rabbit.

Ting was climbing up her, as if scaling a mountain. "Where Daddy gone?"

"We're going to see him today, poppet." She hoped. Half past six, and it was still dark outside. Movement was possible, but not easy. She urged Ting into the bathroom and they showered together. Ting loved that. Ting danced in the shower and slipped and nearly fell. She would have fallen if Minty hadn't got an arm to her quickly. Ouch. Moving quickly hurt.

Back in the bedroom, she found some clothes for both of them. Boom was stirring but not yet awake. No more nightmares, anyway.

It was too early for Serafina to be up. Or Gloria. Ting got into the wardrobe and squealed with delight. "Mummy, watch me! Play hide and seek!"

Boom woke slowly. Minty stroked his cheek, worrying about the nasty bump on his forehead. He smiled up at her. Nice child. Brave.

Once everyone was dressed and more or less in their right mind, they foraged in the kitchen for an early breakfast. There was no toaster, so they had rolls warmed in the oven. Still only half awake, Minty reached for the ground coffee, and then remembered that Serafina had forbidden her to have any. Something stupid about it being bad for her? She shrugged and made do with orange juice and some decaf. She felt better than she'd expected.

Boom was very quiet this morning. Pray God he hadn't got concussion.

"Play bears!" insisted Ting. "Now!"

Minty had a different idea. "We'll start the day with a prayer, and then after breakfast we're going to do some exploring downstairs."

The twins' eyes grew enormous. With exaggerated care, they tip-toed along to the chapel. They liked the chapel and seemed to know without being told that this was not the place to play bears or have a tantrum. The three of them sat quietly on the tapestry kneeler in front of the altar while Minty asked them to join their hands in prayer, thanked God for keeping them safe through the night, for the wonderful people who looked after them, and for the presents Daddy had given them. Finally she asked Him to look after them all in this new day.

She'd been doing a lot of thinking. Patrick had been right when he said she'd been overprotective of the children. They were growing up fast and were no longer babies. Also, Minty had been very struck by Carol's comments on her upbringing; if she'd been brought up at the Hall as she ought to have been, she'd have known what was good furniture and what wasn't. She owed it to the children to help them understand their heritage.

She started by saying they were going to have an adventure that day. Ting sucked her thumb, but Minty didn't chide her. Ting wasn't showing obvious signs of distress about what had happened; she was just sucking her thumb. She'd stop when she felt safe again.

"You know that Daddy spends most of his time looking after other people …"

"That's his work," said Ting, around her thumb. She nestled up to Minty.

Boom sighed. "I want Daddy."

"Soon," promised Minty. "Can you think of anybody else who helps other people?"

"'Fina?" said Ting, after some thought.

"Definitely Serafina. What about Reggie?"

"I like Reggie," said Boom.

"So do I. Who else?"

"Glory?" said Ting. "She looks after us when you're busy."

"Yes, my poppet. She does."

Boom nudged Minty. "You?"

"Yes, me. My job is to look after you, and everyone at the Hall. I think you are old enough to help me, don't you?"

They weren't sure about that.

"Not *all* the time? We can play sometimes?"

Minty laughed and kissed them both. "Of course you can. There's going to be lots of play. To start with, we're going to have an adventure. We're going to go into different rooms at the Hall, places you haven't been allowed to go before, and we're going to find out about things. We'll start this morning after breakfast, right?"

Ting could smell bacon cooking a mile off. She slid away from Minty. "'Fina's cooking breakfast."

"Wait for me!" It was surprising how the children could want more to eat so soon.

Minty saw them safely into the kitchen and without thinking made for the ground coffee, which still wasn't there.

Serafina said, "Decaf for you. I've asked Reggie to have a look at the toaster. It looks to me as if busy fingers have put a teaspoon down it."

Oh. Did that mean one of the children had been experimenting? That it wasn't down to Judith? Or, it could still be ...

Minty took a glass of cold milk and some aspirins and went through to Patrick's room. His schedule must be there somewhere. In the middle of the night, she'd had a thought about that.

She delved through the files until she came to the one dealing with the conversion of three cottages into two. She read off the address and grinned. Clever. He wasn't abroad. He was close at hand, had probably returned to this country immediately after his meetings in Brussels.

Patrick and Minty had spent their honeymoon in the largest of three Mill Cottages on the outskirts of the nearest town. Patrick had used it as a bachelor pad, and still spent the odd night there. The mill stream ran under the bridge and past the greensward of the garden. The ancient building had been filled with the music of its waters, sometimes lulling to a serene, slowly moving stream, and sometimes rushing noisily by.

Patrick had bought the three cottages many years ago, letting two of them out at an affordable rent to local people. The middle one was occupied by the widowed Mrs Mimms, who had relations in the village. And the end one? Had he told her the tenant had moved away? She rather thought he had. Now he was converting three to two? Why?

Had he said anything to her about this recently? He might have done, and she—single-mindedly concentrating on the twins—had probably not listened. So, there was a schedule inside the file. Planning permissions ... windows added at the back ... a corridor along the first-floor rooms, old bathrooms and kitchens to be removed and new ones added. A conservatory was to be thrown out along the back of two of the original buildings.

The schedule gave dates when this and that was to be started, walls rebuilt, conservatory foundations, electrics, central heating, plastering, new kitchen units.

What was happening this week? Ah. Garden furniture was to be delivered. Was that all? Then the new accommodation must be ready to receive them.

Minty didn't try Patrick's mobile, because contacting him on that wouldn't prove to him that she had worked out where he was. He had to know that she'd tracked him down to the right place.

She keyed in the number of the landline telephone at the cottage, and after a heart-stopping few minutes when she wondered if she'd guessed wrongly, he answered the phone.

"It's me," she said. "What time are you expecting us?"

"Oh. You, is it?" He didn't sound very welcoming. And why should he? She had pretty well pushed him out, to use Reggie's phrase. "I hear you've been in the wars."

"I'm surviving, just. Do you want me to crawl?"

"That would be a sight for sore eyes." He still sounded stiff.

"Are your eyes sore?"

"Are you joking?" His voice rose to complain. "The decorators are still in, the new kitchen units have arrived without doors, the garden furniture isn't going to arrive till next week, and it's raining. Oh, and Mrs Mimms said she'd bring some eggs down from the farm for my breakfast, and she hasn't arrived yet."

"What have you done with Mrs Mimms?"

"She wanted to down-size. Not my idea, hers. She's tried retirement up at her daughter's farm and doesn't like it. She wants to live in a granny flat at the end of the cottages and look after you and the children at weekends, to give Serafina a break."

Minty slid down in his chair. A weekend retreat. Really? "How long have you been planning this? Does Serafina know?"

He sounded weary. "Everyone knows, Minty. Except you."

"I know now. So what time are you expecting us?"

"Come when you're ready."

"I have to attend the weekly Heads of Department meeting."

"Good," he said heavily. And rang off.

Chapter Twelve

At half past eight, Minty helped the twins down the curling stairs from the chapel and through the base of the tower into the library.

They looked around with wondering eyes, and it occurred to her that they'd probably never been in this room before. They knew the Great Hall, of course, because they went through that to access the Park. They knew the Long Gallery because they sometimes played there on wet days. But she'd not wanted them let loose in the State Rooms, which were filled with antiques—or not filled with antiques, according to Carol.

Minty felt now that she'd been wrong to keep them out. She ought to have seen to it that they were familiar with every aspect of the Hall from birth. Well, she'd make a start now.

"This is a finding-out game," she said. "I want to know what is your favourite thing in here. It can be a big thing, like the desk, or a tiny thing, like a cushion or a clock."

"Can we touch?" asked Ting.

Minty nodded permission, and the twins wandered around. Finally Ting got under the kneehole of the desk and said, "This is best. Look, Mummy. Hide and seek!"

Boom was climbing the library stairs, holding onto the pole. He got to the top and shook the pole. He held out his arms to Minty. "Mummy! It wobbles!"

Carol had said something about doubting the library steps. Minty decided to investigate its provenance later. She helped Boom down and tested the pole herself. It did wobble. Carol had said something about it being made from two different types of wood, and a close look confirmed that the pole didn't match the steps. She must ask Carol about it.

Later on, she'd have a look in the book on antique furniture which Patrick had so carefully left behind in their bedroom. Clever Patrick. Had he foreseen all this? Probably.

"I like it here," said Ting. "Where do we go now?"

"The Red Room." The Red Room was rather gloomy, as both wallpaper and curtains were dark red. Apart from a few pieces of Victorian furniture, it housed a collection of Moorcroft pottery on shelves above and around the fireplace. Minty lifted the bowls and vases down one by one, pointing out the glorious purple, blue, and red colours to the children. She upended each one. Some were signed. Some weren't. And the signature on all but one of those that was signed didn't look much like the signature on the pieces in Patrick's den.

Ting crooned over the fattest piece of pottery which, Minty was amused to see, bore what looked like an authentic signature. Boom fingered them but didn't seem very interested. Both twins liked the fireplace in the Red Room. Ting tried to get inside it, to look up through the chimney. Boom kept well away from the chimney breast—fireplaces didn't have happy memories for him—but he liked a brocaded sofa and climbed all over it so that he could jump off onto the floor.

"We won't bother with the music room," said Minty, leading the way. The music room was so called because it contained a small pianoforte, but the walls were crowded with gilt-framed pictures, so tightly packed that it was almost impossible to work out what the pattern was on the paper behind them. Was this where a fake picture was to be found? Well, it could wait, because it was more important to see what the twins thought of the last room along.

The twins followed her into the Chinese Room and stared around them.

"What do you like in here?" said Minty, interpreting their expressions but unwilling to ask leading questions. She touched the curtains, which had been protected with a net covering, but which were definitely shredding with age. The fabric was beautiful, muted, authentic. She wondered if it wouldn't be best to leave them as they were, rather than replace them with some modern copy—even supposing such a thing existed.

The chairs, she thought, lacked elegance, though they were supposed to be Hepplewhite. Or was it Chippendale? She wished, fiercely, that she knew more about such things.

"Don't like nothing," said Ting. "It's all silly."

Boom ran his hand along the top of a marquetry side table and recoiled. "It scratched me. Look!" He held up a reddened forefinger.

This was the table to which Carol had objected so violently, and which Minty herself had never liked.

Minty ran her hand along the top and felt the unevenness which Boom had discovered. Marquetry pieces did sometimes come loose and fall out. The piece seemed firmly fixed but was standing proud. Minty had always felt that the table top seemed too brightly coloured for her taste. With Carol's opinion to guide her, she now guessed that a couple of centuries ought to have faded the originally hectic colouring to muted pastel shades. And surely the surface ought to be smooth?

She bent down to look underneath. The underside looked rough, badly finished. Carol had been right. It was a fake. Minty held back a sigh. What was she going to do about it?

"What about the chairs here, twins? Do you like them?"

"They're all silly." Ting had taken to the word *silly* in a big way.

Boom was still favouring the fake Regency table with a glare. "Bad table. I don't like it."

"Can we play now?" asked Ting.

"Yes, of course. Let's go and see if Gloria's up yet, shall we?"

Minty's thoughts shot ahead to the day in front of her. The Heads of Department meeting was due to start soon. Would Toby have remembered to bring Carol's list?

Had Toby taken Judith out last night, instead of ... or with ... Carol?

Gloria appeared, and the twins settled down with her happily enough. Minty tried to sort out what to do next. She took Gloria aside to say, in a low voice, "Gloria, I'm so sorry, but Boom wet his bed. If I've got time, I'll change it before the meeting."

Boom was a little heavy-eyed this morning, but otherwise seemed none the worse for his tumble and a disturbed night's sleep.

Gloria nodded. "I'll deal with it and pack for the twins as well. I've brought my rucksack with me."

"Wait a minute. You're only supposed to be working five days a week."

"Plus this weekend. Patrick asked if I would and I said, of course. So just tell me when you want to be off, and I'll have the twins ready."

"Where we going?" asked Ting.

Minty left Gloria to answer that one, because Serafina was waving her hands around like an agitated hen. Serafina had painted her nails, which she'd never done before, as far as Minty could remember. Now she was trying to dry them.

Minty remembered with a rush of alarm that Serafina was going away today. Minty wished she'd been more generous about it. What could she do to atone?

"That's a pretty colour of nail polish, Serafina. It suits you. Shall I help you pack?"

Serafina was surly. "I'm all ready except ... well, it's not so easy to reach my feet nowadays, and I did want to paint my toenails, too."

Minty couldn't help smiling. She gave Serafina a gentle push towards her bedroom. "Let me do it for you. It would be a pleasure."

Serafina objected, but not very hard. As Minty knelt before Serafina, she said, "Don't get me wrong. I'm really delighted for you that you're going to see your family, and I do hope it all goes well, but I'm scared you'll not come back."

"You'll do all right if you accept the help Patrick's offering you."

Minty unscrewed the bottle of nail polish and began to stroke the colour onto Serafina's toenails. "It's selfish of me, I know, but you understand me and understand Patrick, in a way that no one else does. Gloria's wonderful, but she's young and hasn't got your experience of the world. She's not a close friend, as you are. You've been as good as a mother to me."

"And you as good as a daughter to me."

Minty began to pray. *Dear Lord, I'm in such a mess and ... That's not the right way to pray. I ought to begin by praising God for His wonderful world, and then thanking Him for all the good things He's showered upon me, and only then ask for help. But I'm in such a muddle, Lord. Won't You sort me out?*

She finished one coat and sat back to judge the effect. "If anyone deserves a holiday, Serafina, it's you, and I pray that everything goes smoothly for you."

Serafina snorted. "I dread meeting them again, after so long. Maybe they'll welcome me back, maybe they won't. But go to see them I must."

Minty nodded. Yes, Serafina must go. She applied the second coat and sat back to admire her work. "I must go, too. I said I'd attend the Heads of Department meeting this morning. If I don't see you again before you go, take care, won't you?"

She kissed Serafina, then left her alone to wiggle her ankles around to dry the nail polish.

Minty rushed through into her bedroom to sort out something suitable to wear: a silk shirt with a warm top over it, a long skirt which matched the top. As she was getting dressed, Iris tapped on the door and came in.

Iris had been looking anxious but seemed relieved to see Minty up and about. "Can I have a word? Are you feeling better? That was terrible, yesterday. I thought you'd be killed for sure, or Boom. Judith's going around saying ..." She bit her lip. "She doesn't know you, of course."

"Yes, she does," said Minty, putting her hair up in front of the mirror. "Judith Kent is her real name, but you met her before under the name of Maxine."

Iris sat down with a bump on the window seat. "So that's it. I thought something was familiar about her, but Minty, she's poison! Why did you give her a job, if you knew who she was?"

"Because she said she'd changed. Because she said she'd become a Christian. Because she challenged me to show that I was a Christian by giving her a second chance. I know it wasn't wise, Iris, but I was sorry for her."

"She's saying that you're showing signs of paranoia, that you've invented and arranged attacks on yourself." Iris threw out her hands. "She's got to be stopped!"

"Yes. Will you arrange for her to work in one of the rooms in the north wing, preferably secluded from the chatter in the Estate Office? I'm not a hundred per cent sure what I'm going to do about her yet, but I do know I want her out of my rooms up here."

Iris nodded and got onto her mobile while Minty sought for her pearl earrings, which she hadn't worn for ever. Had Patrick put them in the safe along with her good jewellery? No, here they were, tucked into a tissue at the back of her top drawer, safely hidden away from busy little fingers.

Iris shut off her mobile. "All fixed. Now, Minty, I don't know how to say this, it sounds awful, but if you're coming to the meeting this morning, you won't overrule Clive in front of everyone, will you? I mean, it's a question of the chain of command. If you contradict him in front of everyone, then he loses face. If you want something tackled differently from the way he's suggested, then would you just have a quiet word with him about it afterwards?"

Minty grimaced. "You're right. I mustn't undermine his authority in front of other people, but I do need to talk to him—and you—about Carol."

"I know she thinks there's a problem with some of the furniture in the house, but she's quite wrong, you know. There's a letter come in the post today which makes it even more urgent that we get her to back down. Clive didn't want me to talk to you about it, but I said you really must be told and then you'll help us stop her."

Minty settled the collar of her white silk blouse. It helped to wear business gear when you had a difficult meeting in sight. "Thank you for warning me, Iris."

"You know what Carol's been saying?"

"She told me. Also, the twins don't like anything in the Chinese Room."

Iris tried to laugh. "As if you could rely on children to—"

"They knew," said Minty. "They can detect a fake at fifty paces. They hated Judith Kent the moment she walked in on them. By the way, Iris, Judith is aiming to take what I have: the Hall, Patrick, and the twins."

"Ridiculous!" Iris twisted her hands. "Why, even suppose you'd been killed yesterday ..."

Minty nodded. "Patrick would have run the Hall and been the twins' guardian till Boom was old enough to take over. Judith would have made a play for Patrick and ..."

"Patrick wouldn't be interested. Would he?"

Minty held back a sigh. She no longer knew what Patrick would or would not do. It made her frightened for the future, knowing that she'd pushed him so far away; she no longer knew if she could rely on him or not. He'd been her kingpin, her mainstay and strength for so long ... she couldn't bear the thought of losing him, and yet ... he'd been so distant on the phone. Had she pushed him so far that he wouldn't come back? And how would she bear it if he stopped loving her?

She consulted her watch. "On with the fray. But before we start, what's the problem with Chef?"

Iris opened the door for her. "Getting lazy, been top dog for too long. Clive's dealing with it. Chef says that if you knew about it, you'd back her up, which is nonsense, because it's a straightforward matter of what the wages bill can bear. Oh, and I must warn you that Reggie's immobilised the lift and put an Out of Service notice on the door, so everyone's having to walk up the stairs, which won't improve their tempers."

"I asked him to do so," said Minty. "We can't find the keys to lock the door between our rooms and the office, so I thought that immobilising the lift would be the best way to stop the twins escaping. We'll all have to climb stairs till we can sort something else out."

When Minty had inherited the Hall, she'd decreed that she should meet with the Heads of Department every Friday morning. Sometimes it was a bit of a squeeze to get everyone into the tower office and they'd used the library for their meetings. Today it seemed they were going to use Minty's office, sitting round the big dining room table.

Judith Kent was already seated at the table, talking to Clive. Judith had prettied herself up a bit, wearing a rose pink lipstick and a pink top. Clive's body language said he liked what he was hearing. And seeing. Perhaps Iris was right to be extra wary of Judith Kent?

When Clive saw Minty, he stood up slowly, his smile fading. His eyes darted to Iris, and she must have signalled that Minty was not going to buck his authority in front of everyone. He relaxed.

Toby was hanging around by the window, looking miserable. As Minty came in, he jerked his head towards a couple of files on her desk. So he'd seen Carol the previous evening? With or without Judith?

Minty's mobile phone rang, and she went over to the window to answer it, turning her back on the others. It was Reggie, saying, "I checked with Hodge, Minty, and you guessed right. The man's living in Judith's caravan. I'm annoyed with myself; I ought to have put two and two together. Clive says he doesn't need either of us for the meeting today, but you know where I am if you need me. Oh, and Hodge says don't forget to tell the Ranger that it's hands off that bit of land by the oak tree, right? He says you know all about it, right?"

Minty said, "Thanks, Reggie. I won't forget," and turned back to the others as two more people entered the room: the housekeeper, fanning herself and exclaiming at having to climb the stairs instead of taking the lift, and Venetia Wootton, who would be representing the team of stewards. But no Ranger.

Spotting Minty, Venetia rushed into speech. "My dear, I've questioned every single one of the stewards who were on duty yesterday, and none of them will admit to having spilled anything on the floor in the Great Hall. I really don't know what to think about it. I've always found them truthful, and to be frank, I really don't think any of them was responsible."

"It's a disgrace, what's been done to that floor," said the housekeeper, hovering. "And I've got to get back. There's a new cleaner started, and one of my regulars said she wants to use aerosols on the antiques. The very idea!"

Clive gave her his toothiest smile. "Then I'm sure we can excuse you, for once. All right by you, Minty?"

Minty nodded. "Judith doesn't need to stay, either. Judith, Iris has sorted you out somewhere to work downstairs in the north wing, so you don't have to traipse stuff all the way up here every day."

"I don't mind, really," said Judith, her eyes meeting Minty's, calculating risks. "I'd like to give the meeting a preliminary assessment of what I've found."

Minty smiled but put some steel into it. "I think it's too early for preliminary assessments. I'll be down to see you safely settled later on."

Iris nodded. "Someone in the Estate Manager's office is sorting you out a room. Ask them for anything you need."

There was nothing for it. Judith retired, trying to pretend she didn't care. The housekeeper went with her, and in came Chef, bearing a clipboard and looking hard at Minty as she seated herself at the table.

Minty was annoyed with herself. She'd intended to see Chef before the meeting, and it had slipped her mind. Iris had said Chef was getting too big for her boots. Minty wasn't sure she believed that. She gave Chef a big smile.

Chef relaxed enough to smile back. "You all right now, Minty? Nasty fall. And that little rascal and his trike? I didn't know you were coming today, but seeing as you're here, you may as well listen to what I've got to say."

In came Tim, the Estate Manager, gangling, stammering, young but not inefficient in his own way. He apologised all round for being late—the lift was out of order, it seemed—said he'd arranged for Judith Kent to have a room next to the one which Neville used, and—only slightly out of breath—he took the chair closest the door.

This left a couple of chairs vacant. Where was the Ranger who looked after the Park, and why had Clive told Reggie and Hodge not to attend? Did it matter? Was it worthwhile making a fuss about it? In view of the problems they might have to deal with that morning, perhaps the fewer people involved, the better.

Clive, at his smoothest, assumed the chair even as Minty picked up the files Toby had left for her to see. Minty didn't interfere as he opened the meeting by welcoming everyone and saying they'd a lot to get through, so he hoped they wouldn't mind if he got started.

Minty thought that whoever had described Clive as a Hooray Henry with brains had known what they were talking about. Clive whipped through a report on the accounts, which seemed to be healthy ... but why hadn't Clive asked Neville to be present? Because Clive was expecting ructions?

Iris was asked to report on future events; Toby was asked to report on party bookings; the Hall was becoming increasingly popular as a venue. Clive thanked Iris and Toby for their input and moved smoothly on.

The housekeeper had told him that the curtains in the Chinese Room needed replacing, and she'd got a quote from some people who specialised in reproducing old brocades, which elicited a low whistle from Minty. The repairs to the slate roof over the restaurant block were proceeding to plan, but next year the whole roof ought to be replaced ... another hefty outgoing ... but only to be expected in a house this ancient.

Minty's mind drifted. Clive knew his job. In many ways he was the right man in the right place. Only when it came to ethical matters, it was a different matter.

Tim, the Estate Manager, gave his report, stammering less than he used to. The South Farm was behind with its rent; he was going to visit to see what that was all about. Some of the Home Farm outbuildings had become redundant since they'd built new barns to house their up-to-date machinery. An architect had been asked to advise on converting the old stabling and barn into holiday lets. One of the cottages in the village had become vacant and would be advertised to rent in the usual way.

"Good," said Clive. "Next, have you got the Ranger's report?"

Tim cleared his throat. "S–speaking on behalf of the Ranger, he's embarking on a programme of lopping some trees and replanting where disease has forced the removal of others. There's been an attempt already to steal some of the Christmas trees from our plantation, but he's based a security guard in a caravan nearby to keep watch round the clock, and that should do the trick.

"The great oak that came down in the storm will have to be sawn up and removed, and the Ranger proposes that that piece of land be drained and ploughed over. It's no use to man or beast as it is, and the Home Farm could probably do something with it."

Minty stirred in her seat. "I'd better speak to the Ranger about that."

"Really? Oh. All right, I'll tell him." Tim returned to his notes. "Hodge has taken on a part-timer in the garden to help with the Christmas trade ..."

Yes, indeed! thought Minty. Reggie had just confirmed her guess about this stray male, and it explained a lot.

Then it was Venetia's turn. As Minty might have guessed, Venetia was not pleased that the Christmas decorating event had been cancelled. She was restrained about it but wanted her protest put in the minutes. "The cancellation has upset many of the local community, and if the village is upset, I can't get any more stewards to man the rooms."

Clive was soothing. "We have so many corporate hospitality dates booked this winter that I had to consider giving an integrated, professional look to the rooms. Some of the arrangements in previous years—" he managed a gently deprecating laugh— "were charming, but as each room was decorated in a different fashion, the overall effect didn't convey quite the right message."

Minty lifted her hand. "Venetia, Clive. You're both right, of course. We must maintain the highest standards. Clive, I always thought the flower-arranging clubs were very professional. Have we had any complaints? No. I take your point about having a theme running through the rooms. On the other hand, flower festivals are extremely popular. Venetia, what do you think about staging one in the summer—in June, say? We could run it for a long weekend when we're due to host the parish garden party. It would be a great tourist attraction, wouldn't it?"

Toby came to life and scrabbled in his enormous diary. "Yes, that weekend would be good for it. We've got a couple of party bookings for the evenings already, but they're only for the Great Hall and the numbers are not enormous. The flower arrangements won't get in people's way, while being an added attraction."

"A splendid idea," said Clive, smiling toothily to disguise his annoyance that Minty had spoken up not once, but twice in the meeting. "Of course. June. Delightful people, delightful arrangements." Clive turned his beam on Venetia. "By all means, tell the dear people locally that we're planning something special for them in June next year. So, if there's nothing else, we won't keep you."

It was a dismissal. Venetia narrowed her eyes at him and treated Minty to a wide-eyed stare. She said, "I'll catch up with you later then, Minty," and removed herself. She was still unhappy about the way things had been done, but she'd go along with it.

Chef glanced at her watch and clattered her clipboard onto the table. "I think this is where I come in. Young Toby's sent me down the list of functions booked for December, and I'm telling you here and now, that what he wants is impossible. I cannot and will not work seven days a week. Yes, I know the restaurant's only supposed to be open from Wednesday through to Sunday, but just lately there've been so many evening functions added to the rota that I've been working six days a week. And from now on and throughout the whole of December, I won't get a day off at all."

Clive's eyelids flickered. "No one expects you to work unreasonable hours, Chef. Surely you understand that this is the only time of the year when we make money."

"Not at the expense of my health."

Minty was alarmed. "Florence, dear. You are all right, aren't you?"

"Yes, yes. But I am not going to risk going down with something by working such long hours, seven days a week."

Clive steepled his fingers. "Surely you can delegate ..."

"I need a sous chef. Now."

Minty nodded. Chef wasn't being lazy or unreasonable, and her workload was clearly over the top.

Clive pinched in his lips. "Out of the question. The cost ..."

Chef pinched in her lips. "Then there's nothing for it but for me to give in my notice."

Minty remembered her promise to Iris not to overrule Clive in front of others, and realised that Iris and Clive had manoeuvred her into a corner. She had promised not to go against Clive in public. But, setting apart the fact that Florence Thornby was a good friend of Minty's, the Hall simply couldn't afford to lose such an efficient chef. What to do? She must not upset Clive, but ...

She said, "Florence, dear. May I come to see you about this later on today? Clive, I do see your point, but perhaps there's some way round it. Will you leave it with me?"

Clive reddened but gave her a stiff nod.

Chef looked hard at Minty, looked back at Clive, and nodded. "All right. I'll withdraw my notice for the time being and leave you to think it over." She bustled out.

"We'll excuse you, too, if you like," said Clive to young Tim. He blushed and thanked them — for what? — and left.

Which left Toby eyeing his fingernails, Iris eyeing her notebook, and Clive.

"I think that's all," said Clive, smiling widely at Minty. "It's nice you could spare the time to drop in on us. As you can see, everything's just fine."

"Except," said Minty, "for Chef ..."

"Oh, you'll talk her round, I dare say."

"... and," said Minty, "the fakes."

Chapter Thirteen

Clive tried to stare Minty down. "My dear Mrs Sands, do you think for one moment that I'd be recommending a reprint of the brochure if I imagined there were fakes at Eden Hall?"

Minty braced herself. "I trust Carol's judgement."

"Of course." He continued to smile. "Carol is your oldest friend. But—forgive me—a young lady with a temper, and perhaps not quite as sound a knowledge of antiques as she pretends? I must admit that her report threw me. At first I wondered, could she possibly be right? Could we be misleading our public?

"It was a nightmare. I could see the headlines in the newspapers already ... 'Tourists duped!' Writs would fly. We'd be up in court, charged with goodness knows what! Frankly, I was terrified! Then I calmed down and looked at the facts. Here was a young woman, hardly more than a girl, declaring that everything in the Hall was faked ..."

"Not everything," said Minty, but he overrode her.

"... that we'd been buying and displaying furniture which had been made yesterday in some back street forger's den. That we'd been deceiving the public for years. No, no. Impossible. This was the first big inventory she'd handled. Perhaps she'd been overanxious to impress you with her expertise? She must have felt she must find something—anything—to justify your faith in her ability. And so she ... ah ... was a little overenthusiastic, shall we say?"

Minty put her elbows on the table and her chin in her hands. What the man said was reasonable. But ...

He gave a slight smile, shook his head, deprecatingly. "So naturally, I did what any sensible person would do. I arranged for a second opinion. I went to a big, well-known firm in London and had them come down to do an inventory. Yes—believe me, I was quite pleased when they found three or four repro pieces. It proved, you see, that your Carol was not completely off the mark. Again, anyone collecting furniture as your stepmother did for so many years may well have made one or two bad bargains. I can tell you, I was extremely relieved to get their report."

Minty glanced at Iris, digging holes in her notebook with her pen, and Toby, who was staring out of the window, arms folded and face bland.

"So there we are," said Clive, happy at having proved his case. "A storm in a teacup. Mind you, Carol can't expect to be paid for bringing me a scare-mongering report. I've no doubt she's been complaining about that to you, but ..."

Minty leaned back in her chair. Ouch. Her ribs hurt. "It won't do, Clive. I don't know why your London firm gave us such a glowing report, but I do know that we can't afford to risk anyone querying what's on show at the Hall. I myself am not happy about one or two items. I don't know all that much about furniture ..."

"There you are, then."

"... but I do know that the buck stops with me, and not with you. We can't risk reprinting that brochure until we've got this sorted out."

Clive decided to exercise immense patience. "If you could, perhaps, point out one or two items which have distressed you?"

"The chest in the Great Hall. The clock which sits on it. All the furniture in the Chinese Room, most of the Moorcroft pottery in the Red Room."

"And ...?" He was humouring her.

"I have to study the files, take advice. I don't know what else ... yet. But I will. Until then, we don't reprint the brochure."

Iris was doodling in circles. Toby sighed sharply and shifted his feet.

Clive became even more patient. "Very well, my dear Mrs Sands. You've condemned some perfectly good antiques to the storeroom. What would you suggest we put in their place? Are you suggesting we empty the Chinese Room completely of its furniture? What would you like done with it? Put on a bonfire? How should I explain that to the insurance people? And what literature, above all, do we give to visitors as they come through the door?"

"I don't know yet." Minty pushed back her chair. "But this I do know. Two wrongs don't make a right. We won't be printing any more brochures till I've decided what to do about the fakes ... and yes, before you speak, I know that some are not deliberate fakes, but items that have been altered over the years. Either way, we can't go on claiming that items are valuable originals when they're not. I'll give the matter some thought over the weekend, and let you have my decision on Monday."

Clive took a deep breath. "If you'll take my advice ..."

"I regret," said Minty, smiling sweetly, "having to go against your advice this time. I do think you do an excellent job, Clive. I appreciate I've had to burden you with far more than you anticipated when you came here, but there are some things I have to decide for myself. I will not allow a brochure which deceives the visiting public. I know that some of what we're showing is not right. I trust you to work with me to discover a solution to the problem that this gives us. Understood?" She put some steel into her voice.

Iris flashed a glance at Minty and gave her a nod. Iris certainly understood, even if Clive was still frowning.

Toby sent a grin in the direction of the window, which was approval enough.

"Now," said Minty, "I have to take the twins visiting."

"Before you go," said Clive, "I'd like a word in private. Iris, Toby; give us a minute, will you?"

Iris and Toby removed themselves to the tower office. Minty sat up straighter in her chair. She didn't think she was going to like whatever Clive had to say.

He swivelled in his chair to face her directly. "We ought to get one or two things straightened out. So long as I am the Administrator here, I run the place. I don't think you fully understand the position, because you've been out of touch for so long. We're under threat. The position is serious. I imagine Carol's been leaking her report to the press, because …"

"She wouldn't. When you brought in a London firm to check on her work, yes, that would have started tongues wagging, and I believe one of the stewards has been making noises?"

"Silly old fool. Thought he knew better than the experts. I had to get rid of him."

"Which caused more talk."

"If it were just rumours, they'd die down eventually. This morning I received a letter from a national magazine wanting to do a feature on Eden Hall. They are particularly interested in the Chinese Room."

Minty digested that in silence. "We'll have to put them off."

"How can we? The feature would set the seal of approval on us for all the tourist agencies that visit the Cotswolds. If we put them off with some lame excuse, they'll smell a rat and come sniffing round …"

"So you do think there's something amiss."

He cleared his throat. "No. Of course not. We have to hold the line, somehow make them see that …"

"Are you suggesting that we bribe them to accept the fakes as antique? No."

His colour rose. "I didn't mean that. You're missing the point. We've been trumpeting the fact that Eden Hall is full of antiques for years, ever since your stepmother opened the place to the public.

Thousands of brochures have gone out—are still kept in people's homes—all extolling the beauties of this place. How will it look if ... well ... if someone tries to undermine that?"

"You mean, what will you do when people find out? Because people will find out, won't they? There's some talk already—though not from Carol, believe me! Also, the magazine won't be fooled as easily as your London firm. How did you square them, by the way?"

"This is outrageous!"

"Shall I ask Neville to tell me how much you paid them to deliver a 'sweetened' verdict?"

"I resent that suggestion, and I resent the suggestion that you'd have Neville check my accounts. The London firm was paid not a penny more nor less than was usual."

Yet he'd got at them somehow. Minty was sure of it. She said, "Very well, we have a conflict of opinion here. Carol says the Chinese Room is full of fakes. Your Londoners say it isn't. At least, I assume that's what they say, but I want a look at their report first ..."

"Here it is. See, there's just one item in the Chinese Room they weren't too happy about. Everything else is kosher." He thrust a file at her. She ran her finger down the list of items in the Chinese Room. Yes, they'd cleared everything except the marquetry table, which Boom hadn't liked. Nor Minty. Carol had been pretty vitriolic about it, too. So far, so good.

"As both reports condemn that table, why hasn't it been removed from view?"

"Because it's in the photograph of the Chinese Room in the brochure."

"Well," she said, "suppose we ask the magazine to decide?"

He was horrified. "You can't do that! It would be common knowledge overnight ... the papers would have a field day ... we'd be ruined!"

"Only if there's something wrong," said Minty, silkily. "Which you've just assured me there isn't."

He drew himself up. "You are questioning my judgement again? This is the outside of enough. I really must ask you to hold back ..."

"We can't. We might have been able to sit on this time bomb if it hadn't been for the magazine wanting access, but now we've got to deal with it, and quickly. I don't know how, yet. I'll work on it this weekend."

His eyes narrowed. "They tell me you've been overdoing things. Perhaps the time has come for you to consider withdrawing altogether from interference in the way the Hall is run. You have an heir and a spare ..."

Those words again? Had he been talking to Judith?

"... and everyone's observed how absent-minded you've become of late. And imaginative. Some people are openly talking about paranoia. You're seeing threats to yourself everywhere. First there was that absurd claim of yours that you'd been attacked in the courtyard. When nobody believed you on that, you tampered with the toaster, so that you could claim someone was trying to electrocute you, and then you spread oil on the floor of the Great Hall to cause an accident. Oh, I'm sure you didn't mean it to have such consequences, which could easily have cost you the life of your child, but you must see that it raises questions about your competence to run the Hall. May I suggest a visit to a specialist?"

So he'd been listening to Judith, had he? "Judith Kent has her own axe to grind. Did she tell you that? No? Well, you'd do better to stick to your job and help me find a way out of this impasse, than spending time worrying about whether I'm sane or not. And I assure you that I am. So, unless you have something else to say ... No? Then we'll call it a day, shall we? I'm taking the children away to stay elsewhere for the weekend, but I'll be back here this afternoon, and we can talk again then."

She saw him take in her schedule and wondered if he'd relay it to Judith.

"One other thing," he said. "Reggie tells me the lift is out of order, but he hasn't asked me to get on to the people who service it. Did you order it put out of commission?"

"Yes." She smiled sweetly at him. "It's to prevent the children falling down the shaft. They've learned how to operate it, you see. So until we can work out how to stop them, the lift's out of order."

"Or," he said, slowly, "were you afraid of falling down it yourself?"

She laughed in his face. "Sorry, Clive. That hadn't occurred to me. Thank you for pointing it out. After all, if anything did happen to me, you'd probably lose your job because Patrick would take over, and he has far less patience than me when it comes to dealing with sinners."

"Are you calling me a sinner?"

She gave him an old-fashioned look. "Are you ever going to make an honest woman of Iris? Because if not, you should let her go. And remember this, if I ever find you've been involved in anything underhand, you're out."

He grew heated. "You and Neville seem to think you can run a business today with whiter-than-white Christian principles ..."

"Yes. We do. And don't forget it. I must go. I'll see you later." She took the files Toby had left her and swept off to put them in a safe place, to be looked at later.

Reggie was collecting the twins' luggage to take down to Minty's car. The twins were excited. They each held a large black plastic sack into which they'd been allowed to stow their favourite toys. They were talking a blue streak, except when it came to mention of their trikes.

"The tricycles are nowhere to be seen, Minty," said Gloria. "I've looked everywhere, and the twins won't say what they've done with them."

Had the twins hidden them because of the scare they'd had the day before? Yet Patrick would want the trikes — his latest gift to them — to arrive with them. Minty went swiftly through the rooms.

Serafina was putting her suitcase on the kitchen table. "Reggie's taking me to the station as soon as he's got you off."

Minty kissed her, clung to her, and wished her well. "I'll miss you terribly. I hope your family are horrid to you … no, I don't mean that. Just don't forget us, will you?"

Her bedroom … she hadn't packed for herself yet, but that didn't matter. She wasn't moving over there yet … was she? No, she had to come back to face Judith that afternoon. And Chef. And Clive? And think about the fakes. She wasn't avoiding Patrick. Of course not.

The chapel. Minty hesitated at the door. Surely the twins wouldn't have gone in there by themselves, would they? True, the door was ajar and the handle low down and within their reach. She went in and set her back against the door, not knowing whether to laugh or cry. The twins had left their trikes on the tapestried kneeler, nudging at the altar.

As gifts?

An offering to God to ask Him to keep them safe?

Perhaps they didn't know why themselves. They often acted in concert, out of some deep instinct, and not from reason. It would be Boom who'd devised this, not Ting.

Minty lifted her eyes to the cross on the altar. *Thank You for looking after them, for keeping them safe. Be with them … be with all of us … please?*

She picked up the trikes and rejoined the others. It was Babel — the twins shouting, Gloria laughing, Reggie saying, "Now, now!" But smiling, too. Heavily laden, they toiled their way down the stairs, across the Great Hall, and out into the open air where her car awaited them. The twins were strapped in. Gloria sat up front. Kisses all round. Drive safely.

The twins were silent on the drive, their eyes everywhere. Boom clutched his grey rabbit. Ting sucked her thumb. Gloria chattered about her fiancé, pleased to be going to the cottage because he lived not far off and it would be easier to see him in the evenings.

Mill Cottages looked much as they had always done. They were so ancient, they seemed planted in the ground. As the car drew up outside the first one, Patrick opened the door. The twins erupted into screams of excitement, tugging at their seat-belts. Patrick opened the car door, released them, caught them up in his arms, and disappeared into the cottage before Minty could greet him.

She took some of the luggage and followed him into the low-ceilinged living room with its thick walls, small and unexpected windows, and slightly uneven floor. The room had been enlarged since she'd seen it last. Ah, she could see now that he'd taken down the wall between the living room and the old kitchen quarters, to make one large, comfortable room. There was a huge new settee and chairs grouped round the ancient brick fireplace, but the old table by the side window held his usual flurry of papers and laptop. There was a smell of fresh paint in the air, but the decorators had vanished.

She went through into a new large, light conservatory at the back of the house. This had been fitted out with bamboo furniture, a brightly coloured climbing frame, and a huge old wooden doll's house. The outlook was superb, overlooking the greensward leading down to the mill stream—carefully fenced off—and beyond that to a field in which cows grazed. Patrick was seated in a huge padded chair with the children on his knees.

Boom had his head pressed to his father's heart, with his eyes closed. He still held his rabbit.

Ting had her fingers in her father's waistcoat pocket but hadn't withdrawn the watch. Both children were hugging him as if they could never let go. Or perhaps it was he who was hugging them.

Did I really think I could separate them? They love him so much, it hurts. And he loves them. I can't separate them.

Oh, why did I think that? I don't want to separate them from their father, do I?

He kissed the tops of the twins' heads and looked up at Minty. "You look comparatively unscathed. Good journey?"

He was keeping her at a distance. Well, perhaps she deserved it.

At last the twins stirred. Patrick looked from one to the other. "Well, Ralph?" He used the original pronunciation, which was "Rafe." "Well, Petronella?" These were the names they'd been christened with, but hadn't been used since they'd decided to be Ting and Boom.

Ralph said, "My trike went woosh!"

Petronella held up her finger. "Toaster bit me."

"We went in Mummy's bed!"

Patrick said, "So I heard." Hard grey eyes flicked at Minty and returned to the children.

Minty felt the blood leave her head and sat down with a bump on a nearby chair.

Was he going to ask for a divorce? Had he taken her rejection of him at face value, and created this comfortable second home for himself, in which he could have the children at weekends? He'd never particularly wanted to live in a stately home. He'd never cared for the obvious signs of wealth. All he'd wanted was her, and half a dozen children.

Ouch. They'd lost their first child, but she'd given him the twins, hadn't she? Weren't they sufficient?

Anyway, he didn't believe in divorce. Neither did she.

Yet she'd pushed and pushed and pushed him away from her till he might have thought that was what she wanted.

The children were still talking, telling their father what they'd been doing. Gloria was bringing the luggage in, including the children's trikes. Patrick's eyes checked over the pile, and he looked at Minty. "Not staying, then?"

She felt her colour rise. "No. I mean, yes. That is, I have to get back this afternoon to see people, but after that ... if it's all right with you?"

"Do you need to ask my permission?" Oh, but he was cool.

"Yes, I rather think I do. I need ... I need your advice."

His eyebrows peaked. She thought he'd probably make her beg for it. He would have had every right to make her humble herself, but being Patrick, he just nodded.

"Come on now, twins. Let's explore, shall we? Let's see who can find the stairs first."

The twins scrambled off his knee, Ralph dropping his rabbit and Petronella forgetting to put her thumb back into her mouth. Shouting, "Me first!" they disappeared through another door into what turned out to be a brand-new kitchen. Serafina would love this new kitchen—if she ever returned to them.

Patrick hefted Gloria's rucksack and the twins' black bags. "There's a rumpus room through the kitchen, with access to the living room. We kept the old stairs, which are a trifle narrow, but original. Gloria, your room's at the top of the stairs at the front of the house, with a shower en suite. The twins are over the kitchen. There's a new en suite next to our old bedroom, Minty, and a corridor down the middle leads to another small guest bedroom and the door into Mrs Mimms' cottage."

Shrieks from the twins announced they'd found the stairs. They went up them slowly, because they weren't accustomed to such steep, twisty stairs. Gloria followed them, laughing.

Minty said, "Patrick, I'm sorry."

"For what?"

He was still keeping her at a distance.

She followed him up the stairs, noting the immense improvement he'd made to what had been three tiny, inconvenient old cottages.

Gloria's room was fit for any guest, the twins' was large and airy, but there weren't any cots in it. Only two low beds.

Ralph and Petronella considered the beds, looking doubtful. Petronella had her thumb in her mouth again.

"Of course you can have your baby cots put in here if you wish," said Patrick. "But you're growing up so fast, I thought you might have more room in a bed, to turn somersaults and jump up and down. All that stuff that's tricky in your baby cots."

"Not a baby," said Ralph.

"I'm a big girl now," said Petronella, removing her thumb from her mouth.

Ralph ran and jumped onto the bed, crowing with laughter. Petronella followed.

Clever Patrick. Come to think of it, he's been manipulating me, as well. He tried to get through to me in the normal way, and when I resisted, he altered everything around me, so that I'd start looking at things differently. Serafina, gone at his urging. Gloria, brought in. Then he removed himself, so that I'd feel the cold wind of criticism blowing on me, the winds that he's been protecting me from.

I suppose it helped that Judith Kent was, at the same time, trying to make out I'm going round the twist. He knows what she's been up to. He knows about the oil slick and the toaster . . . though the toaster might have been down to the twins . . . oh, I'm so confused. One thing is clear; my friends have been keeping in touch with him, haven't they? Serafina and Reggie and probably Chef as well.

She looked at her watch. She must get back to see Chef.

Patrick threw open a door into a new, airy bathroom. He'd even remembered to include two low stools for the twins to climb up on when they wished to use the basin. "Mrs Mimms is giving us lunch in the kitchen in five minutes, so you can wash your hands in your own bathroom now."

"Me first!" shouted Ralph.

Petronella trailed her hand across her father's, as she followed her brother into the bathroom.

How was it they obeyed his every suggestion, whereas I'd have had to fight to get them to wash their hands before eating?

Why, now that I'm trying to get through to him, is he holding me at arm's length? To teach me a lesson? Well, I've learned it, Patrick.

To punish me? No, that's not his style.

Why, then?

She touched his elbow and he moved away from her, as if he hadn't noticed her action. She flushed, and then remembered that she'd given him the same treatment time and again, of recent months. Now she knew what it felt like. Horrible. She wished she had time to deal with it now, but she didn't.

She looked at her watch. "I have to get back. Can you spare a moment, Patrick?"

"Lunchtime. Eat first. Talk later," he said, without looking at her.

Chapter Fourteen

Mrs Mimms said how much it perked her up to have young children around the place again. Her hair was as curly and her tongue as long as ever. Though she wasn't perhaps as good a cook as Serafina, she won the children's hearts immediately with a promise to take them up to her daughter's farm that very afternoon to see the cows being milked.

Minty tried to eat what was put in front of her. Patrick smilingly helped Gloria mop up the orange juice which Petronella spilled in her haste to eat as fast as her brother, and there was only one short business telephone conversation for Patrick to interrupt the meal. As fast as the twins finished their plateful, Gloria helped Mrs Mimms put everything into the dishwasher, and the two women took the children away.

Peace and quiet. Minty looked at her watch. She had to get back to the Hall, but before that, she had to make things up with Patrick.

He'd gone back to the sitting room and was lighting the fire. The sun had come out in weakly fashion, but it was a chilly day. He sat — not on that inviting big settee — but on a chair apart. He didn't look at her but patted his pockets, looking for ... his cigarettes? No, surely not. He'd given up smoking ages ago, even in times of stress.

He took his hands out of his pockets and laid them on his knees, crossed his legs, and looked across at her. "Now, how can I help you?"

He might have been a bank manager interviewing a poor prospect for a loan.

She thought of several things to say but could only come up with, "I'm sorry."

He inclined his head. Apology accepted. But his manner didn't thaw.

She said, "I don't know why I got like that. It was just ... I couldn't cope."

"Will you come up to bed with me now?"

She stared at him, surprised and if truth be told, a little taken aback. Then she steeled herself. "What, now? Well ... yes, if that's what you want."

"I can see it's not what you want."

"Of course I ... it's just that ... how long do you think the twins will be?"

It was the wrong answer. He turned his head to look into the fire. "If you're in trouble, I'll help you. That goes without saying. What is it you want?"

"I want you back at the Hall."

"Really? When you arrived without any luggage, I thought you'd come to ask for a divorce."

She flushed. "No way. That's the last thing I want."

"You don't act like it. Before you arrived, I imagined I'd fall on my knees at your feet if you asked me to come back, but it seems I can't. I suppose, if the truth were known, that I'm afraid."

"You? Never!"

"Oh, yes. Consider the facts. Golden-haired moppet, daughter of the lord of the manor, befriends lonely village boy who becomes her faithful slave. When she's sent away, he learns what it is to be lonely again. He waits twenty years for her to grow up and when she does and insists on marrying him, she takes him off to the Hall to live. All right—" he raised a hand to silence her objection—"I admit he wanted it as much as she did, even though he was afraid that one day she'd get tired of him. After they married, he forgot what it was like to be lonely. They lost their first child, but soon enough they have twins. It seems that that's all she wanted of him. A couple of babies. He becomes, so to speak, redundant."

"It's not like that." Yet she could feel her whole body hot with embarrassment.

"From where I'm sitting, it looks exactly like that. I've been trying to accustom myself to the idea of being lonely again. It was hard, but I've more or less managed it. Now you come waltzing in to say you want me back at the Hall and in your bed. I find that I don't believe you."

She stood up. "What do I have to do to make you believe me?"

"To make me trust you again? I don't know." He patted his pockets again, and this time he did find an unopened packet of cigarettes. He looked at it, turned it round and round, then threw it at the wastepaper basket. "Look how strong-willed I've become. I can even throw away my crutches." He was mocking himself.

"Please," she said. She could feel tears come into her eyes. Perhaps they'd move him.

"Pretty please," he echoed. "It's not that simple, Araminta. I don't think you know what you want. As for me, I don't want to be hurt again. So let's give it some time, shall we?"

Time? She brushed tears from her eyes and looked at her watch. "I don't have time. I have to get back. There's all sorts of problems. Chef..."

"You don't need me to tell you what to do there."

"If I give her what she wants—and I think she's being very reasonable—then Clive will object that I'm undermining his authority."

"So? Who pays his salary?"

"Yes, I know, but ... then there's the problem of the furniture. You know about that, don't you? Carol's report condemns forty-seven pieces either as fakes or as pieces which have been substantially remodelled. Yet Clive's managed to get a respectable London firm to give the thumbs-up to practically everything. How did he get them to do that?"

"I expect Carol worked that out in five minutes. I certainly did."

"Won't you tell me?"

"No. Try the Internet. You've got to work these things out for yourself, Araminta."

She took a deep breath. "All right. What do I do about the magazine that wants to come to do an article on the Chinese Room?"

He didn't know about that. He steepled his fingers, put them to his chin. "I wonder who put them up to it? Well, you don't need me to tell you what's right and what's wrong."

"You and your Puritan conscience." She said it lightly, half amused and half annoyed.

"Precisely. What would Jesus do, etcetera."

"And Judith Kent?"

"Ah. She's made a couple of attempts on your life, so why haven't you thrown her out? Aren't you afraid, now she's spreading rumours about your sanity?"

Yes, she was afraid, but didn't want to admit it. "I think—I'm almost sure—that she's deeply shocked by what's been happening, but for some reason is acting a part. I suspect she's covering up for someone. I have to get to the bottom of that before I decide whether or not to throw her out." She held out her hand. "Come back with me?"

He uncrossed and recrossed his legs, looking away from her. He shook his head. "You can leave the twins with me this weekend. I'll keep them safe for you."

"I can see that it's sensible for them to be away from the Hall for a while, yes. But I'd really like you to come back with me."

He grimaced slightly. "Perhaps one day you'll say that as if you mean it."

"I do mean it."

His eyes were hard, looking at her and through her. He knew her better than anyone else in the world. Almost as well as God knew her. She tried not to flinch but knew he'd seen that she wasn't being entirely honest with him. It was equally clear to her that he was not going to like what she'd been hiding.

She quailed. "I'm afraid, too. I think ... I'm not sure ..." Her voice died on her.

He got to his feet. "Let me know when you are sure."

She felt like a small child, caught out in a lie. "May I come back here tonight?"

"Do you have to ask? What's mine is yours." But he didn't smile. "Now, did you have a coat when you came in?"

He saw her to her car and waited in the doorway till she drove off. She stopped once she'd got round the corner, to blow her nose. It was not sensible to drive when you couldn't see straight.

⁂

The fallen leaves on the driveway made a swishing sound as she drove back to the Hall. It had been raining again. Not much, but enough to create a light mist over the Park, and to make the Hall come alive with lights on in all the rooms on show to the public.

She garaged the car in the inner courtyard and went straight to the restaurant. Chef's helpers were clearing tables and taking away the few unsold sandwiches and plates of home-cooked ham and salad left over from lunch. In their place cream teas were being put out, with home-made jam sponges, treacle tarts, and fruit cake. All traditional fare produced by Chef.

The place was full of tourists, enjoying themselves and appreciating the food. Chef's latest purchase — a huge Gaggia — was producing assorted coffees and scenting the air.

Minty passed through into the kitchens, where Chef was overseeing one of her helpers in the production of individual steak and kidney pies while another was creating tiny pastries, presumably for one of the functions for which the Hall was becoming famous.

When she saw Minty, Chef's frown eased, and she gestured that they go into the tiny office at the end of the kitchen. Here everything was businesslike: computers, diaries, bills, menus.

Minty refused an offer of coffee.

Chef eased off her shoes, sighing. "How's Gloria working out?"

"Brilliant. I ought to have had her ages ago."

Chef was tolerant. "You wanted to do everything yourself. I remember how it was when mine were young. By the way, I've found you a woman to come and help with the washing and ironing. She'll start tomorrow. Even if Serafina returns, there's far too much for her to do."

Was this Patrick's doing? Did Minty care? Probably not. She smiled, nodded. "So, Florence, your workload."

"I like working here. I don't mind pressure, so long as it's not twenty-four/seven, but Mr High and Mighty believes in handing down orders for the impossible and not listening to anything we serfs might have to say." She tapped figures up on a computer screen. "The restaurant is doing well, opening Wednesdays through to Sundays. There's queues at weekends, particularly for ice cream in the summer months.

"I'd like to start a kiosk in the courtyard for ice cream in the summer and take-aways and hot dogs in the winter. Food that people can eat in the picnic area—if we had a picnic area—but they use the car park for eating their sandwiches anyway, so why not? Only, the Great I Am says I can't have any more money for wages, and I can't ask any of my girls to take on extra duties or they'll give in their notice. They work hard enough as it is.

"Now, since I started serving hot meals in the restaurant at lunchtime, we're getting a lot more older people coming in on weekdays. They want good plain food, which I can do with one hand tied behind my back. If I could only work out how to seat more people, we'd do even better, but we're limited for space."

She flipped to another file. "I can manage the restaurant five days a week, and if I had more staff, I could open the kiosk as well. That's not the problem. The problem is the evening functions. At first there were only one or two a month—wedding receptions, birthday parties, functions of all sorts—and I could cope by working a few hours extra each week.

"Toby's done a good job advertising the Hall for private functions. Each month the number of functions has grown. Sometimes it's finger food for fifty. Sometimes it's a sit-down banquet of four courses for thirty. Sometimes it's a buffet for a party of anything up to a hundred. To make it worse, these people don't want the restaurant, they want the Great Hall, which means traipsing hot dishes across the courtyard and back again. These parties make money, of course, but it means shift work for my girls, and a very long day for me."

Minty was amazed. "This is on top of the restaurant work?"

Chef nodded. "I can't count on Mondays and Tuesdays off anymore. This week I had Tuesday night off and actually had supper with my husband at home, but it's not enough. I'm worn to a frazzle."

She didn't look it. Chef was a powerhouse, but Minty knew that even powerhouses can break down under pressure. "If you had some extra help, could you last till Christmas, when presumably trade will fall off?"

Chef tapped up another file. "The restaurant is supposed to close from Christmas till the end of March, yes. That's when I booked a holiday. But Toby tells me he's continuing to take bookings after Christmas for birthday and office parties, plus some business functions, right through January and February. Anything from three to five nights a week."

Apart from what this might mean to Chef, it also meant that the Great Hall was going to be in use almost every day of the year. So when would the winter cleaning take place? What about the wear and tear on the furniture and furnishings?

Minty was thoughtful. "I'll have a word with Clive. Long term, I wonder if we could employ a sous chef for the restaurant—under your control, of course—so that you could concentrate on serving fine food in the house and we could still open the restaurant during the day to tourists, but ... yes, you must have a holiday, and you can't continue working at this pace. Do you know of anyone who could help you out straight away, and take over when you go on holiday?"

"There is someone I trained with, who could come as sous chef. He's been working at a pub in town, but he's not happy there. I could have him over, ask him to prepare you a sample meal, and, if you approve, he can start in a couple of weeks' time. One thing, though. We'd have to find him some accommodation."

Minty remembered something. "Didn't the Estate Manager mention there's a cottage become vacant in the village? I'll check it out. Meanwhile, Florence, please don't give up."

Chef nodded. "Be warned, Mr High and Mighty will fight you tooth and nail if you want to spend more money on wages."

"Worth it," said Minty, eyeing the restaurant accounts with respect.

Chef eased her shoes on again. "How's the twins?"

"With Patrick."

"Ah. They'll be safe there. When's he coming back?"

He'd only been gone a couple of days and everyone seemed to miss him. Did Chef think—like Reggie—that Patrick had gone for good? "Soon."

"Good. So what are you going to do about her?"

"Judith Kent? I don't know. Prayers needed, Florence."

"Will do. Now, back to the fray." Chef heaved herself out of her chair and went back to shout at one of her minions.

Minty fought her way out of the crowded restaurant and eased up in the courtyard. She liked Chef's idea of a kiosk. Would it be a mere barrow on wheels? Well, with a canopy across, that might be all right for warm summer weather, but not for winter. Was there any unused space in the buildings on either side of the courtyard?

Beside the restaurant was a staircase leading up to a self-contained flat; it had been rented out for the winter season, but perhaps one day they could extend the restaurant up there? Next came the gift shop—also doing a good trade—and the only other space was taken up by the toilets. There was no room for a kiosk on that side of the courtyard.

On the other side lay the bulk of the great house. In the corner was the tourist exit from the house into the courtyard, and a doorway that led into the bowels of the earth, where Minty's stepmother had created an Olde Worlde kitchen out of the first two cellars. Some tourists did go down there but many didn't, put off by the steepness of the uneven, winding stairs.

Next came the kitchens which had once served the Eden family, but which had been closed down when Chef took over the restaurant. After that were the Estate Offices, and a rather splendidly appointed reception-cum-office which Clive Hatton had adopted for his own use. There were no rooms which they could adapt for kiosk use on the ground floor, except possibly the one Judith had been given to work in. Minty could see her head bent over her laptop in the end Estate Office. Or perhaps they could use part of the now redundant family kitchens?

She watched a family of sightseers emerge into the courtyard from the house and peer down the steps to the basement, wondering aloud whether or not to bother, especially since the attractive restaurant beckoned nearby. One of the tourists disappeared down the stairs and came back pretty quickly. "Don't bother. There's just one kitchen and a bit of a pantry down there. Everything else is blocked off."

They were blocked off because they contained the junk of past generations. When Minty had thrown out her father's stiff modern furniture in favour of Patrick's family antiques, they'd had to find somewhere to put the discarded items. Hodge had said they could probably find room to store it in the basement, but before doing so they'd had to clear a cellar by throwing out half a ton of useless, bent, and broken nineteenth-century kitchen paraphernalia. Carol and her father had bought the lot, saying they could sell them to a firm that needed such things to decorate themed public houses.

The rest of the basement was indeed blocked off by a heavily padlocked door which guarded entry to an unknown number of cellars stretching right under the north wing. With so many other demands on her time, Minty had never explored that far. She'd been told the rest of the cellars were full of junk, but she was beginning to realise that one generation's "junk" might be valuable antiques a hundred years down the line.

There, if anywhere, might be some long-forgotten treasures, something to replace the fakes and altered pieces in the rest of the house. In particular, it seemed to her that the Chinese Room must once have held a collection of good furniture, since the silk which lined the walls and the fragile curtains showed they'd been chosen to complement a room furnished and decorated in early eighteenth-century Chinese style.

So where had all the original furniture gone? It might, of course, have been sold off, or given away ... perhaps passed on to another member of the family for some reason. Or, it might have been thrown into one of the cellars, too good to throw away, but not fashionable enough to keep. Just like Sir Micah's furniture, which might yet appeal to his grandchildren.

There was a problem; no one—not even Reggie—seemed to know where the key might be to the padlock. She must ask the housekeeper, who kept a small chest full of redundant old keys. Perhaps the housekeeper also knew where the keys to the tower rooms might be?

Minty paced along the frontage, walking round a couple of families who were queuing to get into the restaurant. In her mind's eye she traced the steps the waitresses would have to take to get food into the

Great Hall. Across the courtyard, into the north wing, through a maze of passages into the cloisters around the Fountain Court. They'd have to walk two sides round the Fountain Court to get into the Great Hall. It was a wonder anything ever arrived hot enough to eat. Something would have to be done about that.

Could they set up another kitchen within the north wing, nearer even than the one the family had once used? The ingredients for the meals were delivered to the courtyard, and no one would want to hump them through the narrow passages that criss-crossed the north wing ... even though the cooked food had to go that way. It was a puzzle. She must give it some thought.

She stared up at the façade of the ancient north wing. Some of the rooms on the first floor were of a decent size. Once they'd housed the offices for her father's educational charity, but that had long since relocated to London, and the rooms had been used for temporary art exhibitions and the like ... not a very satisfactory arrangement, but it brought in some rent.

The top floor was a self-contained flat which had once been occupied by her stepbrother, and this had been let out on a short-term lease. She had lots of space to play with, but it was all in the wrong place, and temporarily unusable.

Of course it made sense to rent out parts of the enormous house. The upkeep of the Hall would drain anybody's finances, and their tenants were usually quiet, considerate people. Minty hardly even knew them by sight.

"Minty, there you are." Venetia, pulling on a big winter coat. "I was hoping to catch up with you. What's going on?"

Minty temporised. "About what?"

Venetia gave her an old-fashioned look. "I don't think you're going round the twist, but there's no denying that some very odd things are happening to you and the twins. Who spread the oil on the floor in the Great Hall? What's all this about the electrics having been tampered with? And where is Patrick?"

"Patrick's looking after the twins to keep them safe, and I'm joining them as soon as I finish up here."

Venetia drew Minty under the archway into the inner courtyard where they couldn't be overheard. "Toby kept dropping hints till I skewered him to a chair and got him to tell me about Carol's report. I said I was inclined to believe her, and he says he's sure she's right, but that Clive won't listen. If there are fakes among the antiques, what are you going to do about it? And are you in danger because you're trying to expose the fakery?"

Minty considered this theory for ten seconds. The idea that Clive would make attempts on her life to protect his job was laughable. Yet Venetia's expression told Minty that she was really worried about it. So Minty kept her face straight. "No, I don't think Clive's mind works that way. It's true he wants to operate a cover-up, but the attacks on me are down to someone else."

Venetia drew in her breath. "If it's not Clive, then it's that girl, isn't it? Judith. As soon as I laid eyes on her, I thought, *You're trouble, my girl*. I was hoping that Toby and Carol ... I mean, it's not perfect, but maybe he needs someone to tell him what to do now and then, and I really like her as a person. But Judith ... she's not exactly ..."

"Not good daughter-in-law material?"

"You can laugh," said Venetia, looking put out. "But I don't want him tied to a woman who only thinks of herself and what she wants. Carol would take good care of Toby, wouldn't she?"

"Yes, I think she would."

The two women contemplated the future with identical wry expressions.

"So," said Venetia, "what are you going to do about, well, everything?"

"I'm going to pray. I'm going to tell Judith to stop it, and I'm going to find some genuine antiques for the Chinese Room."

"And," Venetia prompted her, "sort out the arrangements for a June flower festival?"

"I promised to get back to Mrs Collins on that. I'll try to ring her this evening, but if I don't get round to it ...?"

"It will come better from you than from me, but yes, I expect I'll be seeing her this evening." She looked at her watch and gave a little trill of alarm. "Must go. Keep in touch, won't you?"

Minty rubbed her forehead. She needed to go up to the chapel and pray. She needed to sort herself out before she could sort other people out. She needed to face the fear that had surfaced when she'd been talking to Patrick.

She fished out her mobile and phoned him.

"How are you getting on with the twins?"

"Fine. I joined them up at the farm. They were somewhat taken aback when faced with cows at close quarters because they'd only seen them at a distance before. Close to, cows must have seemed like giants. Petronella was so startled she tripped over her feet and fell backwards. Ralph stepped in front of her to protect her, even though he was shaking with fear. They've rather gone off cows. They prefer hens, but even they have to be kept at a distance. It's their first introduction to live animals, you see."

"I wish I'd been there. Ought we to get them a dog?"

"Something old and large and slow-moving? Possibly. They're having an early tea now with Mrs Mimms' grandson. He's telling them 'what!' about the countryside, and they're listening with what looks to me like hero-worship. He's five years old, you see. Nearly grown up."

"I wish I were there, but I've got to deal with Judith. And Clive."

"And Chef?"

"Yes. We need a sous chef straight away, but Clive doesn't want to pay for one. I wish you were here."

"You almost sounded as if you meant that."

"I did. Come home?"

A long silence. He switched off his mobile.

She made a face at hers, and went to find Judith in the north wing.

Chapter Fifteen

Wool had made the first Edens wealthy, and they'd built the north and west wings solidly in the local Cotswold stone, but the rooms were mostly small and, being wainscoted, dark. The mullioned windows let in wintry daylight, but Judith—like the others who worked in that wing—had switched on overhead lights to see what she was doing.

Judith was wearing white gloves and bending over a huge folio laid out on a table. She looked up when Minty came in, and for a moment looked dismayed. And then resumed her usual bland expression. "You think the children will be safe away from me?"

So there was going to be a fight. Minty seated herself. "I said I'd send you away if you made trouble, and you have."

"Promises, promises."

"I know how you managed the attack in the courtyard."

"What attack? I didn't see anything. You imagined it."

"I was attacked by your accomplice, lover, whatever. The man who's living in the caravan with you, and who's been taken on by Hodge to work part-time in the gardens. You didn't think I knew about him, did you? But I do. When I offered to see you safely down from the tower and through the house, you made an excuse to go into the rest room and alerted him by mobile phone. When we reached the courtyard, you lingered to fiddle with the door, leaving me at his mercy. Luckily I'd turned back, thinking to help you with the door, so he missed my head and only got my hip."

"What a strange story. A pity no one believed you."

"I followed you after the attack to make sure you got safely to the caravan. I noticed there was a light on inside and that the curtains were drawn. I thought at the time that you'd left them like that as a security measure, so that you wouldn't have to return to the caravan in the dark. But Reggie confirms that a man is living there with you."

Judith shrugged.

"I'm not sure about the toaster," said Minty. "It might have malfunctioned without your interference, but I suspect not. Was that your lover, as well?"

"I have no lover. And anyway, how could a stranger have got in and out of the house? It's like Fort Knox in here."

"Venetia gave you the codes to get in and out, and you passed them on to him. You tried again yesterday. At teatime you heard I was bringing the twins down to the Great Hall, so you rang him on your mobile, alerting him to the opportunity. He took a bottle of oil from your caravan—he didn't get it from the restaurant because Chef doesn't stock that brand—slipped into the house, did the deed, and got out again. Everyone could see it wasn't you, because you hadn't had time. But you knew there'd been an 'accident,' because although it was out of your way, you came straight to the Great Hall shortly afterwards, to gloat. A mistake, that."

Judith leant back in her chair. "You'd be a laughing stock if you tried to take that story to the police. If you try to throw me out, I'll sue you for false dismissal."

Minty rubbed the back of her neck to ease the tension there. "No, I'm not throwing you out, or dismissing you, but I must ask you to stop trying to kill me."

Judith laughed. "You really do amuse me."

Minty considered Judith's bland expression. She was still beautiful, even though her skin was marred.

Minty unsheathed her own claws. "Of course," she said slowly, "*I* could easily arrange to have *you* killed. There's any number of people here who'd be happy to arrange an accident for you. A fault in the electrical wiring which serves the caravan, leading to a fire in the night?

A slip on the stairs? A strange-tasting sandwich from the restaurant which gives you stomach cramps? Do you read me?"

Judith was silent, breathing rapidly. Finally, she said, "You won't, though. Will you?"

Minty smiled. She was imagining how Patrick or Chef or Reggie would receive a request from her to kill Judith. Patrick and Chef would stare at her and say "Nonsense!" in a sharp tone. Reggie would give her a scolding. But Hodge? Ah, he might well take such a request seriously. Hodge's allegiance was to the land, and anything that threatened his territory might well seem to him to be worth defending. He was a Christian, yes. Of sorts. But he could, perhaps, be tempted to do wrong in order that the desired result was reached. Minty thought it might be just as well not to tempt him too far.

Judith looked scared for the first time. "You wouldn't!"

"You mean that it's all right for you to try to kill me, but it would be all wrong for me to try to kill you?"

Judith flushed. "It's not like that."

"Isn't it? Is it all right for you to try to kill me, thinking that as I'm a Christian I'd never retaliate? Perhaps you've read me wrongly. Perhaps I think I should defend myself, or even counter-attack."

Silence.

"Do you really think I'm so weak that you can attack me with impunity?" said Minty.

The tiniest shake of her head. Judith didn't think that, no.

"It's true," said Minty, "that I haven't fulfilled my threat of throwing you out—yet. You probably thought that, once I'd decided to give you a chance, I'd bend over backwards to keep you here, that I'd overlook minor transgressions. You were right to think so. But trying to murder me wasn't exactly a minor transgression, was it?"

"I wasn't trying to murder you. It was just that ..."

"You wanted to hurt me, as you've been hurt. I understand that, in a way. But it's got to stop."

"So what are you going to do? Throw us out?"

"No. I'm not at all sure that you are a Christian nowadays, but I don't sense any evil around you, or not in the same horrible way as when you came here before. Rather, you seem to me to be mischievous. You give way to impulses to hurt people, without thinking of the consequences. I don't sense much good, either, and that is a bit of a worry. Have you come across the bit in the Bible when Jesus talked about an evil spirit being driven out of a man?"

"I told you, I've been healed of whatever it was that took me over for a while."

"I believe you. But Jesus warned that an evil spirit which has been driven out of a man would go looking for another home, and if he doesn't find one, he will return. If he then finds your house clean and tidy—and empty—then he will return with seven other evil spirits, and you will be worse off than before."

Judith took in a sharp breath but did not speak.

Minty was gentle. "Unless you fill yourself with the light of God, temptation will slither in, and little by little, you may find yourself back in the power of the evil thing which once ruled your life, and which nearly destroyed you."

Judith turned her head aside. "You're trying to scare me."

"Read your Bible, Judith. Make some Christian friends, and listen to them. Have you asked my uncle to help you? Or Cecil? Both of them know how. I think you should build defences against the dark."

"Much you know about the dark, Miss Goody-Two-Shoes!"

Minty swallowed. "I'm not perfect, Judith. Far from it."

Judith examined her fingernails. "All right, I played a few practical jokes. You made it so easy, I couldn't resist. If it's any consolation, I didn't mean for you to get badly hurt. I just wanted to even things up a bit. You have so much, and I . . . nothing."

"Listen to yourself. Hear the evil creeping in? What about the man in your caravan? Is he helping you to be a Christian, or leading you astray?"

"The man in the caravan is my little brother. His name is Craig. I rescued him from my abusive father a couple of years back, and he's been devoted to me ever since. I don't suppose you noticed him particularly when I was here before. He was one of the electricians. He thought he wanted to be a dancer, but he's no particular talent, though I helped him when I could. He was the only one to stick by me when I was taken off to hospital. He blamed you for what happened to me."

"Then you'd better set him right, hadn't you?" Minty got to her feet, leaning on the table to help her up. "No more tricks, mind?"

"You're really not throwing us out?"

"I'm praying for you, instead. Oh, before I go. One piece of advice. Hands off Toby Wootton. He's someone else's property."

Judith flushed. "The carrot-top's welcome to him. He's not man enough for me."

"Probably not, but then ... who is?"

"Your husband, maybe?"

Minty tried to laugh, but she sensed the threat to Patrick was very real. Had it come to this, that she felt jealous of this woman? She couldn't blame anyone but herself if Patrick did look for a kind word elsewhere, for she'd driven him from her with her coldness, her refusal to share his bed.

She shook her head at Judith and left her to her books.

The barbed question stuck in her mind. Could Judith now take Patrick away from her?

There were still plenty of visitors around, so she couldn't visit the Chinese Room, which is what she really wanted to do ... except that she didn't know what she was looking for if she did go there.

She made her way across the Fountain Court and up the stairs to the tower office. There wasn't anyone there. No Iris. No Toby.

She looked for the folders Toby which had given her. Her ears were stretched to hear the twins crashing through to her ... and then she remembered, with a stab of pain, that they were no longer in the building. The place was incredibly quiet. No Serafina. No twins. And she couldn't even look forward to Patrick coming in from work.

She could do with a cup of coffee.

No ground coffee. Patrick had thought too much caffeine might be contributing to her inability to sleep soundly. Well, she should sleep tonight, without the twins waking her. Or Patrick, if she couldn't get back to the cottage that day.

She made herself open the files and started to compare the list of articles bought for her stepmother by that slimy, unctuous, so-called "expert," Guy Hertz ... with the inventory prepared by Carol.

Minty shuffled papers. Had Toby been clever enough to include a copy of the inventory done by the London firm? Yes, he had. It was at the back of the second file.

She took a red pen and started to make notes.

The "Jacobean" chest in the Hall had been there long before Guy had appeared on the scene. Carol had marked it down as an oak chest from the seventeenth century, with later carving. The London firm had marked it down as a fine example of Jacobean furniture without any mention of the carving having been done at a later date. So this was an example of the "dicey" furniture handed down through the generations.

The clock which Reggie so much disliked had been bought by Mr Hertz, who had sold it to the Hall as early eighteenth century. Carol had it down as a mid-nineteenth century copy of an earlier piece, with a twentieth-century movement, and Reggie concurred. The London firm had got it down as early eighteenth century, with no mention of its being a copy or of having been altered in any way. This was verging on fakery. The descriptions of both these items needed to be amended in the new brochure.

The library ... nothing to query here except the library steps, which Mr Hertz had not bought, but which Carol believed had been cobbled together in the early twentieth century, from parts of an earlier structure.

The London firm had passed everything in that room as genuine, no mention of alterations. Maybe that description could stand, as the library steps were not described in any detail in the brochure.

The Chinese Room. Mr Hertz seemed to have bought everything in this — at enormous expense — except for the painted silk panels on the walls and the curtains, which presumably predated his acquaintance with the Hall. Minty tapped her chin with her pen. Clive had mentioned that the curtains needed to be replaced, but she rather thought it would be best to retain them, showing the wear and tear of centuries. At least they were the genuine article.

Carol had declared the spindly chairs to be recent reproductions of eighteenth-century Chinese Chippendale. She'd condemned them and the marquetry side table as fakes. The London firm had passed everything as genuine except for the table, which they had the grace to say they considered doubtful.

Minty leaned back in her chair. What was the London firm playing at? When she'd asked Patrick this, he'd advised her to use the Internet.

She switched on the computer in her office and Googled for the London firm. There they were. Solid and trustworthy. Everyone swore by them.

How could they possibly have given bad advice?

Minty's brain went into free-fall. Carol must be mistaken.

Of course, the twins hadn't liked anything in the Chinese Room, either. But you couldn't take the word of two tiny children before that of the London firm, could you?

She scrolled through pages of this and that, catalogues, sale dates, viewing dates, terms, and conditions. Directors. Experts in this and that. Forthcoming ...

She looked to see if by any chance Guy Hertz had managed to inveigle himself onto the board of directors, or become one of their experts. No, he wasn't there.

She was stuck. She'd been stupid to think there was something wrong at the London firm. Had she really imagined that such a respectable company had taken on a shyster like Hertz? So he'd been around a long time, but surely someone would by now have tumbled to the fact that he could give unreliable advice?

Her mind was awhirl with facts. She pressed the Print button. She'd go through it all again later.

Perhaps Hertz knew someone, somewhere ... one of the directors ...? Had brought in a lot of business? Had been highly recommended by Minty's stepmother, who now lived in London and still had money to spend on antiques?

No, this was ridiculous. They wouldn't be swayed by such things. They were above suspicion.

Probably.

She picked up the printed paperwork and sat with it in her hands, idly thinking that the quality was extremely good on this printer. So good, in fact, that you could easily be fooled into thinking this printout was the real McCoy. Suppose ... suppose the report from the London firm was a fake? Anyone could run off a heading from the Internet and then fill the page with any old nonsense. With a faked inventory.

Suppose that when Clive saw Carol's report, he panicked. Wanting to cover his own back, he might well have gone to the files and unearthed the name of the man who'd been acting for Lady C all those years that she was in charge of the Hall. And asked Guy Hertz's opinion.

How would Guy Hertz have reacted if he'd learned that another antique dealer had denounced much of the furniture he'd bought for the Hall? If Carol's report were to be accepted and it became common knowledge that he'd been responsible for stocking the Hall with fakes and altered pieces, his reputation would suffer ... never mind the possibility that he could be sued for fraud. His living would vanish.

What would he have done about it? Offered to arrange for a second opinion and then rigged it in his favour?

Minty liked the sound of this theory. So, how could Hertz have managed it?

Reggie had said that two youngsters had come down from the London firm to do a quick fix on the inventory. Suppose they hadn't come from the London firm at all, but had been people whom Guy Hertz had arranged to visit, pretending that they'd come from a big London firm but in reality people in his pay?

Could he have arranged that by printing off some letter-heading of the big firm from the Internet—just as she had done? He could have provided them with details of what to put in the report, they could have run the faked letterheads through a printer, adding a faked report, and ... it would look real enough. Real enough to please Clive, who didn't want to hear about fakes.

On the other hand, would a big name in the business, like Guy Hertz, stoop to such lengths?

Minty rested her head on her hands. Suppose the London firm's inventory was all right ... then all she had to do was remove that one nasty side table. The magazine could come and photograph whatever they liked. An article on Eden Hall would help boost tourism.

The problem was that at bottom she didn't believe they were right. She had no proof that Carol's judgement was good, but she believed in it, all the same. In which case, the Hall did face a crisis. When the magazine people came to photograph the Chinese Room, they would expose the fraud, and then it wouldn't only be Guy Hertz's reputation on the line, but also that of the Hall.

It was so quiet up in her office.

She missed the twins dreadfully. And Serafina. And Patrick, who'd provided himself with another comfortable home. He didn't need to expose himself to her coldness any longer.

She made her hands into fists and hit her desk. It was better to be angry than to weep.

She turned her thoughts back to the fakes. How Judith would laugh, if she were to guess . . . !

Minty was pretty sure Judith had guessed. Judith hadn't trumpeted the news from the chimney-tops, but maybe she had passed the news on, quietly, to the magazine? A magazine which was shortly coming to investigate?

No, Venetia had been pretty sure that it was the sacked steward who'd been responsible for getting the magazine interested in the Chinese Room.

What to do?

Patrick had one of the most active consciences that she knew. He wouldn't fudge the issue. He'd say, "Tell the magazine we made a mistake, that the furniture in that room has been taken out of commission, that we're trying to put it right."

Only, she didn't know how to put it right.

Her mind switched back to Patrick, sitting opposite her at the cottage, talking about loneliness. She pushed her hair back from her face.

Dear Lord Jesus, how did I get in such a mess? I didn't mean to push Patrick away. I just wanted some time to myself. He ought to have been more understanding. He could see how tired I was.

She had a flashback to a night when she'd fallen asleep early and woken in the early hours to find him missing from beside her. Rushing into the twins' room, afraid of she knew not what, she found him asleep, propped up in a chair, with his tiny son spread-eagled on his chest, also fast asleep, a blanket thrown over them both. She'd been furious with herself for failing to hear his cries. Patrick had important meetings the next day. He couldn't be expected to be nursemaid at night as well.

As clearly as if He was standing beside her, she heard, *Come off it, Minty. You resented his help. You wanted the children to be yours and yours alone. Yet he's been a brilliant father to them, hasn't he?*

Well . . . yes.

And a tender husband in the months after the children were born, when you brushed his hands away every time he wanted to show how much he loved you? He brought you flowers and books and little treats to tempt your appetite. He thought of a hundred different ways to make your life easier — most of which you rejected. When he would have drawn you back into his bed, you found excuses . . .

I was too tired. The twins drained me.

You were too proud to admit you needed help, too scared to tell him what was wrong . . . so the Hall suffered, and so did your husband. You broke your marriage vows.

He's older than me. He should have understood.

How could he understand, when you didn't explain what was wrong? No. You can't push the blame on him.

Minty put her hands over her ears to shut out that inner voice. She thought how sweet it had been to breast-feed the twins, to change them, to cuddle them and play with them. Really it hadn't been so hard to get up in the night. She'd loved being alone with them in the small hours when everything was quiet. She could sing them a lullaby and comfort them if they cried. They had been totally dependent upon her.

Knowing that she became anxious at night, with the tower between their bedroom and the twins', Patrick had rigged up a good alarm system. Even so, she'd found it hard to stumble all that way to them when they needed her.

Patrick had suggested moving their bedroom next door to the children in the east wing, but she'd vetoed that straight away, saying their four-poster wouldn't fit, and that she'd miss the wonderful view over the south front.

Now, facing the gaping hole she'd created between herself and her husband, she acknowledged that they could have moved there, temporarily, and she wouldn't have begun to sleep in the room with the twins, instead of at Patrick's side.

No, be truthful, Minty. Look deeper. Patrick was hungry to have his wife back in his arms when the doctor gave you the all clear after the twins were born. But you refused him. Why?

I was so tired, I couldn't cope.

Try again. The truth this time, please.

Because I knew he wanted more babies and I was ashamed to admit that I'd changed my mind, that I couldn't face another pregnancy again. Or not so soon, anyway. He kept on and on about it . . .

He thought you meant it when you said you wanted more children, too.

Minty put her hands over her ears. *I did at the time, but the twins wore me out.*

Putting her hands over her ears didn't stop the voice. *He could see that, which is why he offered you help — which you refused. How could he interpret that, if not as a rejection of himself?*

But it's just not practical to keep on having children. I couldn't give each one the attention they needed if I kept on having children, and I looked such a mess I didn't think that . . . and besides, I have to look after the Hall as well. More children means less time for the Hall.

What was that you very nearly said a while back?

I looked such a mess that I . . . breast-feeding the twins was the right thing to do. Everyone says so.

Silence.

Well, I did feel a mess. I'd put on weight and none of my good clothes fitted me, and I felt, well, disgusted with the way I looked. It's part of nature's way of making sure I didn't get pregnant again too quickly.

Silence.

Patrick always looks so immaculate, even when he's been under his car, or gardening.

Silence.

All right, I know I ought to have seen that he had a patch of land for a garden, but ...

Silence.

She thumped the arm of her chair. *I WAS AFRAID TO TELL HIM!*

Now we're getting somewhere. You didn't trust him enough to say you'd changed your mind about having more children. You didn't trust him enough to let him lighten your load. You didn't—and don't—love him enough to admit your faults.

She rocked to and fro, keening.

He trusted you, Minty, and how have you repaid him?

She got to her feet, moving like an old woman. Arguing with God was tiring, but it made her look at life in a different way.

Patrick thinks you no longer love him. He's never thought highly of himself, has he? How else would he understand your rejection of him?

She flushed, ashamed.

She would make it up to him—if it was not too late.

Chapter Sixteen

What next? She felt worn out, but had to keep going. The sooner she sorted things out here, the sooner she could get back to the cottage and Patrick. She took the stairs down to the ground floor. She must find Clive and tell him not to print ... She must phone ... who was it? She wasn't feeling up to much, and that was the truth.

Clive wasn't in his fine office in the north wing. She met Reggie in the courtyard. "Have you seen Clive?"

"In his flat, I suppose. Can't stop. Got to set up in the Great Hall."

"Another function?"

Reggie looked harassed. "Dairy products seminar; set up for their buffet, chairs for fifty. They're bringing in their own food, using our kitchens. Clear away at ten tonight. Tomorrow there's a Golden Wedding party; tables for fifty, buffet and urns for coffee. Clear away at eleven. Sunday there's a lecture—can't remember what it's for—but chairs for sixty, coffee and tea urns for the interval. Clear away at ten thirty."

"You manage this all by yourself?"

"Usually Hodge helps me—when it doesn't interfere with his television programmes—and his nephew lends a hand sometimes."

"However many hours are you working?"

"Same as Chef."

"This can't go on, Reggie. I'll speak to Clive about it. Shouldn't he be helping you, anyway?"

"He says he's got a bad back." Reggie's tone was level, non-committal.

Minty bit her lip. She didn't want to criticise Clive to Reggie. "Reggie, another thing, what do you think about letting the Great Hall out every night? Isn't it damaging the furniture there?"

"Mm, I'd like to take the good stuff out every time, but I doubt I could manage it by myself, and of course, it's what the punters want to see."

Minty nodded. "I'll have to think about that."

She set off through the dark passages of the north wing, touching the time-switch lights as she went. Into the Fountain Court. No moon tonight. She shivered. She thought she saw a tall, spare figure crossing the Court in front of her, and for a moment she felt a leap of joy. And then she saw it wasn't Patrick. How could it be? It was probably Clive, who was also tall, though not as tall as Patrick. Oh, come on; it was probably Clive.

The figure disappeared into the far corner and Minty followed, pressing buttons to let her into the tower, and then taking the steps down to Clive's flat.

It was a spacious apartment; because of the slope on which the house was built, the flat had windows at ground floor level looking out over the Park.

She knocked on Clive's door, and Iris opened it, tucking her blouse into her skirt.

Of course. Minty suppressed a comment about this being a "cosy, domestic scene." That wouldn't help.

"Helloo!" said Clive, at ease in a big chair. "What brings the Lady of the Hall visiting at this time of night?"

Minty waited to be asked to take a seat. The invitation was not forthcoming, so she took a seat, anyway. She would see what soft words could do. "I'm glad I caught you. There seems to be so much unfinished business hanging around."

"Everything's hunky-dory as far as I'm concerned, so you can go off and enjoy yourself playing with the twins, and leave me to get on with the job you pay me to do."

Minty felt anger rise in a wave to her forehead. She made herself count ten. She knew she was impulsive and inclined to act without thinking things through. Patrick had taught her that saying absolutely nothing could disconcert your opponent. Clive had suddenly turned into an opponent. Therefore she made herself count ten.

One, two . . .

Patrick said that if you lose your temper, you lose your advantage in an argument.

. . . three, four, five . . .

She observed that Iris was flushed, avoiding her eye. Iris wasn't convinced that Clive was in the right, but she had divided loyalties.

. . . six, seven, eight . . .

It was pretty clear that Iris and Clive had just been rolling around on the settee. Had probably been down here for some time.

. . . nine, ten.

Iris was fidgeting. Iris never fidgeted. She was avoiding Minty's eye, but she wasn't looking at Clive, either. Iris wasn't a happy bunny. Perhaps it would be better to have Iris out of the way, if Minty was going to have a show-down with Clive?

"Iris, will you give us a minute?"

Iris inclined her head and went into the next room.

"Now what?" said Clive, sure enough of himself to be amused.

Minty tried conciliation. "I admit it's my fault that we've been at cross-purposes lately. I know you like to run the Hall your way, and I think you do a terrific job. I'm sure I couldn't do as well in many respects. It's just one or two niggles that we've got to sort out. Let's start with Reggie. He hasn't complained about the extra hours he's working, and I don't suppose he will. That's not the point. We can't expect him to work every evening, setting up for functions and then clearing away, if he's working a full eight hours during the day as well. Who's helping him out? I thought your duties covered the odd evening function?"

"Well, yes. I have been giving him a hand when my back's not bad." He winced. "I've got a bit of a slipped disc. He can always get the gardener to help."

"I'm sorry you've got a problem with your back." Though she rather doubted that he had, it was politic to accept his excuse. "Perhaps we can employ a part-timer to help Reggie out on these occasions and stand in for him when he's on holiday."

"We can't afford it."

"We can't afford not to. Can't you factor in the labour costs when you work out how much to charge for these functions?"

He shrugged. "If you insist, I'll get Neville to look at the figures. I suppose he'll side with you. He usually does."

Minty didn't rise to that. The two men had never liked one another, and the fact that Neville still hankered after Iris didn't help. "Good. Now, about Chef . . ."

He was annoyed. "I run a tight ship here, and I won't put up with whingers. There are plenty of other good cooks who'd like to work here."

"No, Clive, there aren't. Florence Thornby is one in a million. She has personally been responsible for the success of the restaurant and for the increase in bookings for the evenings. If you put in a second-rate chef, our bookings will dwindle. I propose we give her a fat bonus and involve her in future planning, because she has some excellent ideas which will raise our profits even more."

He made as if to protest, so she raised a hand to stop him. "Now, this is what I suggest, that you and I meet tomorrow morning first thing and look at the problem from Chef's point of view. I'm wondering whether we could employ a sous chef for the restaurant; Florence could oversee everything but be relieved of the day-to-day preparation.

"We could open up the old family kitchen in the north wing again for Chef to use—perhaps with a separate part-time staff—just for functions. And somehow, we've got to cover her for the holidays she's already booked."

He was seriously annoyed. "You're mad! How do you think we're going to pay for that?"

"Out of the profits she's making for us."

"They told me you knew nothing about finance, and it's clear you don't."

"I know when something is good value."

He jumped up from his seat, but she held up her hand. "I haven't finished yet."

She reined her temper again. She must try to get him to see reason, to work with her and not against her. "I've thought over everything you said about the new brochure, but I've decided we can't risk printing lies. We must go through the brochure, reclassify anything that's dicey, and remove anything that's a fake. That won't take long—a couple of days, perhaps. We must also physically remove everything from the Chinese Room, and all the other suspect items from the rooms which are open to the public."

He started to pace the room. "What! And leave great gaps in the collection? And what do you propose to do with the Chinese Room?"

"We leave it empty for the time being. Put a notice in it that the furniture has gone for restoration. It's often done, isn't it? Reduce the print run for the brochure. By the time those brochures have been sold out, we'll have something else to put in the Chinese Room. I'd suggest turning it over to another design style if it weren't for the original Chinese silk panels on the walls, and the curtains—which I rather think I want to keep, even through they're showing their age. At least they're genuine."

He turned on her. "A pity you didn't think of this earlier. It's too late now. The order's gone to the printers."

Minty was silent, holding onto her temper, trying to think clearly. Iris and Clive had just been enjoying themselves down here, so would Iris have made that phone call herself, or would she have asked Toby to do it? In which case, Toby—knowing how Minty felt about things—might not have put the call through.

Minty said, "I don't suppose they're working over the weekend. If they are, then we'll have to junk the print run and start again."

"Start again? And pay for having it printed twice?"

"If necessary, yes."

"You're mad. We can't afford extravagant measures like that. Besides—" he calmed himself with an effort; he even managed a smile "—we can't alter the brochure because the magazine people know what's in it, and that's why they're coming to do a feature on the Chinese Room." He seemed to think that was a clinching argument.

"Put them off for a bit. Say we've found that the curtains are falling to pieces, and we need to send them for conservation. Buy us some time."

His voice rose. "And the insurance people, who'll want to know why we've taken so many perfectly good antiques off display?"

"We'll let Neville work that one out. One thing, demoting them from antiques to 'fakes' or 'restored pieces' should reduce our insurance premiums."

He was breathing hard. "How can you be so flippant!"

"Better laugh than cry. Come on, Clive. You know this makes sense."

"Sense! You talk of sense, while you propose to throw away everything I've worked for all these years? They told me you were having a breakdown, having delusions. I didn't believe them before, but now! The sooner you see a doctor, the better!"

Minty got to her feet. "Clive, you'd be wise not to start slinging mud at me, or I might ask you one or two uncomfortable questions."

"For instance?" His spittle landed on her sleeve.

"For instance," she said, keeping her voice steady, "how did you arrange that fake London inventory? Do you have a connection with Guy Hertz that you've kept secret all this while? Has he been paying you to keep quiet about the faked furniture here ... or have you been paying him to supply a faked inventory?"

His eyes looked black in a whitened face. Shock.

He breathed, "How dare you!"

She saw she'd hit upon something like the truth. "When you got Carol's inventory, you realised it threatened your position here, because if it came out that the Hall was showing fakes, we'd have to close down and you'd lose your job. Did you contact Hertz for reassurance that everything was all right? If so, he must have realised that he had even more to lose than you. He'd probably never envisaged that the pseudo antiques he'd bought for my stepmother would ever be called into question. But if they were, then it would all come out about the enormous sums she'd paid for them. He'd be disgraced, possibly prosecuted. So did he suggest arranging for a faked inventory which would back him up — or did you?"

"That is ..." He lost words. He raised his arm, and for a moment Minty thought he was going to hit her.

Her own voice seemed to come from a long way off. "I think you'd better resign. I won't prosecute if you leave quietly. Make any excuse you like. Your bad back, perhaps? Just get out as soon as you can."

There was a flurry of movement and Iris appeared, holding onto Clive's arm. She'd been listening, of course.

"Minty, you can't sack him. We're getting married at Christmas."

Clive gaped at her.

Minty blinked. Was Iris bluffing? Yes, probably. Iris was trading on Minty's affection and trust for her, to save Clive's job. Minty didn't know whether to call Iris' bluff or not. If Clive did marry Iris, would that be a good thing? Instinct said it wouldn't, but it was what Iris had wanted for some years now. Should Iris have her chance at happiness? Minty seriously doubted whether Clive would make Iris happy, but ...

Iris said, "It wasn't Clive's fault. He was only thinking of you and the Hall. You mustn't blame him." She shook Clive's arm. "Tell her, Clive.

Tell her that you rang Guy Hertz as soon as you got Carol's report. Tell her Guy blackmailed you into accepting a second inventory."

She said to Minty, "You see, Guy said that if it all came out, he'd lay the blame on your stepmother, saying she's known all along that some of the furniture wasn't right but hadn't cared what it cost, because she was so anxious to get the place open to the public. Guy said he'd kept letters of hers to prove it."

"I don't believe that," said Minty, and she didn't. It wasn't that she didn't think her stepmother incapable of deceit, because she could swallow that. Just. But the suggestion that Lady C had allowed Guy Hertz to keep proof of wrongdoing . . . no, the woman was far too clever for that.

"Tell her." Iris shook Clive's arm again. "Tell her we're getting married at Christmas."

"I . . . yes," said Clive, bemused but picking up his cue. "That's right."

Minty didn't believe that, either. She shook her head, more at herself than at them. "I congratulate you, and wish you well. But you'd better stop that brochure being printed. As for the rest, we'll discuss it quietly in the morning."

She stumbled over the last step as she reached the ground floor, clutching her upper arms to keep warm. She was shivering. November evenings can make one chilly. So can a lost friendship. If Iris married Clive, she would have to side with him in any dispute with Minty.

Should Minty still sack him? Probably.

The security lights were on in the cloisters. They were on a time switch, so someone must have passed through just before her . . . or still be there? With rising excitement, she wondered if Patrick could possibly have returned. And if so, had he been searching the place for her? A tall, spare figure was disappearing into the far corner. She called out, but he took no notice, so she set off after him.

Shadows played hide and seek as she crossed the Fountain Court, running ahead of her, then switching to her heels. She paused halfway across. There was no one there. Her eyes had been playing her tricks. Patrick was looking after the twins, keeping them safe. If it had been him ... oh, if it had been, she'd have run and clasped her arms around him, telling him how sorry she was that she'd been so cold lately, telling him how much she loved him.

Even if it meant having to undergo yet another pregnancy? Because she didn't want another baby yet, did she? Only, if Patrick needed her to have another baby to save their marriage ...? Nonsense. Their marriage was not in danger. Was it?

She started, hand to mouth, for part of the shadow under the opposite cloister had broken away and was moving towards her. She shaded her eyes with her hand, trying to see what was lying there in the dark, waiting for her. Then saw that the shadow was Judith Kent.

"You startled me."

Judith took a step further into the lighted area, her shadow moving before her. For some reason a little voice in Minty's head reminded her that ghosts don't have shadows. Judith Kent was not a ghost in that she was still a living person, but she carried some ghostly luggage with her.

"I was waiting for you."

"Let's go inside. It's cold out here."

Judith was wearing a heavy coat, but Minty wasn't.

Judith put out her arm to bar Minty's progress. "It might not be safe."

Minty shook her head to clear it. "What's going on?"

"My little brother. I told you about him. He wants to speak to you."

Minty shivered. "Well, let's go inside and find him."

Judith hesitated a long moment, then dropped her arm, turning away. "I'm afraid."

"What of? Your brother?" Minty took a quick scan of the cloisters, but there were too many shadows to see everything clearly. Too many places in which a tall, thin man might lurk, waiting to speak to Minty ... or not to speak to her, but to ... do what? Attack her? Was this the man Minty had glimpsed twice before that evening?

"I was never afraid before," said Judith, turning to vanish into the gloom.

One moment she was there, and the next, she'd disappeared. Minty hesitated, and then followed her. There was no point in staying where she was. If Judith's brother wanted to attack her, there was nothing to stop him. She could, of course, run back the way she'd come, pound on Clive's door, and ask for sanctuary.

Sanctuary from what? Clive would say it was all in her imagination.

Minty couldn't prove that the man had tried to attack her before or caused the oil slick in the Great Hall. Was Judith trying to say that she'd warned him off, but that the warning hadn't taken effect? Surely Judith could control him. It would be best to stick close to Judith, and see what happened.

Was that a footfall behind her? Judith seemed to glide over the ground, leading the way into the old wing. The ancient door creaked as Judith opened it. Minty just managed to catch it before it closed.

Holding the door open, she touched the light switch in the corridor beyond and turned back to face ... whoever had been stalking her.

A tall, thin lad stood there, skin tight over his face. A gangling youth. There was a certain elegance, a swagger about his shoulders which hinted that he might one day be a handsome man, if life treated him kindly.

At the moment he looked half-starved and almost wolfish. His eyes were fixed on her with the expression of a hunter. She was his prey and he'd run her to earth.

What to do? Scream and run? What good would that do?

Face him down? Say something to knock him off balance? He didn't have the look of a drug addict, so reason might get through to him.

Judith had disappeared. Minty stood her ground. "Are you Judith's brother? I've been wanting to meet you. Do you like working here? Do come in, it's so cold outside." She held out her hand to draw him inside.

He hesitated, then stepped inside, letting the heavy door close behind him. Minty relaxed a trifle, but thought it unwise to turn her back on him. "I know where the light switches are, so you lead the way."

Again he hesitated, but then did as he was bid. He went ahead of her through the passages to the door into the outer courtyard. He even held the door open for her to follow him out into the night. Judith was rounding the corner . . . going back to her caravan?

The restaurant was closed for the night, but though Chef and her team had departed, a team of contract waiters and waitresses were shuttling food past them into the tower and from there to the Great Hall. Minty reminded herself to talk to Clive about the inefficiency of this system tomorrow.

The lanky lad led the way round the corner and past the three staff cottages to where the caravan sat, its windows lit up and curtains drawn.

He opened the caravan door for her, and sending up a quick prayer for God to watch over her, Minty went in.

The caravan was spacious. Its décor was muted, its design well thought out.

Judith was making coffee in a tiny but adequate kitchenette. The place was clean and tidy. There was nothing to indicate that this was the abode of someone who had once been a charismatic pop singer, except perhaps for the acoustic guitar laid down on one of the benches.

"Do you take it black?" asked Judith.

Minty shook her head. "I'm off coffee, especially late at night. Have you a herbal tea?"

Judith nodded, reaching up into a cupboard above her head. The youth was hunching his shoulders, his face twitching. Perhaps he was angry with himself? Had he intended to fall on Minty as she came through the cloisters? Probably.

Minty tried to calm her breathing. She was still in danger. No one knew she was here. They could kill her and no one would hear, especially if they switched on the radio.

Judith switched on the radio ... country and western, muted. She gave Minty a cup of camomile tea and pushed a mug of black coffee towards the youth. She was wearing a spicy scent, quite unlike the heavy perfume she'd used in the past.

"This is Craig, my little brother. Craig, this is Minty, who's given us both a job."

Craig muttered something into his mug, avoiding Minty's eye.

Minty said, "Tell me, Craig. Have you done any gardening work before?"

He pulled his shoulders up to his ears and dropped them.

Minty persevered. "We're actually short of help in various departments at the moment. The kitchens ... no? Have you met Reggie, our Houseman? He's short of help, too."

No reply.

Judith sat quietly by, sipping a mug of tea. Her face was hard to read, but if anything, she looked anxious.

Minty closed her eyes and leaned back. She was, she discovered, extremely tired. And—she shifted her position—her bruises hurt. Without opening her eyes she asked, "Judith, have you got any arnica, or aspirin? Something to help my bruises?"

Judith set down her mug with a click, and Minty opened her eyes to see the boy looking at her in terror.

He reminded Minty of a child who's done something silly and expects the sky to fall on him. Judith had said her brother had been abused by her father. Did he think Minty would beat him, too?

"It's all right," she said. "I'm not calling the police. Judith thought I was her enemy and might want to hurt her, and you tried to protect her, right? But I'm not your enemy and I don't want to hurt either of you. Of course I wish you hadn't jumped on me the other night, and it was horrid trying to save my little boy from the oil slick. He had a nightmare about it last night ..." Was it only the previous night?

"I didn't mean ... at least, I did ... but not, not ..." He couldn't get the words out. "Anyway, no harm done." Now he was getting cocky, trying to wipe out any murderous thoughts.

Judith silently put a tube of arnica pills in front of Minty. Minty smiled her thanks and took a couple with her tea.

The boy bolted for the door and vanished into the night.

Chapter Seventeen

Judith shut the door after Craig. "He's confused."

"And you've been covering up for him all this time. The attacks on me were his idea, not yours, weren't they?"

Judith turned her head away, but gave a tiny nod.

"And you're afraid he might actually succeed in killing me, now you've set him off?"

Judith flexed her neck and shoulders. "I'm treading water. I'm not sure I can swim much longer. As for life-saving ..." She shrugged.

Minty tried to work this out. "You want me to save you and your brother? I've given you jobs and a place to keep your caravan. Granted, neither of these is permanent, but in time you'll be strong enough to go after a better job. This is only a temporary haven for you, isn't it?"

Judith's lips twisted.

Minty pushed the hair back from her face. "You're afraid ... of what? Of the dark powers that ruled you in the past? Are you afraid that this time they're after two prizes, not one? That they're after your brother as well?"

Judith made a sharp movement but didn't reply.

"First you give him the opportunity to attack me, and then you ask me to rescue you," said Minty, trying for humour. "You sap my strength and ask me to carry you. You've got it wrong. It's not me you should ask for help, but Jesus Christ, who loves you so deeply, so much that it hurts Him to see you in pain. And that poor lost soul, your brother, too. Have you asked Jesus Christ to come into your heart? He is anxious to wipe out your sins if you only turn to Him in sorrow and repentance. Ask Him to fill you with His grace, and to armour you against everything that the Evil One can devise for you. And your poor brother, too."

A single tear ran down Judith's cheek, but still she said nothing.

Minty got to her feet by numbers. "You only have to ask for help, and it will be given to you. I will pray for you, and I will ask others to do so, too."

Judith made a dismissive move.

Minty said, "There are some powerful pray-ers at Eden Hall, and if they know you are asking for prayer, then you will have it. My uncle, too. You know where to find him, don't you? At the vicarage in the village. He's long past his three score and ten, but he's a major in the prayer army. He lives with the Reverend Cecil, who's also a man of God. There is help available, if you can bring yourself to ask for it."

Judith inclined her head.

Minty touched Judith lightly on her shoulder. "I take it that's a yes. Consider it done. But remember, you have to pray, too. And include your brother."

Judith did not reply, and Minty left her staring into space.

Minty stood outside the caravan, looking up at the stars. She shivered. There was frost in the air. Was the boy, Craig, watching her? She moved her shoulders uneasily but didn't get the feeling there was anyone around. The staff cottages were all quiet and dark. Even the cottage between Reggie and Iris—the one occupied by Hodge—was dark.

She consulted her watch. Seven o'clock? When had she eaten last? At Mill Cottage with Patrick and the twins? She'd promised to get back there tonight, but ... there was still so much to do. And something Iris had said ... someone had asked her to ring them urgently? She'd remember who it was in a minute.

First she must ring the cottage to see if the twins were all right. She had her mobile with her, but not the number of the cottage. She tried ringing Patrick's mobile. It rang and rang. Finally he answered.

our message across. As for Hodge, his language tended to be pictur-
esque at times, and adorned with Anglo-Saxon words. He meant no
harm by it, and Minty was sure that God understood.

What was the time? It was cold and dark in the house, the heating
kept on minimum during the winter months. She would ring Carol
and then jump into her car and make her way to the cottage.

Then she remembered who else she was supposed to ring. Mrs
Chickward, the terrifying She Who Must Be Obeyed, who organised
charity events for half the county with her left hand while directing
the affairs of the village with her right. Except that Mrs Chickward
seemed to be feeling her age at long last. Minty sighed. How sad!

She punched in the time switches on the lights leading up the
stairs to the tower room and her office. It was deathly quiet on this side
of the house, far from the cosiness of the kitchen or the busyness of the
dairy company's presentation in the Great Hall. She noticed in passing
that the Out of Service notice was off the doors to the lift. Good. With
the children out of the way, they could use it again now. She switched
on her desk light and found Mrs Chickward's number.

Mrs Chickward answered correctly—she was always correct—
with her telephone number.

"Minty here, Mrs Chickward. You wanted me to phone you about
the flower festival."

"Yes, my dear, I did. Venetia's just been on the phone saying you're
trying to arrange something for June. An excellent idea, but as I told
her, I don't feel I can take on any more responsibility at the moment.
You will have to find someone else to make the arrangements for you.
I am sure that Mrs Collins will be happy to do so, and I believe she
will do a good job."

"That is very gracious of you, Mrs Chickward," said Minty, appreciating the subtext here, as one grande dame ceded importance to
another. "I am really sorry that you want to cut down your workload.
You've been a role model to me for so long, and I don't know how I

shall manage without you. Would it be possible—if it's not asking too much—for me to call on you for advice now and then?"

"You have very pretty manners, my dear. Of course you may call on me for advice, though I'm not so foolish as to believe that you will take it. Now, to the second reason for my wanting to speak to you. I met an old friend for lunch today in town. We don't see one another that often, even though she and her husband live not far away. They're both about my age, perhaps a little older, but they keep themselves active. Her husband recently retired as one of the stewards at Eden Hall, and she's very concerned about him, because he's sitting at home all day getting under her feet."

Minty tried to put two and two together. "When you say 'he retired,' do you suspect some unpleasantness?"

"Yes, my dear, I do. My friend wouldn't come right out with it, but that's exactly what I think. He's a retired professor, you see. Very interested in the Regency period. Which made him particularly suitable as a steward ..."

"For the Chinese Room?"

"Precisely. My friend says that he was convinced all was not well with the current display, and that he'd had an argument with Mr Hatton about it. Apparently my friend's husband threatened to invite down an acquaintance of his who works for one of the glossy magazines, to ask his advice."

"I'm afraid that's exactly what he has done, Mrs Chickward. I, too, am unhappy with the Chinese Room, and with one or two other items bought in recent years."

Mrs Chickward went on a fishing expedition. "Your little friend Carol has been very tight-lipped about the work she's done at Eden Hall."

"Carol put in an adverse report about certain items of furniture, yes. I'm thinking of emptying the Chinese Room and trying to put the magazine off. It won't do us any good to be written up as having fakes on show."

"I've been trying to remember what was in that room years ago, in your grandfather's time. I rather think he used to sleep there towards the end of his life, in one of those beds with a canopy, you know? Goodness knows what happened to it. And then your stepmother changed things round again ..."

Minty felt prickles run down her back.

"... when she brought in that man Hertz to turn the place into a museum. Can't say I ever took to him. Far too charming in quite the wrong way. He and she had a fine old time throwing out some of the good old furniture and bringing in pieces he'd found for her. Yes, I rather think there was a four-poster with a pleated green silk canopy in the Chinese Room originally. I suppose it's around somewhere still. Mr Hertz wanted to go through all the storerooms and buy some of the junk that the Edens had thrown out over the years, but your father wouldn't allow it. He said his wife could buy what she liked—within reason—but that nothing that belonged to the family was to be sold off while he was in charge."

"Mrs Chickward, you are a bearer of good tidings. I was so afraid that the original Eden antiques might have been sold off over the years. Bless you, bless you. I wish I could start foraging tonight. We'll have a wonderful treasure hunt tomorrow, and see what we can find."

"Delighted to be of assistance," said Mrs Chickward, and put the phone down.

Minty tapped her chin. Now who would know where the old furniture had been put when it was thrown out by Lady C? And before that, by previous generations?

Perhaps the housekeeper would know? She'd been there for some years. But—Minty glanced at her watch—that could wait till the morning, because she must throw a few things into a bag and get out to Mill Cottage. After ringing Carol, of course. And hadn't she promised to ring Mrs Collins back?

She tried Mrs Collins first on the principle that difficult conversations should be dealt with first. The phone rang and rang but was not switched through to an answerphone. Ah, Mrs Collins would perhaps be on her way to a meeting that night?

Carol's number — she put it into her mobile phone before she rang her. Carol answered on the first ring. Minty could hear noise from a television in the distance, and then a man's voice saying, "Don't be long." Was it Toby?

"Carol, it's Minty here. I've been doing some digging, and of course you're right. The London inventory is a fake, and I think I know how it was done. There's a magazine wants to come down to photograph the Chinese Room just as it is, and I'm considering jumping off the top of one of the towers here."

Carol laughed. "Oh, Minty, sweetie. Don't jump. Think how it would mess up your non-existent make-up. Seriously, I'm relieved. I'd got to wondering if I'd been taking too much junk food and it had affected my judgement. What do you plan to do about it?" And then, with her hand half over the mouthpiece, she said to the other person in the room with her, "Minty says she agrees with us about the furniture. Keep mine hot?"

Minty was amused. "Is that Toby there with you?"

"Mm-hm. His turn to cook. Spaghetti bolognaise with a sauce to die for. You should join us."

"Can't. I should be on my way to Mill Cottage now. Did Toby put the order for the new brochures through?"

"No, poor lamb. He's quaking in his shoes at what Clive's going to say to him in the morning, but he hasn't done it."

"Thank goodness for that. Of course we can't reprint at the moment. Oh, Carol, I tried to sack Clive this evening, but Iris jumped in and said they were engaged and getting married at Christmas, and

I gaped ... and he gaped ... and none of us knew what to say next, so I ran away, saying I'd see him in the morning!"

Carol shrieked with laughter, and relayed the news to Toby, who hooted, too.

Carol said, "I demand to be a bridesmaid. Do you think he'll go through with it?"

"I rather hope not, for Iris' sake."

"Same here," said Carol, serious for once. "Lovey, I must go. Lots to think about."

"Hang on, Carol. There's something else I've got to say. I warned Judith Kent off Toby. I said he was already spoken for."

Silence for a long minute, and then Carol said hurriedly, "The subject doesn't see it in that light."

"About time he did," said Minty, and snapped the connection, smiling to herself.

She rushed through into her bedroom, seized an overnight bag, and threw some toiletries and her nightie into it. Went back for her bedroom slippers and hairbrush. Clean undies? Another blouse to wear tomorrow, or perhaps a sweater?

She looked around. What had she forgotten? Well, she'd be back tomorrow, so it wouldn't matter if she had forgotten something. She switched off the lights and returned to the lift via her office to collect the files on the various inventories. Perhaps Patrick could confirm how the faking had been done. She pulled open the gate of the lift and then remembered something else. The book on antiques which Patrick had left at the side of their bed. She might have time to ask him about replacement furniture for the Chinese Room, with luck.

She shoved her bag forward so that the lift gate wouldn't close on her and went back for the book, reflecting that by this time she could easily have gone down the stairs at the other end.

Book in hand, she rushed back, bending to pick up her bag ... and with one foot in the lift realised that she had still to turn off the lights in the office.

And at that very moment, the lift jerked and began to descend ... with the gate still open, and her with one foot inside!

What!

The lift wasn't supposed to descend until she'd closed the gate!

God, have mercy! She was going to be killed! Trapped in a lift out of control.

Her babies! Patrick!

She threw herself backwards and sideways onto the floor of the office, panicking, imagining the lift crushing her, halfway in and halfway out of the lift ... drawing up her knees to her chest ...

The lift was going to take her feet off at the ankles ...

She had no strength to drag herself further away from it ...

She felt the lift pluck at the soles of her shoes ...

Hearing the swish as the lift descended ... faster and faster and ... crashing down two floors below! A cable slap-slapped, running free onto the top of the lift as it descended.

The sound of the crash echoed through the tower room.

The lift doors were still open.

She couldn't move. She was shaking. Sobbing. The lift shaft gaped at her.

She told herself she must push herself back, away from the void.

She couldn't move. Perhaps she'd died, and it was just her lifeless body lying on the floor there.

Lord, have mercy. She inched herself backwards. She clutched at a chair nearby, using that to pull herself away from the dark void of the lift shaft. The gate hung open like a hungry mouth.

She could have been killed. Easily.

Someone had meant to kill her. She curled up, making herself a smaller target.

Judith's young brother? Judith had said he was an electrician, who'd wanted to be a dancer. Electrics. Toaster. Lift.

Reggie would only have taken the notice off the lift if it was work-ing properly and he knew the twins were out of the way. So it wasn't Reggie who'd taken off the notice.

She heard herself whimper.

There was a light, rapid footfall on the stairs.

Was Craig coming back to see what had happened to her? Had he heard the crash and looked inside the wreckage of the lift, expecting to see a corpse?

And, not seeing it, had realised that she'd survived again? And come up to finish off what he'd started?

She couldn't think straight.

The door opened from the staircase ...

Minty tried to scream but made no sound. She squeezed her eyes tight shut.

Chapter Eighteen

Someone came into the room and scooped her up off the floor. She dared to open her eyes, hardly believing it was Patrick.

"Is it really you?"

"Minty? Whatever . . . ?"

He carried her to one of the chairs in the window. She clung to him, biting into the soft wool sweater he was wearing to stop herself from screaming, clutching him as if she could never let go. Shaking uncontrollably.

He held her just as tightly, murmuring inarticulate sounds now and then.

Gradually the worst of her shivers passed. Every now and then she still shuddered, but at last she was able to lift her head and move into a more comfortable position, while still keeping fast hold of him.

"Are you hurt?" said Patrick. "What happened? I heard the lift coming down and it seemed to me it was too fast. When it crashed, I thought you might be in it, but there was no one there. Just some papers and your overnight bag."

"The lift started off without me. I got out just in time." She started to shake again. Her teeth chattered. "I had one foot inside and realised I hadn't turned off the lights and then it started without me . . . my weight must have set it in motion . . ." Her voice went up an octave into a wail.

"Hush," said Patrick, rocking her to and fro. "Hush."

She could hear her voice going too high, the words coming too fast. "I thought Reggie had taken the chain off, but it can't have been him. He meant to kill me."

He stilled. "Not Reggie. Then ... who? Judith?"

She tried to sit up but desisted when he pulled her back to him. She tried to slow down, but the words still tumbled over one another. "Judith's little brother, Craig. He thinks I was responsible for Judith's injuries. It was he who attacked me before. She's been covering up for him, trying to keep him out of trouble. She's afraid *for* him and also afraid *of* him. I don't know. I don't know anything anymore." Her voice rose in another wail. "Oh, Patrick, I nearly died! I don't want to die yet. My babies! And you!"

"Hush. I'm here, and the babes are fine."

"I should be there with them."

"They're fast asleep. Mrs Mimms and Gloria are in competition to see who can do the most for them." He went on talking, quietly, to calm her down. "Mrs Mimms is playing the card that she's brought up four children and five grandchildren. Gloria trumps her by saying she's been looking after the twins since they were born — which is not quite true, but near enough. And the twins look from one to the other. I wonder how long it's going to take them to see that they can play Mrs Mimms off against Gloria. So everyone's happy."

"Except me." She pushed herself away from Patrick to look at him. "Why are you here? I mean, I'm terribly glad you are, but ... I was on my way to the car when ... your book's down there, and the inventory files and my overnight bag with my best nightie in it, and ... I am not going to start crying again!"

"Just as well," said Patrick, heartlessly. "You know I never have a handkerchief on me."

She snuffled into laughter and sneezed. She always kept a spare tissue in her pocket to wipe the twins' noses. She found it and blew her nose. "So why are you here?"

"You sounded as if you needed help. You asked for prayers. The twins were fast asleep, so I thought I'd better come and see what was up."

"Ralph had a horrid nightmare last night. I ought to be there." But she didn't try to get off his knee.

He renewed his clasp of her. "If they do need us, it won't be till the early hours of the morning. So relax."

She lay quietly in his arms. She could feel the rise and fall of his chest as he breathed. Could she hear his heartbeat? Yes. She could stay like this for ever. He seemed to have forgiven her for her recent behaviour. What a man! And how little she deserved him.

"Now," he said, "if you're calm enough, we must report what's happened to the police."

She said, "And Reggie. He'll need to know about the lift. I think Craig cut through the cable at the top. Will the insurance cover the damage?"

He took out his mobile. "One thing at a time. Reggie, is that you? Patrick here. Can you spare a minute? Come up to the tower office. Don't try to use the lift. It's out of order, crashed. Minty nearly got caught in it, could have been killed, but she's all right. Make it as quick as you can, will you?"

He listened to Reggie's response, and clicked off the phone. "He'll be up in a minute. They're just putting the chairs and tables back from some function or other."

"A marketing firm for dairy products. Lots of different cheeses." She began to shiver again. Her teeth were chattering.

"If you'll let go of me for a minute, I'll give you my sweater. Have you eaten? Shall we heat up one of Serafina's home-made soups?"

He helped her to her feet. She stumbled and would have fallen if she hadn't been clinging to him still. "Can we trust the microwave? Craig interfered with the toaster, didn't he? What other booby traps are there lurking for me? Poor Judith. I really do think she tried to rein him in." She heard her voice going faint, and found herself sitting down with a bump in the chair opposite, with Patrick shoving her head between her knees.

"Breathe slowly. That's it. I'm calling the doctor, get someone out to check you over."

She didn't reply. It was a good thing he'd taken charge of things, because she was too far gone to help.

❧

She woke slowly next day. She was lying in their great four-poster. She threw out her arm, but Patrick's place beside her was empty, although she seemed to remember he'd joined her in bed some time in the night.

She tried to sit up. She was still groggy — had the doctor given her something last night? She couldn't really remember. It was all a fuzz ... then events came back into focus.

Reggie, white-faced, shocked at what had happened, declaring that he'd left the lift working properly, but locked it up all right and tight ... the police taping off the lift, talking about taking finger prints, and another policeman tight-lipped, listening to her story ... the police doctor testing her reflexes and someone photographing her bruises and then ... yes, giving her a pill to take.

She remembered Judith appearing in the doorway, hand to mouth, weeping, saying that Craig had disappeared. Something about a motorbike? It seemed that Reggie, Hodge, and Craig had been clearing away chairs when Patrick had phoned down to say Minty had nearly been killed in the lift. Craig had overheard. Craig had disappeared.

Judith, shaking her head, saying she didn't know where he'd gone. The police were looking for him.

Minty managed to get her eyes to focus on her watch. It was late, nearly nine o'clock. She staggered into the bathroom, showered, felt marginally better. Pulled on jeans and a sweater. Craved black coffee. Bother. No ground coffee. Made some instant. Drank it. Wasn't hungry. Made two more cups of instant coffee. Her head was full of cotton wool.

Where was Patrick? It was urgent that she speak to him. If she'd been killed in the lift the previous night, he'd never have known why she'd been pushing him away all these months. He deserved to know. She ought to have told him ages ago. She must tell him, now!

She quailed at the thought of how he'd react, but it must be done.

Only, where was he? Had he gone back to the cottage? No, he wouldn't leave her to face this alone. He'd be in his den, of course.

He wasn't there. Nothing seemed to have been touched since her last visit there.

He wasn't in any other room in their suite. So he must be in the chapel.

Patrick was sitting in his usual chair, a Bible at his side and his head in his hands. He looked up when she came in. "Feeling better?"

She didn't know how to begin. She nodded. Handed him a mug.

"Have they found Craig?" She hated herself for making small talk, but she didn't know how to start making her confession.

He shook his head, sipping coffee. "They took Judith down to the police station to question her. I suppose they could charge her as an accessory."

She slid into the chair beside him. "I don't want her charged. She was afraid of him and of what he might do."

"She started it. She must take her share of the responsibility."

"She cried real tears."

"For him? Is she capable of remorse, or of love?"

"I hope so." Minty sipped her own coffee. Set the mug down on the floor. "Are the twins all right?"

"They've been looking at the cows from the safety of their bed-room window. They say they might want to visit the farm again, but they're not sure. Ralph did wake in the night, but Gloria gave him a hug and he went off to sleep again."

"I feel dreadful about leaving them, but they are safer there, aren't they?"

He nodded. "I'm pulling a team off an old house I'm rebuilding to go over everything here, make sure it's safe. The police are coming back this morning to examine the lift and to take your statement. Reggie's told Clive to get on to the lift people and get them to come over and assess the damage. I phoned Chef and told her what's happened, and she's having someone come in early to make us breakfast."

"You always know what to do in an emergency." She heard the sarcasm in her voice and could have bitten her tongue. "Sorry. Didn't mean it that way." She put her hand within his, because he'd left it lying near enough so that she could.

She nerved herself to confess. "Patrick, I've something important to say ..."

It appeared that he didn't want to hear it. "Can't it wait?"

"No. It's waited far too long already. I need to explain. I don't expect you to understand, really, because it's ... because I got it all wrong. Could you ... could you hold me tightly, please?"

She slid onto his knee. He held her fast, her head on his shoulder. She twisted her fingers into the back of his sweater, holding onto him as if she could wind herself into the very heart of him, so that he could never walk away from her again. "You know we always said we wanted a big family ...,"

"Useful to live in a big house when you want a big family."

"Well, I did, too. For ages. Even after the twins were born, I thought the same way. Only, when I started looking after them myself, I got too tired, and although I knew you still wanted to have more children, I began to dread the idea of getting pregnant again."

He seemed to have stopped breathing. What would she do if he was angry with her? She couldn't bear the thought of his being angry with her. And yet she deserved that he should be.

She forced herself to go on. "I tried to make myself want them. Sometimes I succeeded, but often I didn't. Only, I couldn't tell you because you were so looking forward to having more babies. I began to feel guilty about it, and then I got angry—not with me, but with you—trying to blame you for not understanding, when it really was all my fault."

He still seemed to be holding his breath.

"So … I … gradually … not really thinking about it … I sort of avoided going to bed at the same time as you. I was always tired. That was an excuse, but it was also true. I'm really, really sorry." She braced herself. "If you can forgive me, then of course we must have another baby as soon as we can."

He dumped her on the floor.

She was shocked. Patrick wasn't a violent man, but that had been a very violent reaction.

He stood up and brushed himself down. In a carefully controlled voice he said, "I don't think I've ever wanted to hit a woman before." He wasn't looking at her.

She clung to his nearest leg, just as the twins did. And said nothing at all. She could feel him tremble at her touch. He said, "Let go of me."

She shook her head and clung more closely.

He said, "Not in here, Minty. Not in here."

His mobile rang, and he answered it. "My team have arrived. I must go and let them in. They'll go through everything, see if there are any more booby traps. We can have breakfast down in the restaurant, if you'll let go of me."

"Do you hate me?"

"No, of course not." His voice was cold. He picked up his empty mug. "Did you make us coffee in our kitchen? Well, at least the kettle seems to be all right."

She released him, and he left her sitting in the chapel.

She would have wept, if he'd still been there to see.

She looked up at the cross on the altar. The chapel was the heart of the house, and at the heart of their relationship.

Dear Lord above, show me how to get through to him. I suppose I ought to be praising You and thanking You, but ... I'm a bit stuck. I can't believe I'm still alive and warm, and I've actually managed to confess, even though ... he will come round, won't he? He won't shut me out for ever?

And I do thank You and praise You for keeping the twins safe, for good people to look after them. And, please ... don't forget to tell me what I ought to do about the Hall.

About Judith — why do I feel so sorry for her, when really she could be plotting my death at this very minute? But no. I don't think she is. Look after her.

Craig. Oh dear. I sense so much violence and anger ... but not that terrible, choking evil that surrounded Judith before. I wish him well, and I pray that he comes to no harm.

And my beloved husband, keep him in Your hands.

I'm in such a muddle.

Her thoughts went off at a tangent. Her bruises hurt. She was sitting twisted in her chair. She was incredibly hungry.

The morning sun broke through the clouded sky and filled the chapel with its radiance.

Perhaps he'll forgive me, in time. Do You forgive me, Lord?

Hustle and bustle. Workmen, testing, probing ... the freezer had been turned off and the door wedged open. The contents were spoiled and would have to be dumped. Petty malice on Craig's part. They had very little food in the flat. They'd have to eat in the restaurant. As if that were a hardship!

The police taped off the lift and the stairs from the tower office, so everyone had to use the stairs at the other end of her rooms. She took a load of spoiled food down to dump it in the refuse containers at the back of the restaurant. There'd been a hard frost in the night, and her breath steamed in the air.

She saw Patrick, unsmiling, consulting Reggie and Chef in the courtyard. Patrick hadn't shaved that morning and was wearing good but ancient casual gear; not that that mattered. It was obvious, looking at him, who was the real Master of the Hall. He had a hundred business affairs of his own to attend to and he didn't interfere often at the Hall, but when he lifted his little finger, everyone jumped to attention.

Minty hovered, hugging herself against the cold. She found herself included in the group but couldn't understand what they were talking about, something about codes and updating systems. She wanted to weep but wouldn't give in. She went back upstairs for a jacket and another load of spoiled food. She wondered what would have happened if she'd refused Judith a job.

The people who serviced the lift arrived, but the police said they weren't allowed to touch it till after they'd finished their work. Minty directed them to the restaurant and phoned down to Chef, asking her to provide them with a free breakfast.

A policewoman accosted Minty, suggesting they go into the restaurant so that Minty could give her a statement. Chef plonked food and coffee in front of Minty and the policewoman. The policewoman seemed to be on Minty's side this time. Minty ate about half of the food Chef put in front of her, but the policewoman made appreciative noises and finished off her plateful. The restaurant wasn't officially open, but people kept wandering in and asking if Chef would oblige with this and that ... and Chef beamed and came up with the goods.

Minty wandered outside again. Patrick had disappeared, as had Reggie. Flakes of snow whirled into the courtyard but didn't settle.

Tourists wouldn't start arriving till noon, but the cleaning teams were going in and out. Doris and her new helper were taking delivery of boxes of Christmas decorations at the gift shop, while Hodge the gardener was backing in a truck containing freshly cut Christmas trees, produce of the estate, to stack against the wall. People came from miles around to get one of their trees. Minty thought she might as well make herself useful and offered to help, but Hodge told her not to bother dirtying her clothes and he could manage by himself.

He swung the largest trees around as if they were matchsticks. She retreated, feeling useless. It occurred to her that the courtyard was going to get too crowded if they did open a kiosk there while Hodge was taking up room with his trees for sale ... and then there were his home-grown vegetables and potted plants. Could they find an alternative place for him to sell his produce? And could she trust him to take money and hand it over?

Yes, she rather thought she could. In the old days he'd sold estate produce on the side and pocketed the money, but that had been before Minty took over, when he'd been living on an inadequate wage. He'd been loyal to her ever since. Yes, she rather thought she could trust him now.

Judith, looking older and more careworn after her night at the police station, was decanted from a police car and scuttled along to her caravan with her head down.

A policeman went by on his walkie-talkie. Minty overheard him say that Craig's motorbike had been found at the railway station above the village. He might be anywhere in the country by now.

The police forensic team said they'd finished, so the people who serviced the lift went in to see what they could do.

Minty found a sheltered corner and rang the twins on her mobile. They squeaked and shrilly laughed and told her that they'd gone right up to a big big horse and the farmer had put Ralph on its back and he was so high up it was higher than the clouds, higher than a mountain even, and then Petronella had said she wanted to go up there, too, and she'd sat behind Ralph and she hadn't cried.

Toby Wootton arrived and stopped by Minty long enough to say he'd told his mother that they were not reprinting the brochure, and that she was pleased because she didn't like what was in the Chinese Room, either. He said Venetia would be briefing the stewards about it this morning before they opened the house for the day.

A grocer's van appeared, and the driver exchanged friendly insults with Hodge.

Clive and Iris were expected to be on duty at weekends, but a pile of mail arrived for the Estate Office, which wasn't open on a Saturday. Minty took it in. Kitchen staff arrived. The loos were cleaned.

There was no sign of Patrick, and somehow she didn't feel inclined to ask anyone where he might be. The stewards were arriving in dribs and drabs.

Venetia did stop by Minty long enough to say, in a worried tone, "Toby said you won't reprint the brochure, and I think you're right. I suggest we close down the Chinese Room for the time being. I'll get them to turn the lights off in there, say it's being revamped, hustle people through. Any idea what we can put in there instead?"

"I thought I'd go on a treasure hunt this afternoon. We hardly know what's been stored in the basement and on the top floor in the east wing. We should be able to find enough good furniture to dress the room again."

Venetia's frown cleared. "Good idea. I've got to go to town this afternoon, but I could be back in time to help you in the early evening. I'll ask around, see if any of the stewards would be free, too." She hurried off into the house.

No one else needed her help, or asked her opinion. She might as well not be there. More flakes of snow fluttered through the air. The restaurant was doing a roaring trade. Delicious aromas of cooking seeped out ... hot breakfasts, soup ... good coffee ...

Hodge trolleyed in pots of flowering azaleas and cyclamens from the greenhouses, setting them up for sale on trestle tables outside the gift shop. Minty helped him display them to advantage. "Where's your nephew? Doesn't he usually help you?"

Hodge grunted. "Gone all arty-farty. Making holly wreaths, back of the big greenhouse. Thinks it'll impress little Miss Daydream in the shop."

"Good idea. It probably will."

"Leaves me short-handed. That Craig, not much notion of what hard work means, but I could have taught him."

"You know what he's been doing?"

"I told him, 'There's a good job here for you if you want it, but you lay off our Minty.' Scared of his own shadow one minute, and boasting what he can do the next. Seems his father used to tan his backside something wicked. My father used to tan my backside regular, but it never did me no harm. The young think the world owes them a living, without their lifting a finger."

"He'll be back, won't he?"

"Where else will he go? Back before nightfall, I shouldn't wonder. Now you clear off and let me do this my way."

He reorganised what she'd arranged, and Minty, chastened, looked for something else to do.

Ah, there was Clive Hatton striding into the courtyard, immaculate as always. "Are the police still here? Have the lift people finished yet? Can't we get them out of sight before the first visitors arrive?"

Iris wasn't with him. Why not?

Chef disentangled herself from her kitchen to speak to him, and Minty joined them. Chef talked at Clive, and for once he listened. Minty went along for the ride, nodding now and then, listening to them both. She felt numb. Wondered if her hearing might have been affected by all she'd been through. Clive was opening and shutting his mouth, and for all the good that did, he might as well have been a goldfish in a bowl.

Minty pressed her hands over her mouth, fearing hysteria.

Chef was prodding Clive with her forefinger, and Clive was giving way. Clive was being overruled. Clive wasn't his usual bombastic self. Was he actually going to listen to reason for once?

No, that was unfair.

Minty heard herself say in a bright voice, "Then that's all settled? Chef contacts someone to act as sous chef. We reopen the old kitchen so that Chef can provide food for functions from there. Next, we find somewhere else for Judith to work, and fit out that small office next door to the kitchen to serve as a kiosk with a window onto the courtyard from which to serve extra teas and coffees. Well done, Clive."

Clive harrumphed and departed.

Chef put her arm round Minty, gave her a hug, then hustled off to her kitchens.

Minty said aloud, "I don't think I'm functioning very well today."

The police congregated in the courtyard, told her that a cable which went over a flywheel at the top of the lift had frayed and broken. The firm who serviced the lifts ought to have spotted it, and Minty might have a claim against them because of it. They'd taken photographs but were writing it off as an accident, and were now off.

Minty wasn't sure whether to believe it was an accident or not. Probably not. But ... without proof, what could she do? Reggie paused on his way through to say he and Patrick were altering all the security codes for the building. Patrick was currently retrieving Minty's belongings from the lift, unless she wanted him for anything else, no?

She shook her head. What she wanted was a quiet time with Patrick, but it seemed she'd have to wait for that. The foreman of the lift-servicing team came out for a quick word. The damage to the lift itself wasn't as bad as it might have been because there was a fail-safe mechanism or brake or something that had slowed the lift's downward progress, but of course the cable would have to be replaced. They couldn't understand how it had happened that it had got through their last service, and they were going to have a word with someone about that. He couldn't promise to get it working again for maybe anything up to a fortnight. Maybe longer.

She asked, "Was it sabotaged?"

He shrugged. "Looks like ordinary wear and tear, though I admit it's not usual for the cable to part so completely."

She nodded and thanked him. She still had the feeling that it had been interfered with, but at least the lift being out of commission solved the problem of the twins getting out that way.

The foreman of Patrick's builders' team appeared and said the kitchen seemed all right now, but they'd hardly started on the rest and had already found exposed wires from a plug connecting the television, which would have given her a nasty shock if she'd turned it on. Had the children been playing with it? It looked as if they had. They were going to have a break and get back to it again in a while. He ushered his team into the restaurant, loudly demanding sustenance.

A few flakes of snow drifted into the courtyard, and Minty turned up the collar of her jacket.

Chapter Nineteen

Minty wandered along the courtyard, turned into the alley by the cottages, and stopped short. Reggie's cottage was silent, but Iris' next door showed signs of life. Minty could see a television screen shimmer and flash through the window.

Iris never took time off, unless she was ill or . . .

No, she wasn't with Clive. Clive had been all by himself today.

Last night Iris had declared she and Clive were getting married before Christmas. Clive hadn't given the idea a rapturous welcome, but he hadn't denied it, either. It might be worthwhile finding out what had happened between the two of them after Minty had left.

She knocked on the door, and Iris let her in. Iris was frowning, immaculate as always in her black and white office gear, but without her shoes. Minty stepped from the alley straight into the sitting room, which Iris had decorated in cool colours and modern pieces of furniture.

"I wondered if I could cadge a cuppa," said Minty. "Everyone's so busy this morning. Everyone but me."

Iris gestured to the coffee table, on which sat a cafetière of coffee, two bone china teacups and saucers, and a plate of biscuits. Also Iris' mobile phone. Had she been expecting Clive?

Iris resumed her seat and picked up the remote control for the television. She muted the sound but started channel hopping. Minty had never known Iris to watch television during the daytime before.

Minty helped herself to coffee and a biscuit. The coffee was cold. She remembered Serafina warning her that too much coffee was bad for her, and she sent up an arrow prayer that Serafina's journey back to her roots should go well.

Minty looked at Iris' calm profile and wondered how to get through to her. There was no engagement ring on her finger, but then Clive had hardly had time to get her one. Minty tried out various congratulatory noises in her mind and rejected them all. Iris was not giving the impression of a happy bride.

"Are congratulations in order, then?"

Iris sighed, blinked. Was that a tiny shake of her head? She switched to another channel on the remote.

Minty replaced her cup on its saucer on the table. "If you'd like to talk ...?"

Another tiny shake of the head.

"There really is no reason why women shouldn't propose to men nowadays, is there? I had hard work to get Patrick to accept me."

Iris muttered something about that being different.

"Well, we were childhood sweethearts." Minty told herself not to let her thoughts stray to Patrick's present coldness, but to concentrate on Iris.

Iris sighed. Flicked the television off. Decided to talk. "Clive took it well, in a way. Downed a schooner of whisky, said his father was going to live for ever and his elder brother would inherit, so he didn't suppose it mattered if he did marry me. He said you'd be bound to give us a good house to live in, you being so fond of me and all."

Minty bit off the words, "Hardly romantic!" But then, Clive didn't love Iris. He probably didn't love anyone except himself. "And now ...?"

Iris flicked the television on again. "I could say I'm over the moon with happiness, but you'd see through that, wouldn't you? I felt—I still feel—humiliated."

"It's what you've wanted for ever."

"And now I've got it, I don't want it, okay? If I'd had a gun or a knife in my hand, I'd have killed him, I think. Luckily I hadn't. He reached for the whisky bottle again, and I walked out."

Minty sat back in her chair. So that was it? There was nothing so perverse as a woman who'd got what she'd wished for. Except, of course, that Iris hadn't got what she'd wanted, which was for Clive to return her love. Iris knew very well that Clive didn't love her. Ouch. Not nice.

Iris turned the sound up on the television. A squeaky cartoon. Not really her kind of thing. Minty waited. Perhaps Iris would open up, and perhaps she wouldn't.

The cartoon ended and Iris flicked the sound off, while keeping her eyes on the silently gesticulating figures on the screen. "Do you want to say 'I told you so'? You'd be within your rights. I knew he was a weak man and only capable of loving himself. I've seen the real thing often enough to know the difference. I've watched Carol and Toby circling round one another; it won't be long before they make a match of it. I've seen the loving care my father has always given my mother. I've seen you and Patrick light up when you meet. I've been wild with envy when I've seen you or Patrick lifting the twins to cuddle them. That's what I want out of life."

"No one's perfect." Minty was cautious. "Clive's a good Administrator, within limits. We'd find it hard to get anyone better."

"I've been sitting here, half hoping that he'll come bursting through that door with his arms outstretched, saying he really does love me. I made coffee for him, rehearsed what I'd say. It won't happen. He doesn't love me, Minty. He'd have married me, cold-bloodedly, to save his job. Part of me despises him for it. I'm working hard on that part. I'm worth more."

Minty nodded. "You certainly are."

"That's what Neville Chickward says."

Minty blinked. Iris hadn't begun to spend time with Neville, had she?

With a steady hand, Iris poured herself out a cup of cold coffee. It was a symbolic act, because both cups—which had been put out for

Clive's appearance—had now been used. Iris was making a definite move away from the past.

She sipped her coffee, her eyes on her mobile. "Once a month Clive visits his father. He's never suggested taking me. Some time ago I agreed to go out with Neville for a meal on those occasions. At first I went thinking to make Clive jealous. That didn't work, did it? What did work was that I discovered what it was like to be valued by a good man who has never once tried to overstep the mark. And yet I know that if I only lifted a finger ..."

"Iris, no! I know you've been badly hurt, but you mustn't take Neville on the rebound. He doesn't deserve that."

"No, he doesn't." Iris set down her cup. "You may be surprised to hear that I value his friendship too much for that, too. I knew he was going to be up in London this weekend, but I rang him after I'd walked out on Clive last night, and told him what had happened. We talked for hours. He says he's willing to take a chance, if I am. I admire and respect him. He knows everything about me, the good and the bad.

"Clive doesn't even remember my birthday. Neville's never forgotten it, and he's such good company. I enjoy being with him. Lately I've begun to look forward to our meetings. We can talk about anything. We laugh at the same things. Neville wants the same things out of life as I do. We're going to give it six months, take it slowly, see if anything develops between us."

Minty pushed back her hair from her face. "Iris, you can't just switch his emotions on and off like that. Another thing: Neville's a Christian."

"And I'm not? He's been talking to me about that, about what it means to him. He's no pushover, you know. He made it clear that he would want me to think about it seriously. I tried to talk to Clive about it, but ..." She gave a hard little laugh. "Clive isn't interested. I've gone on thinking about it, though, about people I know who are Christians, and the difference it makes to their lives. Particularly Neville, who is the kindest, most thoughtful of men. Then there's you and Patrick, Serafina and Chef, Reggie and even that old scoundrel Hodge. None of you go on about your faith, but you act it out, don't you? Look how you were about Judith Kent. And about the fake furniture."

Minty tugged at her hair, trying to concentrate. "Yes, but ... could you love Neville, really, the way a woman should love a man? I mean, he's not exactly handsome, is he?" She meant that Neville's fair hair was gradually thinning on top, and he seemed to be taking a larger size in suits every year.

Iris smiled. "Neville's all right. And when I have the job of looking after him ..." She blushed, and busied herself clattering the cups and saucers together to hide it.

Minty sat back in her chair, marvelling. Iris was actually ready to fall in love with Neville. Who'd have thought it? "And Clive?"

"I'm going to have to tell him that I've changed my mind. I do see that this might make things difficult for you. Do you want me to resign? You need to keep Clive, don't you?"

"I don't want you to resign. I need you to help me sort out the brochure, banish the fakes, and find new stuff to put in their place. There's no way I want to lose you, Iris. As for Clive, I think I'm a little sorry for him. I'll ask Patrick if we should advertise for someone else, but on the whole, if only Clive will agree to listen to me now and then, I think I'd like to keep him. If it's not too uncomfortable for you."

"Awkward, but by no means impossible," said Iris. Her mobile rang. She checked the display and accepted the call. "Neville? I'm all right, really." She was smiling, yet tears began to slide down her cheeks. "I thought you said you'd be tied up in meetings all day today."

Minty tiptoed out, wondering whether she felt more like crying or laughing, and came face to face with Clive.

"Morning, Minty. My bride-to-be hasn't turned up for work this morning. Is she within?" He was jaunty, but perhaps a little nervous, too.

For a second, Minty wondered whether to tell him that Iris didn't want to see him, but then she held the door open for him to enter. Iris had to make her own decisions. Minty sent up a quick prayer: *Please, Lord, guide her to the right man.*

Where was her own man? She wanted Patrick so badly it hurt—along with all her bruises—but it might be best to let him be for the time being. Minty remembered Judith making for her caravan, moving like an old woman. Someone ought to be with her. Minty knocked on the caravan door.

Judith opened it, looking grey and drawn. She probably hadn't had any sleep last night. "Have they found him?"

"They found his bike up by the station, but not him. May I come in?"

Judith stood aside to let Minty enter. They sat opposite one another. Judith had a mug of tea before her. She offered one to Minty, who shook her head.

"Why should you care?" said Judith. "He's done his best to kill you, and he may still want to do so, for all I know."

"Mm. Scary. Well, it's up to you to stop him, or he'll end up in jail."

"I did try." Judith looked exhausted. "He rang me on my mobile while I was at the police station. I did my best to get him to turn himself in. He wouldn't listen. I handed over my mobile to the police inspector, asked him to have a go. I'd rather Craig were caught now and jailed for assault, rather than have him left free to murder you and end up with a life sentence."

"So would I," said Minty, trying to laugh. "Hodge thinks he'll be back here before nightfall."

Judith took off her glasses and rubbed her eyes. "I've been trying to pray for him. The words are there in my head, but they don't mean anything."

The hairs rose on the back of Minty's neck. "Do you think you're under attack, Judith? The powers of darkness fight hard to reclaim a lost soul. You have asked Jesus to forgive you for what you've done in the past, and to make you one with Him?"

"I've asked, but He's not listening. Why should He listen to me, anyway?"

"That's the devil dripping poison into your ear. Remember that Jesus is far more powerful than all the evil in the world. You have asked Jesus into your life, haven't you? Well, then. Nothing and no one can separate you from the love of God—unless you yourself wish it."

"I ... don't ... wish ... it."

Minty took Judith's hands and held them firmly in hers. "Then I'll pray with you now. Dear Lord Jesus, You have promised that where two or more of us are gathered together in Your name, You will be there, too. We are in desperate need of Your ..."

There was a knock on the caravan door, and a well-loved voice asked if Judith was in.

Minty started. Patrick? He'd come looking for Judith?

Judith withdrew her hands from Minty. A sea change came over her. She smiled, visibly drawing on her resources to banish her depression. Even as Minty watched, Judith seemed to grow taller, her lips lifting in a self-conscious smile. She undid a button at her neckline and fluffed out her hair.

"I'll be with you in just a minute." Judith's voice was low, caressing. She smiled at Minty. "Now it's your turn to listen and learn!" She pulled Minty up and whirled her into the tiny shower area. Minty, taken by surprise, careened off the wall and slid to the floor, half stunned. The air smelled of shampoo.

It took a moment or two for her to realise where she was, and as she did so, she heard the latch click. Struggling to her feet in that confined space, she tried the handle. Had she been locked in? No, surely the catch must be on the inside? She must be turning the handle the wrong way. She turned it the other way, but still the door refused to open. She pressed her ear to the door, and through it she heard Judith invite Patrick inside. She drew in her breath, prepared to scream to him for help.

Patrick wouldn't realise he'd walked into the lioness' den. He'd turned Judith down once, but that was before Minty had driven him out. This time, Minty didn't know how he'd react. Judith could be seductive. Suppose he allowed himself to be attracted to her? If he did, could she blame him? Perhaps his Christian principles would protect him, but ... suppose he felt so bitter about Minty that he forgot them? It would be all her own fault if he fell for Judith.

Minty could have wept with frustration. Should she yell for help? Or pray for it? Yes, she could do that. And pray for Patrick, too. *Dear Lord above ...*

She could hear them clearly enough.

Patrick said, "Someone said Minty came this way."

"Been and gone. I'm so glad you came. I was beginning to give way to despair. And then you came. Oh, Patrick, I'm so afraid!" Judith's voice throbbed with feeling.

"So am I. But I don't think we're afraid of the same thing."

"If it weren't for you ... but now you've come to my rescue ... oh, hold me tightly!"

Minty tensed.

Patrick's tone didn't alter. "Are you going to faint? Sit down. That's it. Put your head between your knees. Shall I fetch you a glass of water?"

"No. No, I'm not feeling faint, or not exactly. Give me your hand. I feel so ... lost. Everyone looks at me as if ... but I had no idea that Craig would ... I know I can count on you, can't I?"

"It depends what you want. When did you eat last?"

"I was afraid you wouldn't come, that they'd somehow keep us apart."

"Do you need a doctor?"

"No, no. Just you, Patrick. Just you."

Silence. Minty screwed her fists up, holding them against her mouth. How could Patrick refuse Judith in this mood? In any mood.

Yet it seemed that he could. His tone was as measured and as courteous as if he were in court. "I'm sorry to disappoint you, but ..."

"Don't say that. I know you desire me. I've seen it in your eyes. I know you've always been loyal to that pale wife of yours, but she doesn't need you any longer, and I do. Oh, I need you so much, Patrick. I hunger for you."

Still Patrick failed to catch fire. "I realise most men would be thrilled to hear you say this, but ... well, the fault is mine, entirely."

"Fault?" The beautiful voice lost some of its mellowness. "What do you mean?"

Patrick hastened to explain. "Not your fault. Of course not. But I expect you've noticed that men and women tend to admire their physical opposites."

"You mean that my looks don't appeal to you?" Yes, the voice was definitely becoming ragged.

"You are a very beautiful woman." He said this as if he were reciting from the telephone book. "As I said, the fault is mine entirely."

"What's wrong with me? Is it the way I'm dressing now? Or the colour of my hair? Am I not glamorous enough for you? I promise you, all that can be changed in half an hour."

"No, no." Patrick was almost laughing, indulgent. "I'm sure you're most men's dream. It's just that to me ... well, there's really no need to go into details, is there? I wonder where Minty went to?"

"Tell me!" There was iron in the voice now.

"Mm? Oh, it's nothing important. You've a figure to delight clothes designers everywhere. Now, if you don't mind, I really think that I ..."

"You mean, not enough bust?" Judith was outraged.

"Something like that. Put it down to my being a very odd sort of person. Did you hide Minty in the bedroom?"

Silence. "In the shower. The door sticks."

Minty kicked the door, turning the handle at the same time. And it gave way.

"Ah, there you are." Patrick gave her a cool nod and held the door of the caravan open for her. Judith turned her head away as Minty passed her by.

Once outside, a swirl of snow nearly blinded her. Patrick put his arm about her shoulders. "It's bedlam up at the house. Let's go where we can be quiet for a bit, right?"

He rushed her — not back to the house, but round the corner into the lee of the walled garden. The snow was beginning to lie on the ground, and a gusty wind was blowing it into their faces.

Double doors led into the walled garden from the visitor parking lot. Patrick wrestled one open, and they passed inside. The snow lay thinly on the ground inside, and they crunched over it to the warmth and peace of the largest of the greenhouses, half filled with cyclamens, chrysanthemums, and Christmas cacti which Hodge had grown for sale.

There were the remnants of holly wreaths on part of the staging, where Hodge's nephew had been creating works of art, but the place was deserted.

Minty inhaled the scents of winter flowering plants as they stamped snow off their feet and loosened their jackets.

She was uncertain of his mood. "You handled Judith well. You knew I was there?"

"Hodge told me he'd seen you go into the caravan and not come out. He was worried about you."

They were awkward with one another.

She said, "I didn't mean to eavesdrop. She took me by surprise, rushed me into the shower, and then I couldn't get out. When you came, she was trying to pray, and failing. I ought to have been able to help her, but I'm not much good at this soul rescue business. Perhaps I ought to get my uncle onto it."

"I'll ask him if he can spare the time. Do you want to spend the weekend at the cottage with the twins?" He was treating her as distantly as he'd treated Judith, and it hurt.

"I want to be here with you. Or rather ... yes, I want to be with them, but ..." She pushed her hair back. "I'd rather be with you. If you'll let me."

Silence. He was looking away from her. She told herself to take it slowly. He wasn't ready to hear her speak of love yet. What else could she talk about? "Another thing: I need to look through the stuff that's been stored upstairs and in the basement, to refurnish the Chinese Room."

"Yes. Venetia told me. I should think everyone in the house and village will know that's what you want to do by the time the house closes for the night. It's very dark down in the basement. Who's going to guard your back?"

Now it was her turn to be silent. If he didn't volunteer, how could she ask him?

She touched his sleeve, where snowflakes were shining on the fabric.

"Patrick? Forgive me?"

He put his arm around her and she turned into his shoulder. In a muffled voice she said, "I really am sorry. I've been a bad wife."

He held her fast. "I ought to have worked it out, but I was always afraid you'd go off me one day, and that's what it looked like."

"I don't think my fear of another pregnancy is something that would occur to a man."

"I dreamed of having a big family because I was an only child. I never looked at it from your point of view."

"It was cowardly of me not to tell you."

"We don't need to have more ..."

She put her fingers over his lips, steeling herself to say the right thing. "Yes, I would like to, one day. But perhaps not straight away?"

"We could leave it to God's timing, not ours."

She wasn't sure that God would be on her side in this, but she nodded anyway. She tried to lighten up. "I don't know why you put up with me. I dragged you here to live when you'd have been happy to live in some ordinary house ..."

"I'm happy to live anywhere so long as I have you and the twins. I ought to have been praising God for setting my feet in such a pleasant place, instead of which I was always asking for more. The twins should be enough for anybody, and I've grown to love the Hall. I let you carry too great a burden far too long, just because ... inverted pride, I suppose. I didn't want anyone to think I was trying to take over. I should have stepped in to help you long ago. Stupid of me."

She took his free hand in both of hers, and put it to her lips. "So will you help me run the Hall now?" Her hands wanted to wander over his face, re-acquainting themselves with what had once been so familiar to her, the sharp tilt of dark eyebrow, the clever, mobile mouth, the upright line of concentration between his eyes.

He took her hands in both of his and kissed the fingertips. "I've been praying about this. I think the answer is no. Advice, yes. Action, no."

She didn't like that. For a second she allowed herself to be angry that he wouldn't help her—and then she saw the trap and avoided it just in time. "I'm desperate enough to take what I can get." She freed her hands and pulled him down gently to kiss his lips. How sweet they tasted, and how long was it since she'd kissed him properly? He picked her up and set her on the staging, moving some of the flame-like flowers of the cyclamens to one side.

"I do love you, you know," she said.

His breathing quickened. "Minty, this is not the time and place ..."

"When do you have to go back to Brussels?"

"Monday morning first thing. Perhaps I can put it off ..."

"No, you mustn't. I'll be all right, now we're all right."

He touched her cheek lightly, holding himself back. "You're a mass of bruises, which makes me very angry and reminds me that I haven't yet thanked God properly for keeping you comparatively unharmed."

His mobile squawked and he answered it. "My men have finished checking out our rooms, and they say everything else is as it should be except for the plug on the television set, which they've replaced. It's safe to go back."

"Do we bring the twins back? I miss them dreadfully, but ..."

"We'll leave them there till Craig's been dealt with. You don't mind that I created a bolt-hole for us for weekends?"

"It's a brilliant idea."

Chapter Twenty

A squeaking trolley announced Hodge's return to the greenhouse. Patrick and Minty exchanged rueful glances at being interrupted. He lifted her off the staging and set her on her own feet.

Hodge said, "So that's where you two have been hiding, eh? You can name your next child after me, right? Such ructions with Clive and Iris. She threw him out and chucked coffee after him. Splashed from head to foot, he was!" He harrumphed with laughter. "Serve him right!"

Minty put her hands over her mouth. "Oh, dear. He's such a proud man, he'll never get over it."

Patrick's lips twitched. "Minty, it sounds as if you have to soothe some ruffled feelings."

Hodge was piling more plants onto his trolley. "Drat this weather! Sales will be right down if the snow settles."

Minty tried to tame her wild hair. She needed a mirror and a hard brush. What must she look like? "Hodge, do you think we should put signs up in the courtyard and in the car park to let visitors buy Christmas trees and everything that you grow from a booth in here? It would save you traipsing everything round to the courtyard all the time."

"Trust me with the takings, will you? Well, why not? But I'll need that Craig to help out, as well as my nephew, right?"

"Talking of your nephew. Where is he?"

"Canoodling with that dolly bird you've got in the gift shop. And her barely out of school, skirt up to here, and neck down to there."

Minty was scandalised. "She's got a boyfriend of her own, hasn't she?"

"A pimply lad, lives with his mother and three younger brothers in a council house. He's nowhere near ready to be wed, and trust me, she is. Now my nephew, he's got his own little house behind the church, that my sister passed on to him when she went into a home. Love's young dream is one thing, but if she's ready to pup, she'll take my nephew within the year, right?"

Minty suppressed a giggle, because Hodge was probably right.

He was looking out through the glass. "The snow's stopped for a bit. Now I've got you two here, there's something I want to show you." He set off without checking that they were following, but of course they did.

Hodge led them through the courtyard and the formal garden, up the slope to the folly on its man-made mound, and over the top to where the crippled oak lay in all its devastation. An icy wind swept up the slope. The Park looked bleak today.

Patrick was frowning. "What is it, Hodge? I thought you'd have cleared the tree away by now."

"You leave him be, and him goes back to nature nicely. I said to Minty, the master's fond of this place, and she'll want to make something of it for him."

Patrick shook his head. "Make a garden here, you mean? I haven't time to tend a garden, Hodge."

"Not a garden. A wood."

Patrick looked stunned. "Hodge, a wood takes years to grow."

"Not if we brings in some mature trees, which I've always wanted to do. And some we transplant from round the Park, at one year old or two. The wildlife would soon follow."

Patrick surveyed the slope below with fresh attention. He smiled, whispering to himself, "Oak, ash, and beech. Glory be."

Hodge gave Minty what was almost a pleading look. "He needs two or three acres from the Park. My granfer said that *his* granfer told him there was a spring up here that fed a stream running down the hill to a big pond. That's where the monks used to keep the fish they needed for their food in the old days. That old pond would be where the lake is now, I reckon. The spring up here is what makes this bit of land no good, now it's all spread out. But if we dig out a course for the water, to make a little stream running this way and that down the hill ..."

"With a pond halfway down, all fringed with trees," said Patrick, in a hushed tone. "And waterlilies. Then there could be a pipe with an overflow into the lake below ..."

"We could start tomorrow, laying out the boundaries. Then we dig out the course of the stream and pond, and work out the line of the paths," said Hodge. "That is, if Minty agrees. Because the Ranger wants this bit to throw into the Home Farm, not that they'd know what to do with it, mind."

"Consider it done," said the Lady of the Hall.

The snow started up again, swirling around them, but as they trudged back to the house, Minty heard Patrick talking to himself. "Hawthorn, blackthorn, and hazel ... honeysuckle and wild briar ... a glade filled with bluebells? Primroses; yes, I think so. A temple to God in the wild."

Minty laughed without sound, tucking his hand within her arm. What pleasure to give such pleasure! She could see that a wood would give Patrick exactly what he needed, a place apart from the world.

Back in the greenhouse, Hodge collected his squeaking trolley and went off, grumbling at the falling snow.

"Best get back," said Patrick. He enclosed Minty in a bear hug, which almost cracked her ribs, before setting her back on her feet. "A wood? Really? I can hardly believe it." He touched the tip of her nose with his finger, and gave her a little push. "You deal with Clive, and I'll catch up with you later. You'll need a new code to get in with. Your birth date this time, day and month."

The snow had more or less stopped by the time she reached the courtyard again. She was surprised to see how many visitors were still around, despite the snow. The restaurant was full with a queue of people waiting for tables, while Hodge was selling Christmas trees as if there were no tomorrow.

She punched in the new code and the door opened into the north wing. Clive wasn't in his office, so where would he be? Hiding his face, thinking that everyone would be laughing at him? She crossed the courtyard thinking that there was something else she ought to be doing apart from finding Clive, but she couldn't think what it was.

Carol. She stopped to phone Carol on her mobile. The snow lay like a thin skin over the courtyard. The water in the fountain in the centre had been turned off for the winter, but Hodge had planted trailing ivies in pots around the rim. It looked good.

"Carol? Minty here. When you've finished at the shop for the day, do you fancy a treasure hunt? I want to have all the dodgy stuff moved out of the Chinese Room, and need replacements. Toby can come, too, if he likes. Bring torches. I suppose you've heard I stopped the new brochure? And of course I'll see you get paid for what you did."

"Toby's just dropped in with the latest gossip. Did Iris really empty a coffee pot over Lord High and Mighty?"

Minty groaned. "Is it all over the village already? I might have known. Poor Clive!"

"Poor Clive, my foot! I wish I'd seen his face. I'll be up later. Wouldn't miss it for anything."

So far, so good. Smiling, Minty accessed the tower and made her way down to the basement. There was no light under the door to the housekeeper's flat. Bother, that meant she was away visiting her sister for the weekend, as she often did. Who else could tell Minty where to find some good furniture?

Clive's flat was the next one along. She knocked on his door. Perhaps he'd been expecting to see Iris, because he opened up with a frown, which only deepened when he saw who it was. He gestured her in, looking over her shoulder into the corridor to see if she was alone.

There was a tumbler of whisky on the table beside his big chair, but he seemed sober enough. He'd changed his clothes since she last saw him, which added strength to the tales she'd been hearing about coffee having been thrown over him.

"Want one?" he reached for the whisky bottle.

She shook her head. He didn't ask her to take a seat, but she did so anyway. "I came to see if you were all right."

He stared at her and through her. Didn't reply.

She sat on her impatience, reviewing what little she knew of him. A younger son, from a county family. Father still alive and kicking. Elder brother due to inherit. Perhaps Clive had been unwise to choose a career where he'd always be serving others, instead of being master? He really wasn't good servant material. Yet in his own way, he'd served her well enough, and he must be feeling humiliated at the moment.

She said, "Clive, I don't want to lose you. I realise this must be a painful time for you, but ..."

He drained his glass and set it back on the table with a click.

Her voice sharpened. "Drinking won't help, Clive. Our previous Administrator used to dip into the bottle. He ended up nearly running over a child in the village and had to resign. I don't want you resigning. I need you to help me out of this nasty hole we're in. The London inventory was faked—don't argue, I can prove it was—but I'll put that out of my mind if you're willing to admit you were misled, and will help me put things right."

He refilled his glass.

She set her teeth, then made herself relax, muscle by muscle. "I'm rather surprised you've kept your relationship with Iris going for so long, but if it is over ..."

He flung his glass into the stone hearth, where it shattered.

Minty raised her eyebrows. "We all have to take responsibility for our own actions. I'm not clearing that broken glass up, and I don't think Iris will, either. Now, there's plenty of good fish in the sea, so to speak, so shall we agree to put this nasty little matter behind us, and move on? I came to ask if you'd join me on a treasure hunt this evening."

"I thought I was sacked."

"Do you want to keep your job?"

He threw his arms wide. "Where else would I go?"

"Then we'll start again, shall we? I'm going to attend all the business meetings in future, and you're going to take on board the decisions that I make, right? You let Iris get on with her life, and find yourself a Hooray Henrietta instead ..."

"A ... what?"

"Sorry. Someone from your own background."

He didn't reply. She got to her feet, thinking she'd handled this badly. "Well, I must be going. I have to dig out some replacement furniture for the Chinese Room. You don't know where any might be, do you? Almost anything in the way of good antiques would do."

His voice was hoarse, but he was trying to follow her lead. "I'll stay on, since you've asked me to do so, but Iris goes and I'm not having Carol up here, either."

"Grow up, Clive. You made a couple of bad mistakes, but you'll get over it. Be gracious and laugh it off. You can do it. And now, have we the housekeeper's telephone number at her sister's? I need to ask her if she knows where I might find some good furniture to replace the fakes."

"Forget it. She's gone up to London for the weekend to do some Christmas shopping. I did ask her to leave me a number where she could be contacted, but she hasn't done so."

"Oh. Well, I'm going to make a start. The sooner we get the fakes out of the way, the better. Now I seem to remember the lighting down in the basement is not particularly good, so if we can find some torches, we'll get to it after the house closes for the day. Half past six, say?"

He nodded. Maybe he'd come, and maybe he wouldn't. But at least she'd tried.

Now, did she have time to drive to the cottage and see the twins before she had to be back for the treasure hunt? Probably not. She longed to be with them. She'd never been apart from them for so long in all their lives. Would her absence give them the feeling they'd been deserted?

She hesitated, wringing her hands. She wondered if she'd time to go up to the chapel to pray for a while. From where she stood in the cloisters, with flakes of snow slowly tumbling to the ground, she imagined the chapel as being the heart of the Hall. Although it was only at the top of one tower, its influence seemed to spread out through the whole. She had the odd fancy that rays of light were spreading out from it, except where small patches of darkness covered the fakes.

Please, dear Lord. Help me to be a better person. To be a better wife to Patrick ... how like him to relinquish his hunger for more children, for my sake. Give me courage to do better, to give him more children if that is Your will. And help me to serve You better. Look after the twins for me?

There hadn't been much praise in that prayer, but Jesus would understand. She recalled that favourite prayer of Patrick's, the one she'd been trying to remember the other day: *Lord, Thou knowest how busy I must be this day. If I forget Thee, do not Thou forget me.* That had come from a famous general on his knees before a battle. She felt as if she were going into battle, too.

What next? Carol's words came back to her, about each generation throwing out the treasures of the previous one. She'd seen for herself how that worked, when she threw out her father's furniture in favour of Patrick's. Who knew what gems the Victorians might have thrown out?

In particular, what furniture had been in the Chinese Room before her grandfather had thrown it out so that he could sleep there in his canopied bed? And where was it now?

The housekeeper wasn't available, but she wouldn't have done the physical shifting of furniture herself, would she? Perhaps Hodge might have helped. Or Reggie?

She ran them to earth in the restaurant, which was still almost full, but serving last orders for the day. The snow had stopped again. Christmas trees, plants, and the latest decorations in the gift shop were flying off the shelves. Chef was nowhere to be seen. She was probably hard at work preparing for that evening's Golden Wedding Anniversary party in the Great Hall. Minty grabbed a plate of food at random and joined Reggie and Hodge at a corner table.

"How's Clive?" asked Hodge, grinning around a giant sandwich.

Minty shook her finger at him. "Don't give him a hard time. He's been humiliated enough as it is. Now, look; I know you've got to clear the trees and the pot plants away yet, and then there's the Great Hall to be got ready for this evening, but I need to get rid of the dicey pieces around the house, and in particular find some good furniture for the Chinese Room. When my family cleared stuff out in the past, do you know where it went? When I first came, I tried to explore everything, but I must admit I didn't get far into the basement."

Reggie shook his head. "I was your father's driver, remember. Hardly around here much."

Hodge slurped tea. "None of the Edens ever threw anything away. I've worked here in the gardens man and boy. So did my father afore me, and his father afore that. They wasn't let in the house much, 'cause there was a big indoor staff in the old days afore the War, but they was useful when it come to shifting old things out to make room for the new. Stuff that was thrown out went down the basement under the north wing and up into the storerooms atop the east wing."

He laughed hoarsely. "My old dad used to tell of a ghost walking down in the cellars, and when he'd got me properly wound up he'd allow it were only the under footman and one of the upstairs maids. Any road, the housekeeper—not this one but the one two times afore her—had a padlock put on the door, and that stopped those goings-on.

"By the time your grandfather died and your mother and father took over, there wasn't much indoor staff, and most of the house was shut up. Your father liked all that newfangled furniture, so your grand-father's bits and pieces—some of it bought by his mother and going back mebbe a hundred years—went up top. I helped move it. Solid stuff, mahogany, mostly. Family mementoes, boxes of old clothes, cur-tains, and the like."

Minty nodded. "I've seen all that. Now Mrs Chickward said my grandfather used to sleep in the Chinese Room on the ground floor in a green canopied bed. Is that right?"

"I took it to pieces myself after he died, and we moved it upstairs next to the room with the old oak four-poster that your father and mother used to sleep in. The curtains were falling to pieces, and your mother had them redone in blue. That bed's still there.

"When your mother died and your stepmother took over, every-thing got changed around again. Lady C wanted to open the house to the public, but instead of foraging in the basement for family antiques, she bought stuff from that tame 'expert' of hers to fill the gaps . . ."

"Which is where we got into trouble," sighed Minty. "He brought in some good things, but some fakes as well."

"Lady C was mad keen to have an Olde Worlde kitchen, but the rooms on the ground floor in the north wing were all being used by the Estate Office and for your father's charity work, so she had to go down into the cellars for her kitchen. She got me to saw off the padlock to the door at the top of the stairs—the key had long since gone miss-ing, and we got in all right. She took a tumble down the stairs, and I thought it was like the old house was taking its revenge on her.

"Now you've got to understand the layout down there. You go down the stairs and you come to three little rooms together. That's where she faked up her kitchen and pantry for the tourists to gawp at. The third room was half full of old pots and pans that weren't no use to nobody, which is what we cleared out to get your father's furniture in.

"Beyond those three rooms, you come up against another gurt big door. Lady C wanted that open to have a look-see beyond, so we sawed the padlock off for her. She didn't look far before saying it was all a load of junk. She had me put another padlock on that door and turned her back on it. There's rooms down there as hasn't seen the light of day for years."

Minty grinned. "Being you, you had a good old nose around first?"

"Dust sheets over most things. Broken bits and pieces. Table tops leaning against the wall. A bear ..."

"A bear?"

"Stuffed. Gave me a turn, I can tell you. Taller'n me. Lotsa stuffed animal heads and fish and birds in cases. Wreaths of flowers, bridal wreaths, maybe. A room full of chairs and tables, everything all mixed up so you can hardly tell what's what. Some rooms you couldn't hardly get in. It's dark down there. One dim light bulb here and there and the rooms go on for ever, right under the north wing and maybe under the Great Hall, too, though I didn't get that far, for there's another locked door as stops you. But dry as a bone. They knew how to build in those days.

"You want to take a look? The key to the padlock on the first door's in my cubby hole at the back of the greenhouse. It'll be labelled, so I should be able to lay my hands on it. I'll rout it out and leave it in the padlock for you."

"Half six, with torches, if you can spare the time."

"Best get going, then."

The staff were clearing people out of the restaurant now. Minty hurriedly ate whatever it was she'd grabbed and fingered her mobile. She'd forgotten something important. What was it?

She hesitated in the courtyard. Hodge and his nephew were clearing away the few unsold plants. Doris in the gift shop was closing up, her young assistant helping her. Minty took a hard look at the girl and silently whistled. Hodge had said the girl had her "skirt up to here, and neck down to there." Minty suppressed a grin, thinking Hodge had been right and the girl was more than ready for marriage.

The snow was lying on the ground, but it was only skin deep.

Minty went round the corner to knock on Iris' door.

"Come in," said Iris, who had changed her clothes for the evening. She was still wearing her favourite black and white, but the office look had been superseded by something softer. Even her haircut seemed less severe than usual.

Minty wouldn't have been surprised to see Neville sitting there, but Iris was alone.

"Neville's collecting me in a minute," said Iris. "I'm sorry I made a scene when Clive came round, but he assumed I could be had for the asking, and I couldn't get him to understand that it was over."

"Did you really empty the cafetière over him?"

There was a guilty silence. "Half a cup of cold coffee, actually. I'm sorry about that. Is he asking for my head on a platter?"

"And Carol's. I told him to grow up, laugh it off, and find himself another girl. I hope he will because I need you both. And Carol, too."

"If it will help, I'll apologise to him."

"Thank you, dear Iris. That would be generous of you."

"I'm only sorry I can't join in the treasure hunt this evening, but Neville says he wants to take me somewhere special. You can borrow my good torch, if you like. I've heard it's haunted down in the basement, though I don't believe that, of course. But there's probably lots of spiders." She shuddered.

Where had Patrick gone? Nobody seemed to know. Iris disappeared. Reggie, Hodge, and his nephew turned their attention to getting the Great Hall cleared and ready for the supper party. Chef's minions melted a pathway over the snow, humping food into the Great Hall. Clive didn't show his face.

Carol came rushing up from the car park just as Toby appeared from the upstairs office to give her a friendly—though not loverly—hug.

Venetia arrived, having returned early from her expedition to town. She had rounded up three of her stewards to help, including—now this was a nice surprise—the knowledgeable steward who'd expressed his doubts about the furniture in the Chinese Room. The stewards were all elderly and wearing clothes too good for tumbling around in the basement.

Minty greeted them all warmly—especially the steward whom Clive had sacked—and asked Venetia to take them up to search through the storerooms in the attics. They promised to make a note of anything they thought might be useful.

Still no Patrick, and neither Reggie nor Hodge were free as yet.

Minty switched on her torch and gestured to Carol and Toby. "Courage! Let's explore!"

Chapter Twenty-One

Minty led the way to the door from which tourists left the Hall at the end of their tour. "So few visitors risk these stairs that I'm wondering if it wouldn't be better to take Lady C's kitchens off the tour."

"I see what you mean." Toby was anxious that Carol shouldn't slip. "Careful! Hang on to me, Carol."

Minty remembered Hodge's story about her stepmother falling down the stairs, and grinned. "Actually, I'm amazed that the Health and Safety people haven't forbidden us to use these steps."

They peered into the first cellar, which housed a reasonably authentic array of old kitchen ware, and had a small pantry leading off it. A dim light came through from windows set high in the wall of the kitchen, which would be at ground level in the courtyard.

Carol wasn't impressed. "Surely the original kitchens would have been up above? These would have been cellars, storerooms, that sort of thing." She caressed the stonework. "This looks older than Jacobean. Much older. Do you think the Hall was built on the remains of an earlier building?"

Minty said, "Patrick thinks there might have been an abbey here at one time. I suppose that if there had been, it would have been destroyed at the Reformation and the stones of the original building reused for other purposes, perhaps in the village. When the Edens bought the land, I suppose they might well have built on the foundations of whatever was here before."

They turned back into the corridor; opposite lay the room where Minty's father's furniture had been laid to rest. They didn't bother with that.

Just as Hodge had said, beyond those three rooms, a padlocked door guarded the entrance to the rest of the basement. The door was several centuries old, its oak planks girded with iron. It was intimidating, and Minty felt duly intimidated. A large padlock hung open on its hasp, though there was no key in it.

Minty wondered if the others felt as daunted as she did. They had certainly fallen quiet. She said, "Shall I lead the way?" She tried to pull the great door open, but it resisted her efforts till Toby helped her. It grated on the stone floor, and they all laughed, made nervous by ... they didn't know what.

"Definitely pre-Elizabethan," said Carol. "Any ghosts around?"

"Whoo-whoo!" Toby gave a bad imitation of a ghost. He put his arm around Carol's shoulders. "Bring on the ghosts. I'll protect you!"

The corridor beyond was in darkness, but an ancient wiring system burst into life when Minty groped for the switch. One low-voltage bulb dangled from a bare wire some way along, and dark doorways led off to left and right.

"Ladies and gentlemen," said Minty, trying to lighten their mood, "you see before you what were once the engine rooms of this great house. As Carol suggested, here are the original butteries, storerooms, and larders from which perhaps forty or fifty people were fed three times a day."

Toby tried to follow her lead. "They drank home-brewed ale then, didn't they? The water wasn't safe."

Carol brushed dust from her sleeve where it had touched a wall. "Aren't there any windows down here? Why is it so dark?"

Minty had forced open the first door on the left and felt for the light switch. There was one, but the light it gave was not cheerful. She shone her torch upwards to where the window onto the courtyard ought to have been, but unfortunately it had been boarded over.

Dust sheets covered piles of broken chairs and stools. Rolls of ragged carpets. Stepladders missing a rung. Boxes of ancient, hand-carved garden tools, grey with dust.

"I suppose we could use some of this to fit out a room somewhere at the back of the house or in the walled garden, to show people what tools the gardeners used to use," said Minty. "Can anyone see anything else of use?"

"Making notes," said Carol, doing just that.

Toby retreated to the corridor and managed to open the next door along. You could hardly move in this room for furniture. More dust sheets. He pulled some off. Six Victorian table tops were revealed. Carol inspected them. "Where are the bases? Some of these could be restored without too much difficulty."

"Here," said Minty, falling over a pile of them. "Oops. Haven't I enough bruises?" She looked back over her shoulder. They couldn't get locked in here, could they? No, Toby had taken the key out of the padlock, hadn't he?

Something slithered along the floor, though it was hard to know which direction it came from. Carol jumped. "I hate rats. And mice."

"It doesn't smell of mice," said Toby, seemingly impervious to atmosphere. "And it's surely too dry for rats?"

Minty found the darkness unnerving. Shadows danced up and down the ceilings as Carol played her torch over her finds.

"Do we want Victoriana?" said Minty, wanting to get out of this room fast. "I'd really like some kind of display which would look at home in the Chinese Room."

Carol was being brave, but her voice cracked. "You don't have to match the wallpaper." She levered up the lid of a trunk. "Velvet curtains. Good velvet. We might make something of these."

Toby whooped. "A rocking horse!"

"The twins would love that," said Minty, trying to be positive.

Toby found a pile of picture frames. Some had paintings in, some didn't. Gesso flaked off as he lifted one.

"I'd better have a look at those in daylight," said Carol.

Toby sneezed. "Dust!"

Minty started. Was that a footfall behind them?

Toby had disappeared back into the corridor and could be heard pounding on the next door. There was the most almighty crash, and both girls jumped.

"Toby!" Carol rushed to rescue him. "Eeeeek!"

"What is it?" Minty edged into the room behind her. And then laughed. Or tried to. In his fall, Toby had pulled the dust sheet off a giant stuffed bear. The one Hodge had mentioned? A great grizzly, possibly from the Rockies of America. Its glass eyes reflected the light, its teeth looked sharp, and its paws were outstretched to grab.

Minty put up a hand to stroke its paw, and it seemed to nod its head towards her. It was leaning forward, perched unevenly on a pile of planks. She attempted a laugh. "Isn't he enormous! I rather like the look of him."

Toby thought it hilarious. "Look what I fell over! A fox in a glass case! Do you fancy decking out the Great Hall with these, Minty?"

"The bear's in pretty good shape," said Minty, fascinated by the huge animal. "Perhaps my grandfather shot him? I wonder how old he is."

Toby was pulling off dust sheets left, right, and centre, to display more glass cases. "Birds and beasts? And yes, isn't this a stuffed pike? These ought to be in a Natural History Museum."

"Could we could turn the Chinese Room into a Victorian gentleman's den?" said Minty. "With all these around the walls? Perhaps not. I don't think the twins would like it."

Carol was clambering over the cases of stuffed animals. "This room goes back a long way. It's bigger than the others, isn't it? What's this? Oh, the top of a roll-top desk, I think. And this is ... a cache of cache pots? Oh, no!" She crowed with laughter. "Minty, come and see. Chamber pots, potties to you, my love. Put one in each bedroom, right?"

Toby was working to dislodge something. "I think this might be part of a bedframe. Are we looking for a bed?"

"How many chamber pots?" Carol was counting. "Three ... four ... that one's broken, what a pity. Is that an embroidered fire-screen over there? We could use that, too. And another one, on a pole. Looks like it's Queen Anne. It's pretty and quite valuable."

Toby was still tugging at his timbers. "Carol, we've got a pile of old junk at home at the top of the Manor house, too. We must have a poke around some day ... ah." He dislodged a timber and held it up. "Solid oak. Heavy enough. This must be from the framework of a big bed, don't you think?"

Shadows shifted across the room, and yet both Carol and Minty were holding their torches steady. Toby had even put his down on the floor while he wrestled with the bedframe. Minty backed into the bear and tried to laugh. "What a place. I don't believe in ghosts, of course, but ..."

"Look, it's a tailor's dummy!" said Carol, prodding at something in the gloom. "Judging by the shape, it's Edwardian. Eeek!"

She threw her torch upwards and a giant spider shape enveloped her from behind. A man-sized spider, dressed from head to foot in black, with a black hood over his face. Launching himself out of the darkness, a glistening sliver of steel in his hand.

Carol screamed.

Minty froze.

Toby acted, swinging the heavy oak beam round to connect with Carol's assailant ... missing his body, but snatching at his upraised elbow ... catching him off-balance, so that he staggered and would have fallen if he hadn't been holding Carol so tightly.

It was Craig, of course. He'd heard Minty would be down here. It was no secret. He'd known where the key to the padlock was, because it was labelled and hanging up in Hodge's sanctum. He must have got in early and lain in wait for them behind the great bear.

In the badly lit room, he'd mistaken Carol's bright red hair for Minty's blonde mop, and his knife was pointing at her throat.

Minty could think of only one thing to do. She stepped forward, shining the torch on her face, trying to keep her voice steady. "You've got the wrong girl, Craig. I'm here if you want to talk to me."

Craig dropped Carol. Toby stumbled forward to pick her up and haul her out of range of Craig's knife.

Carol had dropped her torch when she'd been seized and it lay on the floor, sending a silhouette of the tailor's dummy onto the wall behind it. Toby's torch lay on the floor where he'd left it, pointing under another sheeted pile of furniture.

The strongest light now came from the swinging overhead bulb, disturbed by Craig's leap onto Carol, and from the torch which Minty was pointing up at her own face. Its light blinded her, so that she could no longer see where anyone was.

"What do you want, Craig?" Minty tried to keep her voice low.

A slither of sound. The door to the corridor shut. Minty sent her torch searching for Craig, but he'd already moved on. Then the overhead light clicked off.

"This makes us equal," said Craig, his voice lifting high with excitement. He switched on his own torch, a powerful one. It illuminated Minty, but left the rest of the room in darkness. She put her hand up to shield her eyes, but could see nothing.

She could feel her heart beating strongly, too fast, too fast. Patrick had warned her. "There's nothing equal about one person having a knife and the others being unarmed."

"You're three to one," said Craig. "The knife helps."

"Your sister is worried about you."

"No, she isn't. I told her I'd be back and would even things up for her."

"In what way? Everyone knows I'm down here with my friends."

"Once you're dead, you can't testify against me."

"And my friends?"

"I might let them live, and I might not. It depends. I might just put the padlock back on the outer door and leave them here. Someone will find them before they starve to death, I suppose. It'll give me a head start, anyway."

"You saw the key in Hodge's shed and pinched it?"

"Stupid old fool. Thinks I'm going to slave for a pitiful wage in his garden for the rest of my life. Get real, man. Judith and I are off tonight, to travel the world."

"Using what for money?"

"The treasure you're looking for down here, of course."

Minty would have laughed, if Craig hadn't been so serious. "There's no gold or silver down here, Craig. Only old furniture. That's the treasure I was looking for."

"Wha-a-at?" His screech made her shiver. "You're lying!"

"No, I'm not. Ask Carol. Ask Toby."

"It's true," said Toby. Carol was welded to him. Or he to her. But his voice was steady. "We were looking for things to replace some of the furniture up above. So put the knife down, and let us out of here before the police arrive."

"I put them off the scent by leaving my bike up at the station. They think I'm in London by now."

"Hodge said you'd be back by nightfall," said Minty. "He and Reggie are due down here any minute."

"You're lying again!"

She could see the glint of his eyes in the holes he'd cut in a black hood, and the sheen on his knife as he brandished it, but he himself was part of the darkness behind him.

Toby shifted Carol within his arms, so that he was between her and Craig. The boy whirled round and Toby recoiled, taking Carol back with him.

The moment that Craig's light left her face, Minty stumbled to her left, but was quickly caught in its beam as he heard her move and swung his torch back to her again.

"Well, if there's no treasure, I can at least finish what I started."

He leaped towards Minty, who lifted her arms up to defend herself, knowing it was too little, too late, praying that Patrick would look after the twins for her ...

The door grated open. A powerful torch flooded the room with light, while a dark figure hurtled into the room.

"No, Craig, no!" Judith darted between Minty and her brother, arms outstretched. He couldn't halt his momentum but crashed into her as Minty tried to twist herself sideways out of range of his knife. She half fell, half scrambled into a sheeted pile of furniture, ducking down, looking for a hiding place because the two struggling figures were between her and the door ... Her feet tangled in the dust sheet, bringing her down ... She bumped her head against something hard ... She couldn't see anything but darkness.

Someone screamed. Judith or Craig?

Toby was yelling, "Carol ... this way!"

Minty could hear someone screeching thinly. Judith? Craig was shouting at her. There was a confusion of voices. Someone was shouting, "Minty! Where are you?"

Was it Patrick? Where was he? Why couldn't he see her? Why couldn't she see him?

Oh. She was on the ground, out of sight. But why had everything gone black?

Judith was whimpering. Why?

Craig howled, a horrifying sound.

Her name was being called again, but there was so much shouting going on ... however many people were down here now? She blinked, trying to clear her sight, and realised that something dark had fallen over her head. A dust sheet had descended over her as she twisted and fell, and she supposed, muzzily, that she was now invisible to everyone in the cellar.

She said, "I'm here!" But her voice was lost in the general hubbub.

If she came out from under the dust sheet, would Craig stab her with that lethal knife of his?

She sought for the edge of the dust sheet and lifted it a little way to see what was happening ... to see if Craig was standing over her, waiting to pounce.

Legs ... lots of legs. Someone's skirt whisked across her vision. Carol was being rushed past her by — presumably — Toby. Minty raised the dust sheet further and saw Reggie standing in the doorway, reaching out to take Carol from Toby.

But where was Craig?

Ah, on the opposite side of the room, standing right in front of the great stuffed bear, looking horrified. He wasn't looking for Minty. He was looking down at Judith, who was kneeling before him, weeping, holding one of her hands up with the other while something dark dripped down, down, down ...

"Oh, Craig. It's all my fault. I must have been out of my mind!"

Craig had stabbed his sister by mistake? He was devastated. Now he was crying, too.

Minty began, with care not to attract attention to herself, to crawl out from under the dust sheet, aiming for the door. Perhaps he wouldn't notice her.

An authoritative man's voice. "Hold, in the name of the Lord!" Her uncle? What was he doing down here?

A confusion of voices. Patrick — she still couldn't see him, but he was there, somewhere in the room, she could hear him — while Reggie was shouting to the old man to "Stand back, let me deal with him."

"Peace, boy!" Her uncle's tall, stooping figure towered over Craig. "It's over now. Give me that knife."

And then ... and then ... Minty tried to close her eyes but couldn't.

"I won't let you take me!"

Craig lifted the knife high, in both his hands. Everyone could see that he was going to bring the knife down to kill himself. The Reverend Reuben Cardale lunged forward, clasping the boy and the knife to his own body.

Craig howled, trying to free himself.

The two men rocked to and fro while Judith made a mewing sound, reddened hand to her face ... and the two, shouting, whining, battling age against youth, stepped back into the path of the great bear and it rocked ... and slowly, slowly, fell forward on top of them, while Judith screamed herself into silence.

The bear's fall was thunderous. It crushed both men to the ground.

Craig's hand, still holding the knife, relaxed.

Reggie darted forward to kick it out of sight.

Judith whispered, "No!"

Patrick emerged from the shadows behind the bear while Minty slowly, painfully, pulled herself to her feet. "Minty, my sweet heart!"

He held her tight, while she said, over and over, "I'm all right, I'm all right."

Hodge appeared. He and Reggie tried to lift the bear off the bodies beneath, but it was only when Patrick put Minty down and went to help them that they could lever it off the floor and back onto its feet, where it towered over them all.

Neither the old man nor the young moved when the bear was lifted off them. They lay side by side, the older man spread-eagled over the younger. Neither seemed to be breathing.

Reggie got out his mobile. "No! No signal. Someone will have to go upstairs to phone for an ambulance."

"I will," said Toby, sweeping Carol out of sight.

Patrick kept one hand in Minty's, while leaning over the older man to touch his neck. "There is a pulse. I told him to wait upstairs, but he wouldn't listen."

Hodge was feeling Craig's neck. "This one will live."

Judith whimpered to herself. "What have I done, what have I done?"

The Reverend Reuben Cardale began, feebly, to move his head. "Help ... me ... up." A spasm contorted his face, and Minty felt her own pulse quicken. Was he having another heart attack?

She tried to speak but could only manage a whisper. "We oughtn't to move him before the ambulance gets here, ought we?"

"Won't make no difference," said Hodge. "He's had it."

Patrick shot him a glance, and Hodge shut his mouth.

The old man's eyelids fluttered. "Take ... me ... upstairs!"

Patrick was calm. "Lie still. We've sent for the ambulance."

The old man's face convulsed with pain once more, and then relaxed. His voice was reedy, and the words came with difficulty. "I refuse ... to die ... down here. Take me up ... where I can see the stars."

"Why not? Give the poor old codger his last wish," said Hodge. "Give us your hands, Reggie, and we'll set him on them like a chair and take him topside, right?"

Minty would have objected, but Patrick stayed her protest. "Hodge is right. Who would want to die down here? I'll help them up with your uncle, and you can follow. Reggie, stay with the boy."

The two men departed, carrying the Reverend Reuben between them. Judith crouched down beside her brother, stroking his face with one hand while holding the other, wounded one, close to her breast.

Reggie tried the light switch. It flickered on. Off.

Minty caught the glitter of Craig's long knife as the light flickered and died. Reggie had kicked it under the pile of shrouded furniture which had protected Minty during the fight. She couldn't leave the knife there, so close to Judith's hand.

As the light came on again, it thrust Judith's silhouette against the wall, stooping like a great bird over the body of her brother on the floor. She eased off the black hood her brother had been wearing and wiped spittle from his lips with her sleeve. Her left hand was bleeding, reddening her dress. "Don't die, Craig! You're all I've got left! The Reverend says I'll be all right now, though I'll always have to take care. Don't leave me!"

The boy turned his head and opened his eyes. Like a child, he said, "Hurts!"

Judith was between Minty and the knife. Reggie seemed to agree that Craig was still dangerous, because he'd armed himself with a broken table leg. She caught his eye and nodded towards where the blade lay, but Reggie couldn't see it from where he stood.

In the struggle, Craig's side had been pierced, but it didn't look like a mortal wound to Minty. The old man had taken the weight of the bear, and by doing so, had probably saved the boy's life.

Minty felt rage and sorrow mounting within her. Why should her uncle have put his own life in danger for this worthless creature? She took a noiseless step towards the shrouded pile under which the knife lay.

Craig tried to sit up.

Minty cried out, "Don't let him get up!"

Judith pushed Craig back, holding his hands fast in hers.

Reggie was standing over Craig, looking as if for two pins he'd use his table leg on the boy, but Craig had no more fight left in him. His eyes closed and he sank back to the floor. Judith wept, without sound.

Minty wondered how long it would take for the ambulance men to get there. In reaching for that murderous knife, she stumbled on one of the torches that had been dropped in the struggle and grabbed at something, anything, to prevent herself falling. She steadied herself with an effort, but the dust sheet that had protected her, hiding her from Craig's eyes, now slid completely off the furniture it had been covering.

She gasped ... for as it descended, she realised that what she was seeing now was indeed a treasure trove.

A tottering pile of fragile-seeming, dusty, but exquisite Chinese Chippendale chairs, balanced on and around a couple of delicate side tables. Behind them what looked like a spinet. The brocaded seats of the chairs had long ago disintegrated, but the delicacy, the craftsmanship, screamed quality at her. She let out her breath slowly. Perhaps these were the original pieces of furniture made for the Chinese Room?

She wondered what young bride had banished them to the basement, and what she'd put in their place. Victoriana?

These pieces would refurnish the Chinese Room. Eden Hall was saved.

But what about her uncle? And Judith? And Craig?

Chapter Twenty-Two

Patrick crashed back into the cellar, looking for her, worrying because she hadn't followed him upstairs. She stumbled into his arms, shivering, still grasping the knife. Patrick extracted the knife from her grasp and gave it to Reggie, murmuring words of comfort, asking if she was all right, did she need to sit down, was she hurt?

"No, no," she said, trying to think straight. Her uncle needed her, she must go to him, she must tell Patrick about the furniture, and she couldn't seem to get the words out. Shock, of course.

"Calm down." He stroked her hair, muttering comfort, helping her out of the cellar into the corridor, saying he was sorry he hadn't got there earlier, but Hodge had said no one could get into the basement till he found the key to the padlock, and that he'd had to finish getting the Great Hall ready first. So Patrick had gone to fetch Cecil to talk to Judith. Only Cecil had been out, and Reuben had insisted on coming back with Patrick.

Down the uneven stairs came two stout paramedics. Reggie filled them in on what had happened.

Minty said she'd be all right now, really she would. Patrick asked if she could walk or if he should carry her. She tried to laugh, saying that of course she could walk; she wasn't hurt, only shocked. But she let him help her along the corridor towards the kitchen, which seemed a haven of bright light by comparison to the cellar they'd just left.

She thought she was doing all right until they reached the stairs, when she felt everything go black around her. She came to in the kitchen, with Patrick forcing her head down between her legs. "I'm all right. I'm being so stupid!"

"Mm," said Patrick. "There's no water in the taps here. Sit still for a moment, then I'll carry you up the stairs."

She sat, feeling numb. The paramedics went past the door, carefully carrying Craig on a stretcher. Judith clung to her brother's side like a shadow.

Minty tried to force her brain into action, but it was still replaying the moment when Craig lifted the knife high in order to kill himself, and her uncle had thrown himself forward to stop him . . . and then the great bear had fallen slowly, so slowly, on top of them . . .

She tried to stand and didn't make it. "Uncle Reuben? Have they taken him to hospital? I must go with him."

"You're not going anywhere. As for your uncle, he refused to be taken to hospital, and I agreed he shouldn't be moved. He wanted to see the stars, but it's snowing, so . . . anyway, we took him into the cloisters."

She made it to her feet, holding onto him. "I must go to him. I'll be all right now, really I will."

He helped her up the steps, and indeed she did feel better when she got out into the cool night air.

He said, "I left Carol on her mobile trying to locate Cecil, but he may not get here in time."

Minty made it to the cloisters on rubbery legs, supported by Patrick. The Reverend Reuben Cardale had been laid on a mattress in the cloisters, where snowflakes drifted in to touch his chilled face and hands. Carol was beside him, helping to cover him over with a blanket, gulping back tears. He was trying to smile at her.

Hodge stood at her uncle's feet, with head bowed.

Minty knelt beside her uncle and took one of his hands in hers. His breathing was light, and his eyes had gone beyond her to fix on what he could see of the sky. There were no stars to be seen. The cloisters were always lit at dusk, and the ancient arched passage provided a fit setting for a dying man of God.

The sky was dun coloured, promising more snow to come. Minty shivered, and Reggie put a blanket around her shoulders. Her uncle seemed serene, his lips moving now and then. Patiently awaiting the end.

He'd been a harsh guardian to her in her youth, but she'd learned to love him in the end, and he to love her. She didn't want him to leave her now. She bent her forehead over the hand she'd clasped in hers.

Patrick knelt on the other side of the dying man. Reggie stood guard at his head.

"Minty . . . Patrick . . . my dear children." The words were breathed out on a sigh. "Carol . . . Cecil . . . you've all been so good to me."

"I'm here, Uncle. I love you." Had he heard her?

"Agnes, my dear . . . wife."

Minty couldn't speak.

"Lord . . . into thy hands."

There was a stir, and Chef ushered the Reverend Cecil into the cloisters. Patrick moved aside so that the younger clergyman could minister to his old mentor and friend. Venetia and two of the stewards came through to join them. Toby stood with one arm round Carol and the other around his mother. There was nothing to be heard but the murmur of Cecil's voice and the whisper of settling snow.

Minty was aware of other figures joining them. Was that Doris from the gift shop, huddling into her winter coat? Tim from the Estate Office appeared, with the Ranger from the Park . . . and behind him hovered Clive. Minty was glad Clive had come.

And then — she really must be very tired — it seemed to her that the cloisters were filled with other shadowy figures, men in long robes with hoods over their heads, watching with them for the passing of a brave soul. The rough-hewn pillars at this side of the cloisters looked far older than the Jacobean building which it was supposed to be. Had the cloisters once belonged to a monastery, as Hodge said?

Minty shut her eyes tightly, and when she opened them again, she saw only the shadows cast by the real people whom she knew.

Cecil's voice died away. There were tears on his cheeks. He'd been a protégé of the old man's in his youth, though of recent years their roles had been reversed. Cecil would miss him. Patrick took Cecil's place.

The stern face of the old minister convulsed with pain once more. Someone behind Minty whispered, "His heart."

The old man said, "I thought I was so far from home ... but it's not far now." His lips relaxed into an enigmatic smile.

Minty had the odd fancy that the snow would soon cover him, and then he'd look like one of the stone figures carved on early Eden tombs in the church.

His hand lost its warmth, and she laid it over his breast. Patrick did the same with the hand he'd been holding.

Hodge fumbled in his pockets and came up with two coins. Before Minty could stop him, he closed the old man's eyelids and placed the coins upon them. An ancient country custom. Well, why not?

Patrick helped Minty to her feet and kept his arm around her. He said, "Cecil, will you see to the tolling of the passing bell? The village will like to know that he's gone to join his Maker."

Cecil nodded and disappeared with Chef, who was blowing her nose as quietly as she could. It was over.

A time to mourn.

❧

The Hall returned to normal within days, but Minty took time to recover.

The twins returned and threw a tantrum because they were not, not, not going to sleep in baby cots again! They wanted proper grown-up beds like the ones they'd had at the cottage. Patrick organised that their new beds were brought over from the cottage and the cots were banished to a storeroom.

Another giant step towards normality occurred when Serafina returned from visiting her family. Minty was thrilled to welcome her back so soon, though she sorrowed with Serafina when told why.

"I should have realised they wanted something from me. They said they were booking into a hotel in Knightsbridge and that they'd arrange accommodation for me there, as well. When I arrived, I was sent up to their suite. No expense spared for them. They didn't even ask me to sit down, but treated me as if I were a servant they were interviewing for a job. Do you know what they wanted? They wanted me to go back home to take care of a distant cousin who'd become a burden to his family. That was the only reason they wanted to make contact with me again. They thought I'd be delighted to be welcomed back into the family on any terms.

"I was chilled by their reception of me, but family ties are strong, and I hesitated. Can you believe it? I actually considered doing what they asked. I said I'd go to my room and think about it, and would give them an answer in a couple of hours. They said they hadn't booked a separate room for me but that I could sleep on the settee in the sitting room when everyone else had gone to bed. They treated me as if I were a slave, a woman of no account.

"So I told them that I was neither penniless nor friendless, that I had a good job with you, and plenty of money to buy my own house. That's when they changed their tune. You could see them calculate what this might mean for the family. They still thought they had the right to dispose of me without asking my opinion, but when they realised I had money ... ah! Perhaps it would have been better if I had not told them."

Minty was fascinated. "What did they want you to do?"

"I was to buy a house in Central London with my own money. Then I was to sponsor my nephews who wanted to be educated there. I was to housekeep for them, provide them with food and accommodation at my expense. Two of my nephews were there in the room when my brothers explained what my role was to be in future. They'd treated me like dirt from the moment I arrived. From the way they talked, I could tell they were a work-shy lot who intended to live the high life at my expense.

"I told my brothers there and then that I didn't see any sense slaving for them night and day when I had you and Patrick and the twins to look after. I told them that here I had my own quarters, I was given a good wage, and was treated as a member of the family. They were not pleased. They said that I owed them, that it was my duty to return to the family to work for them, but I called for a taxi and booked in to another hotel. Then I went to Harrods and bought myself three pairs of expensive shoes, a leather wallet for Patrick, an evening purse for you, and some toys for the children. And now, I'd better see about restocking the freezer."

On Monday Patrick had to fly off to Brussels, but he made it back to the Hall late that night. Also on Monday, the professional decorators arrived to make a start on the rooms open to the public, Iris and Reggie began to strip out all the questionable items of furniture, and Toby laboured to alter the pages for the new brochure.

Clive disappeared for forty-eight hours and came back looking the worse for wear. He was soon back in control again, though noticeably curt when Iris was around.

Minty found herself weeping at the drop of a hat. She couldn't settle to anything. She took the twins up to see Mrs Chickward in the village, and she spent time with Carol in her shop, evaluating what needed to be done to restore the "treasure trove" furniture.

She talked to Hodge about setting up a sales booth in the walled garden, and she helped Chef work out how best to put the old kitchen back into service. She played with the twins but handed them over to Gloria without too much of a pang when she was needed elsewhere.

She slept in Patrick's arms.

She grieved for her uncle.

One fine winter's afternoon Patrick returned early from his office and suggested they take the twins for a walk in the Park. Or rather, give the twins an opportunity to run wild, and the adults to saunter behind.

The snow had vanished overnight, but hard frosts had glazed over the edges of the lake and caused the visiting ducks and geese to slither and slide as they landed. Patrick had begged scraps of food from Chef for the twins to throw to the birds.

The twins' shrill voices echoed in the still air and the setting sun glowed red across the Park.

Minty was indignantly bringing Patrick up to date with the latest news. "... and Hodge went to visit Craig in hospital, and told him there'd be a job waiting for him when he gets out! Also, Reggie's told Judith she can leave her caravan where it is. I was so angry with them both, I couldn't think what to say. All right, I know I can't prove he laid all those traps for me, but he did try to kill me down in the cellar. You can argue that it was Judith who led him into trouble, but she did try to set him right and he wouldn't listen. I think he needs a prison sentence with psychiatric attention."

"Granted," said Patrick. "Then what happens when he gets out? I'm going to suggest that on his release we may be able to make something of him."

"No way! The sooner Judith takes off the better, and I never want to see Craig again."

Petronella ran to Patrick. He picked her up, threw her into the air, and set her down on her feet again. Satisfied to have touched base with him, she ran off after her twin.

Minty tucked her hand within Patrick's arm. "You do agree with me, don't you?"

"Does it matter what I think?"

"Yes, of course it does." She was cross with him. "I can't possibly risk having them around, for the twins' sake."

Ralph ran back to his father, grasped his leg for a moment, then ran off again.

Patrick shaded his eyes from the glow of the sun. "I've been doing some research. Hodge was right in thinking the foundations of the Hall are a lot older than the brochure says. Hodge says the north wing was built on the foundations of an abbey that once stood here, and I've found some documentation to prove it."

Minty was silent, remembering that odd moment when she'd imagined monks standing around her uncle's deathbed. Hodge had put some beautiful ferns in that corner of the cloisters only that morning. In memory.

Patrick went on, "Abbeys were places in which men gathered to worship God, but they also took in and cared for the sick and the homeless. They were a focus for good in the community. Maybe the Hall's getting to be that way."

Minty was horrified. "You think I ought to allow Judith and Craig to come back, after all they've done?"

"Judith came back here wanting to be done with her old life, and she did struggle through, didn't she? As for poor Craig ... well, we don't have to think about that for a few years, do we?"

Minty set her lips in a firm line, but Patrick had stooped to help Petronella with her bobble hat, which had come adrift, and he didn't notice. Petronella always grew tired before Ralph, who could keep going long after everyone else was worn out.

When Patrick straightened up again, he said, "Did you read the files I left out for you?"

"Yes. I ought to have paid more attention when you tried to talk about them before. What does this other charity want with you?"

Petronella had run in a wild circle, and now returned to their side. She was beginning to slow down. Minty took her free hand, and Patrick adapted his stride to Petronella's short legs.

"They want my life-blood, as if sorting out the affairs of your father's Foundation wasn't enough. It's a can of worms. As you know, it's an international charity supporting crisis centres anywhere in the world where there's trouble. Their finance director has taken an overdose and may not recover, there doesn't seem to be anything left in the kitty, and someone has tied up their finances so that it's almost impossible to work out where the money's gone.

"The directors are beside themselves. It isn't just a matter of easing out this person and that, and somehow making good the deficit. If the news gets out, the scandal sheets will have a field day. It's not too far-fetched to say that there would be a national crisis of fund-raising for charity. It's one big headache. If I take it on, it's by no means sure that I can rescue them, and I'd have to spend a great deal more time than I'd like abroad. I don't really want to get involved, and I'm aware that you want me to be here more often to help you with the Hall. So I need to know what you think. If I did take it on, could you cope here without me?"

"What!" She felt faint and stood still. What did he mean? Surely he wasn't going to leave her?

He stopped, too. Petronella pressed her face into Minty's skirt.

He said, "I've a good life here, haven't I? A short day's work in the office in town with occasional trips to London, some evening meetings on local councils, then back to this wonderful house, the twins ... and you. And now—" he smiled—"the wood. Neville wants me to come on board to help run the Hall. Well, I suppose I could manage that, somehow, as well. But I can see that if I do what these people at the charity ask, I won't be home much."

Of course Patrick didn't mean to leave her.

Petronella held up both her arms, wanting to be picked up. Patrick did so, and Petronella laid her head against his shoulder.

Minty was silent. Troubled. Patrick was not a man who settled for an easy life. She had always known that, but she'd let the knowledge slip out of the forefront of her mind recently.

He said, "When I was young I had fantasies of holding down high office to prove I was worthy of you, but God said He wasn't interested in furthering my career, though He'd let me earn money so that I could help others. I wasn't at all sure He'd want me to work for your father's charity when we got married, but yes, that proved to be what He wanted me to do. Then came all the work for local committees, tiresome at times, but He seems to think it's the right thing to do, and I've done it. I've grumbled about it at times, but I've done it. And now . . . this. It would be hard, thankless work. I'm not really experienced enough. I don't want to leave you here to struggle on your own. I don't know whether to accept or not."

She didn't like the thought of his being away from her more often, either. "You've prayed about it?"

"Yes. I consulted your uncle, too. He was all for it, but he didn't realise you needed more help here. The question is, can you cope without me, running the Hall, taking in the poor, the sick, and the needy, and helping them to make the best of themselves? Putting up with my frequent absences?"

Gut feeling said she couldn't. The prospect was frightening. Suppose she got pregnant again soon and went back to neglecting her responsibilities?

He paced along beside her, tall and straight, gazing into the distance, and not looking at her. In recent months she had hurt him unbearably, unthinkingly. How stupid she had been! So selfish! Now there was a slight, a very slight withdrawal on his part. She was going to have to work hard to restore his faith in her, but she would do it.

Of course she could weep and wail and hang on his arm, adding to his already heavy burdens. He would turn his back on his chance to fly high, and settle for the quiet life at her side. Or would he? There was steel in his backbone. If he felt that God had asked him to do something for others, Patrick would probably do it. Or live to regret it.

Once before she'd had a choice, to let him go or keep him by her side. It had taken an enormous effort on her part, but she'd managed to set him free to continue with his work—with God's help.

She'd got herself into a mess recently, by thinking she could manage her life without help from Patrick or from God. Now she had him back at her side, and he was asking her to let him go? No way!

She tried to calm herself down. She knew it was wrong to think that any man—even Patrick—could take the place of God in her life. She knew in her head that with God, all things were possible, but in her heart, the prospect of life without Patrick always at her side was still appalling.

She saw now where she'd gone wrong. She'd not trusted anyone, not Patrick, and certainly not God, to help her. *Dear Lord, I really am a complete mess, aren't I! How stupid can I get? Please, forgive my blindness. Please, help me to remember that You are always there, waiting for me to turn to You. I can't do this in my own strength. Do You really want me to let Patrick go?*

Ralph had run himself to a standstill, and now he dropped to the ground and lay there, unmoving. He wouldn't ask to be picked up and would probably resent it if she did. Patrick handed the sleepy Petronella to Minty and lifted the boy onto his shoulders. Ralph's head wobbled with fatigue, but he kept himself awake, just.

Minty's battle was short but sharp. She gave up her own wishes, and in return, was filled with a sense of peace that she hadn't known for a long time, if ever.

She said, "I still have some growing up to do, haven't I? Of course you must do it."

Chapter Twenty-Three

The house would not be open to visitors till noon, but Minty took the twins downstairs to the Great Hall, thinking they'd like to see the professional team decorate the giant Christmas tree that Hodge and Reggie had installed.

The twins held hands as they gazed up and up at the huge tree, which towered above them in the angle of the carved oak staircase. Two of the decorators were on tall stepladders, testing the strings of lights they had already put in place. Two more were arranging swags of stiff gilded ribbon around wreaths of fir laid on the mantelpiece and down the centre of the long oak dining table.

"That's tremendous." Minty gave praise where it was due. "You will remember to leave enough room underneath the tree for the presents we give the staff at Christmas?"

There was a commotion at the front door, and in came Hodge and Reggie, perspiring as they trolleyed in the giant grizzly bear. The twins took refuge behind Minty's skirt.

"What!" said Minty.

Reggie was grinning. "I thought we'd put him in place of that no-good oak chest." He introduced the twins to the bear. "Twins, this here bear is called Friendly. He came from overseas with your great-grandfather, and he's here to help guard the family in times of danger. Right, Minty?"

"Right," said Minty, faintly. She wasn't going to contradict Reggie in front of strangers, and anyway, the bear did look good in that space between the two windows.

Hodge said, "You'll be wanting a Yule log in the fireplace, won't you? I got just the thing, eight foot long if it's an inch, bringing it in this forenoon, right?"

"Right," said Minty, wondering if the chimney had been swept within living memory, and checking to see that there were indeed a couple of fire extinguishers within reach. There were. Reggie and Hodge departed with their squeaking trolley—why didn't they put some oil on the wheels?

The front door opened a crack and a frail figure drifted in.

Judith Kent.

Minty stiffened and looked around for the twins, but they hadn't noticed Judith. They had clambered up onto the long oak bench beside the table and were fingering the blown glass ornaments which the decorating team were passing along to hang on the tree.

Judith had washed the brown colour out of her hair, which was now back to its original auburn. She had discarded her dun-coloured clothes and was wearing a rose pink sweater over black trousers, with a dull red parka over all. But her features looked pinched and she seemed to be shivering, although the house was warm enough that day.

Minty was alarmed to discover that she wanted to rush at Judith and slap the make-up off her face. She held onto the mantelpiece to stop herself.

Did Judith remember how nearly Minty and little Ralph had been killed by crashing into this very fireplace? How dare Judith approach them now?

Judith looked around her, as if trying to imprint the scene on her memory. When her eyes fell on the great bear, she shivered and bowed her head. She had never lacked for courage. She made her way round the table to where Minty stood.

"I came to say goodbye, and to thank you for letting me stay so long."

Minty nodded.

Judith twisted her hands. "It was terrible, your uncle dying like that."

Minty gave her another stiff nod.

Judith flushed dark red. It looked painful. "I could have taken the caravan and gone without a word, but I wanted to see you, to apologise for what I did, and for what Craig tried to do ... which was all my fault. I ... I am ashamed."

She looked away from Minty, and then forced her eyes back. She lifted her right hand, which still bore a bandage. "I'm always going to have a scar on this hand and I'm glad, because it will remind me ... and remind Craig. He realises now, what he so nearly did ... what he so nearly became."

"Did he interfere with the lift?"

"The cable was already fraying. He says he helped it on a bit, frayed it a bit more, that's all." She bit her lip. "'All.' No, I'm not making excuses. He's not making excuses. He took the 'Out of Service' notice off the lift and hoped the lift would fall and give you a fright. He didn't think that it might have killed you! All this has shattered him, made him grow up. He's prepared for the fact that he will have to go to jail." She looked around at the busy scene. "I'm sorry to interrupt. I'll be on my way."

"Where will you go?"

Judith shrugged. "Where the wind blows. Don't worry, you won't see me again."

Minty surprised herself. "I think you should stay, Judith. You came here for healing, and your instinct to do so was right."

"I killed your uncle."

"No, you didn't. His heart was weak, he was more than ready to go, and it was an accident. Come, sit with me in the window." Minty led the way to a window seat.

After a moment's hesitation, Judith followed. "I had no right to come back here in the first place. When I think how I tried to bargain with you, I'm ashamed."

"You made the common mistake of thinking that the Hall belongs to me. It doesn't. I hold it in trust for my lifetime. I'm only a steward here. My job is to look after the Hall and all the people who depend upon it for a living. Some are Christians. Some are not. But none are perfect."

Judith's lips twisted in mockery. "Not even you?"

"Definitely not me," said Minty, thinking of the way she'd behaved recently. "But I try, and my friends encourage me. Judith, you have friends here. I think you should stay."

"Even if I wanted to, and really I have no right to be here ..."

"As much right as anyone else who works here. You pointed out that we had no official guide to take parties around the house. I think you'd be ideal for that job. And yes, we do need someone to catalogue our books and perhaps delve into the archives, do some research on the origins of the house."

"You may need someone, but that person can't be me." Judith's voice was hard. "You may find it easy to forgive, but I can't forgive myself. I will go and leave you in peace."

Petronella ran up to Minty and deposited a painted red bauble on her lap. "For you, Mummy. Lady give it me."

Ralph carried another bauble over, holding it in both hands with great care not to drop it or trip over anything on the way. He reached Minty and looked up. Seeing that she already had a bauble in her lap, he transferred his gaze to Judith, who hadn't. He looked at her long and hard, as if he'd never seen her before.

"There you are," he said. He handed her a glittering star and ran back to the table.

Judith held the star in both hands and closed her eyes. Tears ran down her cheeks.

Minty put her arms about Judith. "That's settled, then. You're staying."

"I can't. I can't get your uncle's death out of my mind. I've nothing to give you."

"You have yourself and your talent. One day you may sing in public again, perhaps. But you could sing at church ..."

"No, no! Everyone would know!"

"Yes, they would. And we, your friends, would be there to show that you are forgiven and belong here. You could sing 'Amazing Grace' for us."

Judith began to laugh and cry, both at once.

She stayed.

Patrick had been right to rely on God's timing for the conception of another child. Although they resumed their loving relationship, Minty did not get pregnant again for some time. Not after the skating party they held on the frozen lake in the Park, or even after Carol and Toby's wedding in February.

As the months passed, Patrick began to laugh again, and Minty to busy herself with new projects to improve life at the Hall. Now and then she even joined Patrick on some of his frequent trips to London and Brussels, where she was thrilled to hear him praised as a force for good in some of the rather murky waters he now frequented.

Perhaps she became pregnant the day that Judith triumphantly discovered the eighteenth-century receipt covering the Chippendale furniture, now resplendently restored and on view in the Chinese Room ... setting the seal on the article which eventually appeared in the respected magazine?

But no. It happened after an ordinary, busy day at the Hall, with Patrick home to spend a quiet evening with her and the twins. As if to reward her for her surrender, she had an easy time with this pregnancy and the birth.

One frosty December evening, Minty sat contentedly nursing her new son in Patrick's den. This baby was a redhead with a peaceful temperament when he could see everything that was going on. When laid on his back in his cot, he turned into a fighting, red-faced fury, so he spent most of his life strapped into a harness on someone's chest. Patrick had been known to get into his car to go off to work, with his son happily gurgling away in front of him.

The twins were—at long last—asleep, having caused much alarm that day by disappearing for an hour, only to be found by a steward, oblivious to the tourists passing through, happily playing with their ancestors' toys in the Victorian nursery on the first floor.

"Never a dull moment," said Patrick, greeting Minty with a kiss and his son with a touch of his forefinger, before going to lay his laptop on top of his desk, and riffle through the post which had accumulated in his absence. "Doris popped out of the gift shop to tell me the twins had escaped again, Hodge waylaid me to demand I meet him in the wood at eight tomorrow morning to help him heel in some wild rose cuttings, and Chef called out that she wants me to try her new recipe for a game pie. I got away from them with some difficulty, only to have Iris trip me up on my way through the courtyard, to say I've got to talk to you about your latest plan for using one of the barns for ... some ploy or other."

Minty smiled. She knew that all this was happening because he'd become the Master of the Hall, even though he never thought of himself as such. She deduced this last trip of his had gone well; he looked tired but content.

He picked one envelope out and slit it open. "So what's upsetting Iris?"

"After the twins, my brain seemed to turn to cotton wool, but this little redhead seems to egg me on to think of more schemes to help the Hall. I'll tell you about it when you've eaten. Serafina kept some food back for you."

He wasn't listening but staring down at a letter in his hand. She said, "Something's happened?"

"Mm. Something unexpected. I never thought I'd be up for a gong, but someone seems to think otherwise. How would you like to be Lady Sands?"

Minty shook her head to clear it. "Did I hear aright? They want to give you a knighthood? You'll be Sir Patrick?"

"Services to charity, and all that. I'm sure there are many worthier people, but they seem to think ... I don't know whether to accept or not."

Minty put her son over her shoulder, and he burped obligingly. "Of course you accept. Not for my sake — how strange to be called Lady Sands — but because it will give you an edge in your work. It's proof that you're doing the right thing, fighting for those who can't fight for themselves."

He fingered his chin, which needed another shave. "I never looked for praise or reward. I'm not sure I ought to accept. From village boy to 'Sir Patrick' is quite a leap."

"To God be the glory."

"Oh, well. If you put it like that! What did you say there was for supper?"

Eden Hall

Veronica Heley

After twenty-four years, she's learning the truth that was hidden from her as a child. Now the fate of many people depends on what she will do with it.

At the age of four, Araminta "Minty" Cardale was exiled from Eden Hall on the wings of a scandal. Twenty years later, summoned by her half-sister, she has returned to see her dying father. But her hopes of a warm family welcome are shattered, and she is rejected once again.

Making a place for herself in the village at the gates of Eden Hall, Minty begins to learn the truth about her father and her long-dead mother. She has yet to understand the threat she represents to family members who care only for money, power, and self-advancement, or the hope she offers to the community she is growing to love. And there are some who will do anything to prevent her finding out until it's too late.

Thankfully, Minty has friends to stand by her, and, in this modern Cinderella story, she find an unlikely and unpredictable champion. At stake are the soul of her father on his deathbed—and the future of the entire village.

Softcover: 0-310-24963-5

Pick up a copy today at your favorite bookstore!